Ask Me No Questions

Cindie Miller

PublishAmerica
Baltimore

© 2009 by Cindie Miller.

All rights reserved. No part of this book may be reproduced, stored in a retrieval system or transmitted in any form or by any means without the prior written permission of the publishers, except by a reviewer who may quote brief passages in a review to be printed in a newspaper, magazine or journal.

First printing

All characters in this book are fictitious, and any resemblance to real persons, living or dead, is coincidental.

PublishAmerica has allowed this work to remain exactly as the author intended, verbatim, without editorial input.

ISBN: 1-60813-799-6
PUBLISHED BY PUBLISHAMERICA, LLLP
www.publishamerica.com
Baltimore

Printed in the United States of America

The following story is dedicated to the thousands of women and children who suffer in the name of love; innocents who, through no fault of their own, live in danger. To my parents, who did their best to protect and guide me, and loved me when I made all the wrong decisions. And to my family, my heroes, who have given me the strength to survive and tell the truth. You are the wind beneath my wings. Thank you.

Every book has its champions; this one is no exception. Throughout the years, people have heard or read my story and encouraged me to pursue its publication. I thank all of you for your kindness, your honesty, and your willingness to read, reread, and read some more as this book took shape. Thank you Sherry Brooks, the angel who made me promise to never give up. Thank you, Tom Armstrong, "Poet Laureate of Music Row," who told me years ago that the manuscript was "perfect" and that I shouldn't accept a minimal offer. Thank you Lucy Adams, for your words of praise and for your prayers. Thank you Margaret Lefevre, for your suggestions and your editing expertise. Thank you, Nashville YWCA Women's Shelter, for your support and encouragement, and the opportunity to speak to students and victims of all ages about domestic violence and related issues. Thank you Sharon Poppen, for reading and asking questions that needed to be answered. And thank you most of all, Doug Miller, for nagging me and helping me, and taking care of everything else so I can write.

Chapter 1

I hit the bed like a rag doll, slid across the quilted cotton bedcover I'd sewn with my own two hands, and smashed head first against the corner of the laminated oak veneer headboard of my brand new second-hand bed.

The night was black, an impenetrable Stygian abyss. Lights danced in the darkness, but I couldn't tell whether they came from the fire in the living room or that inside my head. My eyelids clenched together and I prayed a silent prayer. *Please, God. Please, God.*

A shadow crossed the threshold. The door whispered shut and the darkness swallowed me and I strained and ground my teeth to still my breath, and I heard his step—so light, so sure—on the carpet. *PleaseGodpleaseGod.*

Then I heard only the thud of my heart as the fear rose quick and tangible and overpowering, and suddenly I had to vomit. But I couldn't move, couldn't flinch a finger as I heard first one shoe drop and then the other.

And that was when I knew that God didn't listen anymore. I was alone.

His hands were on me and I squeezed my eyes shut so tight they hurt, and somehow whatever went on then went on without me, and I just floated away, disappeared, and just before the black night claimed me, I heard Beth Kiltrain's voice rise out of my past. "Isn't he wonderful?" she said.

* * * * *

April 1965

"Well? What do you think? Isn't he wonderful? Isn't he brave? Have you ever met anyone like him?"

Beth's copper curls caught the last rays of the dying sun, and as she tossed her head, it appeared to burst into flame. Beth's hair was her trademark. It sprang from her head in a wild tangle of burnished brass, and she knew its effect—she flaunted it just as she flaunted her alabaster complexion and verdant green eyes.

Beth was the most confident girl I had ever known. If truth were told, I was envious of her: envious of her brazen ability to stand up for herself and talk back to everybody from teachers to parents, envious of her precociously matured knockout figure, envious of her raucous family, which contained, in addition to Beth, seven siblings ranging in age from six to eighteen. Beth Kiltrain was everything I was not. The only thing we had in common was our love for theater.

No—Theatre, with a capital "T" and an auspicious "re" spelling.

On that particular April afternoon in 1965, Beth's eyes flashed and danced into the lowset sun as she gushed on ad nauseum about her latest boyfriend. They'd been dating only about a month, which was, for Beth, a long-term commitment.

I kept still, half listening with the tolerance of best friends, while in my head a litany chanted. We won! We won! I can't believe we won!

"Stephani, where are you?" Beth wailed. "You haven't answered me—don't you think he's wonderful? To give up his day off to drive us to the competition, and then to drive home even after he hurt his ankle! He must be in agony!" She hugged herself, her green eyes ablaze with virginal ecstasy.

"I'm really more excited about the fact that we won the competition, Beth. Can't you stop with your boyfriend long enough to realize what this means? We won! Two of us beat out hundreds of the top drama students in the state. That's got to be nigh on to impossible!"

"Oh, Steph, of course we won. We're the best, aren't we? We're going to be stars. Rita Hayworth and Doris Day, look out!" She was Rita, of course—strong-willed, sexy, and bold. I was Doris Day, the girl next door, blonde and naive and always getting into some kind of jam. The two movie stars were icons in the sixties, their larger-than-life images molding the dreams of idealistic teenage girls all across the country. For Beth and me, those dreams were as real as shooting stars. We just had to reach out and catch them.

Beth caught my arm in hers, and, linked together, we skipped a few steps down Dorothy's imaginary yellow brick road before collapsing breathlessly against Beeman Photography's red brick wall.

"Oh, God," Beth gasped, "I can't make it home. Why are we walking, anyway? Where's our limousine?"

"Off to the hospital, remember? You sent him there to x-ray his ankle." I slid down the wall, my brand new white cotton blouse pulling out of the waistband of my equally new pleated skirt as I settled on the sidewalk. Rolling my feet beneath me, I tucked that skirt around my knees. "Do you think we'll really make it, Beth? Will we really be great actresses? Will we even get to the actress part, much less be *great*?" Uncertainty slashed across my mind.

"Stephani, you worry too much," she said. "We've got it made." She held our trophy, won just hours ago, so that it caught the path of the sun's rays. "Tomorrow is ours."

I reached out and covered her hand with mine. We held the piece of wood and gilt-painted plastic aloft, and we watched the light deflect from the gold, and it all seemed real, possible.

"Ours," I repeated.

We looked at each other and giggled. Then, groaning, we clambered up from the sidewalk, linked arms again, and continued our walk home.

"You never did answer me, you know," Beth said. We had reached our corner; she would go left, I to the right.

"I know," I said. I hugged her and she pulled me in tight, and we laughed, embarrassed, as we parted.

"Well, what do you think? I'm not going to let you go until you tell me." She kept a grip on my hand. "Isn't he terrific?"

"Sure, he's terrific," I said as I crossed the fingers of my free hand. Victor Charles Brian was just the latest in a long list of Beth's admirers. Each one had been "terrific" until she got bored. "Why wouldn't he let me look at his ankle?" I asked her. "It's not as if I haven't had my share of broken bones. I could have told him whether it was broken or just sprained."

"Pride, Steph," she said with the smugness of experience. "Pure, male pride. He probably didn't want us to know how badly he was hurting. You couldn't have done anything, anyway, despite your many broken bones. You're just mad because you don't have a boyfriend. You would, you know, if you'd come out of that fog you're always in and join the real world. It makes you look like you think you're too good for anybody."

She grinned as she spoke, knowing that I would be offended if she didn't. She knew me too well. "Anyway," she said, "Victor's mine, so keep your hands off."

"Don't worry," I smiled back, pricked by her words despite her attempt to temper them. "He's not my idea of a knight in shining armor. See you Monday," I said, withdrawing my hand from hers.

"See you," she replied, and she turned her way as I turned mine.

So there you have it. The beginning. Unremarkable in every way. Except that on that April day of 1965, the pebble had been tossed into a pond and the ripples were just beginning to roll.

The truth was, I couldn't tell my best friend what I really thought of Victor Charles Brian. Oh, I was as hormonal as any sixteen-year-old girl. I dreamed—secretly, of course—of the Right Man, the Man who would love me with undying passion for the rest of my life. Trouble was, I knew it would never, ever happen to me. I was the "smart one" in my family, the one with the brains. Everybody knew that boys didn't like girls with brains. And I wore glasses, which is the biggest turnoff there is. And despite the fact that I religiously followed those exercises Miss Cromby led in gym class, I was as flat as a pancake on top: when every other girl was strutting around in the shower with her breasts proudly displayed (carelessly draping the towel over her shoulders, of course, careful to be casually ignorant of the fact that her body was being assessed by every other girl in the room), I wrapped myself up like a cocoon and stepped behind the cement walls while I turned the water on and my back to the room to disrobe. I may have been the girl most asked to be a study partner, but I was always standing on the sidelines at the dance.

Besides that, I lived for my dream—acting. I'd lusted after Hollywood all my life, having watched old Shirley Temple movies on television when I was younger and graduating to musicals like *Oklahoma!*, *The King and I*, *My Fair Lady*, and so many others. I wanted to sing and dance and act—I wanted to make people cry and laugh and reach for a better world because of my words, my voice. So no matter what I thought of Beth's boyfriend, it wouldn't make a piddle of difference in my life. I had better fish to fry.

He's shallow, I told myself. Shallow, immature, reckless, and selfish.

But even as I said it, I remembered the way he'd watched me the whole time Beth snuggled next to him in the front seat of his sky-blue '57 Chevy. Stared at me through the rear-view mirror, his eyes a curious gold, opaque like a coyote. At first I was flattered, then I got nervous. I wasn't used to male attention. I stared back once, briefly, lifted my chin and defied him in some sort of weird answer to an unspoken challenge. He grinned, his eyes narrowing slightly, and sent a dart through the mirror, a bolt of electricity Beth didn't notice. I ignored him the rest of the day.

Until he'd hurt his ankle.

We stopped on the way home from Reno. The competition had started at seven o'clock and finished at three-thirty, so it was late afternoon by the time we headed home. Beth and I were wrung out from three rounds of Shakespearean monologue, running on adrenaline, giddy with our victory, so Victor stopped at a hidden oasis in the northern California desert. It was a perfect setting for two Shakespearean actresses: the long, dry grass blowing in the breeze on the gentle hills; the stream bending under a stretch of railroad tracks that were, in themselves, a lonely effigy, a single sign of civilization in an otherwise uninhabited land. Beth and Vic had disappeared, and I was enjoying the solitude of a miniature pool that gurgled peacefully beneath the railroad bridge when, suddenly, a body hurled from above and behind me, and there was Victor, rolling on the ground nearly on top of me.

"Aaow!" He grasped his ankle, his ruddy face skewed into a grimace. Beth ran down the slope of the escarpment and scrambled to his side.

"Are you all right? Vic, talk to me! Are you hurt?" She fluttered around him, uncertain and scared. The railroad track, from which I assumed he fell, was ten feet or so above us.

Vic stopped rolling around and stuck his leg straight out, his face beet red and tight from the pain. "I think I broke it," he gasped. "I can't move it."

Beth hovered near the ankle, her hands clasped together. She reached, trembling, toward his leg.

"Don't touch it! Just give me a minute. Just—leave me alone."

Watching the scene before me, I squelched an uncharitable thought and offered my help. "I can tell if it's broken," I said. "I've had a few broken bones myself. It might just be sprained."

"Can you?" Beth asked.

"No!" Vic said. Their voices rang out together, but Vic's rejection was louder than Beth's hopeful query. "I'll be all right if you'll just give me a few minutes," he said. He stared at me as he'd stared through the mirror in the car, daring me to defy him.

Suffer then, I thought. "I can help," I said, but I didn't move any closer.

"Stephani, what can you do?" Beth said, her hands resting on Vic's shoulders. "If it's broken, you can't set it, anyway. It's Vic's ankle. He knows what it feels like. Let's just wait, like he said. Okay?"

"Sure. Let's wait." I turned away from them, shut out the cooing sounds behind me as Beth sympathized with her fallen hero, and I let my fingers trail into the cool waters of the spring. I was not impressed by Victor's silent suffering. Eventually he allowed Beth to help him to his car, which he drove home using his left foot on the gas pedal, his injured right ankle stretched out to the side. Beth snuggled close beside him, ready to help if he so much as batted his eyelids. I sat in the backseat, feeling abandoned and alone, my heart still prickling from Beth's refusal to let me help. I knew I could do more than they allowed—after all, I'd suffered a broken arm, a cracked ankle *and* a sprain, and I could surely at least assure them of the seriousness of his injury.

He's a smart aleck, I thought later, as I walked toward home. *A reckless, James Dean wannabe. I hope his ankle is broken. It would serve him right for showing off.*

In that moment, I forgot that I'd always felt a strange fascination for James Dean, the talented Hollywood bad boy who'd died ten years before during a wild ride in a hopped-up Porsche Spyder on a lonely desert road.

I walked into the twilight, past the business section, beyond the neon lights beginning to flicker as the busy streets of Woodsville, California, hummed their Saturday night tune of cruisers and Bobby Vinton, punctuated by occasional shrill laughter. It was a typical spring evening in a stereotypical SmallTown, USA. The "bubble" haircut was in, Elvis was King, and women's lib was about to change American society forever. John Kennedy had failed to save the world, but he gave us a vision to pursue, a reason to hope. His death made martyrs of us all. Beth and I were caught in that in-between place, that world that saw perfection just beyond its grasp, just far enough away to try to reach it. We stood on the precipice ready to jump.

And we would. We would make our mark. We had time on our side, and passion. And talent.

At least, that's what Beth said.

A familiar sense of loneliness crept into me and with it the memory of Victor's oblique gaze as he stared at me from the mirror in the middle of his '57 Chevy coupe. Shivering, I glanced over my shoulder, almost expecting to see that sky blue shade of paint close behind. But the people in the cars that passed by were oblivious to my solitary form in the shadows of the maple trees that lined the sidewalk.

As the residences stretched out and trickled into sparseness along a county road, I tried to recapture the excitement of the competition, struggled to hold onto the confidence of Beth's pronouncement. *We're going to be stars!*

But as the road wound about the hill that signified the entrance to the subdivision in which my family now lived, the weight of the dying sun settled on my shoulders, and I recalled instead Beth's declaration, "You don't have a boyfriend. So keep your hands off Victor. He's mine." Loneliness erupted into self-pity as the moon crept into the sky. I yanked the glasses off my nose, folded them into my purse, and stared blurry-eyed at the tips of my new, color-coordinated, yellow pumps. Victor's opaque gaze bored through my mind. *I'm just a misfit*, I thought. *A nerdy, gangly, ugly tomboy. No one will ever love me. No one will ever care.*

ASK ME NO QUESTIONS

For the last half-mile of the walk home, I indulged in moroseness and let my insecurities overwhelm me. Who was I, anyway, to think I could "make my mark" on the world?

I was just a logger's child—the fourth of five children and the second daughter. This placement in my family, by its very nature, pitted me always against the elder siblings: I was doomed to be second in everything from clothing—hand-me-downs—to introductions—"Oh, by the way, this is our other daughter."

I had discovered the thrill of audience applause one Christmas eve during the gift-opening ceremony at my grandparents' house. Upon being presented with a two-foot-high Miss Karen doll—complete with a trunk outfitted with two drawers, a hanging rod and three hangers, *and* the wardrobe that filled the hangers and the drawers—I rose from my place in the circle of family faces, raised my arms above my head, and pirouetted ballerina-style on the multi-colored rug my grandmother had braided with her own two hands. For a few blinding seconds I danced with the sheer joy of this wondrous gift, oblivious to the spectacle I made.

Papa was the first to applaud. I loved my tall, craggy-faced Papa. He was old, for sure—his hair had been white all the years of my memory and his face lined with smile wrinkles. I'd never seen him raise his voice or hand, not in anger nor in any other emotion. He was not reserved, he was just—quiet.

That night he clapped his hands together, his mouth a wide grin, his faded blue eyes lighting upon me in appreciation of my excitement. The rest of the family joined him. The sound and the energy of their applause drove me to even faster steps, more creative, deliberate movements, fingers splayed and wrists extended. I was a ballerina, a gypsy, a queen. I danced for them.

I wanted to dance forever. On the real stage. Dance and sing and entertain. I wanted to bring imaginary people to life.

The morning after Beth and I came home with our acting trophies, I awoke to the familiar aroma of bacon sizzling in the frying pan. My mother was cooking breakfast. I knew she would be already decked out in her Sunday morning attire: dressed for church, her apron carefully covering her Sunday finery as she handled spatula and skillet. I glanced over to the empty bed across my room, the bed that used to be Brandy's. Two years my elder, Brandy had married her high school sweetheart, Guy, in September, and I still missed her morning grumbling. Brandy was the acknowledged beauty in the family. She had dreamed of becoming an artist, but an unplanned pregnancy put a stop to that. She seemed happy, though.

She and Guy lived with his parents two blocks away. Their little boy had been born after a long, complicated labor the day after Christmas. If my parents were disappointed, they sure as heck never said anything around me. Brandy never could do anything wrong.

Still, I missed her.

I headed for the shower, the extra bathroom in this house still a luxury in our lives. Now that there were just Ricky and me at home, it was even better. When we moved here, there had been all four of us Stevenson kids—Travis, Brandy, me and Ricky, in that order. The bathroom had been a big bonus, and all of us took full advantage of it. Travis, my elder by four years, had first dibs, of course, and spent every morning in the shower, as if water was perpetual. It *was* kind of a miracle, after the pumped-up spring water we'd used all our lives. Mom had regulated the water usage with military rigidity: for baths, we were allowed two inches in the bottom of the tub once a week. We never did take showers in the old house.

Travis loved the shower. Loved the steam, loved the heat, loved the constant stream that came from the shining chrome head. He could spend all day in the shower, I'd bet. As much as I used to yell at him in the mornings as I waited my turn, I missed him, too. He'd moved out after an argument with Dad last year. Of course, he was an adult, so it was time anyway. He worked for the forest service and visited us frequently. He and Dad still went fishing and hunting nearly every weekend. So the argument—about Travis not finishing college—hadn't split them up permanently. And now I had first dibs on the shower.

I locked the bathroom door and turned on the water, stuck my head in and let the stream pour over my hair. It was still stiff with the spray Beth had used yesterday. I hated hairspray and was glad to get it out. But my hair, long and heavy and fine, was a flyaway mess if I didn't spray it for the roles I played. As Portia in *The Merchant of Venice* yesterday, I'd worn it in an old-fashioned, mannish-looking creation that Beth had dreamed up. It must have worked, since I won Best Actress honors at the contest. My parents hadn't said much about it when I got home. I'd waited for one or the other to say something—"How'd it go?" Or maybe, "I'll bet you put all the other actors to shame!"—but then, Dad was late getting home from fishing and Mom was busy making blackberry jam. She'd nodded a "hello" from behind the steam on the stove and continued stirring the pot. By the time Dad came home with a string of rainbow trout, it was time for a late supper, and Ricky grabbed the limelight with the update on his baseball practice. My big victory in Reno somehow didn't get into the conversation.

ASK ME NO QUESTIONS

Oh, God, please let them be proud of me, I prayed as the water ran down. *Please let them see that this is what I was meant to be!*

"God, Steph, are you gonna take all day?" Ricky's voice came through the haze. "I need to go to the bathroom!"

"Just a minute!" I yelled. "I'm almost done!"

Guiltily I stepped from the shower and dried off. Ricky was only six years old, but he was everybody's friend. Tall and blonde and Nordic as the pictures in the history books, he had an endearing personality and a self-assurance borne of unconditional love.

"There you go," I said as I opened the door. The cool air from the hallway dissipated the warmth that had enveloped me. The cocoon of dreams melted away just as quickly. I had to get ready for church.

"Breakfast is on the table," Mom called.

Several days later, I was walking toward home on Main Street when I heard the peculiar throb of Vic's car as it pulled up beside me, slowing despite the traffic whizzing by on the busiest thoroughfare in Woodsville. I was still high, flying on the thrill of my victory in Reno, still sure that somehow my parents would hear destiny calling. Couldn't they see that I had a gift? That I was meant to be an actress? Mr. Erickson, my drama coach, had some connections in Hollywood. He was going to get me a screen test. Surely, I told myself, with that kind of endorsement, Mom and Dad would have to see that my future lay not in college, not in some boring, practical career like medicine, but in acting.

Deep in my thoughts, I ignored the car that was keeping pace with my every step.

"Hop in!" a voice yelled above the din. I looked up, startled, and met those strangely hooded golden eyes. Victor. Daring me to accept. Daring me to refuse. One side of his mouth curved upward, a miniscule break in an otherwise straight line.

"No thank you," I replied without breaking stride. I lifted my chin, straightened my back despite the load of books in my arms. They felt very heavy all of a sudden.

There was a hollow "click!" as the door opened, then it swung toward the sidewalk as the car kept its chugging pace. "Get in!"

He's mine, so keep your hands off! Beth's words leaped into my head. A horn honked behind us as traffic began to build up on the busy street. I sneaked a glance from the periphery of my eye. He was still looking at me, disregarding the street ahead of him. He was not smiling.

No, his gaze instead was intense, as if assessing just how long I would resist the inevitable. Several cars began to blast steadily on their horns. Ignoring them, Vic continued to escort me down the street, acting as if the world would stop just for him. I wondered if it would.

A stationwagon with an angry-looking woman at the wheel shot past, tires squealing as she turned to avoid an oncoming pickup. A vision of twisted metal and bright red blood popped into my brain as the stationwagon careened around a corner. Vic seemed oblivious to the danger and the commotion.

"Oh, all right," I muttered. "You win this time. But just because I don't want you or anybody else to get killed." Amid the honking of the horns behind us and the glares from passing motorists, I stepped to the open door and slipped into the seat beside him, struggling to keep my chin high and my books balanced. Somehow I must appear composed, aloof, nonchalant. Somehow I must keep him from knowing how fast my heart pumped inside my chest.

The moment I touched the seat, the engine roared as Vic floored the gas pedal, and we thundered down the street.

He was silent as he drove, his attention focused on the road. He seemed to need to pass every vehicle ahead of us, as if we were involved in some strange, one-sided race. "Don't worry," he said without taking his eyes off the car in front of us. "I haven't killed anybody yet." He flashed a lopsided grin my way, then he jerked the wheel to the left and streaked past the other car just as we reached the curve that marked the beginning of the familiar county road.

I hugged the door on the passenger side, my fingers crossed under the pile of books, that flash of fear crystallizing, clarifying, as I watched the countryside blur by. I shut my eyes. *Dear God*, I prayed, *please don't let us have an accident...please...*

He laughed, and I popped my eyes open and stared out the window until I saw my house at the far end of the cul-de-sac. God was listening to me. We were alive. Exhaling cautiously, I uncrossed my fingers. Vic jerked the vehicle to a sudden stop.

"Thanks," I said awkwardly, my hand on the door handle. He didn't attempt to help me, didn't move, just sat there and stared enigmatically. James Dean reincarnated. His eyes mesmerized me, and I couldn't think of anything witty or sarcastic or memorable to say.

The door swung open on its own weight, and as I hefted the books into my arms for an awkward exit, the thought flashed into my brain.

"How did you know where I live?"

One side of his mouth twitched upward. "I know a lot about you," he said with that lopsided grin. "More than you could possibly imagine."

Disconcerted, I looked down; another realization dawned. "Your ankle," I murmured. "It's not in a cast."

"No. It wasn't broken." His eyes, gold eyes, bored into me, dared me to say it. *I told you so!*

"I—I'm glad." The silence stretched. Then I tore my eyes from his and clambered out of the Chevy, my head thick as if I was moving in a fog. I was inside the house before I heard the engine rev angrily, then Victor floored the gas and disappeared down the street.

A week or so after that day, Beth reported that she and Vic had had a fight and were no longer seeing each other. "He's not the only fish in the ocean," she sniffed, with a toss of her flaming red hair. "If he thinks he can get the best of me, he's got another think coming." Beth soon had another poor sucker snagged on her hook, and after that, Vic seemed to just show up wherever I happened to be.

Chapter 2

The bed creaked and his hand brushed my thigh.

"No-o-o!" I wailed, my voice high as a banshee wail in the night. Thin and high and totally useless. I opened my mouth to scream, gasped and filled my lungs, when the faces of my children flashed behind my eyes—four precious daughters sleeping in the three rooms upstairs—and I bit my lip and kicked out in the darkness; kicked but found only air; black, impenetrable air.

His hands were on my shirt and they yanked and I felt the shirt rip, and I gritted my teeth and fought him, the gasps of our efforts mingling, dancing in syncopation briefly in the blackness as I flailed balled fists uselessly in the dark.

He laughed.

The sound of his laughter was the most terrible sound I ever heard. It was a lover's laugh, a soft chuckle of enjoyment, a sound I'd heard hundreds of times over the years of our life together. I hated him for that laugh: like everything else, it was a lie.

I flailed, and he laughed as he held me. He ripped my clothes easily with one hand and held me down with the other, and when I was naked he straddled my body and grinned at me beneath him. I knew then that, this time, I would not escape. Later I would wonder how I could not have seen, not have known this side of him. I glimpsed the white of his teeth as his lips swooped down to graze my mouth, cover my screams, stop my breath. The flash of his teeth, the glint of his eyes—images in the darkness that once had been dear—how had this happened?

*****

May 1965

"How would you like to go fishing next Saturday? I know a great spot up the river."

ASK ME NO QUESTIONS

Vic and I were alone in the auditorium. Play practice was over; everyone else had gone home. Outside it was dark, past ten o'clock, and I had a long walk ahead of me. The streets of Woodsville were still safe in the sixties; you could walk in the dead of night and expect to get home intact.

"Fishing?" I asked. Somehow I couldn't see him with a fishing rod. He was full of surprises.

"Fishing. Or don't you fish either? Beth's idea of fishing was reading a book in the shade."

"Beth? You took Beth fishing?" The idea was ludicrous. I had a sudden vision of the ivory-skinned redhead reclining under a tree in an effort to protect her complexion from the sun. Scarlet O'Hara circa twentieth century. I giggled. "That's really funny," I said.

"You wouldn't hide under a tree, would you, Stephani?" His grin was engaging, after all. His smile changed his face entirely.

"No, Vic," I replied, "I don't hide under trees. I hide in them," I teased, suddenly wanting to see him smile once more. He was really quite attractive in a rough-hewn kind of way. His smile was crooked, stretching more on the left side than the right, exposing slightly crooked teeth. Those imperfect teeth made him more human, less a mystery man. Kind of like James Dean. I noticed a deep dimple on his left cheek.

"Well, how about it then? You can climb trees, I'll catch us some dinner. We can celebrate."

"Celebrate what?"

"The end of the school year. The beginning of summer…and maybe something wonderful." His voice trailed off, hinting.

"Something wonderful? What can that be?" My heart began a nervous drumming.

"Who knows?" he evaded. "The future…who knows what the future will bring?"

He turned then, toward the door of the auditorium, extending his arm in a courtly way. I joined in the game, making the most of the pretense. *He can really be sweet,* I thought. *Why am I always so nervous around him?*

Perhaps it was his serious intensity that unnerved me. Or perhaps it was just that he was four years older then I. He was a world traveler, after all, an ex-Service man, a mysterious, dark and kind-of-handsome stranger. He attracted me even as he repelled me with his habit of staring without a blink of his strange, golden eyes.

His brief smiles never reached those eyes. I was fascinated. I wanted to make him smile all the way to his fingertips, all the way to his eyes. I wanted to see him let go of his serious man-of-the-world facade.

I had become accustomed to his watchful scrutiny, used to his silent presence on the perimeter of my life, nicknaming him my "shadow" in the days since his breakup with Beth. It was a game we played. But even as his attention flattered me, I told myself it meant nothing, could mean nothing. I had plans for my life; Victor Charles Brian was not in those plans. But still, what would it hurt? It was just a little picnic.

As we left the darkness of the auditorium that night, I shivered. The back of my neck seemed to prickle with a thousand tiny needles.

"What's the matter?" Vic asked. "Are you cold?"

"No," I smiled self-consciously. "A ghost just walked over my grave."

I straightened my back, lifted my chin, and told myself not to be stupid. What could happen on a simple little fishing trip? It was just a date, after all. Defiantly, ignoring those prickles of apprehension, I agreed to a picnic and a fishing excursion the following Saturday. And I got a ride home in the process. It didn't seem so scary the second time.

I didn't see him the rest of the week, and, strangely, I found myself looking for him in the darkness after play practice. Maybe he was kidding, I thought more than once. Maybe he isn't going to remember about Saturday. It wouldn't be the first time someone had stood me up.

Saturday dawned, a clear May morning with the promise of a hot afternoon. The mountain stream sang a familiar melody as it traveled lazily to the valley below. Vic had shown up after all, his Chevy announcing his arrival at my door before the sun rose. I was ready, and I sneaked out of the house as quietly as possible, aware that my parents were probably listening for my departure. I'd told them of my plans, told them a little about Vic, but they liked to meet my friends. I'd promised to bring Vic in later.

The day was glorious, with bright yellow and blue and deep green all sparkling in the sun. I laughed aloud, apprehension forgotten. While these lodgepole and tamarack and fir didn't resemble my redwoods in any way, the forest was still Home. Nothing bad could happen here.

He laughed with me, his full lower lip stretching in a crooked smile as the rich ha-ha-ha's resounded through the forest, bouncing off the pines to boomerang back to us.

We fished all morning. I kept pace with him as he followed the stream through the mountain, casting into clear pools where the river widened before plunging on over lava rocks. Vic was an aggressive fisherman, knowledgeable and sure of himself. He moved from spot to spot along the stream, hunting out the deep shady holes where trout lay hidden and teasing them onto his hook with the ease of an expert. He was obviously very comfortable in this setting, a fact I tucked away at the back of my mind.

After a few hours, I left my pole to explore the wild terrain as Vic fished on downstream. I was in my element, and I let my imagination wander as my feet fell soundlessly, barely disturbing the pine needles on a deer trail that wound through the woods. The woods always took me back, back to the origins of my birth. This was where God lived. Unlike some of my suburban counterparts, I was never afraid in the forest.

I thought of the play in progress—*Li'l Abner*. I, of course, was portraying Daisy May, the ultimate hill girl. I loved the music, the large cast, the interaction of the characters. Mr. Erickson had even pointed out to the male lead—who was flubbing his lines—how I came to every rehearsal prepared. His comment had made me work even harder. The play would be another nail to hammer into the marquee of my successes in the theater, another name to add to the list of arguments I was preparing for my dad.

Dad. Oh, God, how was I going to convince him? We'd had a terrible argument when I'd shown him the trophy from Reno.

"See, Dad?" I'd jabbered. Full of myself, full of possibilities. "I won this! All by myself! There were hundreds of kids at the competition. Other schools sent dozens of people in several plays. But Beth and I won over all of them! Isn't that wonderful?"

Dad had grunted, barely glancing at my trophy before he resumed cleaning his tackle box. He and Travis were taking Ricky out that weekend—not the same place Vic and I were—and he wanted everything to be ready for my little brother.

"Dad, look!" I said, shoving the trophy under his nose.

He swatted the six-and-a-half-inch trophy away as if it was a piece of junk—a fly, a pest—and it fell from my hand. Tears stung my eyes.

"Don't you care?" I pleaded. "Don't you see what this means? I can do this! I was meant to do this!"

I was whining, I knew. I hiccupped and gasped and tried to control my voice, but this was too important. He had to understand. He had to approve.

"Anyway, I'm going to become an actress. I'm going to get a screen test and I'm going to go to Hollywood with Mr. Erickson. He thinks I've got what it takes."

Dad still didn't look at me. Intent on his hooks and flies and fishing line, he kept his eyes straight down.

"Do you hear me, Dad? I said I'm going to be an actress."

"No daughter of mine is going to live like that," he said. The words bit like a steel trap; he took the line in his teeth and knotted it around a sinker. I might as well have kept my mouth shut.

"I'm going to be an actress," I repeated. "You can't stop me!"

"I won't have to," he said, and he looked at me full in the face. "You can't go anywhere without my permission. You don't have any way to get there."

"Mr. Erickson—"

"He's not going to take you anywhere without my say-so. You're a minor."

He resumed his work on the fishing rod. The fishy stench of bait rose from the depths of the box; I was dismissed.

I picked up the trophy and threw it across the yard, blinded by my tears. Then I ran out and headed for the hills that rose in the distance, crying uncontrollably.

When I returned home later, I retrieved that award from under a rose bush and, exhausted and dirty, headed into the house. Mom shook her head at me as if I should have known what would happen, and I slipped into my bedroom to cry myself to sleep. The next morning, Dad and I avoided each other's eyes and pretended that nothing had happened.

But surely, I told myself now, surely Dad would come to his senses when he saw how good I was! His voice reverberated in my brain: "No daughter of mine is going to live like that. It's not for you, Steph. Not for my daughter."

But I couldn't stop dreaming of the day he would change his mind. He'd be in the audience, watching under protest, and at the most dramatic point he'd suddenly *get it*, he'd understand and approve. Then he would smile and clap wildly, his eyes shining with pride. *Someday*, I thought, as I watched a deer leap from her cover in the trees, *someday you'll be proud of me, Dad. You'll see.*

It was in this pensive frame of mind that I returned to the clearing where Vic had parked his car, and I settled on the grass to enjoy the sun. It was there that Vic found me, completely given up to the warmth of the day.

His breath was on my cheek, his lips grazed mine. Startled out of a half-doze, I stiffened and turned away.

"What's the matter?" he murmured. "Relax."

"Stop it," I stammered. His arm snaked around my waist.

"Don't you like me? I like you. A lot."

"Like you? I hardly know you! I'm not the kind of girl who meets a guy and just…" My voice trailed off to nothing. I couldn't say the words. I could barely think them.

"There's nothing wrong with it," he insisted, refusing to let me up.

"There is for me! Now let me go!"

His arms released me abruptly. I scooted away from him, stood and paced toward the car. He didn't move.

Glancing over at him, I felt a twinge of uncertainty as he remained motionless, his eyes studying the ground. "I'm sorry, Steph. Come on back. I won't touch you if you don't want me to."

I rejoined him warily, alert to any sudden move. The ground wasn't as comfortable as it had been minutes before; there were tiny little rocks in the grass beneath the blanket. I fidgeted nervously.

"Have you ever been in love?" he asked.

"Yes," I answered frostily. What did he think I was? Some kind of dateless wallflower? I'd had a boyfriend. I'd been in love. And I'd lost. "And I don't intend to be so foolish again."

"Not ever?" His voice was muffled, his face averted.

"Never," I said flatly. This conversation was skirting forbidden ground.

"Did he hurt you, Stephani?" Vic whispered, his voice floating to me just above the breeze. Frowning, I began to pull my legs beneath me, ready to stand and walk away. His hand, suddenly hot on my arm, detained me. "I won't hurt you, Stephani."

Hesitating, entranced by his sincerity, his intensity, I moved imperceptibly toward him. His hands caught my cheeks in a gentle vise and he turned my face to his. "I won't ever hurt you, Stephani."

Slowly, cautiously, he lowered his head until his lips were just a skin-depth away, his breath warm and sensuous over my mouth. Gently, carefully, he kissed me, his mouth scarcely moving upon mine. I trembled. I was afraid, but curious too. No one had ever kissed me like that. "Trust me, Steph," Vic murmured against me, "I don't want to hurt you. I only want to love you."

His tongue grazed over my lips, moist, probing. His arm was around my shoulders, supporting me. I liked kissing, but hadn't spent much time doing it. Vic's lips were soft and he kissed with his mouth open. Somehow, I had fallen back; my head touched the ground. Somehow Vic's body was pressing down on mine. A bell clanged somewhere in the back of my brain.

"No!" I wrenched away, tried to get out from under him. He held me fast, his arms hard.

"What's the matter?"

"Don't," I said, my heart pounding against the fear inside. "Let me up."

"Why? What's wrong?"

"I'm not—I'm not *that* kind of girl," I stammered, uncertain just what "that" kind of girl was. Mom's face loomed before me, frowning in disapproval.

"What are you talking about?"

"I want to stop. Let me up!" He didn't move. The fear within me grew. *What now? What if he doesn't let me go?* My heart thumped against his chest.

"What are you afraid of?"

What, indeed? What did I imagine might happen? I closed my eyes, feeling foolish and impossibly immature.

Vic wouldn't let me up, wouldn't stop touching. He smiled down at me as his fingers brushed my skin. I had to stop him, had to get away.

"Look, I don't plan on getting pregnant," I spat with as much heat as I could muster. "I'm not going to have to get married!"

His smile turned upside down. "I'm not going to jump your bones," he shouted in my face. "I don't seduce little girls." His voice softened, he looked into my eyes, and he smiled. "And when I marry you, it'll be because I want to." And he kissed me once more, his lips soft, gentle, unsexy. A chaste kiss. A kiss of promise.

He pushed me gently to the ground, his leg lying heavily over my own. Fear made me wary, unable to respond; confusion kept me still, frozen in place. The words "when" and "marry" resounded in my brain, and I thought, fleetingly, that he was going to exercise marital rights there and then. Whatever that meant.

But I need not have worried. True to his word, Vic restrained himself. He proved he was trustworthy, proved he really cared. I couldn't get pregnant from kisses. I was limp with relief. I was safe, my virginity intact.

Mixed with my relief was a sense of embarrassment. *What is wrong with me, anyway?* I asked myself as he kissed me, his tongue exploring my mouth. *He hasn't given me any reason to be afraid!* I pushed the memory of Sam Jones back in its hole and concentrated on Vic. I kissed him back, mimicked his moves, tested the sensation of his tongue against mine.

Then I felt my waistband move, felt his hand against my skin. The fear rushed back, the soft-spoken words vanished. Panic made me strong. I pushed him away, pushed and rose in one motion, and then I was running toward the car, my hair whipping behind me.

ASK ME NO QUESTIONS

"Damn!" I heard him swear as he gathered up his fishing gear. In a minute he would be beside me. *How stupid!* I felt silly and childish and scared. *Now he'll really think I'm an idiot*, I thought. But I couldn't help it. I wasn't ready for this.

"Why'd you run away?" he demanded, his arms full of fishing rods and tackle. Opening the nearest car door, he heaved the armload into the back seat.

"I'm sorry," I cried. "You—you scared me." Gone was the wood nymph, the joy in the sun and the sky. Gone was the fantasy of romance. I was just a sixteen-year-old girl standing uncertainly beside a dirty Chevrolet.

Sixteen going on twelve.

Vic stared at me, a long, hard look I could not meet. Turning away, I saw my reflection in the car window, and my embarrassment grew. I looked like a little kid, a little girl with wind-blown hair hanging down my back, my shirt askew and my cheeks flushed. Wood nymph, sure! More like wood rat. *Skinny wood rat*, I amended. Suddenly I was filled with self-disgust.

Vic must have been disgusted with me too, for he got into the car and started it, revving the engine. He looked so angry I thought he was going to leave me there alone, but he reached across and opened the passenger door. "Get in," he shouted over the car's roar. "I'm taking you home."

I obeyed silently, relieved and embarrassed and strangely ashamed. The bump-thud! of the car on the rough mountain road was the only sound all the way back to the pavement. Lighting a cigarette, Vic smoked in contemplative silence while I huddled against the door. *Darn it!* I thought. *I've really acted like an idiot. All he did was kiss me!* But I knew, somewhere deep inside, there was more to it than that. His kisses weren't the groping explorations of a clumsy boy. They were the demands of a man used to getting his way. And I didn't have the experience to know how to deal with it.

Surely he doesn't expect every girl he dates to make love with him, I thought. I know Beth hadn't. Belatedly, I tried to remember what she'd said about their breakup.

"Stephani."

His voice interrupted my thoughts. Glancing about, I noticed that the car was parked beside the highway, pulled off into a wide spot shaded by tall pines, sheltered from inquiring passers-by. *Now what?* I thought, frightened once more.

"Stephani, I apologize."

I looked at him fearfully, questioning with my eyes.

"I shouldn't have rushed you." He exuded humility, contrition, apology. "I know you're still very young. I have no business even dating you." He gazed out the window, his voice suddenly distant, determined—a master of self-control. "It's just that—I don't—no. I can't involve you."

"Involve me? In what? What is it?" Curiosity made me bold. Forgetting my confusion, I gave him my full attention. "Vic, is something wrong?" His hesitance was an invitation, his uncertainty endearing.

"I can't tell you, Steph. At least, not yet. Just—Stephani, please trust me." Looking straight at me, his eyes serious and sincere, he reached for my hand, grasped it tightly within his. "You do, don't you?"

I met the entreaty in his face. "Yes, Vic, I trust you," I whispered. I was hypnotized by those eyes. I heard the words, heard myself say them, but I wasn't sure if they were true. Yet how can I not? I asked myself, meeting his gaze. I've never met anyone like you, you're so patient, so understanding.

I was embarrassed by my lack of experience, embarrassed by the accusations still resounding in my head. Vic wasn't Sam Jones.

I thought of the weeks just past, when Vic had stayed in the background, watching me from a distance. Most boys just rushed right in, making one clumsy attempt after another, using whatever lines came to them at the moment. Vic was different. He didn't have a line. He wasn't afraid to be honest. I could truly trust him.

"You don't have to tell me now," I said. "Not ever, if you don't want to. It's all right. I'm sorry I acted so silly...."

"That's what I love about you, Stephani," he said, shushing me with a finger to my lips. "You're not like other girls. You're not cheap. I'm willing to wait." He turned then, away from me, away from any reply I might have made. He started the car and cautiously, for him, re-entered the highway. "How about a hamburger?"

"Sure," I replied, relieved to return to a mediocre conversation. Yet I wondered, as we drove down the dusty road toward town, if I had imagined those moments in the forest, if I had imagined his anger at my obstinate refusal to go all the way. Or maybe I had just misunderstood his intentions altogether.

I learned more about him that night. Vic took me to the drive-in movies, another new experience.

My parents had strict rules regarding dating. Before we had moved to Woodsville, places like drive-in movies were not a concern. They didn't exist. The logging town in which I was born consisted of a few cabins, nothing more. Later, when we moved to a 125-acre farm, the nearest village had a grand population of 500; the biggest social event was the annual Halloween party put on by the local fire station. I had never been trick-or-treating; had been invited to only one high school party; had never had a beer or a drag on a cigarette. Although my great uncle Axel had once given me a plug of his tobacco to try. I'd gagged and heaved it out, spewing black chunks of the stuff all over the barn floor. I never had the urge to sample the weed again. The high point of our move to Woodsville when I was 13 was the availability of a real movie theater; it was tradition for all the high school kids to go to the movies on Friday night.

But the drive-in movie was different. Mom called it the "passion pit." I didn't know if my sister Brandy had ever gone, but she wasn't home to ask, so when I called home from the A&W and told Mom we were going to the movies, I didn't elaborate. Let her think I meant the theater. I didn't want to argue, and I didn't want Vic to think I was a total nincompoop. Who ever heard of someone who'd never been to a drive-in?

Between crunching popcorn and sipping watered-down Coke, I told Vic an abbreviated story of my life and status in my family.

"We're really a very ordinary family," I said. "My dad is an old-fashioned, hard-working family man, and Mom has always been home for us kids. I've gone to church nearly every Sunday of my life, I know how to butcher out a deer or a chicken, and I love the outdoors. I'm going to be an actress someday. Now how about you?"

"Me?"

"Yeah, you. Did you go to school here? Where's your family? Just who are you, Mr. Victor Charles Brian?" I said it lightly, teasingly, but I waited impatiently for his answer.

"I'm no one," he said gruffly. "No one you want to know." His hand muffled his words as he shifted in the seat, his breath fogging up the window.

"I wouldn't ask if I didn't care, would I? I wouldn't be here."

"Look, we're missing the movie. The best part's coming up."

"I don't care about the movie. Tell me about Victor."

His eyes focused on the screen. I glanced at it briefly, then turned back to him. "You don't have to be afraid to tell me, Vic. Anything, even your deepest, darkest secret. Who are you?"

"Bond. James Bond," the voice from the speaker announced. Victor's eyes never left the screen.

I stared at him, willed him to answer me. The screen exploded into gunfire.

"I'm not going to let you get out of this, you know," I said, as I tossed a buttery kernel at his mouth. "No matter how sexy James Bond is."

"My mother tried to kill me," he said, his voice flat. His eyes never moved from the screen: the picture there reflected on his face. James Bond was kissing his female nemesis. My stomach clenched at the sight of them as a background to Vic's words. "She chased me with a butcher knife. That's when I joined the Army."

The smile left my face.

"She's always hated me. My older sisters used to try to distract her when she came home from work, 'cause she was always in a bad mood. She'd take it out on us kids. Mostly me, 'cause I was my father's son. She'd beat me so many times I didn't even feel it anymore. Until she took after me with that knife. Then I knew I had to leave."

I touched his hand hesitantly. I'd never heard a story like that, never knew anyone who was beaten by his parents.

"Is this what you want to hear? Are you happy now?" He glanced at me, his eyes as flat as his voice. Then he returned his attention to the screen.

"I'm sorry, Vic. I didn't know."

"Yeah, well, it's not as if I advertise it. People don't want to know the truth."

"I do, Vic. I'll listen."

And I did listen, listened as my heart broke for him. Besides being abused by his mother, he was deserted by his father. Acceptance had come in the Army, where he had served as a mess sergeant until his medical discharge. A tiny piece of shrapnel had pierced his left eye during a training exercise; he was partially blind. So much for a military career. That's when he'd returned to Woodsville, his home. His parents were in Korea, where his stepfather was a civilian advisor to the military.

Vic recited this story as if it was unimportant, insignificant, his eyes rarely leaving the light of the giant James Bond before us. I felt as if he'd left me somewhere, as if he'd split and only a small part of him was beside me in the car. And that part was there just to satisfy my curiosity, or to somehow make me regret my questions. Like knowing his painful past was a punishment. I sat in silence, mesmerized and somehow ashamed. I didn't want to hurt him.

Vic had nothing but respect for Jorge Mendiguran, the man who raised him. "He took us in," he said, "all three of us, and raised us as if we were his own. Even after he and my mom had kids. He worked his way up through the ranks and became a missiles expert, despite having only an eighth-grade education. He's the best."

Mendiguran had tried to protect Vic, too, but it did no good. "My mother hates me," he said, his voice remote and lost. "I can never please her." Later, I learned that he had three younger siblings as well, two brothers and a sister. "Six of us, altogether. Four different fathers. My mother is nothing but a slut."

But that wasn't the worst. What was harder, more horrible than anything I'd heard so far, was Vic telling me that he could never have children. "I was tested when I was in the Army," he said. "Part of the medical tests they take. I'm sterile."

I felt something crumple in my heart, some little piece of me reach out to him. To be unable to have a child had to be the saddest thing a person could ever face. I planned to have a large family.

"You see why you don't have to be afraid of me," he said. Finally he looked at me, looked me eye to eye, his face as hard as stone. "You'll never have to marry me. I can't have children."

I didn't know what to say, how to comfort him. I reached out, across the width of the seat, to touch him in silent condolence. Then, somehow, I was in his arms. He buried his head in my hair, and I didn't know who was holding whom, and it didn't matter. I couldn't bear his pain.

And I couldn't reject him, either. He already had so much hurt inside. My family was so different from his, so *Happy Days* normal. I'd taken it for granted that everybody lived like us. We had our problems, but we didn't go around beating each other. If anything, we were too close, too interwoven. If I lost any one of them, I'd have lost my self. They loomed, larger than life, in my mind as I compared my family to Vic's.

Unlike Victor, I was blessed with a structured family environment that I assumed was the norm back in the sixties: two parents, one working at his job—the breadwinner father—and one working at home—the nurturing mother. There are the four of us Stevenson kids: Brandy is two years older than I, while she is two years younger than Travis. Ricky, the latecomer, was born when I was nine. And, of course, there had been the eldest, Danny, who was killed at the age of two by an errant log truck driver.

Though he made his living as a logger, our father was a hunter by nature and upbringing. Deer, elk, moose, javelina, duck, quail—anything edible eventually found its way to our dinner table. We were fortunate that our home was situated in the midst of the coastal mountains, just a few miles from the Pacific Ocean. Our grocery store included the redwood forest, the numerous rivers, and the sea. Dad knew them well, knew all their secrets, and their bounty was our daily bread. The forest provided venison, the fields quail, even pheasant, the sea was rich then with crab and abalone, the rivers gave us trout and salmon. Moving to Woodsville hadn't changed it much, except that we didn't have a vegetable garden or an orchard.

Dad was the undisputed ruler in our home, the king of his castle. He had merely to glance at the four of us to get instant obedience. But he seldom touched us, even as disciplinarian. Never in anger. That look was all we needed. Spankings came at the direction of my mother, who, I imagined, would calmly tell Dad which of us deserved the punishment, and why. Dad would take the designated culprit into the appropriate bedroom and quietly mete out the required number of whacks with the palm of his hand. I hated the spankings, of which I remember two, more because of the shame they brought to Dad than the fleeting physical pain. He disliked his role as much as we did.

Our father was a man who loved to laugh. He lived every day as if it were a precious gift, never allowing the harsh labor of logging to deprive him of his innate joy in living. He shared his love of sports with his children. After school, after the chores were done, we'd be out in the field beyond the house, playing two-man teams of baseball, or football, or basketball. Mom never joined us, and Ricky was too little, so it'd be Dad and me against Brandy and Travis, or Travis and me versus Dad and Brandy. Sometimes, on weekends, there'd be cousins and uncles, too, while the aunts joined Mom in the house, providing us with refreshments when we'd all tromp in, sweaty and noisy and winded from hours in the field.

More than a playmate, Dad was a teacher. He was never impatient with us, never demeaning. If we dropped the ball or slipped and fell or struck out or did anything that makes you feel stupid when you're trying so hard to please, he never made a big deal out of it. As long as you were giving it your best, that's all that mattered. Pay attention. Swing hard, run fast, watch the ball. These were the lessons we learned after school, lessons that affected every aspect of living. I thought everybody knew them.

Dad was Paul Bunyan, Daniel Boone, and Mickey Mantle all rolled into one six-foot-three frame. He was my idol.

And Mom was my role model. Unlike Vic's mother, mine seldom raised her voice, never a hand against us. She ruled with a kind of silent dispassion—always there, always watchful. Mom was always waiting for us after school, always had dinner on the table at five o'clock sharp, always put her needs—if she had any needs—after everyone else's. As far as I knew, she never made an important family decision, never wanted anything other than marriage and motherhood. Her self-effacement became my martyrdom; her modesty my humility.

People say I look like her; when I was sixteen, I hoped I would. At forty-two, Mom was frequently mistaken for a much younger woman. The boys who occasionally squired Brandy or me always came to life around my mother. She was the essence of femininity—slender, soft-spoken, quiet. Her many talents, especially her artistic abilities, were formidable. The fact that she never exhibited these talents only made her sacrifice of them bigger, nobler, purer. She never had to talk about herself—her very presence changed the atmosphere in a room. I knew I could never live up to her example. Or her expectations.

Where Dad provided the athletic outlet, Mom introduced us to the world of performance art. It was she who saw that Brandy and I were tutored in piano and ballet; lessons began when we were barely out of our toddlerhood. When we were little, both Brandy and I sang unselfconsciously as the music came from nowhere to flow through our bodies. Later, Brandy's music came through her fingers to grow into exquisite pictures on canvas, while I secretly dreamed of becoming a famous Broadway star.

"Secretly" because my dreams were the source of discomfort and the object of ridicule. "Discomfort" because everybody knew you had to be beautiful to make it in show business; "ridicule" because everybody knew I wasn't beautiful, and never would be. Brandy was the beauty of the family. I always knew that, and knew, too, that I could never compete. She had the thick, burnished auburn hair of our mother, while mine was lank and straight and fine, a dirty blonde with no body or beauty whatsoever. She had the perfect nose, short and straight with a refined little bulb at the end, while mine was longer, straighter, larger, a sure indication of "less than" which I have never lived down. And perfect brows, winged and arched without the need to ever pluck, and, of course, perfect bow lips. These things she pointed out to me during our adolescence. I would glare at her and then into the mirror, but try as I might I could never tame the thatches above my eyes nor reduce the generosity of my mouth.

Brandy's eyes were her only defect. Hooded by drooping lids, framed by short, straight lashes, she would always have difficulty with the finesse required to enhance them cosmetically. But, as if to make up for this slight error, Nature had given them a bright, clear azure, a blue that never changed no matter what her mood.

I simply paled, literally, in comparison. My eyes were, as I said, seagreen; sometimes grey, sometimes a washed-out grey-blue, sometimes a murky green. And while they often shone with curiosity or laughter, they were just as often somber, as I am. My lashes may have been longer, and gently curled, but they were, like the hair on my head, fine, demanding quarts of Maybelline to even make them noticeable.

No, I could never compete, although, as the younger sister, I did. And, it seemed then, I always came out lacking. Last. Least. Less than. Despite that constant sense of inferiority, the bond between my sister and I was an almost tangible force, a force that would survive anything. Or so I believed back then.

And then there was Danny. As a young girl, I secretly mourned Danny. Because I never knew him, he became everything I lacked from other family members. He was my savior, my knight, the brother who always stood up for me, rescued me, applauded me. No one ever talked about him. His picture hung in my grandmother's bedroom, one of those black-and-whites with tinted cheeks. I talked to him whenever I was alone. I imagined that he answered.

This was my family. As a child, this family comprised my entire world—with grandparents, aunts, uncles and cousins, of course. School and church provided social stimulation and training, even friends, but family was the core of my existence.

And the source of all my problems. For I was cursed with the stubborn, silent pride of my mother, the need for approval from my father, the call from the divine from my maternal grandmother, and the yearning for adventure from my paternal grandfather.

That is why it was so easy to fall for Victor Charles Brian, this idealistic, mysterious man who had no close family.

Our second date convinced me that meeting Victor was part of my destiny—a sign from God. Our second date took place at church. I had been invited by the pastor of my church to join the college-age youth group, even though I was only a junior in high school, ostensibly because of my "maturity." I was always told I was "mature" for my age, probably because I took life seriously, held aloft impossibly high goals, and was idealistic to the extreme. One day in Sunday school, I'd self-righteously declared my stand against smoking, announcing that it was a sin against the "temple of our bodies." The next thing I knew, Reverend Smith was extending an invitation to join the older youth group. Of course, I was flattered and proud.

Vic could quote the Bible with such authority that even the Reverend was impressed. That he was a religious man was like a direct anointing from God, as far as I was concerned. I was caught by surprise, then overcome with pride that I had brought him to the meeting. Within minutes, all the others were listening to him as he entered into a rousing discussion over certain scriptures.

"I didn't know you knew the Bible like that," I babbled later. It would be great to talk to someone about God without feeling shy. I could imagine Vic and me getting into some really heavy religious discussions.

"There's a lot you don't know about me," he teased. "I've thought about becoming a preacher many times. God means so much to me, has been such a big part of my life that I want to share Him with others." His eyes glowed with missionary zeal; even his voice changed, as it had in the group. He sounded a lot like Oral Roberts.

"That's really awesome," I said, excitement welling up within me. "I've often felt that way, too. Only it's hard to talk about it to most people. They think you're weird. Even my family doesn't know how much Jesus means to me, how I talk to Him all the time."

We looked at each other for a long moment, Victor's eyes seeming to draw my soul right out of my body. I felt so strange, not a part of myself any longer. Was this an epiphany? A sign? How deep was this man, how much was there simmering beneath the surface? Suddenly I was in his arms, and he was kissing me, and it was all so *right*. I knew then that I belonged to this man, that he was my destiny.

I introduced him to my family when we returned home that night. They were all there, gathered in the living room as if by prior arrangement. Brandy and Greg and Travis. They all turned their heads away from the TV when I led Vic inside. They all listened politely when I introduced him. Vic had dressed in a somber dark blue suit, a dark tie. Even his shoes gleamed with a proper shine.

Vic addressed my parents as "Ma'am" and "Sir" and smiled respectfully at my older siblings. Ricky ignored us, his eyes glued to the tube. A few awkward moments passed while everyone tried to think of something to say, then Vic politely excused himself, leaving me to face the judgments I knew were coming.

"He drives too fast, Stephani," Mom said. "The whole neighborhood heard you leave today. And he's too polite. I don't like to be called 'Ma'am.'"

"He's too old for you," Travis said. "I'm going to find out more about him."

"He looks like a hood," Brandy chimed in. "Greg says he has a bad reputation."

"I don't like him. I hope you don't see him again." This from Dad, my father the King. Furious, chagrined, I told them all they didn't have enough information to pass judgment, and stomped to my room.

So it began, the dream before the nightmare. The forest became our retreat. In the small town of Woodsville it was soon known that Stephani Stevenson was not allowed to see Victor Charles Brian, the bad boy returned from who-knows-where, for my father was not impressed, as I was, with Vic's incredible knowledge about everything and anything, any more than with his ultra-politeness to his elders. Rumor had it that Victor had run away from home when he was eighteen, had been trouble all his young life.

But I would not listen to rumors. I knew the truth. Whatever he showed the rest of the world, he showed me what was really in his heart, the tenderness he was truly capable of feeling, the love he had stored up inside for his entire life and was ready to give to me.

So I believed.

For the first time in my life, I was ordered to stay away from someone I liked—for the first time in my life, I disobeyed. My father was wrong about Vic, I knew that as surely as I knew my own soul. Dad would see, in time, I told myself. Then he would approve, even applaud my choice.

But the schism between us tore me into pieces, fragments of guilt, and pride, and stubborn righteous belief in Vic's goodness.

"They just don't understand," Vic assured me, as I cried in anguish over our estrangement. "They'll come around. Don't worry. Our love is all that matters, Steph. Our love will win them over, you'll see."

He said what I needed to hear, what I wanted to hear. Besides, he believed in me, in my talent, as my parents never had. "You're going to be famous someday," he'd tell me. "You're going to be great, Stephani. I want to be there when they finally realize what a genius they have for a daughter." Shallow words, words meant to flatter. As they did. In the aftermath of rejection of both my chosen profession and my love, they were words I needed to hear. Victor understood me as no one else ever had. He was my ally.

So Vic and Stephani ran away from prying eyes and meaning-well neighbors to discover each other where no one could see. We fished in the streams, we cut down dead trees to sell for firewood, we talked about our dreams and hopes and aspirations. We created a world entirely our own.

"He understands me!" I shouted to my father, when he discovered we were stealing away together. "Don't you see, Daddy, he really cares about me." He shook his head in resignation, throwing me that look, that obey-me-or-else look, and I glared back at him, my heart turning to ice. "He loves me, Dad! Please, please understand." He sighed, this man whom I wanted to please more than anything in my life, and in that sigh was a silent rebuke.

I ran to my room, slamming the door behind me. The echo reverberated down the hall and back again; his sigh returned to mock me. I pulled the pillow over my ears. *You just don't understand, Daddy,* I sobbed silently. *You refuse to see him as he really is!*

Chapter 3

I moved off the bed, slowly, quietly, willing my mind to numbness. *Don't think,* I thought. *Don't remember.* Moving to the door, I caught a glimpse of my image in the bureau mirror. *Oh, God. Is that me? That creature?* The reflection was vague in the dim light; the bedroom curtains were drawn against the weak winter sun. But I didn't want to see more. I didn't want to see the mottled bruises, the pink blotches, the ravaged eyes. My long, pale hair frizzed out in a cloud about my face, tangled and limp. A harridan's face, a witch's hair. Forcing myself to move quietly, I opened a drawer, slid it just far enough to reach inside and grasp a piece of cotton flannel. I nearly had the nightgown out when I heard the doorknob turn. *Caught.*

"What are you doing?" he demanded. "You shouldn't be out of bed. You'll catch cold running around like that. Come on, let me help you…" Taking my arm, he led me back, one arm around my waist, guiding me. Tucking me in, he said, "We have all weekend. We're totally alone. I'm going to show you how much I love you, Steph, how much you love me."

He unbuttoned his shirt.

I tried. God help me, I tried to comply. I wanted to die. But something was growing within me, something that refused to give in. All the time that he "loved" me, I fought the impulse to strike him, fought the shudders of repulsion, fought the need to scream, and scream, and scream.

No one would come to my rescue. I knew that, just as I knew I could not fight him with my body. I had to beat him with my mind. Against every instinct and impulse, I kept still, allowed him to "love" me while I concentrated on how I was going to escape. *Getaway.*

My thoughts drifted. Pictures of our life together skated across the mirror in my mind. Behind those brief flashes, a child wavered, a toddler standing in a river, a fawn beside her, the forest behind her. *Where is that child now?* My resolve deepened. *You will not win this war,* I cried. *You will not!*

"See, Steph? I can make you happy. Just be patient, darling, just be patient. I'm the only man who can make you feel like this."

He moved over me, adjusted my arms and my legs, and was inside me. I felt a tear dampen my cheek.

I blinked the tears back. *I will not cry anymore!* Crying was weak. Crying didn't help. I clamped my teeth together. Every muscle tensed, every nerve screamed. His flesh grated against mine. *You will not win,* I thought as his rhythm increased. *You will not win this war.*

"God meant for us to be together, Steph. Always. What God put together, no one can take apart. Remember? We made a promise to each other. No one can break that promise."

"Yes, Vic," I said. "You're right. You're always right." *No! No, no, no, no, no! God didn't put us together, He didn't create this mess, I should have known!*

He rolled off me, spooned himself against me, wrapped his arms around me. "Let's just sleep awhile, baby. I'll hold you, I won't let go. We can just relax the entire afternoon."

Sure, sleep. I didn't think I'd ever sleep again. *Why didn't I see it? How could I be so blind?* It was there from the beginning. All the clues had slipped subtly, one by one, from behind the madness. If only I had seen them.

* * * * *

June 1965

"What would you like?" Vic asked, his voice oddly autocratic. Tonight he was dressed in a double-breasted navy blue suit and a gray-and-green tie, his black shoes gleaming from a recent shine.

"I'm not sure," I replied. "I haven't had a chance to look at the menu yet." My nose tickled from the aromatic chrysanthemums nestled on my shoulder; floral perfumes always made me sneeze. I, too, had dressed for the occasion, dragging my peach-colored chiffon—last year's Spring Fling—out from the depths of my closet.

"Might I suggest the spaghetti. It's really quite excellent." Vic's glance flicked over the tall menu, his serious expression quelling the sense of excitement quivering in my stomach. I had seldom been to such a fancy restaurant. Never an Italian bistro. The white linen tablecloths and matching napkins were intimidating; the lighted candles emphasized the elegantly appointed room. The silverware—two forks, two knives, and two spoons—reflected the candle's flame.

ASK ME NO QUESTIONS

I straightened my spine.

"Well?" Vic prompted. "The spaghetti?"

"Yes, the spaghetti." I laid the menu in front of me, folding my hands on my lap in an effort to hide my nervousness. Vic was different tonight. Unreachable.

The waiter approached our table in response to a preemptory glance from Victor. "Are you ready to order?"

"Yes," Victor replied in that stiff formal voice. "The young lady would like the spaghetti. Thousand Island dressing for her salad, and she'll have the soup and—coffee?" His eyes flicked my way in question.

"No, I'd like milk, please," I said without thinking. *Milk! Children drink milk!*

"Milk to drink," Vic repeated.

The waiter scribbled while Victor continued. "I'll have the New York steak, medium rare; baked potato with butter only; and coffee."

"Salad, sir?"

"Yes, Thousand Island dressing. And soup."

"Thank you, sir." He held his hand out for the menus, and, upon retrieving them, glided noiselessly toward the kitchen. In moments, he returned with our soup.

Victor was watching me. His eyes, now so familiar, glistened in the candlelight as he watched me pick up the soupspoon. I smiled reassuringly at him and brought the first spoonful to my lips.

"Soup is eaten by bringing the spoon in, this way, and then turning it away from you, like this," he demonstrated. I stared, my mouth closing over the hot liquid. I swallowed, returned the spoon to the bowl and mimicked his instructions, my face hot with embarrassment. But I summoned up a smile and followed his example. Of course, I couldn't think of anything clever to say.

Salad soon arrived, the soup bowl whipped from its place with alacrity as a mound of shredded green settled in front me. I knew enough to use the outside fork. Glancing at my so-serious beau, I determined to play the game, matching him bite for bite.

"You eat the salad with the fork furthest from your plate," he intoned, obviously unaware I had already chosen the correct utensil. "Always work your way from the outside in." Again I smiled brightly, lifting my eyebrows in what I hoped was a mocking salute.

But my cockiness, what little there was, vanished when the mound of spaghetti, overflowing with its dark spicy sauce, was placed before me. How does one eat spaghetti neatly?

Victor knew. And told me. "Spaghetti is usually cut into edible portions," he said as he sliced into his juicy New York, "and it's quite proper to tuck your napkin into your dress like a bib." I watched him cut his meat into "edible portions" and wished I had a steak in front of me.

"That's all right," I said. "I'm not very hungry, anyway."

Somehow I made it through the evening without further humiliation, but only because I decided there was no way I would let him see my embarrassment. He corrected me only once more, when the ice cream was served, but I stubbornly continued spooning it toward me, defying him to make an issue of my ignorance. He merely smiled knowingly and sipped his coffee in silence.

The evening ended with an uncharacteristically prudent drive home. As we walked to my door, Vic slipped his arm around my waist in the only warm gesture of the evening and kissed me lightly on the lips before retreating to his car.

The aloof stranger was gone next day, and I asked myself if I had just over-reacted to the formality of the occasion. After all, it was our first "dress-up" dinner date, our first encounter with an elevated style of dining—and our first official date since Dad had confronted me about my relationship with Vic. Maybe Vic was nervous, too, stiff and autocratic out of a desire to impress me. There could have been any number of explanations. Rather than belabor the memory, I put it down to getting-to-know-you jitters and concentrated on the Vic I saw before me today.

And today he smiled his wide, crooked smile, his eyes alight with devil-dare as he coached the Little League team to their first victory. Today he held my hand as he guided me over the rocks to the stream we fished; he crowed with delight when I caught and landed a native Rainbow trout and insisted on gutting it myself. Today he playfully tossed the beach ball over my head, his laughter unrestrained when I fell, backside first, into the cold water of Eagle Lake.

When he offered me his class ring in June I accepted it, suppressing the twinge of guilt that threatened to mar my happiness. Knowing what my parents' reaction would be, I wore the ring on a chain around my neck so it would hide beneath my summer tees. I knew what I was doing. After all, it was just a ring! If things didn't work out—if I was, after all, wrong about him—I could always give it back.

Mom and Dad had other ideas. The ring was discovered almost immediately. I was, at this point, still unused to deception, unskilled at lying, unable to hide anything for long. That would come later.

"I thought you didn't want to be tied down this last year of school," Mom said, calmly trying to use logic with an illogical teenager.

"I changed my mind," I said. "Vic's fun, and he really cares for me. He's proud of me, which is more than I can say about my family." This last was muttered as I walked away from her.

"I don't think you know what you're doing," Mom said, abandoning logic for parental wisdom. "He's not what you think."

"What do you mean? Can't you trust me? Why can't you let me make my own decisions?"

"Because your decisions aren't very good ones. Because you're in over your head, and you can't see it. He's not good for you, Stephani!"

"Mom, he understands me! He doesn't try to make me into somebody else! Can't you just let me grow up?"

"Why can't you trust *me*, Steph? Why do you insist on making the biggest mistake of your life? You're acting like a child, not the grownup you think you are! Can't you see that?"

I turned away from her, tears burning my eyes. *I'm a senior in high school!* I shouted silently. *Old enough to know what I want!* But even as I thought those thoughts, even as I protested, part of me felt a curious relief that Mom was putting her foot down. Vic often confused me. His constant pressure to go all the way added tension to our dates, even though his reassurances that he wouldn't hurt me, wouldn't do anything I didn't want, tweaked at my innate desire to trust him. Sometimes I felt like a yo-yo.

"Your father's not going to like this," Mom said to my back. "You're going to have to talk to him." She left my room, shutting the door behind her.

I waited for the inevitable confrontation with Dad. I couldn't fight him, couldn't win an argument with the King. Couldn't even argue. I waited, the tension building inside me.

The summons, when it came, was a denouement to the climax of my own emotional upheaval.

"Stephani!" Meekly I followed the source of that roar; submissively I sat before my father, the man I idolized more than anyone on earth.

The pain in his eyes was unbearable. I gazed instead at the waning summer sun.

"Why are you doing this, Dolly?" Oh, no. He'd used my pet name. Swallowing, I waited for the plea. "He's not the right kind of person for you. You have plans for college, for a career. He can only hinder you. You don't want to give up your dreams, do you?"

My dreams? I thought. *You won't let me pursue my dreams. You don't even want to hear about them. What do you know about my dreams?* "Daddy—"

"When he comes to see you this afternoon, give him back his ring. Tell him you won't see him anymore."

"But Da—"

"Give him back the ring."

"Daddy—"

"Break up with him!"

We stared at each other, each in pain, each in conflict, each hating to hurt the other. *What about my dreams to act?* I cried inwardly. *What about my plans to go on the stage?* But I didn't give voice to the plea. He would reject that, too.

I retreated to my room, defeated. If only we had been able to communicate with each other, it's quite possible that all the years of misunderstanding and heartache would never have happened. If we could have broken through the barriers of pride and shame and guilt, of adolescent insecurity and parental uncertainty, we might have avoided immeasurable regret. But it was not possible. Not then.

When Vic came later to pick me up, I met him at the door, tears streaming down my face, the ring in my hand.

"What's this?" His eyes sharpened, probing.

"I—have to give this back to you." I held it out to him. He took it, palmed it lightly, and then handed it back.

"Now tell me what's the matter."

"I—we—have to break up."

"Why?" His chin stuck out in familiar belligerence. Vic was not one to retreat.

"Because. Because he said to."

Wordlessly, Vic grasped my elbow, ushering me into my own living room. "Mr. Stevenson?" My dad stood, his six-foot-three towering over Vic by a head. "Mr. Stevenson," Vic continued, unruffled, "Stephani has told me you don't want her to see me anymore. Can I ask you the reason why?" That chin jutted out, begging to be struck.

But Dad merely sputtered at the younger man's effrontery. He opened his mouth, but no words came out. Alarmed, I thought he was having a heart attack, as his face darkened in a purple rage. "Get out!" He cried, his eyes bulging. "Get out of my house!"

Vic returned his stare, eye for eye, and in seconds my father—the King—slumped to the couch, gasping for breath. I stepped toward him, my hand extended. Vic drew me back and slipped his ring onto my finger, folding my hand over so it wouldn't fall off. I watched, helpless, as Mom rushed to my father. Neither of them looked at me. "Dad," I said, but Vic's hand kept me close, and I watched as within seconds my father recovered. The purple flush receded from his face and his breathing appeared to return to normal. "Vic," I whispered, my eyes meeting my love's stricken gaze as he, too, watched my parents' reaction to his defiant presence in their home. Assured that my father was not having a heart attack, I allowed Vic to lead me to his car, my mind whirling.

After that, there was no separating us. The small sense of relief I'd experienced at our short separation faded into astonishment at Vic's courage. Here was a man who stood by his convictions, a man who would not let others dictate to him. And he loved me!

But while my parents had lost a skirmish, they had not yet given up the war. Mom was too honest to hide her feelings, but Dad had apparently realized the uselessness of appealing to my "good sense." The summer days passed in a sort of truce; I saw Vic openly now, but had to put up with my mother's occasional dark comments. My siblings, when I saw them, added their ridicule to Mom's, until I felt even more ostracized than before. It seemed I'd always been the subject of my family's scorn. I'd always been Different. Nothing would ever change that.

Vic became my refuge, my strength. Only he understood.

Summer vacation culminated in one final battle, this time a surprise attack. Each year my family made a trip to the coast, back to the logging town where we were raised. Located some 300 miles west of Woodsville, the village of Ft. Henry has not changed since the Great War: it survives despite the cutbacks in logging and the decline of the fishing trade, due largely to an increasing tourist trade. Its three thousand residents have roots there, roots which extend back beyond the War to the dawn of Western expansion. Most of our family still resided there, cousins and aunts and uncles and grandparents. We would stay with my maternal grandmother during our visit.

An idyllic week passed. My cousins and I caught up with each other, sharing boyfriend stories amidst peals of laughter. All was well. All was relaxed.

All was a scam, a plan, a pretense created for my benefit.

One morning I stumbled out of bed only to overhear my parents talking quietly with my grandmother, Nanna. "If we leave late Monday night, she won't be able to do anything about it," Mom was saying.

I crept closer, my stockinged feet soundless on the hardwood floors.

"But how do you think she'll take it?" Nanna asked querulously.

"I hope she'll settle down and forget him."

Oh, no! They're going to leave me here! Trembling with indignation, with fear, I hurried back to my room, threw on some clothes, and ran next door to my aunt's. Reaching the telephone, I dialed frantically, ignoring Aunt Judy's questioning glance.

"Winkler's," a voice announced crisply.

"Is Vic there?"

"Yes, just a minute."

I waited, my heart thumping in my ears.

"Yeah?"

"Vic, they're going to leave me here! They're going to leave in the night and just—go!" Panic welled up as I spoke. How could my parents do that to me? How could anybody do that to a child? Abandon her?

"Don't worry," Vic said. The determination in his voice calmed me. "If they leave you, I'll just come and get you." I could almost see the set of his mouth as he spoke. "No one's going to take you away from me."

"Oh, Vic, I'm so scared."

"Don't be, Steph. Just go on back and enjoy yourself. I can get there in a few hours if I have to."

Relief flooded through me. Replacing the telephone, I took a deep breath and walked back to Nanna's to face them.

It went surprisingly easy, that confrontation. My aunt had overheard my side of the conversation with Vic—I hadn't even noticed her standing there—and was in Nanna's kitchen when I returned. Mom and Dad looked so old. No one said anything.

"I know," I announced boldly, my heart hammering in my ears. "Vic's going to come and get me if you leave me here." I sounded stronger than I felt. This was bravado. Vic would come and get me, sure. But my parents, while dwindling in stature, shrinking in power, were still my parents. The ultimate authority. If only they had known it.

They didn't. They caved. Mom looked at me, a look of such pain I couldn't return it. There was resignation there, and sorrow. I recognize it now, having children of my own. But at sixteen, all I saw was scorn. And pity. *You always think you know best!* I thought. *You don't, you don't!* I wheeled and left the room.

We returned to Woodsville in silence. Ricky, now seven years old, said little, his attention diverted by a lap-game. Mom and Dad were lost in their inner reflections. I had nothing to say to them: they had betrayed me. Never again could I trust them.

ASK ME NO QUESTIONS

Barely had the car parked in the drive when I was gone, running to Vic's apartment. He was waiting for me, arms spread wide in welcome. I fell into them. Straight into his arms, and into his bed.

The losing of my virginity was, after all, anticlimactic. Painful, too. But those things were unimportant. What was important was that I belonged to Vic now. Fully, all the way. There would never be anyone else.

We clung to each other long after the blood had dried on the sheets, long enough for my tears to dry up. They were tears of joy, tears of love. And tears of regret. Now I would not be a virgin bride.

But Vic was ecstatic. He kissed my tears away, he held me and promised that no one would ever hurt me again. "You're mine, Steph," he said, over and over. "Mine. I'll always protect you."

Finally, it was time to go home. I cleaned myself in his minute bathroom, rearranged my clothing, stared at myself in the filmy mirror. *Do I look different?* I wondered. *Will they be able to tell?* Already, guilt was replacing relief, shame crept in to cover joy. The little girl was gone. I had chosen my path; now there would be no turning back.

Vic took me home and dropped me off, reassuring me with a quick embrace. I went in, the aroma of fried chicken assailing me immediately. Mom and Dad greeted me as if nothing had happened between us. We ate together like the family we weren't, our thoughts concealed under a banter of chitchat.

Two weeks, just two weeks after our homecoming, just when the world was once again settling into a sense of calm, my worst fears were confirmed.

The phone rang one Saturday morning. Mom had taken Ricky shopping with her, so I was home by myself. "Steph? Vic's quitting." It was Tim, a friend and classmate, calling from Winkler's Coffee Shop. "He had a big fight with Frieda, and he just walked out of the kitchen. I can't convince him to stay." Tim knew how much I loved Vic, how close we were. Frieda was the head waitress, an old-timer who'd been at Winkler's since the turn of the century. She had a lot of clout, figuratively and literally. Why fight with her, of all people? Frieda liked Vic!

"Is he gone?" My heart pounded in my chest. *Don't be gone!*

"Not yet. He's sitting on the back step, smoking a cigarette. Says he's leaving right after his shift."

Thank God. "I'll be right there."

I ran the mile and a half as if my life depended on it, which of course it did, praying with every thunk! of my tennis shoes hitting the pavement. *You can't leave! Oh, please, God, please don't let him leave!* My prayer life had grown considerably since meeting Victor Charles Brian, I have to say that for him. It seemed that every day brought a new crisis, a different set of problems. And every prayer ended with an exclamation point.

I reached Winkler's, panting, my legs rubbery. Vic was still on the back step, sucking a cigarette. "Vic," I cried, reaching out. "Tim said you quit. He said you're leaving town. Why? What's the matter?"

My plea was met with a chilling silence while my love, my life, contemplated the stub of his cancer stick before taking one last draw.

"It's time to go, kid. It's been nice."

"Nice! It's been 'nice'? What about us, Vic? What about our plans! We're supposed to get married! You can't just—give it all up! What happened?"

"Look, I'm going. Leaving. That's that." He snubbed the butt on the ground beside him, stood, and stalked back into the restaurant.

You got what you wanted, I thought. *Now you run.* How would I ever face my family?

But I wasn't ready to give up. Digging a gum wrapper from the depths of my pocket, I tore it open to reveal the blank part inside, and I found a pencil in the glove box of his car. "Dear Vic," I scribbled, squeezing the letters onto the tiny space. "You told me once to fight for what I wanted, to not give up so easily. How can I, when who I'm fighting for doesn't want me? How can I do anything but give up when the person I love is walking out of my life?" Tears slipped over my cheeks, dripped onto the paper. *Why should he love me, anyway?* The enormity of what I'd done, what I'd given, overwhelmed me. I choked on the shame of it. I turned the wrapper over. "I forgive you, Vic," I wrote, my letters barely legible on the printed label. "I know I'm not good enough for you, anyway. I know I'm just a kid, no matter how hard I try to act grown-up. You deserve better. Thank you for loving me." I didn't sign it, since he should know its author. I stuck it into the edge of the windshield and hoped he'd find it. Then I turned away from Winkler's, away from town and began to walk on leaden feet toward the hills.

It was one of the longest days of my life. I didn't have the slightest idea of what to do. I'd given myself to him. I couldn't change that, couldn't take it back. As liberal as the sixties may have been, "free love" was not rampant in small towns across America. Gloria Steinem had not yet made her mark, and girls who gave up their virginity without benefit of matrimony were marked for life. I had fallen into that pit, and there would be no climbing out. I was ruined.

Watching the sun make its way across the sky, I thought about just staying on the mountain. Maybe a rattler would find me and I would succumb to its bite. How long could I last up here? There was water in the pond we swam in occasionally, cold water that would keep me alive. But I didn't want to live. I couldn't face them, couldn't acknowledge my stupidity, my mistake. I wallowed in self-pity while the sun dipped over Eagle Mountain.

But inevitably I did make my way toward home. Slowly I trudged toward the lights blinking on in the housing development below me. I didn't have anywhere else to go, and I wasn't brave enough to die.

I was nearly home when I felt, more than heard, a car stop behind me. A door slammed, arms caught me up, and I heard Victor's voice in my ear. "I couldn't leave you, Steph, don't you know that? I could never leave you." I clung to him, clung to those words, clung to their promise of forever.

The sun was hidden behind the mountains before I stepped into my home that night, a billion years older than when I had left it. Mom and Dad and Ricky were oblivious to my aging experience: they watched the tube in comfortable silence, no one the wiser. I slipped into my room and under the covers of my familiar twin bed, the quilt Mom had made me a comforting weight. I pulled it over my head and shed silent tears. Tears of exhaustion, tears of relief, tears of mourning. Nothing would ever be the same. For beneath the relief was the knowledge that this new world—this world of love—could disappear in the blink of an eye. There was no one I could trust. *Please, God*, I prayed. *Please, God.*

Chapter 4

"God spoke to me. He said we're meant to be together. Always. Forever. You'll never leave me, Stephani. Never leave me. We're meant to be together. Forever. God said so...." I heard the sounds, felt the words against my hair before I understood them. It was dark, the darkness of death, in which all light was closed out, curtained off, contained. Vic's arm snaked around my waist, clamped me to him in a vice-grip so tight I could scarcely breathe.

I moved the toe of my right foot, felt the prickles of numbness, stretched my left leg. It, too, was numb with the weight of immobility. Vic's arm tightened. "You'll always be my wife, always. What God has put together, no man will part. No man. You'll never leave me, Steph. Never..."

I won't get away from him, I thought. *I'll never get away.* I could have laughed, if there was room to laugh within that embrace. I'd never wanted to leave, I'd only wanted him to love me. I'd fought heaven and all its angels to stay with him, to prove my love was enough. But love was never enough. Not with someone like Vic.

* * * * *

December 1965

"I can't marry you, Stephani. I can't marry anyone. I'm an agent for the CIA."

His voice was low, nearly a whisper, but I heard every word as if we were alone. The people chattering all around us in the busy restaurant were merely making background music for the most important words I would ever hear.

I'm an agent for the CIA.

He looked at me from hooded eyes, eyes that glowed amber in the candlelight. The candles from twenty white-linenned tables reflected there, like an Andy Warhol print, flame after flame flickering in the canvas of his iris, and if I could have found humor in that moment, if I hadn't been stunned by his dual announcement, I would have laughed aloud at their multiple reflection.

But even then, I knew not to laugh at Victor Charles Brian.

You have to marry me, I thought. *You said you would. Tonight.*

I stared at his face, incoherent, confused, and saw only the features of the man I loved, the man who loved me, who'd planned to elope with me this very night. There was pain written there, on his mouth, and sorrow in his eyes, and worry on his brow. And tension in his hands.

I looked down at our hands, clasped together across the table. His knuckles were white and my fingers were pinched inside his, and suddenly I pulled my hands away, nearly upsetting the water glass in my haste. A drop slid over the rim, pooling on the pristine cloth like a tear before it was absorbed.

"Steph, I'm sorry," he said, his voice stronger now, carrying easily, I thought, to the table nearest us. I glanced around, afraid the other diners were witness to my humiliation. How many people were jilted on their wedding night? The room was cold, so cold. I shivered as a chill rolled over my bare shoulders.

He was almost handsome in his navy blue suit. He'd worn a tie, the only one he owned, for this very special night. It was narrow and navy in color, with grey and maroon diagonal striping, and it contrasted with his white shirt in such a distinguished way. I was so proud of him, proud to be with him as he'd escorted me to our table, his hand on my elbow.

I'd worn my strapless white tulle gown, thinking it would make a wonderful wedding dress, and my white fur stole for which some poor rabbit had sacrificed his life, and I'd felt elegant, so bride-like as I'd entered the restaurant, carrying our secret just beneath my heart. I glowed with it, I knew. Trembled with the excitement of it. As I looked around the packed dining room of Winkler's All Night Cafe, I wondered that everyone inside could not guess that I—we—were getting married tonight.

But no, we weren't, after all.

"I'm sorry," he said again. "I do love you. I don't want to hurt you. But Steph—Stephani look at me—I can't risk your life. I can't ask you to take the chance."

I retaliated then, stung by his easy dismissal of our love. "You don't want to hurt me? You can't risk my life? What do you think you're doing? I've given myself to you! I've changed my life for you! Defied my family, estranged my friends, changed my schedule, all for you. And what do you do? You're late for half our dates, you disappear for days at a time, you say you can't marry me, and you don't want to hurt me?"

"Please, Steph, you don't understand—"

"I understand, all right. I understand that you're just like my mother said. You wanted one thing, and now that you got it, you're done. Through. Goodbye. Thanks a lot, Vic. Thanks for ruining my life."

The words tumbled out, but somehow my throat squeezed tight, and I didn't know if he could even hear me and I screamed inside, *You idiot! Don't you dare cry now!* as my hands twisted the tulle into a crumbled net on my lap.

What did I expect? Vic and I had been inseparable for six months now. He was my world. While I was still planning to become an actor, now I had an exclusive audience. He advised me about the Tennessee Williams play I was in, waited for me during rehearsals, and picked me up right after school so we could spend an hour or two together before I had to go home.

But while he praised my talent and spoke frequently of the glowing future that awaited me, he was often preoccupied, late for dates, defensive and evasive when I questioned him.

I had defied my father for him, estranged my family. I didn't even see much of Beth anymore, I was so wrapped up in Vic. I had given him everything, including my precious virginity. All I had left to lose was my pride.

So I lifted my chin, straightened my shoulders, and said as regally as if I were indeed the princess I'd felt like thirty seconds before, "I don't suppose it ever occurred to you that I might be a help instead of a hindrance."

Surprise flitted over his eyes. He, too, straightened, glanced around the room, and, cocking his head warily, asked what I meant.

"I'm an actress, Vic. I was born to play this part. Don't you see? No one would ever know you were anything but a cook in a restaurant. I could be your cover." My voice gathered momentum as the possibilities grabbed my imagination. The shame and humiliation of a moment ago receded, but I knew I was fighting for my life. I would never live it down if my mother was right. I would always be just another teenager who fell for the wrong guy. Everyone would know. "I could even find out things for you," I said eagerly. "I can be whoever you need me to be. I can help you!"

It was a moment of divine inspiration. The sudden twist in conversation was too sudden even for him; he had no retort, no ready objection. He'd obviously never envisioned me taking the offensive, and I certainly had not thought I'd be clawing desperately for survival on this night, and in moments we were out of the restaurant, away from prying eyes and straining ears, and into his car, where I continued to argue my case.

ASK ME NO QUESTIONS

"I know it sounds corny, Vic, and maybe it is, but I've always known I was meant to do more than just be a wife and mother. I've always known I would have to sacrifice a normal life for something bigger, for a calling, or a cause, or—something! This is it, Vic. This is the reason we met and fell in love. We were meant to be."

I babbled on, my head filled with idealistic notions of fate and honor and noble sacrifice, and, yes, glory too. I saw myself as some kind of heroine saving her country and couldn't stop, wouldn't have accepted anything but concession from the man I now knew was my destiny. I was fighting my own crusade and wouldn't accept defeat.

It was an exhausting monologue. Vic usually did the talking when we were together. That was one of the things he loved about me, he'd said, the fact that I didn't insist on being the center of attention. Unknowingly, I had adjusted my temperament to meet his expectations. He could never know that one of my teachers had once called me "brutally frank." With Vic, I was the epitome of modest womanhood. I spoke when I was spoken to and gave my opinion only when it was requested. It wasn't a conscious adjustment; it was done only out of a desire to please.

In the end, he agreed, and in the end, he won. He pulled out the diamond chip engagement ring he'd kept in his pocket, and named his terms.

"You'll never know where I am, Steph. I could be gone for days, or even weeks, and you won't know anything but what I can tell you. We work on a need-to-know basis. You'll have to lie for me at times, pretend you know where I am, but you won't. Your life will never be your own. Our life will never be normal. No one will ever know what we're really doing. It will be hard. You'll be alone. You have to be strong. And you won't ever be able to ask any questions, because I can't give you answers. Do you understand?"

"I love you, Vic, that's all that matters. And all I need to know is that you love me."

I extended my left hand, and he slipped the tiny circlet over my knuckle. It sparkled like the stars in the clear December sky above us. I thrilled with the triumph of victory.

If ignorance is, indeed, bliss, then arrogance must surely be faith. It was blind faith that swept me along the hurricane of emotion that night, arrogance that sparked the fuel of the fire that carried me for the decade that followed. I believed in him, believed in his cause, and his lies became mine.

"I want to do this right," Vic said solemnly. "Instead of eloping, I'd like to ask your father for your hand. Do you mind?"

We drove home, where Mom and Dad were still up, watching Johnny Carson on television. Vic followed me inside, asked my father for a minute of his time, and quietly, formally, asked him for my hand in marriage.

Dad's reaction surprised me. Never accepting our relationship, I knew he had always hoped I would break it off. But Dad didn't know what I had given; he didn't know that I belonged to Vic, that there was no turning back for me. I watched him as he listened to my fiancé's request. He seemed stunned. I waited for the outburst, the angry refusal.

But he nodded his head. Yes, I could marry Vic. I had my father's permission. It was the best Christmas present I could ever imagine.

We were married in late March just as the daisies were popping through the ground, the white petals a vivid contrast to the tender green shoots of grass. Strangely, as I walked down the aisle on my father's arm, I could hear no music. No one sang of everlasting love or of bonds never to be broken. Oh, the organ wheezed "The Wedding March," silencing the sweeter sound of the birds singing outside. But I walked in a vacuum. I thought then that time stood still for this blessed occasion, but I know now that the angels were holding their breath as I joined my hand to the devil's.

It was a small service, the ceremony brief, quiet, serious. Despite their acquiescence, my family had always been against the marriage, hoping I would "come to my senses" after all. Dad reminded me of all our plans, of college and career going down the drain. He may even have consented to my becoming an actress, if it meant I would never see Vic again. But I didn't ask, didn't bargain with my life. I knew where I belonged.

At first Dad tried to convince me to wait at least until after I graduated from high school, perhaps hoping that by then I would reconsider marrying Vic at all. "I want you to graduate a Stevenson," he said. "What's the rush? Why can't you wait?"

There was no time. Vic wanted to be married immediately. I needed to be married immediately. The Army was wrong, Vic's tests were wrong: I was pregnant.

I had ignored those first prickles of apprehension; the markings on the calendar denied the feeling that "something" was different. I shook off the fear. After all, Vic had told me he couldn't have children. I told myself I was being paranoid, when in truth I was ashamed of the weakness that had allowed me to give in to Vic's demands when I wasn't ready. Once the deed was done, I had no further argument. I was his, totally and completely his.

ASK ME NO QUESTIONS

Making love wasn't at all what I had thought it would be. The romantic novels I read and the equally girlish whisperings in the high school locker room hadn't prepared me for the pain; there was, after all, none of the passionate longing for fulfillment, none of the satisfaction of having been fulfilled. Our coming together was always hurried, always silent, always something to be hidden. I was inordinately shy, and not at all sure of what was expected of me.

Vic had some very clear ideas about the subject. "A man doesn't like an aggressive woman," he told me. "It's the woman's job to make sure her husband is satisfied. But you'll learn. You're fine. I love you." That was all that mattered anyway, that he loved me. After we were married, I wouldn't feel so guilty, so ashamed. Then it would be different.

So amidst my guilt and shame was denial—denial of the possibility that I might have another worry, another guilt, to add to the list. My pregnancy was confirmed just two weeks before the wedding.

Even then, at the discovery of my embarrassing condition, my parents had tried to talk me out of the marriage. "You don't have to get married, you know," they insisted. "We can arrange for you to go to school somewhere else until the baby's born. No one need ever know." Of course, they were talking about adoption. Sending me away in shame. Sending my baby away. No. This was my child, mine and Vic's, and I would never, ever give him away. I had no doubts about that. So a hasty wedding was arranged.

The reception at my parents' home was noisy and informal, with a lot of laughter and good-natured teasing. Two families, strangers to each other, met for the first time and covered their discomfort with expected titters over the young newlyweds. My parents had come through, as always, with smiles on their faces no matter what may be in their hearts.

Vic's parents were absent, a sign of years to come, as they lived overseas. Vic's mother had sent him a letter, admonishing him over our situation. "I taught you to be strong," she wrote. "And now you have to face the consequences of your weakness."

But her words didn't matter now. She didn't know the truth, anyway. Our baby would be a blessing during the times that Vic was gone, risking his life for his country.

So I was glad the harridan, Vic's mother, was absent from this most joyful occasion. His older sisters were present, though, with their husbands and children. They were family enough. They seemed happy for us.

I was supremely happy, confident that I was truly fortunate to be able to marry the man I loved and serve my country at the same time. Since his admission to me of his secret life, I was filled with a sense of destiny which nothing could overpower. He had become my reason for living; his secret became mine. I was willing-eager—to sacrifice my life and all my dreams, so great was my conviction in his cause.

As we prepared to leave the reception, Mom hugged me and pulled me close. "You've made your bed," she said in my ear. "Now you have to lie in it. Goodbye."

The farewell was final. I knew without question that I was banished. But I didn't care. Someday they would all know the truth.

Vic and I drove to our new home; it was a one-bedroom bungalow, painted white, with a white picket fence surrounding the miniscule yard. A typical American dream house. Upon reaching the front door, Vic lifted me and swept me over the threshold in the traditional gesture of possession, kicking the door shut behind us.

Inside, the tiny rooms seemed cozy and secure despite the worn carpet and sagging couch. My clothes were stuffed into microscopic closets whose doors wouldn't quite close. Maybe not quite a dream house. But close. What mattered was us, anyway. Mr. and Mrs. Victor Charles Brian.

"God, I thought I'd never get you to myself!" he said, setting me down in the center of the living room. "Let's get rid of all this paraphernalia." He lifted the circlet of rhinestones and lace from my head, impatiently pulling at the hairpins that kept it in place. I felt my hair fall, its weight released from the constrictions of wedding day finery. "I love you, Stephani Brian," he murmured, catching my hair in his hands as he held me, raining kisses on my eyes, my nose, my neck. "You are so precious…"

And so I began the most challenging role of my life, the role of Victor's wife.

Chapter 5

He left me, promising to return in a little while. My body ached with a weariness surpassing anything I had felt in the past. It was a deathly weight, a heaviness that chained me to the bed. *What time is it? Has the night passed yet?* It didn't matter. Nothing mattered. *Was this what it had all been for? The years of sacrifice, of loving and understanding and giving in, giving up? God, what a fool! How could I have been so blind! To think he really loved me!* The tears began again as the pain inside my head exploded into a myriad of lights, so intense that the very act of opening my eyes was torture...It was too much. Cradling my head between my hands, I buried my face in the pillow. *Oh God,* I prayed, *Please help me. Please, please help me to die. I can't live like this anymore*! But I knew that praying was futile. I knew that God didn't listen anymore. I knew there would be no release.

* * * * *

March 1966

"No mission too difficult, no sacrifice too great. Duty first." So read the slogan which governed our lives.

There wasn't going to be a period of adjustment for Stephani Brian. No honeymoon. No time to get used to the idea of being a Company wife. Vic told me that he had to work the day after our wedding, so we'd celebrated briefly by going out to dinner and taking in a movie. Vic wanted to show me off, to announce to the world that we were finally husband and wife. We had dinner at Winkler's, the restaurant where Vic worked during the day—his cover job—and his boss made a fuss over us and stuffed the bill into his pocket. Then we sauntered into the theater, where the Saturday night crowd greeted us cheerfully, inspected my tiny diamond, twin to my engagement ring, and made lewd comments about the night ahead. We left before the first feature was half over.

Despite that fact that I was not a virgin bride, I had dreamed of romance and moonlight on our first night together as husband and wife. Vic's sister had given me a sheer white peignoir as a wedding gift, and I donned it nervously in the tiny bathroom of our bungalow. *Finally*, I thought, *we can be together without haste, without shame or guilt or embarrassment. We're married.*

I touched the tight knot of my belly, sucking in and inspecting my profile. Despite the doctor's prognosis of delivery just two months away, our baby was not very big, making only a little convex bump to my silhouette. I hoped our lovemaking would not be as painful as it had been in the past. I hoped that Vic would not be in such a hurry. After all, we had the entire night.

Opening the bathroom door, I glimpsed my husband in the sliver of light that escaped into the bedroom. He was lying on his side, facing the opposite wall. I switched off the light and crept around the bed. There was a window on that wall, and I parted the curtain to allow the pale moonlight to filter in. Turning to touch Vic's shoulder gently, I whispered, "I love you," as I leaned in to kiss him.

He was asleep.

My visions of a romantic wedding night disappeared as I listened to my husband snore softly in the darkness. I felt the excitement of the day and the nervous anticipation of this night dissipate, the energy drain from my body as I watched him sleep. I'd hoped that we could take our time, tonight, to really make love. I wanted to please him, to learn how to love him. I wanted to find the joy and fulfillment I thought lovers were supposed to feel.

Once again, I would have to wait. I blinked back tears of disillusionment and swallowed my hurt. Lying down beside him, I became conscious, for the first time, of the warmth of another body lying beside me. *My husband.* I snuggled close, turned on my side, and spooned myself against him. *We have the rest of our lives*, I thought. *Time enough to love.* I closed my eyes.

Four o'clock. I glanced over at the clock beside Vic's head. The hands shone in the darkness. It was time for Vic to get up. Surely he'd set the alarm. I waited a few more minutes, then touched his shoulder. "Vic? Honey?"

"Hmmm?"

"Honey, it's four o'clock. Time to get up."

"Nooo. I'm sleeping."

"Come on, you'll be late for work."

"Don't have to work. Go back to sleep."

"No, Vic, you said you had to work today. You'll be late."

"I don't have to work. Go back to sleep."

ASK ME NO QUESTIONS

I lay back, resting my head on the pillow as I tried to remember Vic's exact words in the casual conversation earlier. I was sure he'd said he couldn't get Sunday off. In fact, he'd apologized for the lack of a honeymoon, saying that he'd wanted to get a fancy hotel room in Feather River, a place where we could be alone, away from everyday routine. But Mr. Winkler had only given him one day off, his wedding day. Should I awaken him? I hated to begin our marriage by nagging a reluctant husband to get out of bed. Vic was a grown man, he didn't need me to remind him of his responsibilities. Maybe I'd misunderstood. *I'll ask him later*, I told myself, settling back into the pillow. *I hope he won't be in trouble with Mr. Winkler*, I thought as I drifted off.

But when we finally awoke, Vic was in a great mood, and I didn't want to spoil it by questioning him on our first day as man and wife. We spent the morning as most newlyweds must, enjoying the freedom of unrestricted togetherness and adjusting to each other's morning habits. We were together. That's all that mattered.

That afternoon I noticed Vic's distraction in the middle of a movie on television, and before I could ask him where his mind was, he arose from the couch and picked up the car keys. "I've got to go," he said briefly, "I'll see you later."

"Go? Where're you going? Is it about the case?" I knew he was in the middle of a mission. Excitement rippled through me.

"Yeah," he replied. "I won't be long. Don't worry, I'll be back before you know it."

"Okay," I said, "I'll have dinner ready when you get back." *I wonder what you're working on*, I thought. *Can you tell me about it? Will I read about in the newspaper?*

Dinner was cold and I was asleep when he returned. I had finally succumbed around midnight, feeling good and sorry for myself as I slipped into bed. *So much for a romantic weekend*, I moped, the excitement gone. *I guess this is what it's like to be a spy's wife.*

I'd waited as long as I could, bathed and pampered and dressed in my new peignoir. Alone, I'd clung to the memory of our long conversations in the weeks before the wedding. "No questions," he'd said. "You won't be able to ask me what I'm doing, or where I'm going. I may have to leave at any time, for days, or weeks, maybe months. I'll get in touch with you, but you won't be able to contact me. It won't be in any way a normal marriage. Can you handle that?" *Yes, yes. I can handle that as long as I know you love me. You can have your work, no questions asked.*

I didn't awaken when he returned, didn't hear the car or the door, or Vic's step on the frayed rug. Didn't hear my husband slip into bed. Our first day was over.

On Monday I returned to school. There was just a little more than two months to go before I graduated. There had never been any question about that, at least. Then, since I wasn't headed for Hollywood any time soon, I would earn a two-year degree at Woodsville Community College. It was a perfect way to continue acting and keep my ear on the pulse of the town. And it would keep me busy when Vic was away.

My world divided into two dimensions; the daily "normal" routine, almost unchanged, and the "real" life at home, waiting for Vic. Except for the fact that my name had changed, school was the same as it always had been. Beth chattered on about her latest flame, my teachers made little of my new status. Finals were coming up, and then graduation. I could have been any high school senior on any campus in America.

But I wasn't. Everywhere I went, from the moment I woke up in the morning, I was acutely aware of the fact that life was, indeed, a very precious thing. The excitement of being a Company wife faded quickly into a niggling, nagging fear that Vic would die in service to his country. I worried constantly about the danger, imagined getting a message that he had not survived "the mission." That fear began to crowd everything else out of my mind. In the evenings, I "saw" the messenger knock on my door; at school, I "heard" my name on the intercom, calling me to the office. Always with a dire message, a tragic story. Somehow I knew he would not be mine forever. I could not trust our happiness.

But I could not share those fears with my husband. If I voiced even an intimation of worry, I would get a gruff, "You knew what you were getting into," from Vic. Gradually I learned to hide my anxiety under a facade of calm acceptance.

That was what Vic expected, anyway. A cool head. No hysterics. Not one to accept tears in a woman, neither did he like public displays of affection. They both attracted attention. I had to learn to be inconspicuous, to melt into a crowd. "Don't be so bouncy," he'd say as we walked down the street. "You look like a little kid, not a married woman."

"But I'm happy!" I'd reply. "I can't just walk like some complacent married lady! I feel like shouting, like saying 'Look at me, world!' and running down the street simply because I love life! Can't I be happy, Vic?"

"Stephani, stop it. You're creating a scene. People are looking at you." And he'd walk ahead of me, leaving me behind until I behaved as a proper married woman should.

There were other things I had to learn. Vic didn't expect or want a dinner at night, as my father had expected his. Since he worked at a restaurant, Vic ate there, two or even three meals before he came home. His evening snack usually consisted of something convenient, like potato chips or cookies. Most often, though, he wasn't home at all, so the need to show off my culinary skills evaporated before I ever learned how to cook.

And then there was budgeting. Vic's take-home pay from Winkler's was $280 a month, sufficient, in 1966, to support a family of two, maybe even three. His earnings as a Company man were irrelevant; they went into a bank in San Francisco, where they would accumulate until Vic retired. A portion—twenty-five percent—went to an orphanage in Alaska, Vic explained, so I was not to count on government money while we were young and healthy. "Besides," he said, "if we can't live on three hundred a month, then there's something wrong."

Never having had any experience with household budgets, I accepted his explanation and, as in everything else, never asked questions. Vic handled the money. He gave me five dollars each week for groceries. I learned very quickly that I could just about make do on a loaf of bread, a dozen eggs, a half-gallon of milk, and a few cans of tuna. Then I would have enough left to buy the snacks that Vic liked to munch on late at night.

Vic was very particular about the household accounts, giving me my allowance each Friday with the admonishment to "make it last." Frugality, if not inherent, was soon learned. I enjoyed the challenge, reveled in my tiny victories as I scrutinized the grocery shelves for bargains. Luckily, my appetite was small; I had been eating just lunch and dinner for years, skipping breakfast in the rush to get to school. All I had to do was cut back a little more. I didn't want to gain fifty pounds of baby fat, anyway.

To further our economy, I washed our clothes in the kitchen sink, feeling quite wifely in the process. Vic loved the smell of line-dried laundry.

However, if Vic noticed my efficiency, he never commented. But he did ask, every week, how much money I'd spent, how much was left from my allowance. I made sure there was always some change.

It was a strange world, this wedded life. Not at all what I had imagined.

From the day of our wedding, I saw less and less of Vic, my love, and more of Victor the spy. Especially in public. Always, I had to remember to conduct myself as a "respectable married woman." Subdued, I learned to school my features into a facade of coolness whenever I left the bungalow. I took my cues from Vic. If he was laughing and carefree, then I was also. If he was restrained and businesslike, then I followed suit.

And when he was angry, I withdrew into frozen, frightened silence.

I no longer hear my mother warning me, "Wait until your father gets home," but I remember how we used to cower in anticipation of the deserved punishment. My father stands six-foot-three; he's got the strength in his long, lean body to fell a redwood with a four-foot diameter in less than fifteen minutes, and if you thinks that's a long time, you ought to try it yourself—if you can find a tree that big anymore. Anyway, he's a strong man, a tall man, and when he came home from a day in the woods, he really didn't want to face domestic problems. There were always chores enough on our hundred-and-a-quarter acres to keep us all busy past dark. Thus Dad's spankings were quick and hard, and once they were over, they were over.

"Wait until your dad gets home" was not an oft-repeated phrase because we'd all four learned early on that, worse than Dad's spanking was the look in his eye, the set of his jaw that told us he didn't want to do this, didn't want to have anything to do with punishment, but it was his duty as our father, and he was never one to shirk his duty. So we helped him, as much as we could and as much as we understood, by being "good" children most of the time. It was truly a case of the punishment hurting him worse than it hurt us.

Not to imply that it didn't hurt. As much as he may have hated delivering the blows, his hands were big and hard and strong, and we were all skinny little kids. The last spanking I received ended up being humiliatingly memorable, as I ran to my room accompanied by the warm trickle of urine running down my leg and I realized I had peed my pants. As the tears of embarrassment flowed from my eyes, I promised myself I would always be good.

Thereafter, if any of us misbehaved, it would just take a look from Dad to settle us down. We were well trained.

I did not know how to deal with anger, not other people's or my own.

Vic's anger terrified me. Only once during our courtship had I glimpsed what I called "the Victor side" of him; once had been enough. It had been over a trivial enough matter: when the senior class pictures were delivered just weeks before our wedding, the usual exchanges had taken place, with each person writing his or her message on the backs. I had passed mine out, signing them, as I usually did, with "Love, Stephani." Vic saw one in a friend's possession and immediately exploded into rage, shouting at me, his face inches from mine, before stalking away in furious silence. "How could you sign it, 'Love, Stephani'? Do you love him?" he yelled, emphasizing "love" with ripping sarcasm.

"No, of course not! I love you. It's just a signature, the way I sign my name! You know that!"

"I know you said you 'loved' another person. That means you can't love me—unless you're spreading it around."

I blanched, felt the blood drain from my face as I stared at him in disbelief. "Vic, you can't mean that—"

"How do you know what I mean? For that matter, how do I know if you mean it when you say you love me? You could have any number of guys on your string for all I know!" And he'd stomped off, leaving me gaping after him.

I hadn't heard from him for three days. He'd refused to answer my phone calls, refused to see me when I went to his work or home. Bewildered, I'd finally stopped calling. When he called me on the fourth day, all traces of anger were gone; in fact, he acted as if the incident had never happened. It receded into the past with the same abruptness as it had appeared, making me confused and uncertain.

But I wasn't confused about one thing—I never wanted to see that side of him again. It was Vic I loved, the carefree outdoorsman with a zest for living. Vic, the man who sacrificed his life for his country.

Surprisingly, the days began to resemble a routine, a routine that became the measure of what was "normal" in my life. By the end of our first week together as a married couple, I was confident that nothing would ever come between us. We loved each other.

Chapter 6

I awoke suddenly, my dulled senses struggling to focus. Something was happening. I waited, listening, straining my ears, my eyes remaining closed. My very skin seemed to listen, the nerves reaching beyond the confines of the flesh.

Someone was in the room with me.

I felt him then, felt the eyes upon me as he stared, willing my own to open. "Stephani," he murmured, his words just brushing my ear, "I know you're not asleep. You can't fool me, you know. I know everything. I know you love me. Show me you love me, Stephani. I know you're awake. Don't try to ignore me, Stephani. Your little games don't work." I heard the anger coming from somewhere deep inside him, the frustration building. I knew there was no use in pretending anymore.

I turned over. He was lying just behind me, his head resting on one hand, his eyes unblinking as I turned to face him. *Is that the face of the man I loved?* Those burning eyes, that grim mouth. *Where is Vic, the man to whom I gave my life?*

He reached over me, grabbed my hair, and pulled my face to his. "Show me, Stephani. I know you still love me. Say you'll never leave...."

I groaned, gagged against his breath, his mouth on mine. His hand tightened in my hair, and then he was on top of me, inside me, and I could not fight, could not move, could not feel. "I'll never leave you," I said, my voice coming from somewhere far away.

* * * * *

March 1966

Once again, I awoke before Vic's alarm buzzed. Something had awakened me, something within my seven-months-pregnant body. I listened in the stillness of the early morning, listened to the message my inner being was whispering. I felt so strange.

ASK ME NO QUESTIONS

Today was our one-week anniversary. School had let out early yesterday in honor of Easter vacation. Vic had surprised me by taking me out to a friend's ranch, where we'd spent the afternoon riding horses. I loved horses, had had one before my family had moved to Woodsville. My pregnancy hadn't stopped me from enjoying the rhythm of the horse as we raced over the hills near Woodsville. Vic had laughed as he chased me; we raced and I had won. Later, we stopped in at the bowling alley for a hamburger, and had bowled a few games. My back was aching by that time, but it ached most of the time now anyway, so I'd ignored it. By the time we returned to our little bungalow, I was tired but happy, happy to melt into Vic's arms as he loved me.

But now, now I felt something happening. It wasn't pain, it wasn't the cramping of contractions, it was just—something.

The alarm shrilled. The bed was suddenly wet beneath me. "Honey," I gasped, "Honey, I think it's time. The baby's coming."

"What? It's not due for two months yet! Are you sure?"

"Yes, I think my water just broke. Call Dr. Daily."

Vic stumbled from bed and made his way to the kitchen, where the phone hung from the wall. I heard him mumbling into the instrument. Why don't I feel any contractions? I had spent hours in the town library since I learned of my pregnancy. Now I struggled to remember what I'd read.

"Your mom says I should take you to the hospital," Vic called to me from the kitchen.

"Mom? Why'd you call her? Call Dr. Daily."

"I did, I did. I just thought your mom should know." My parents had not wanted to see me after my marriage; they were too hurt by my indiscretion. I had ruined all their dreams for me.

"I'm glad you called her," I said, "but now I think we'd better go."

Swooping me up in his arms, Vic carried me, blankets and all, into the Chevy, dumped me unceremoniously onto the seat, and ran to the driver's side. I had not prepared a suitcase or a bag, since I wasn't expecting this little jaunt just yet, but I doubt my husband-about-to-be-a-father would have remembered it anyway. I watched him fumble with the keys, amused at his panic. Vic was obviously going to be a typical new father. The car spit gravel all over the drive behind us as he raced the mile or so to the hospital.

Vic always loved racing down the road at breakneck speed—what better excuse than a baby on the way? He made it through town to the hospital in less than five minutes, daring the cops to catch him. Years later he would tell the tale of this mad dash, embellishing it with sirens screaming and brakes screeching in the emergency entrance, but I heard none of that. Just the two of us, arriving with no fanfare other than the grand entrance we made as he carried me in, sheets, blankets, and slightly bulging tummy.

The head nurse was an efficient redhead with a ramrod-straight back who brooked no excuses for a clean, quiet delivery. Her accomplice was a broad black woman with a smile so wide all I could see were her teeth in a midnight moon face. Her name was Trini. The drill sergeant informed my husband that first deliveries take anywhere from eight to eleven hours, so he might as well go off to work. The baby wouldn't be here until after he put in his shift at Winkler's. Vic happily left me in her charge—after all, this was woman's work.

Trini, my nurse-turned-nanny, whisked me into a hospital gown and proceeded to initiate me into this alien world, this place of cold, hard tables and needles and tubes. It was all strange, all different from the description in the books.

Thus I was introduced to the preparation to childbirth. The enema. The shave. The examination of my private parts. Everyone was coldly efficient, silent and impersonal. I hid under the ends of my hospital gown, my face flaming as I submitted to the pushing and prodding and cold morning air. Then I was alone in the sterile delivery room, staring at the blank walls while my body was ripped apart by our little bundle of joy.

Tiffany was born after a mere two hours of unbearable pain. I decided somewhere in the middle of this experience that it was not for me, and unashamedly begged Dr. Daily to make it stop. "Relax," he ordered. "Push."

How one does either while cramps are controlling every body movement is beyond me, but I did attempt to comply. When my bloody little daughter was drawn from between my spread-eagled legs I felt none of the pride and love I had expected, nor did I forget the pain she put me through. I was relieved, and scared, and exhausted.

"Is she all right?" I asked weakly.

Trini held the tiny creature in my line of vision, proudly displaying the baby's perfect form. Wrinkled skin drawn over fragile, impossibly tiny bones. Mouth screwed into a puckered grimace, eyes squeezed shut. *That came out of me? Wow!* I stretched an arm to touch her wrinkled cheek.

I drifted off to sleep, a sense of accomplishment finally, a small sense of satisfaction. She was healthy, heart and lungs deemed satisfactory and in fine working order.

Trini called Vic with the news, a service she did not perform for everyone who came through those corridors. But sometime within those two hours I had struck a sympathetic nerve, and she wanted to reassure my waiting husband that everything had progressed just fine. Though a little more than six weeks early, Vic's daughter was perfect in every way, right down to her ten tiny fingernails.

"How much does she weigh?" Vic shouted through the line.

"Four pounds, eleven ounces."

"She weighs eleven pounds, four ounces," the new father yelled to Winkler's regulars.

Trini chuckled when she reported this to me, and we shared a moment of woman's wisdom over the silliness of men.

The day lengthened, and as two o'clock approached I washed my face, smoothed the hospital gown over my newly-found waist, and brushed my hair a good hundred strokes. Vic would be coming to see us soon.

But it was Mom whose face appeared in the door at two, Mom who asked how I was feeling and assured me of my baby's well-being.

Why don't you leave? I prayed nervously, searching for Vic behind her. *Vic and I want to be alone.*

But Vic didn't appear. My prayer was answered only moments after I thought it, and Mom left, and Vic still didn't come. "The baby," as I was calling her, was brought in for her afternoon feeding—formula fed, I might say. Nursing was out of the question. Was never a question. No one asked me, although if they had, I suppose I would have agreed with my husband. I couldn't take the baby to school with me, after all.

As the shadows lengthened in the afternoon, all the doubts that hid behind the mask of confidence slipped to the fore, and I worried within my mind. *Where are you, Vic? Are you working, on a mission, even now?* I tried to remember conversations, comments, or even uncompleted thoughts that might have been voiced before or during the ride to the hospital. Nothing. If he was working, I just didn't know. As I settled back on the pillows, I heard a tap on the window, and Vic's gleeful grin filled my eyes.

"Vic!" I waved, my heart instantly joyful. "Come in here! What're you doing outside?"

For answer, he held aloft a stringer full of crappie; he'd been fishing. I stared at the fish, and stared at him, and my heart warred between anger and relief. Relief won. "I'll see you later," he said, as he waved the stringer at me. "I've got to clean the fish."

So I settled in again, this time determined to rest and think about nothing but our baby, until he came back.

"Tiffany Anne," he said, later. "We're naming her Tiffany Anne, after my sister and your mother." He sat beside me on the bed, held my hand, and kissed me lightly on the lips. He'd brought me a milkshake. The next morning, he took me home.

Once again, reality belied the fantasy homecoming I'd envisioned. As soon as I was safely deposited in the house, Vic left to catch up on his fishing. He was obviously uncomfortable around all the intimate trappings of birthing—I could barely walk, so tight were the stitches inside. I wanted the support of his arm as I stepped into a tub of warm water and soothing lotions. But there would be none of that.

I hid my disappointment, as I was learning to hide all emotion; besides, Mom was there to take care of me, and men just got in the way. This, too, was woman's work.

Tiffany remained in the isolette in the hospital, for she had some growing to do. She'd lost nine ounces since her birth; she wouldn't come home until she was a bouncing five pounds.

Mom left to attend her own family. Just as I was beginning to feel downright sorry for myself, Vic returned with a wonderful idea, an idea that exonerated his absence over the past two days.

"Mr. Winkler gave me the rest of the week off," he said, pulling me in a close hug. "I think we should go on a honeymoon. How about it?"

"A honeymoon?" I said uncertainly. "A real honeymoon?"

"Yes, baby, a real honeymoon. Let's get away for a few days, just you and me. We haven't had a minute alone. I want you alone! Okay?"

"Yes! Yes, yes, yes! Where are we going?"

"I thought we could go to Lake Shasta," he said, enjoying my excitement. "It's too early for the tourist crowd, so we'll have the whole lake to ourselves."

"I'll get packed right now. When do we leave?"

"I think we can wait 'til morning," he grinned, catching me up again enthusiastically. "We'll get up really early so we can get a good start."

A camping honeymoon in early spring might not be everyone's idea of romance, but for us, it was perfect. Lake Shasta is a man-made reservoir stocked with trout, bass and bluegill, set in the northern Sierras. It would be chilly there at night, but we had our love to keep us warm. Love and youth.

The next day I tolerated the sensations of postpartum cramping while I listened attentively to Vic's enthusiastic anticipation. He was in unusually high spirits, an almost euphoric state, as he raced over the mountain highway, cutting corners and making the tires squeal.

ASK ME NO QUESTIONS

We reached the marina before noon; Vic replenished his supply of bait and asked directions to the secluded campground. I stepped out of the car gingerly, wincing as my stitches pulled against the incision inside me. Vic had been careful, but he'd been unable to avoid tearing them; despite Dr. Daily's instructions, Victor Charles Brian was not about to wait six weeks to make love to his bride.

It had happened last night, during the excitement of planning our honeymoon. Vic had kissed me, really kissed me, and all the longing and disappointments of the past twenty-four hours had suddenly gushed into overdrive as I responded. This was my husband, my new husband, and I wanted him to assure me that he really truly loved me, and that the suddenness of fatherhood was not an imposition, and I was not in the way, or unattractive, or no longer lovable, with my flabby belly and gushing bloody clots. Vic's hands were all over me, and we were all of a sudden on our bed, and he was on top of me and I couldn't stop him, wouldn't if I could, even though it hurt like hell and I wanted to tell him to stop and yet love me all at the same time.

So I walked slowly to the sheltered inlet where the boats were tied, listened for the sounds of fish jumping in the bluegreen water while trying to ignore the chafing pricks between my thighs.

"Pretty, isn't it?" Vic said as he reached my side. "I'll bet there's some good-sized bass in there. Look!" His pointing finger stretched out toward the water. "Did you see that?" Following his gaze, I saw the spreading ripple marking the spot where a fish had jumped.

Vic tore open the package of supplies he'd just purchased. In a few seconds, he'd attached a big green lure to the end of his fishing line and was preparing to cast out over the water. "This is great," he said, "I'll try out my new Whopper. Stand back, Steph, you're in my way!"

I watched the lure sail over my head, the line following it like a kite string in the air. I saw the Whopper land about twenty feet from the shore, the line falling behind it limply. "My lure! It came off the line! Go get it, Steph. I'll lose it! Hurry!"

Like a trained puppy, I jumped into the lake, the cold water closing around me as I paddled to the spot I'd seen the lure drop. I reached it before it had a chance to fall into the bluegreen depths, grabbed it, and returned to shore, swimming with one hand clenched over the runaway lure, the other scooping water furiously as the icy temperature sent chills through my skin.

Vic reached out to pull me from the lake, wrapped a blanket around me, and retrieved the lure from my clenched fist. "Thank you," he said, as sincerely as if I had just saved his life. "I thought it was gone." Carefully placing the offending bit of tackle in his tackle box, he closed the box, restored it to its place in the car, and helped me into my seat. "The sooner we find a campsite, the sooner we can get you dry," he said, revving the Chevy and backing out. "I'll get a fire started and some coffee made. Good thing it's still early."

Soon we were warm and secure, with a cheery fire blazing and a pot of coffee brewing shepherd-style on the grill. Vic didn't wait for the grounds to settle, before he took his fishing pole and tackle box from the car and headed for the water. I poured myself a cup of the steaming liquid and held it in my hands for a time before I sipped, willing the heat to find its way from my fingers to my toes.

The days passed quickly, serenely, like peace before catastrophe. As it was early in the season, we were the only campers willing to risk the near-freezing nighttime temperatures. It was a good way for me to recover from the trauma of childbirth and adjust to the idiosyncrasies of married life, and I felt closer to Vic than in all the past weeks, during the tension of wedding plans, family frictions, and impending parenthood. The only difficulty was at night, when Vic took me in his arms.

I tried at first to protest, to obey Dr. Daily's orders, but Vic was too eager, too loving, and too offended when I suggested that we allow my body to heal. I felt we had all our lives; he felt there was only the present. "There may never be a tomorrow for me, Steph," he said soberly. "I need to know that you love me, no matter what." And of course, I did, I wanted to please him. Forcing my body to relax, I willed my mind to ignore the pain and the gush of warmth, the warm wetness of my blood as it slipped out of me. I was young: I would heal.

We returned home on Sunday, rejuvenated. March melded into April with relatively few difficulties. I began to recognize Vic's habits, his likes and dislikes. I began to settle in to the demands of juggling schoolwork and housework with all the enthusiasm of any bride, never forgetting that I wasn't the bride of just any man.

Chapter 7

"Let's do something really special," he said, his cigarette glowing in the darkened room. *What time is it? Is it still day?* The drawn curtains shut out any light. "How about something special for lunch? A picnic. That's it. We can picnic right here. You won't even need to get dressed. How about that? I'll bring you your favorite. Then we can just enjoy each other. How does that sound?" The glow brightened as he took a drag. *How long? How long will you keep me here? Surely, surely you'll let me out to go to work on Monday.* He turned back to me, his eyes reflected in the glow. "You'll see, Stephani. We can work it out. I just have to show you how much I love you. Then you'll understand. God wants us to be together forever."

* * * * *

April 1966

"Hi, honey," Vic's voice came over the telephone. "How would you like to go out tonight?" The muffled sounds of the restaurant, clanging of dishes, rumble of voices, waitresses ordering, came to me in the background.

"Really? Do you mean it?" *You remembered! I'm seventeen today!*

"Sure I mean it. How about a movie?"

"Oh, Vic, I'd love it! It seems so long since we went out." The moment the words were out, I regretted them. Complaints, or anything that could be construed as such, weren't allowed.

"Yeah, I know. I'm really sorry, honey. It's been pretty rough on you, hasn't it? I'll see what I can do to rectify the situation."

Surprise silenced me. No recriminations? No accusations or offers to relieve me of my misery? He was in a good mood! Smiling into the phone, I felt my spirits soar. A night out with Vic! It was the best birthday present I could get.

"What time should I be ready? Will you be home right after work?"

"I have to go out for awhile this afternoon, but I'll be home by 6:30. Why don't you wear my favorite yellow dress?"

"I'll be waiting. I love you!"

There was a curiously long silence as I listened to the dishes clattering, then voices on Vic's end of the line. Anticipating a cheery, "Goodbye—I love you too," or even a "Happy birthday, honey," I was startled at the change in his voice as he shot out the words, "They're here. Gotta go." Click!

"They" could only be the enemy. I had no idea who or what the "enemy" was, but visions of James Bond popped into my head, and all the anticipation of the moment vanished. "They" had to be drug traffickers, pushers, dealers and the worst sort of people. I spent the rest of the afternoon alternately trying not to worry and praying.

I took a luxuriously soapy bath, washed my long hair, experimented with makeup, tried on the yellow dress. *They're here. Gotta go.* Scrubbed the tub, plumped up the pillows on the bed, looked for something to do in the kitchen. *They're here.* Mended some of Vic's socks. Avoided looking at the clock. *They're here. Gotta go.* Six-thirty came and went. *Please God, let him be all right.* At seven I began pacing the floor, my eyes on the door. *You knew what you were getting in to,* I reminded myself, unconsciously using Vic's words. He might not come home at all. "I don't care!" I said aloud. "Just as long as he's okay!" The hands of the clock crept around to eight. *Why am I so nervous,* I thought. *He's never home before midnight.* But tonight was my night, I argued. Tonight we were going to be normal.

Feeling alternately cheated and guilty over what I construed as selfishness, I continued to worry. At nine I turned on our thirteen-inch black-and-white TV and ate a yellow wedding-cake rose for distraction. At ten, I exchanged the yellow dress for a nightgown and made a pot of coffee. Midnight approached, the television station went off the air, and I was still sitting in the dark chewing nervously on a strand of hair, tense with anxiety. *Please, God, let him come home.* I envisioned the Messengers knocking on the door, their death masks hiding secret smiles.

Lights brightened the driveway; glimmers of metal in the gravel sparkled like minute stars as the car crept toward the porch. Inside the house, I held my breath as I listened to the car door slam; then footsteps echoed on the wooden porch, and the key turned in the lock. He's home!

I rushed to him and threw my arms about his neck, hugging him in a frenzy of relief. "Thank God! You're safe! You're home! Oh, Vic, I was so worried!" Burying my face in his shoulder, I held him close.

Until he pulled my hands away. Wearily pushed me away from him. "Not now, Steph. I'm beat."

"Not now! Not now what? You mean I can't hold you for a minute? I was worried, Vic! You said you'd be home by six-thirty!" I could hear the desperation in my voice; swallowing, I lowered the register an octave or so. "You said you'd pick me up at six-thirty."

"Look. I'm tired, I've been chased halfway across the country, I almost lost an agent tonight, and I don't need your whining the minute I walk in the door! Just leave me alone!"

He left me standing in the middle of the darkened living room, the light from the full moon shining on my face. I could see my hair glistening in the windowed reflection from the bedroom where he'd disappeared. I could see the shine of tears on my cheeks. Angrily I brushed both the tears and my hair away and followed him.

Climbing into the bed, I muttered, "I'm sorry," as I turned on my side, my back to him. *When will I ever learn? No questions. No hysterics. Just accept the inevitable. Nothing matters but that he's safe.* The occasion of my birthday suddenly seemed very small.

The bed wheezed as my husband shifted position. The sound of his breathing filled my ears. The silence was as dense as the darkness.

"I know this is hard on you," he said at last. "I wondered if you would be able to take this life, even with your very convincing arguments. I don't know if we should have gotten married."

Suddenly all my senses were alert, focused on the sounds emanating from the man lying beside me. The words coming from his mouth stilled me; all the fear of the past three weeks rushed up to choke me. *Three weeks. It's taken you three weeks to realize you don't want me.* But were these his words, or the Company's? Please, don't let them be his. I could live as long as he wanted me, no matter what he had to do.

"I'll be okay," I said, forcing the words through my constricted throat. "I am okay. It's just that tonight you said you'd be here, and then you weren't, and I was worried. But I'll learn. I will learn." I strained to keep my voice steady, to hide the tumult within me. Yet fear engulfed me. *He can't be thinking of leaving us*! A shadow of Tiffany, lying in her isolette, flitted across my mind.

"I don't know," he said. "I hate putting you through this."

Silence. I was too frightened to speak: my heart pounded, my throat filled with the pain of choked-back protests. Crying would only anger him, convince him he was right. I lay stiffly beside him, not daring to move. *I have to say something, have to get him off this train of thought.* What was more important, anyway? A night out, or the mission? Our marriage, or our country? I had to convince him I could help him better if we stayed together.

"Vic," I struggled to find words, "I know it's been a strain on you, worrying about me. But I'm okay, really. I just have a few things to learn, that's all. I don't know how much I can say to you, I keep putting my foot in my mouth. It's hard. I want home to be a place where you can shut the rest of the world out for awhile, where you can find some peace..." I drifted off, not knowing how to continue. Everything seemed so trivial compared to the importance of his work. The night closed in on me as silence once again pervaded the room.

"We almost lost an agent tonight." The statement, bluntly made, laid in the darkness like a sudden noxious odor.

"She was set up," he continued in that flat tone, "taken completely by surprise. We watched while they tortured her, burned her legs with a stick heated in a fire...we watched, and we couldn't do a thing about it." I listened, horrified, the smell of burnt flesh, the screams, sudden and nauseatingly real. I felt Victor's anguish. "But she didn't break. She did not break. By the time we got her out, she could hardly walk." His voice broke, the sound grating in the darkness. I held my breath, not daring to distract him. This was the first time he had spoken to me about the realities of his work. "She's tough, all right. The best. We got the whole damned gang."

In my mind, I could see them, the pictures vivid against the cloak of darkness. Pride filled me, pride in the man beside me. Gone was the anger, the worry, the fear. My husband is doing something important! Dangerous, yes, but vital. Of what importance is my birthday? I didn't ask the name of the agent. No questions, that was the rule. So I listened, and made a private vow to keep my petty problems to myself.

Vic fell into an uneasy sleep shortly after his monologue, while I lay staring into the night. *Please, God, give me strength,* I prayed. *Help me to bear whatever I must. No complaints, no whining. Help me be the wife he needs. Even if it means losing him. Even if it means giving him up. Give me courage.* And as I prayed, my mind strayed to the tiny little being still lying in an isolette just a mile or so away. Would Tiffany lose her father before she even knew him? I couldn't let that happen. Somehow, there had to be some way to keep our family together without Vic having to give up his work. *Please,* I thought to the universe. *Please don't let us lose him.* Finally, I slept, dreaming of babies being tortured with burning sticks.

Awakening the next morning with a new determination, I put on my best dress and prepared for church, thinking about Vic. He'd left for work as if nothing had happened the day before. That was how I should be: accepting things as they were, instead of wishing for something else. I had my part to play—it was time I grew up and began to be his partner in earnest.

I pasted on a bright smile and greeted my friends at church, a steady flame burned in my eyes as I sang familiar hymns with new conviction. *Vic needs me. He needs me to be his helpmate. Only I can give him the semblance of normalcy he needs. Only I can comfort him after long hours of mind-numbing, painstaking work. I'm the only one there for him to talk to.* Such was my pride, the arrogance that framed my downfall. These thoughts gave my life renewed purpose. If he needed me to give him freedom, I would do that, too. But I refused to think of that possibility.

Returning home, I changed into jeans and a knit top, fixed a cup of coffee, and put our little house into order. There wasn't much to it, the bungalow was so small, and I hummed as I worked, envisioning the house as a cozy haven of rest for my husband.

Promptly at two-fifteen, the Chevy roared up the drive; a moment later the familiar footsteps sounded on the porch. Opening the door before he could reach it, I smiled, feeling my face, my entire being, light up at the sight of him. He looked so tired. His wavy brown hair was disheveled, as if he'd been running his hands through it. His shoulders sagged, his face was pale. Reaching out, I touched his cheek in a wordless greeting. Soundlessly, he pulled me to him, his mouth crashing down on mine. His heartbeat pulsed against me, his arms were tight bands imprisoning me inside their circle. Before I could catch my breath, we were tumbling into our own private world. The world of lovers with no time to lose.

He slept peacefully. Watching him, I wondered at the constant changes in his mood. One minute serious, the next laughing, the next passionate. Would I ever get used to him? One thing is certain, I told myself, life will never be boring! Slipping out of bed, I found my clothes, put them on, and went into the kitchen to catch up on my schoolwork. Finals would be coming up soon, and I had no intention of falling behind. An hour or two of concentrated effort would do me good.

"Steph?" His voice interrupted my focus on the words in front of me. Shoving the pile of books aside, I walked into the bedroom. "What time is it?" Already he was up, pulling on his clothes.

"About three-thirty. Are you going out?" *Silly question.*

"Yeah, I've got to meet someone. Where's my shirt?" Distractedly he threw aside the blankets on the bed, finding his things among them. Finally dressed, he picked up his car keys and lunged out the door.

This is it, I thought, watching him leave. *This is how it always is. Why can't I get used to it?* Gone was the strength of the morning. Deflated, I wandered outside, sat on the porch and stared with unseeing eyes into the street. *One minute I feel so good about us, so strong. The next minute, I'm a blubbering baby. No wonder he gets so impatient with me. No wonder he wants to leave.* Remembering our brief moments together, I thought, *He loves me. I know he loves me. That's all that matters right now. His work is important. More important than our happiness. Our life will come, eventually. Someday, we'll really be together. And I'll have the satisfaction of knowing that I was beside him during the hard times.* I had to be satisfied with that. I had to draw strength from within myself.

The afternoon dragged along as I tried to focus on my school work. I called the hospital to check on Tiffany. I missed her. It was so strange for my body to have expelled this child, and for my arms to be empty. I wanted her home, to hold her while I waited for her father.

The sun went down, I turned on the kitchen light and drank coffee for dinner, and kept my eyes on my books. When my ears picked up the sound of a car approaching, I resolutely stayed at the table. I was beginning to fear his homecoming; he might tell me he was leaving.

"Stephani? Where are you? Stephani!" He burst into the house bellowing my name, his voice demanding, impatient.

"I'm in the kitchen, hon," I called out, rising from the chair, my voice controlled. "Be right there."

"Come here, I need you."

Well, that's a relief. Rushing into the living room, I stopped abruptly at the sight of blood dripping down his face. "Oh my God, what happened?" Reaching him, I saw only blood, and the ashen shade of his complexion, and I ran to the bathroom for a clean towel. Luckily, first aid was not new to me. Running cold water over the towel, I grabbed a dry one too, and went back to his side.

He was leaning back on the couch, his head resting against the cushions. Eyes closed, nostrils flaring, I knew he was fighting pain.

"Try to relax," I told him calmly. "I have to look at whatever's under the blood." No questions, I reminded myself. Wiping gently, I cleaned as much of the area as I could, discovering a shallow groove along the side of his forehead, not far from his left eye. Blood dribbled steadily from the gash.

ASK ME NO QUESTIONS

But close investigation revealed only a small wound, so I applied pressure, which slowed the bleeding to a trickle. "It doesn't look bad," I said, "Just in a place that bleeds easily. I can butterfly it, and it should be okay." He sat quietly as I finished, his color returning to normal as the bleeding stopped.

Removing the soiled towels, I kept my thoughts to myself. *No questions. That's part of the game.* The wound was minor—but what about the next time? *That's the risk he takes. It's his life. No—it's our life. We're in this together.* Rinsing the blood from the towels, I watched as the water turned from pink to red and to pink again. My mind was detached as I realized that this could be the first of many such occasions. Doctors were only for serious wounds.

Returning to Vic, I sat quietly beside him as he rested, his closed eyelids shuttering his thoughts from me. He wasn't asleep. I felt he was trying to think of what to tell me, what to say that would sound logical. *No. Vic wouldn't do that. He knows I can take the truth—if he can tell me anything. He doesn't have to anyway. I know what happened.* Visions of "gangsters" filled my mind, desperadoes chasing my husband. Would he always get away?

"That was close," he said suddenly, startling me out of my thoughts. "We almost didn't make it."

"You did make it. That's all that matters," I replied.

Heaving himself off the couch, he stood, testing his balance. "I'm sorry you had to see me like that."

"It's okay, Vic. That's why I'm here. For you to come home to."

"Yeah. Well, I sincerely hope I don't come home like that too often," he said, attempting a grin.

He disappeared into the bedroom then, wearily stripped and pulled the bedcovers over himself. In a few seconds I heard him breathing deeply. I tiptoed around the house, knowing I wouldn't be able to sleep for a long while. Finally, long after midnight, I crept in beside him, closed my eyes, and accepted oblivion.

Chapter 8

The bedroom door squeaked as it opened; for a second the light from the living room pierced the darkness of my prison. I closed my eyes, kept still, breathed evenly. *In. Out. Don't move.* I felt his scrutiny, felt the weight of the blankets as he adjusted them to cover me more securely. *Don't move!* The light disappeared and the door squeaked once more upon closing behind him. I heard the familiar click! in the distance as he locked me in once again. It didn't matter. Nothing mattered. Stephani was dead. But someone else was beginning to take her place. Someone else was growing inside her bruised body.

* * * * *

April 1966

"Stephani?" The voice on the telephone was businesslike, impersonal. "You can take your daughter home today. Checkout time is before noon. Can we expect you this morning?"

"Oh, uh…I guess," I replied, thinking fast. Vic would be at work until two. Maybe Mom…should I ask her? While she had been there for me after I came home from the hospital, our relationship was still strained. But she'd said she would watch Tiff while I was at school. So maybe…"Sure," I said. "I'll be there. Do I need to bring anything?"

"Just her clothes," was the reply. "You'll want to bundle her up for the outside air. She's still pretty little, you know."

I called Mom, arranging with her to pick me up and take me to the hospital, where three-week-old Tiffany Anne Brian, now tipping the scales at a whopping five pounds, awaited. I had not seen much of her during her stay; Vic's erratic schedule and the fact that he operated our one vehicle had limited my visits. While I had earned my driver's license a year before, I was not allowed to drive the '57 Chevy. Tiffany was still a stranger, a tiny stranger who was going to add another dimension of stress to my life. Yet I loved her with a possessiveness that surprised me with its fierce physicality. I would protect her. I would keep her safe for her father.

Vic's parenting tendencies had not yet come to the fore, but then, he had more important worries. He had a country to serve. It was up to me to keep our personal life separate from his professional life. And it would be up to me to be both mother and father to our child. Until Vic could really be a part of us.

I gathered the tiny gown, the cotton diaper, the soft blanket and its matching quilted coverlet, and packed them all into the brand new diaper bag Mom had bought. The bottles, sterilizing equipment, and cans of formula were in the kitchen; the borrowed bassinet took up an entire corner of the bedroom. A dresser filled with an entire infant-sized wardrobe rested against one living room wall, clothing loaned to us by an acquaintance who'd had twins. We were as ready as we could be, thanks to friends and family.

Mom was silent on the way to the hospital. We didn't have much to say to each other these days. I was still ashamed of disappointing her and Dad, and yet so aware of their disapproval that I felt like everything they said to me was a criticism. I would be forever grateful for their help, though, especially Mom's. She always came through, no matter what. I hoped I could be like that for Tiffany. Without the criticism. *I will love my daughter no matter what*, I told myself. *I will let her live her own life, whatever that might be. I will never make her feel ashamed and rejected.* So I told myself.

Seeing Tiffany, pink and pretty after three weeks of developing into a normal baby, broke the ice somewhat. "Be careful of her belly-button," Mom said gently. "She's still got a scab there." She watched as I pushed Tiff's toothpick-sized arms through the sleeves of the gown, and we both giggled at the picture of this tiny, tiny baby enveloped by her clothes. Even the diaper was too big, and as Tiff's scrawny little butt disappeared beneath layers of cotton, I wondered how I was ever going to care for such a little being. She could have fit into a shoebox.

We checked her out, stopping to say goodbye to Trini and the other nurses. Mom helped me settle her in at home, and we firmed up the arrangements for Tiffany's care during the remaining two months of school. Then Mom was gone, and I was alone with my daughter. I watched her breathe, afraid she would stop any moment.

When Vic got home from work, we greeted him at the door, eagerness lifting me from my usual caution. We were complete now. A family. Holding our baby securely in my arms, I opened the door as Vic approached, anticipating his delight at the sight of us.

"Hello, honey," I said in greeting, lifting Tiff for her first glance at her father. "Guess who's home!"

A smile lit up his face, that crooked smile that I had grown to love more than my life. He came to us, touched a finger gently on Tiffany's smooth baby cheek, crooned softly to her. She responded, whether to his touch or his voice, or whether her still-immature eyes actually saw him, I didn't know. But she smiled, her thin little lips widening baby-like over her toothless gums. "Where's her teeth?" Vic asked. "How's she gonna eat?"

I laughed, treating his question as a joke. Vic had such a sense of humor. "Silly," I said, "babies don't have teeth. She eats cereal, watery rice cereal, and formula. Here, you want to hold her?"

"No, I can't hold her! You keep her." *He's afraid of her*, I thought, *just like I was*. So I put her back to bed, and by the time I had her settled, Vic had already changed his clothes and was on his way out the door. Nothing interfered with The Mission. Nothing.

"Oh, I almost forgot," Vic said suddenly. He turned away from the door, his hand extended to me.

"What?"

"I picked these up for you. Dr. Daily wants you to take them."

I looked at the amber bottle in his outstretched hand. "What are they?"

"Tranquilizers. He said they'd help you relax."

"Relax?"

"Yeah. I told him you were nervous about Tiffany coming home. He said they'd help. Here," he said, forcing me to take the bottle. "Take one now, and then follow the directions on the label."

I stared at the amber container blankly. *Nervous? I'm not nervous.* "But—" Too late. He was gone. Confused, as I was often confused, I never thought to call Dr. Daily myself, to check up on that prescription. I just set the bottle in the cupboard and forgot about it. Vic was wrong. I loved being a mother. It was he who made me nervous.

Tiffany's homecoming had little effect on Vic's life. There was, in fact, an acceleration of his activities. Where before he had established a routine of sorts, now there was none. I never knew when he would return home from his nocturnal outings, if he returned at all.

ASK ME NO QUESTIONS

Occasionally there was a break in his frequent absences, and we'd act as if they never existed, going out to the movies or to friends to play pinochle. Usually it was pinochle. Movies were a luxury for young couples with a new baby.

It was on one of these evenings that I once again glimpsed the fury which lay banked beneath Vic's golden eyes. We were on our way to Stan and Jean's, the couple with whom we played cards. Vic had introduced me to them shortly after our honeymoon.

"I need to stop at the store," Vic said, as we drove toward their house. "Give me some money."

"I don't have any money," I replied, instantly guilty over spending my grocery allowance.

"The money your grandmother sent. Let me have it."

"But that's Tiffany's money," I objected. "Nanna sent it for her." Nanna had sent us ten dollars. I planned to buy a new dress for Tiff, something special for when she could actually fit into clothes. At the moment, she was still doll-size.

"I'm out of cigarettes," Vic replied, his voice a warning, broaching no argument. But I hadn't yet learned.

"But that money's for Tiffany," I repeated stupidly. Didn't he understand? "Don't you keep money for your cigarettes?"

Suddenly the car swerved as my husband gripped the wheel and pressed down the gas pedal. "Damn it!" he yelled, his voice rolling over me with all the force of a hurricane, "Give me the fuckin' money or get out of the car!" I crouched in terror as we careened down the busy street, dodging cars and weaving through the Friday night traffic. "You think you fuckin' own me now that we're married? A man can't even have a cigarette because his fucking wife says so? Give me the money!"

I did.

We reached our friends' home after he replenished his smokes, buying a carton with Tiffany's money. I got out of the car, trembling. I felt violated, verbally raped. I had never felt so frightened, so small, so dirty. I wanted to never, ever, feel that way again. I could still feel the car careening down the busy street.

So it was with a new awareness, a new apprehension, that I went with my husband to our friends' that night. The ban on questions extended even into our everyday lives: I could not question him, I could not disagree with him. Ever.

We played pinochle until the morning hours, stopping finally when Vic had to go to work. The men had won consistently, as usual, until the last game. I was still a beginner, still learning how to play, but I'd felt pleased that Jean and I had won one game at last.

On the way home, Vic said quietly, "I hate it when Stan deliberately loses. Jean won't have sex with him if he wins too often. She can be a real bitch. I hate a woman who holds her body as a bribe in order to get her way."

I absorbed his words without comment, subconsciously retaining the message behind them: Vic didn't like to lose, and he didn't like a woman to say "no." He won't have to worry about me, I vowed. I never win anyway, and I'd certainly never refuse my husband his rights. I felt sorry for Stan and Jean.

Graduation arrived. It was just one more hurdle to jump, one last impediment to our real life. Once I would have anticipated this occasion, would have made extra efforts to look my best as I accepted my due. But now I knew that high school graduation was just another milestone in the average person's life. There were much more important things in the real world, things only a select few accomplished. And my husband was one of those few.

I stood in the front row with other California Scholarship Federation "lifetime" honorees, willing my husband to look at me from the crowded auditorium. His eyes glowed briefly in silent salute. I smiled back at him.

At the party afterwards, his attention was elsewhere, his eyes always searching the crowd. Crowds were dangerous; you never knew what they concealed. When the others dispersed for a midnight swim, Vic rushed me home, only to make his excuses as he just as quickly left. "I'm proud of you," he said, pecking me absently on the cheek. I flushed with pleasure, but he was gone before I could reply.

I removed my graduation finery, resigned to the inevitable. The powder blue sheath with its rows of lace down the front accentuated my slimness, its sleeveless design leaving my arms bare. Mom had bought the dress for me, her graduation gift. "At least I graduated with honors," I said to the image in the mirror. "At least they can still be proud of me for that." Tiffany was spending the night with her grandparents, so I had not even her presence to take my mind from Vic's absence. It was at times like this that I nearly lost control of my tightly-bound feelings, gave in to the luxury of self-pity.

Padding into the kitchen, I fixed a cup of coffee. "What am I going to do?" I said to the silence. "I wish I could talk to someone! I wish I could at least confide in somebody!" Tears began to blur my vision. "No. I can't be like this." Wiping my cheeks with the back of my hand, I lifted my chin. "I'm not going to be a baby. He needs me to be strong, to support him. We have a child now. I have to stay strong for her."

By the time I went to bed, I had talked myself into some semblance of serenity, drawing strength from thoughts of our child and the sacrifice my husband made every day of his life. "He isn't whining," I told myself. "He isn't complaining. Who am I to do any less?"

And I fell asleep, waking briefly to hear Vic return in the early hours of the morning, taking comfort from his warmth beside me for a short hour before he arose to go to work. Who was I to complain? He was the one making the sacrifices. He was the one who never slept.

When Tiffany was returned to me the next day, I fussed over her until she cried in protest. She was still so small, gaining only ounces each week, sleeping most of the time. I'd read that "preemies" generally took a year to catch up, so I usually left her alone except when she needed attention. I was afraid of spoiling her by holding her too much, afraid of offending Vic by showing Tiffany too much attention when he was home. Vic was uncomfortable with her yet, refused to allow her into bed with us if she awoke in the night, insisted she was too small, too fragile for him to hold, complained about the smell of soaking diapers. I was becoming more insecure every day, torn between my pride in Vic and my loneliness, my love for Tiff and my uncertainty as a mother. I wanted to be held, to be assured and comforted. But there was no one in whom I could confide.

Vic came home from work and fell into bed for his nap before assuming the Victor role in the evening. I got in beside him, grateful for this time together. But he'd already dozed off, obviously exhausted. *I might as well read,* I thought. Vic had gotten some pretty smutty books for me to "study"; he'd told me that they would help me learn how to make love to him. I still didn't know what I was doing wrong, but if Vic thought these books would help me, then I was determined to plow through them, distasteful as they were. It seemed that all the women in them were ornaments for their men, vessels of service. That wasn't how our relationship worked.

The shallow stories did nothing to hold my attention. I couldn't just lie there and think. My thoughts took me down uncertain roads. The more I questioned, the fewer answers came. *No questions. Ask no questions.*

But I have to do something, I screamed silently. Restlessly, I got out of bed—*Careful, careful. Don't wake him up!*—and decided to take a walk. Before I slipped out the door, I left Vic a note so he wouldn't worry about me.

"I'm taking Tiff for a walk," I wrote. "Don't worry. I love you, Steph."

I stepped out into the sunshine, the wheels of Tiff's buggy crunching lightly on the graveled driveway. Thinking about the long summer days ahead, I wondered how I was going to occupy my time. Vic was away so much. The tiny house took very little time to clean, even with washing our clothes by hand. The shopping was done in less than an hour each week. Since Tiffany's homecoming, my five-dollar allowance bought even less than before, since two-thirds of it now went to baby formula.

I'd been snitching the roses off our wedding cake in secret bliss, relishing the sweetness in the long, lonely evenings. The top layer had been saved and frozen as tradition requested, to be shared on our tenth anniversary. Each day I opened the tiny freezer above the old refrigerator, unwrapped the white-and-yellow confection, and waged a battle with my conscience for long seconds before I pried one of the flowers loose. I couldn't help it. I was hungry. The roses were nearly gone; soon I'd start in on the cake.

What am I going to do? I asked myself as my steps took me further away from home. *College doesn't begin until the first of September. Maybe I won't be going to college.* Another thought crowded in: *Maybe I won't even be married by then.* Remembering his comments, his distraction, I worried, *Who knows? Maybe he doesn't even love me any more. Oh, God! Was it all for nothing? I won't believe that! I won't!*

My thoughts raced, and I didn't notice much of the scenery. I was strolling toward the park, which was filled with children playing. Their squeals of pleasure brought me out of my inward journey for a moment, and I glanced over at the mass of youngsters expending so much energy having fun. Wistfully, I thought of the child I pushed ahead of me. I couldn't help but wonder what her future would be. *Will you know your Daddy? I thought. Will you ever have the chance to love him?* Suddenly, someone bumped me, knocking me sideways. The handle of the buggy slipped from my fingers.

"Hey, are you all right?"

"I—I think so. At least nothing seems broken. My baby—" My heart suddenly thumped in panic. *The enemy. You could be out to get Tiffany!* I grabbed for Tiffany, expecting the worst. But the buggy was safely upright; Tiffany was safe. The man was gently inspecting me, his hand lightly supporting me.

Laughing in relief, I said, "I must have walked right into you."

"No, I was trying to catch this ball," he began, brandishing a football in his hand. Then, "Stephani! Stephani Brian, how are you?"

A genuine smile spread across my face, my eyes laughed as I finally recognized Roy Athens, a friend of Vic's. "Roy!" I exclaimed, my troubles receding. "How nice to see you! Gosh, it's been ages! What have you been doing?"

The lanky young man, towering six-feet-plus above me, grinned and leaned close to my small ear. "You would know, if you weren't so occupied with your new husband," he teased, a knowing look in his eyes.

Blushing, I turned away, my smile weakening. "Yeah, I guess we have been pretty busy," I murmured, hiding the sudden tears.

"Hey, where is Vic anyway? I wouldn't think he'd be for letting you wander out here all alone on a beautiful day like this."

"He...had to go out for awhile," I hedged. "You know how busy he is, always working on something."

"Yeah, well, I think he's crazy. Tell ya what, Steph, if you ever have any complaints, come look me up," Roy joked. "I sure wouldn't be too busy."

Glancing suspiciously up at him, I saw only friendly concern. "Thanks, Roy. I'll remember that." His smile was sincere; he had no idea that Vic was gone every day. Suddenly I realized how much I missed the lighthearted banter of my friends. As Roy walked away to rejoin his football players, loneliness descended upon me like a blanket of lead, its weight crushing my spirit. I watched as the football sailed into the sky, and the two informal teams rushed at each other across the makeshift football field. People. Where were the people in my life? Everyone seemed to avoid me since the marriage. *They probably all think we want to be alone*, I thought. *After all, we are newlyweds. If they only knew what it's really like.*

Resuming my walk, I headed back toward home, deep in thought. Neither Vic nor I encouraged visitors, since his secret work was so unpredictable. My parents now welcomed my infrequent visits, but there was an obvious constraint in their attitude toward Vic. It created an awkwardness that I avoided, thereby making it easy to stay away. I just have to be strong, I reiterated to myself. This life has been my choice.

When I reached home, Vic was already gone. The walk had done me good: I was able to keep busy, at least until darkness fell. Then I went to bed, feeling a weariness of soul which I couldn't shake off. When Vic returned, I didn't stir. Unaware, I slept through his four-thirty alarm, waking only when the sun streamed through the window in mid-morning.

Chapter 9

I have to be strong. I have to get out of here. When will he be back? How can I get away? The questions rang out, repeated themselves as I tried to think, tried to shut out the images of the past twenty-four hours and concentrate on the days ahead. I couldn't fight him alone. I had to plan, had to forget the pain. More than that, I had to forget the past. There was no Victor, no CIA agent, no marriage.

* * * * *

June 1966

"Stephani! Stephani, where are you?" His voice reached me in the back yard, where I was hanging out laundry. I dropped the basket immediately, hurrying into the house. Was he hurt again? "I'm here, honey. What's the matter?"

He grabbed me by the shoulders, squeezing hard as he shouted into my eyes. "What's this I hear about you and Roy? It's all over town that you were with him last night." His mouth twisted over the words, grinding them out like hot metal.

"I wasn't *with* him," I stammered. "I happened to run into him at the park. Actually, he ran into me." The hold on me tightened, shutting off my breath. "Vic, you're hurting me." Putting my hands up, I tried to loosen his grip. The attempt only angered him more.

"Don't try to get out of it," he snarled. "Everybody knows! They're all at the restaurant, they could hardly wait to tell me!"

"Who? Who are 'they'?"

"My team, that's who! You can't do anything in this town without me knowing about it! Don't you know you're watched every second?"

"Well, you're *team* is wrong!" I cried, twisting away from him. "I haven't seen Roy or anybody else in over two months, since we got married! He's your friend, after all! He just asked me how we were! My God, this is a small town! I'm bound to run into somebody I know once in awhile!"

"I won't have my wife talked about," he continued, reaching for me again. His face was inches from mine. "I won't be laughed at behind my back!"

"Vic, stop it! Nobody's laughing at you! There's no reason—"

He left suddenly, disappearing into the bedroom. "I thought I could trust you," I heard him say, almost to himself. Then he appeared before me once more. "Do you have any idea the kind of damage you did? Are you so sorry you married me after all? God, I was a fool to trust you!"

He turned away again, throwing himself on our bed. I followed, uncertainty keeping me silent. I didn't want to invite more anger, but neither did I want him to believe that I was in any way disloyal. Hovering over Tiffany's bassinet, I waited for him to speak. He was silent. His eyes were closed against me; it seemed obvious that he had no more to say. As I began to leave the bedroom, however, he asked the question that had been flitting on the edges of my consciousness for days.

"What would you do if we got a divorce?"

His voice was dispassionate. Gone was the heat, the anger, of just minutes before. The question was asked quietly, almost curiously, as if we were discussing the purchase of a new house or car.

"Do?" I repeated stupidly. "I'd…. I'd join a convent." *There is no life without you.* I waited, my back to him, my eyes unfocused. The seconds ticked and I waited for the words that would manifest the end of my marriage, the end of my life.

"Don't worry," he said distantly, "I'm not going to divorce you. I just wanted to know what you'd do."

I felt the breath leave my chest—I hadn't even been aware I was holding it. The bed creaked, he began to dress into his nighttime "uniform" of tee shirt and jeans, and I knew the conversation was over. He was leaving. I didn't hear him come up behind me, wasn't aware of his nearness until he wrapped his arms around me, pulled me against him, back-to-chest, and said softly, "Don't worry, Steph. I love you." And then he was gone. The tires screamed as he raced out of the driveway, nearly ramming a car on the street. A moment later, all I saw was a rapidly retreating stream of vapor emanating from the exhaust.

The day dragged on. I sat on the porch, drained, barely aware the summer sun was burning my scalp, my body. I didn't care. The scene replayed over and over in my mind as I tried to understand what had happened. The meeting with Roy was accidental, innocent. How had it gotten blown out of proportion? And how did Vic hear about it? *Don't you know you're watched every second?* The nerves on my neck suddenly tingled. Watched? I am being watched? Glancing about me,

I could see no one. But eyes seemed to be peering out from behind every bush and tree, behind the curtains of the houses around me. Scrambling up, I stumbled into the living room and locked the door.

I curled into a ball onto the couch, not daring to move. All the blinds were drawn, every bit of light shut out. In the middle of the summer day I sat in darkness.

About midnight, I stretched my cramped muscles and limped into bed.

Vic returned, his key scraping the lock. My ears pricked, but I remained on my side, feigning sleep as he undressed and joined me in bed. For a moment there was silence, a listening kind of silence as both Victor and Stephani waited. I could see the scene with my actress eye, as if the body lying beside him in the bed belonged to someone else.

Suddenly Vic began an oration which kept me spellbound.

"I see life as a golden road," he said, his voice booming in the dark silent night, "A long narrow path on which the travelers seek their way. The road twists and turns, keeping its secrets around each bend until the travelers reach them. There are many valleys on this path, and high mountains. Each valley is a resting place, and each mountain a cross we must bear. Sometimes there are boulders in the road, obstacles we must pass before we can reach our destination. Up ahead, I see a fork in the road, and I know that we must part. But further on, after many detours and much hardship, the paths once again join, and we will be together." His voice stopped, the air still echoing with the cadence of his impassioned speech. It sounded, almost, like a plea for me to understand. He had chosen his path: I had to abide by it.

I forced myself to gulp in slow, deep breaths, swallowed painfully, choked the tears back. Lying on my back, I stared into the darkness and listened as he continued.

"I love you, Stephani. I don't want to put you through any more hell." The silence deepened, our breathing meshed as we each thought our secret thoughts. What would you do if we got a divorce?...*I'd die!* "I'm working with a female agent, Ruth. You know her as a waitress at the restaurant." I pictured the slim brunette, a serious woman with deep brown eyes and a thin straight mouth. "The boys aren't very happy with your actions of the last few days. We have to take corrective action. In order to protect you, and the mission, we have to tell everyone we're separated." My breath quickened briefly, caught before I recaptured control. "We'll have to act like we're not getting along. It will take a few weeks, but if the other side sees that I don't care about you, they'll leave you alone. You're too vulnerable as it is now. And it may be the only way my superiors will allow us to stay married."

I listened as he outlined the plan, my throat and eyes burning with the need to release the tension inside of me. Now and then I responded to a question, keeping my voice level and controlled. Always controlled. The darkness hid the pain inside, the wetness of my cheeks as the tears escaped against my will. In spite of the terror I was feeling, my love for him welled up, battling with the self-pity, with the pain. *This is why I married you, to help. If it means fighting in public, or starting a rumor that we're separated, then so be it. Just don't leave me.* "I'll do anything, Vic," I said. "Anything."

The next day, the plan was carried out. Vic called me from the restaurant, formally asking me, for the benefit of listening ears, if I'd like to go out for dinner. Following the unwritten script, I enthusiastically accepted. That evening I dressed carefully, choosing a turquoise sheath and white pumps, accented by shell-like earrings and matching necklace. I pinned my long hair up, giving this dinner the distinction of a special occasion.

As I stared at my reflection in the mirror, I practiced the expressions I was going to have to portray that evening. *Can I pull it off? Hide the love from my eyes while I pretend anger? Hold back the tears while I nag and whine?* Schooling my mouth to sternness in an effort to age my perpetual baby face, I squared my shoulders and took a deep breath. I had to go through with it. I had to make Vic proud.

He came home in time to take a quick shower and change. Dressing in casual slacks and a knit tee shirt, he smiled encouragement as he opened the car door. "Don't worry," he said, "you'll be fine. Just don't lose your cool. You have to be convincing. We're being watched by my superiors as well as the other side."

"I'll be fine," I echoed, my stomach in knots.

Upon reaching Winkler's, I assumed a tight-lipped smile as I pointedly allowed him to open the door for me. The dining room was nearly full. People were chatting, eating, enjoying the social scene. I glanced about the room nervously, wondering if it were possible to discern the "enemy." Who were Victor's superiors? The heavyset man sitting alone in the corner? He looked suspiciously inconspicuous. Or perhaps the couple over by the window? Women were included in my survey. After all, Vic was working with a woman. Ruth. Was she here tonight?

A hand in the center of my back gently pushed me toward a table. "C'mon, Steph. Don't let me down now."

At his cue, I remembered my role. I smiled, chatting lightly with him as he pulled my chair out from the table. He was really putting everything into this, being the solicitous husband. Maybe it wouldn't be a difficult part after all.

Leaning toward him across the table, I touched his wrist as he picked up the menu. "Honey, this is so nice," I said eagerly, using that special for-Vic-only tone. "Thank you for thinking of it." Allowing my love for him to shine through my eyes, I gave him my best smile. "It's been so long since we were out together."

"Are you complaining?" he replied, his voice carefully bitter.

Despite our discussion before, the swift change in his manner took me by surprise. I reeled back in my seat, my stomach heaving. A glance from him calmed me momentarily. *Keep cool,* I reminded myself quickly. *It's part of the game.* "Why, no, honey. I am just so happy to be here with you." Lifting my chin in an attempt to ignore his jibe, I berated him gently. "Besides that, having dinner is a special treat."

"Are you saying that I don't provide for you?" His rejoinder was barbed with sarcasm. Although his voice was still low, his eyes flashed with intense indignation. "What's the matter, aren't you living in the manner to which you'd become accustomed?" The waitress hovered just out of reach; her mouth hanging open in startled surprise.

"Honey," I began, once again reaching across to him, "I didn't say anything of the kind. I was just thanking you for this evening."

Taking my hand deliberately from his arm, he whispered gruffly, "Stop touching me! They're watching!" Perusing the menu, he spoke aloud, calmly, stiffly formal. "You're welcome. I always enjoy taking my wife to dinner. Now what would you like? The waitress is waiting."

I sighed, hiding the pain of his rebuke behind what I hoped was a woman-wise expression of wifely exasperation. Nodding to the woman waiting patiently beside our table, I said to her with a wry smile, "Men. Sometimes I wonder why we put up with them."

She smirked in conspiratorial agreement, and began to take our order.

"I'll have the New York steak," Vic dictated impatiently, cutting into my open-mouthed attempt, "with a baked potato and salad. The lady will have a chef salad. Coffee for the both of us." He set the menu down, obviously finished.

"But Vic, I want the steak, too," I protested, remembering my role. I really did prefer salad. But, looking at the woman apologetically, I countered Vic's order. "I'll have the New York also," I said, "medium rare. And the baked potato, and soup." I glanced at my husband's scowling face, then back at the waitress busily scribbling on her pad. "And milk, please. No coffee for me."

"Stephani," Vic began.

"Vic, that's what I want. It's my dinner, isn't it?"

"You always have the chef salad."

"Well, this time I want something different. I can do that, can't I?" I smiled pleadingly at our waitress, who was shaking her head.

"Is that it, then?" the woman asked with an understanding smile.

At Victor's nod, she looked my way belatedly, and at my confirmation, went about her business. She was barely out of earshot when Victor turned on me. "How could you do that?" he demanded, his voice rising.

"Do what?" I asked, a carefully blank expression in my eyes. *Keep cool. It's all part of the game.*

"Embarrass me like that!"

"Embarrass you? How? All I did was order what I wanted."

"But I had already ordered for you!" His voice was becoming louder. Keep cool, I told myself.

"I didn't want the chef salad," I exclaimed, still under control but beginning to lose patience.

"Maybe you didn't want to come out to dinner with me, either. MAYBE you'd rather have dinner with Roy." Now he could clearly be heard across the entire dining room. People were looking at us from behind their menus.

"How can you say that?" I sat board straight in my chair, back rigidly indignant, my eyes smarting. "I don't even know Roy that well." *Here it comes! Be calm. Be the wife he needs.*

"Well enough to embrace him in broad daylight," he said loudly, his words clearly enunciated. Several people were openly staring at us by now.

"I did not!" I exclaimed, allowing anger to carry my voice. Part of it was real, anyway, as I remembered Vic's accusation the day before.

Our first course was placed before us, interrupting the exchange. The waitress filled Vic's coffee cup before she scurried away. I splashed at my soup, my spoon making a mess of the steaming liquid as it spilled onto the tablecloth. Despite my resolve, tears were tickling my eyelids. "Keep it up," Vic instructed surreptitiously. "You can't stop now."

Putting the spoon down, I glared at him. "Look," I spit out bitterly, "I can't help it if Roy's around more than you are. Maybe if you'd be more of a husband, I'd be more of a wife."

"And maybe if you knew how to be a wife, I would enjoy being your husband," he replied.

The words chilled me. I knew they were part of the game, but it was becoming difficult to separate the play from reality. I froze, rooted to my chair while those words sunk all the way to the core of my heart. *It's only a game*, I told myself. *He didn't really mean it.* The silence stretched to hour-long seconds: it seemed the whole world was silent. As if in slow motion, the clatter of the restaurant came to a halt.

Then, lifting my napkin from my lap and placing it delicately on the table, I rose from my chair with as much dignity as I could muster, and stood facing him. "Since you obviously don't enjoy my company," I said quietly, "I will leave you to your dinner. Good night." And I walked to the door, my chin high, my heels tapping on the floor in the silence that followed my regal exit.

Vic was after me before the doors closed behind me. The glass front of the restaurant provided a good view of our argument. I could see some of the diners looking our way as Vic solicitously offered me a ride home, and I haughtily refused, shaking my head so that all could see. I was the difficult one, not Vic. I started the argument, I was seen with another man, I had left the table.

As I walked down the sidewalk, Vic returned to our table in the restaurant. Sneaking a glance backward as I passed a hedge along the way, I saw him speaking to the waitress, shaking his head with a certain amount of confusion. And before I turned to take the long walk home, I saw her pat him on the shoulder, fill his coffee cup, and leave him to his lonely dinner.

Chapter 10

My eyes were dry, so dry they hurt. Prayer, which had once been my source of strength, did nothing for me now. I was alone. Entirely, absolutely alone. There were no more tears to be shed. No one knew of my dilemma. No one cared.

So I told myself, as I lay stretched across the bed in the room which had become my prison, my cell. As if from ingrained habit, I felt the eyes upon me, watching my every move...

* * * * *

June 1966

I did it. *I did it!* Triumph lifted the pain in my chest as I strode down the busy main street, head held high. *Everyone will believe it was real. Everyone will think we really had a fight.* A sudden sob choked the breath from me, catching me by surprise. Passersby stared as tears splashed from my cheeks, unheeded. *I told him I could do it!*

Suddenly a pain tore into my guts, a pain that began at the center of my chest and grew until it engulfed my entire upper body. *Oh, God! It hurts!* My stomach cramped, the pain radiated into my back, and I was forced to stop, as, retching, I heaved dry, wracking remnants of the day's meals on the graveled alley into which I scrambled. Hidden from the street, I doubled over, forced by the sudden sickness to empty my stomach. The tension, the anticipation of today's drama took its toll, as the cramps repeated, rolling like aftershocks through my body. When there was nothing left to regurgitate, they continued, bringing with them nausea, dizziness, and a weakness I could not fight. I held on to my purpose as if it were a lifeline. *The mission. That's all that matters. Save the mission.* I concentrated, forcing my breath to slow, deepen, and relax.

Gradually, ever so slowly, the piercing stab lessened, stopped. I straightened, breathing deep, steady gulps of air, focusing on the street ahead as I took one step after another. I felt the eyes of the enemy, of Vic's superiors, on me as I walked. *The mission. I have to think of the mission. Nothing else.* I smiled, a shaky, self-conscious smile that I hoped would fool anyone watching. *I am the bitch,* I said silently. *I started the fight. Smile.* The walk home became a journey into consciousness, a trip beyond time.

Vic was jubilant. "We did it!" he shouted gleefully. "We fooled them! Honey, you were great. You convinced them. It worked!" Whirling me around, he smothered me in kisses, leaving a trail on my neck and shoulder. "You were wonderful! Now we can move on to the next step."

"Next step? There's more?" Tremulous, I looked up at him, the joy in his once-familiar smile fading. *I don't want more. Not yet.*

"Yeah. But the rest will be easy." Dropping his hands, he began to strip off his finery, changing into fresh jeans and shirt. "You have to call Reverend Smith, tell him we're splitting up. I'm going to Alice's tonight to tell her the news." Alice was his older sister, the one member of his family living in the area. Reverend Smith was the minister who'd married us; more than that, he was our friend. Lying to him would be difficult.

"Reverend Smith? I have to tell him we're splitting up?"

"Yeah. We have to make this look real. Unless you want a real divorce."

"No, I'll do it. I just didn't know that everybody would know."

"Well, that's the way it is. I told you, Stephani. No questions. Understand?"

"Yes, yes. I understand." I watched him busily prepare for another night out. "When do you want me to call him?"

"Tonight. Tell him tomorrow. Ask him over here, tell him you need to talk to him. By then Alice will know, and the word will start getting around."

A peck on the lips and he was gone.

I surveyed the places he had been, taking in the evidence of his passing through; the dirty cook shirt on the floor near the couch, his white cook pants by the bed, soiled socks thrown carelessly in the corner. The slacks and shirt he had worn to the restaurant dropped on the bed, as if tonight never happened. *This is my life.* I thought. *This is what I said I'd be happy to do.* Bending over, I picked up the clothing and tossed it into the laundry hamper.

I was folding those same clothes, now clean and fresh from the line, when Reverend Smith knocked on the door the following day. "Stephani?" His cheerful voice called, "May I come in?"

"Oh, hi, yes, of course," I answered, my mind rushing to form the words I had rehearsed. Busily I continued to fold Vic's tee shirts and pile them on our bed. "Just make yourself comfortable, Reverend. I want to fold these before they wrinkle." *Also, I won't have to look at you while I lie*, a voice inside me accused.

"You've made a nice cozy home out of the house, Stephani. It's very cheerful."

"Thanks, Reverend. I love doing it. I like making Vic feel like this is a haven, a place full of love." The words slipped out before I had a chance to think about them.

"Well, you should be very proud of yourself. It feels like a house with love in it."

"Actually," I began to regroup, talking carefully now, "it's not." Facing him, I sat on the bed beside a mound of underwear and shirts. "Vic and I have decided to split up."

My friend stared, the smile gone from his face. For a second the preacher disappeared, and I glimpsed the man behind the white collar. "Split up? You? But you love Vic. You've only been married a few months—"

"Two and a half." *Is that all? It seems like centuries!*

"Two and a half. Are you sure you've given it a chance?"

"It isn't that, Reverend. It has nothing to do with giving it a chance. We just realized that we don't love each other." *I can't believe I'm saying this. I sound so calm, so sure.*

He stared at me, into my eyes and, I feared, into my soul. "I'd have bet my collar that you weren't a quitter, Stephani," he said soberly. "I can't believe my ears, or my eyes. You seem very matter-of-fact about this."

"Yes, well, one might as well face facts, mightn't one?" I quipped, meeting his eyes with what I hoped was innocence. "There's no use in beating a dead horse."

"Yes," he repeated, apparently satisfied. "Well," he sighed, rising to leave, "I hope you've thought about your child."

Those words almost proved my undoing. Suddenly all guile vanished. Turning back to the laundry, I choked, "We have. She'll be okay."

Then he asked me, as I'd been afraid that he would, to pray with him, to ask for God's guidance and protection. He reached out his hand, that same hand that had blessed my wedding barely ten weeks before, and grasped mine. I closed my eyes, trembling, and asked for God's forgiveness while the Reverend intoned, in his quiet way, a prayer of supplication. He squeezed my hand gently at "Amen," his expression holding no rebuke. "Let me know if there's anything I can do."

The door closed quietly behind him. Darkness descended on the little house as the afternoon sun slipped behind the distant hills. And inside, the tears flowed freely as, all pretense of housework gone, I sprawled across the big bed, unable to stop the body-wracking sobs wrenching from deep within. *Oh, God, help me! I've got to go through with this! Please, please. Give me strength.* A breeze lifted the window shade, and I remembered my silent "partners." The watchers. My tears stopped as quickly as a well run dry.

Chapter 11

I was cold. Shivering, I tried to pull the blanket over my nude body, but my groping fingers found nothing to grasp. Goosebumps freckled my flesh: then I felt him there, so close beside me his hair tickled my skin. He was kissing my hipbone. His lips were wet. His tongue made circles on my skin, concentric circles that moved over to the other hipbone, and back to my belly, where then began to spiral downward. I suppressed a shudder. "I'm going to love you, baby," he was saying. "I can make you feel good. That's all you need, just to have me love you…" His voice trailed off as his tongue probed, and I shivered, the cold reaching my soul.

* * * * *

July 1966

The water was colder than I expected, but then it seemed I always felt cold these days. Lying on my stomach, I watched as my sister Brandy splashed in the shallow end of the pool, holding little Shane close in her arms. The sun seemed to have lost its warmth, too. Goose bumps dotted my shoulders, sending a slight shiver down my spine.

"I heard that you and Vic were splitting up, Steph. Is that true?"

The voice, quiet and light and communicating an I-don't-want-to-impose-but-I-want-to-know quality, felt like ice cubes thrown into my consciousness. I glanced at my mother toweling off beside me. Taking a deep breath, I nodded stoically.

"I'm glad. You know we never liked him. It's all for the best, you'll see. Now you can get on with your life." Kind words meant to encourage. Words spoken so carefully, tone held so evenly. *If you only knew. He's really not the scoundrel you believe him to be. He's just a man fighting for his country. And you'll never know.* Conscious that even here at the public swimming pool, I could be the object of scrutiny, I controlled my own words and voice.

"I know, Mom. But I'd rather not talk about it, okay?"

With a sympathetic glance, she complied. I could almost read her mind. Mom was never one to pry. Neither would she reach out. But I felt that her judgment, all their judgments, were not in my favor. I had let everybody down.

Her thoughts seemed to float my way. I could see them in her eyes, in her mouth, the way she looked at me. Stubborn, she was thinking. You're so stubborn. I shook off the resentment that was beginning to glow deep inside. Someday they'd know the truth, I vowed. Someday they'd eat their words.

The afternoon was pleasant, one of the few times since summer began that I'd seen any of my family. They kept a respectable distance, and I did nothing to encourage them. After all, with Vic away so much, it was better that no one knew how different our life really was. We said goodbye as the sun dipped over the mountains, with promises to call soon. Which I knew wouldn't happen.

The rumor spread, as we had intended it would. When I attended church the following Sunday, it seemed as if a thousand eyes followed me to my seat, eyes that were sympathetic and wise and full of I-told-you-so's. It was all I could do to keep from shouting, "It's not true! It's not true, we love each other, we just have to do this!" But I dutifully kept my head bowed and my eyes shadowed, and smiled when I sang. And made sure that I left immediately after the service, before anyone could stop me with his or her prying condolences.

Two weeks went by, two weeks in which I again adapted to the patterns of Vic's comings and goings. Since we were unofficially "estranged," he spent even less time in the little house than before, but I kept busy. I found that writing helped to keep me sane, and I filled countless pages of spiral theme books with my thoughts, my dreams, and whatever Vic said during his short visits. I was able to find some measure of happiness, reminding myself that, however indirectly, I was helping fight the battle for my country.

Then one bright afternoon I was busily rinsing out some clothes in the sink when Vic came into the tiny kitchen. His step was slow, telling me he had something on his mind. I had become adept at learning to read my husband's moods. Knowing the weight of his thoughts, I sought to always reassure him that I could take care of myself. I was determined I would never become a burden to him. I dried my hands carefully, leaving the clothes to soak for the moment. My heart leaped at his sudden appearance—I had seen so little of him lately! But I controlled my emotions, controlled my features. I must let him see that I was handling everything.

"Hello. How are you today?" The words sounded stiff; but then, I was talking to a stranger. I didn't dare go near him for a kiss—the watchers could be nearby.

He frowned, eyeing me soberly. "I have to talk to you." I waited, but no more words came forth. He just stood there in the center of the room, the sun shining through the windows onto his face.

"All right. Shall we sit down?" I motioned to the couch.

"No. Not in here. It's too—public." He walked into the bedroom, throwing himself on the bed in obvious exhaustion.

I followed hesitantly, my heart thumping in my throat. *What now? What can it be now?* He was lying on the bed, his tennis shoes marking up the white coverlet. I crawled to the other side, sitting with my back against the wall. Waited.

"We have to get a divorce," he announced without preamble.

My stomach contracted. My heart thumped erratically. "A divorce? Why? I thought this separation—"

"They want it. That's why." They. The Company. They spelled death to me, to all that I held dear. They held all the cards, my life in their hands. For a few moments of eternity, the only sound was that of our breathing. And my heart pounding. Then, "It will only be for awhile, Steph. Only until this is over. Heck, it won't even be a real divorce."

"Not a real divorce? What do you mean?"

"They're flying me to Mexico. It won't be legitimate. In a couple of years, we'll get back together again. I'll take care of you, I promise." He turned toward me then, his eyes tender. Wrapping his arms around me, he pulled me close to him. "I won't let you suffer, Steph. It'll be better this way. You'll see. When this is over, we can really be married. We won't have to play this game." Stroking me, he whispered encouragement. "Don't cry, Steph. I love you. You know that, don't you?" I nodded, my breath coming in short little gasps as I fought to keep the tears back. *I mustn't cry. I've got to be strong.* And somehow, I smiled, kissing him back, showing him that I loved him, trusted him, and that was all that mattered...

"When are you going?" The night hid our bodies as well as our thoughts. Our voices were soft, matter-of-fact, emotionless.

"I don't know yet. They'll let me know when they're ready." The glow of his cigarette outlined his face. "You'll have enough notice. Don't worry."

"I won't." *Liar. How can I not worry? Every minute, every second of my life is filled with fear.* Once again I imagined those uniformed men knocking on the door. "Mrs. Brian?" they'd say. "Mrs. Brian, we're sorry to have to tell you..." I knew that day would come.

And so, to stave off that numbing, incomprehensible fear, I never thought of tomorrow. Tomorrow didn't exist for Stephani Jean Stevenson Brian. There was only today—less, there was only now, the moment he was in my life. I was seventeen, a mother, about to be abandoned by my husband. Yet my prevailing thought was, "Thank you, God, for this moment. This precious moment with my husband." I felt alive only in those minute slices of time when he was with me. I was playing a part in a role for which there was no script.

The cigarette disappeared, once again his arms imprisoned me. Content, I settled inside them; they were all I had. All I wanted.

We had to wait for the signal. Each day that passed without him leaving was a reprieve from the inevitable. I saw a few people I knew when I walked to the store, or my favorite haunt, the library. But, as I had thought, I did not see my sister or brothers or my parents. They had their own lives to live. Maybe they even had their own secrets. I was glad I didn't have to face them with my lies.

Summer was in full glory, but this year we didn't steal away for afternoons at our favorite hideaway on the river. For the first time in my seventeen years I didn't worry about getting a tan, I didn't revel in the sun's bright rays. I stayed inside the walls of my prison, the curtains drawn, the door locked. The little back yard became my haven, the furthest I would venture into the visual range of the eyes I imagined watching me. Tiffany slept peacefully in the shade of the maple tree while I wrote agonized passages in my spiral theme book.

The strain grew unbearable at times. But I had learned to shield my thoughts from my husband, to wait and mirror only what he was thinking.

I had to be there when he came home from work. That was the rule. If I was ever gone, his own self-control vanished, and all the worry and stress became anger, anger barely controlled by the need to play the game. I didn't ever want to test the strength of that control. So I was home at two o'clock in the afternoons, and most mornings, and every evening, and of course, every night. Waiting.

Except one afternoon, when Vic breezed in, peeled off his cook whites and fell into bed. He'd been out nearly all night, as usual, returning just before dawn to change for work. I'd hardly slept, and when he came in, I'd murmured a sleepy "hello," hoping he'd have time to share something with me of his work. But he'd brushed off my overtures with a hurried frown before disappearing out the back door. I had hopes he would be more communicative this afternoon. But obviously, he was worn out. He was asleep in seconds.

I stared at the sun and the summer outside my door, and I had just *had* to be out there, see some people, hear some voices. The park was only a block or two away. Unable to bear the waiting and the silence another minute, I scribbled a quick note. "Honey," I wrote, "I can't take it anymore. I've got to get out for awhile. See you later." I signed it, "I love you, Steph." Then, gathering Tiffany, I slipped outside.

I was gone perhaps thirty minutes, forty-five max. I had been careful to avoid contact with anybody; I knew my "companions" would report to Vic any indiscretions. The sun and the fresh air worked wonders with my mood, and I returned to our bungalow refreshed.

"Where've you been?" Vic said, his voice muffled by the tee shirt he was pulling over his head. "Where did you go?" He approached me, the note grasped in his hand. "What do you mean by this?"

Startled out of the ambiance of the outdoors, I stared at the note. "I just wanted you to know where I had gone," I stammered. "I didn't want you to worry."

"Do you know what they could do with something with this?" he cried. "They could use it against you. It's proof!"

"Proof of what? I just wanted to get outside for awhile! I just went for a walk."

"They won't look at it that way. 'I can't take it anymore,'" he read, "And, 'I love you!' You know you can't say that! We're supposed to be separated!" He sighed, shook his head and threw his arms wide in exasperation. "Don't you ever listen? You can't put anything in writing! Get it? Nothing. In. Writing!" He didn't wait for my reply, but dashed down the front step to the blue Chevy, revving it angrily as he roared out of sight.

An answer would have been useless anyway. His anger was too close to the edge for me to dare test it. None of it made any sense. Unless...*Maybe he's just acting like he's mad*, I thought, remembering the eyes that watched us daily. *Maybe he's just testing me, just doing this because they're testing him. Maybe it's all part of the plan, that we're arguing because we need to be apart right now.* Could that be it? It made sense. His erratic behavior all made sense. *I have to trust him*, I reminded myself. *He loves me. He wouldn't hurt me.* The litany echoed in my head. Trust me, it said. Trust me.

I sighed, the walls of my prison closing in on me as night began to fall.

Test or not, his words had the desired effect; never again did I leave him a note—but then I had no reason to, for in all the years which followed, I never left the house without his permission.

Chapter 12

God, let me die. Let this be over. I can't take any more. I prayed, disbelieving in any great miracle. Gone was the innocent bride of yesterday, gone the trusting wife. They had disappeared, just as had the knight, keeper of Democracy, hero of the free world. *God, I was such a fool! Will it end now? Will it end here, in this room? Will I ever see my children again?* I lay in the rumpled bed, lay as if already dead, as if there was no hope, no tomorrow.

And the voice inside me said, *Wait. Be patient. Your chance will come.*

* * * * *

August 1966

The days crawled by.

Vic and I talked about our eminent "divorce." It helped me to talk about it, even though it was something I dreaded. I didn't believe in divorce. The vows spoken were real to me, made before God and all my family. But this was different. A Mexican divorce wasn't real, wasn't legal in the States, Vic told me. I know now that he said that to soothe me, to reassure me that he would still be my husband in the eyes of the law. This was for the Company, he said, so he could prove he could distance himself from me, continue his work without worrying about me. It was just an order, a test of his loyalty. It didn't mean any more than that. It was part of the game we played.

We talked about afterward, after we were allowed to reunite. That was my sustenance. I didn't think about the time—years—in between.

But when he was gone, I prayed for it just to be over, that He would give me a miracle, that Vic would come home and say it was all over and we could really be a family. I believed that the Almighty still listened.

And one day I knew my prayers were answered.

ASK ME NO QUESTIONS

It's said that life is stranger than fiction, that the twists and turns in this road don't necessarily flow smoothly. It's not like reading a book, where the plot is planned and the actions all add up to a conclusion. No, life is gritty. It gets into your teeth like sand, filling the hollows and smoothing away the edges until the line between reality and fantasy somehow disappears. It cuts your tongue and cleaves to the roof of your mouth until it hurts to breathe. And when you wash it away, it's as if you can taste and smell and breathe a different kind of air. Fresher. Sweeter. Sharper. But the taste of sand still lingers.

That's what it was like that day.

I had finished the meager amount of housework the cottage required, put Tiffany down for her nap, and was lying on the bed soaking in the sun which filtered through the curtains. It had been weeks since the curtains were opened: they were thin white strips of cotton, just enough to brighten the room a little without letting anyone see inside. Vic was due home in an hour or so. I was writing in my journal, pouring my thoughts into the pages where they could be safely hidden. The lines had grown rather monotonous lately, I'm afraid—"Please, God, give me strength" had become a litany. I was in the middle of such a line when the thought came to me, and, without any reasonable explanation, I just knew. There wasn't going to be a divorce.

I instantly accepted that thought, that feeling, without question. It was so strong that I stopped writing, stopped thinking. I sat there on the bed and just stared, unseeing. *There isn't going to be a divorce.* It was as if the world tipped back on its axis, putting everything back in its rightful place. I had experienced similar instances at various times in my life, but none so strong as this one. After all, I was the child who spoke to wild animals. I was the child who heard the wind sing through the redwoods. Talking to God was only half the process—the other half was hearing Him. So I accepted this inner knowing, and I rejoiced in it.

I didn't know then that this was just the beginning, that there would be many more hours of similar tearful prayers, that divorce would one day be preferable to a life of secrets. I didn't know there would one day be other, darker, options.

By the time Vic got home, the little house had gained a coat of wax, a sheen of dusting spray, a glow of cleanliness. For the first time in months, I felt a song bubble in my heart and find its way through my lips. It didn't matter if nothing else had changed—our marriage was still intact. God had listened. All was right in my world.

Vic arrived, his smile telling me all I needed to know. "We can stay married," he said, and he reached out and drew me to him. I welcomed his arms, welcomed his kiss, melted into his embrace eagerly, feeling the tension disappear between us.

Later, he stretched out on the bed, his back resting against the wall, smoking rather soberly, I thought, for a man who had just gotten a reprieve from a sentence of loneliness. But then, he had things on his mind. "Ruth didn't get off so easily," he said thoughtfully, his eyes shuttered in memory. "She has to marry Benny Armstrong. She's mad as hell."

"Benny? But why does she have to marry him?" I could afford to feel sympathy for the woman now. Benny Armstrong was a fate worse than death. I didn't really know him, but Vic did. I had seen him around town, of course. You don't miss many people in a town the size of Woodsville. Benny Armstrong was a geek.

"Orders," Vic replied, his look reminding me. *No questions.* Not even now, when I wanted to know why this reprieve, why they had changed their minds, what had happened between last night and this afternoon? But I kept silent. "We have to make up, let everybody know we're back together." I could almost see his mind clicking off details. "We'll start tonight," he said, his arms gathering me to him once more. "I'm taking you out to dinner." The way he said it, you'd think we were headed for the Ritz. He kissed me once more, then headed for the shower. "Wear your western outfit," he called over his shoulder, "I want you to look special."

My "western outfit" was simply a pair of skinny black jeans and a fringed satin shirt, complete with a leather belt and calf-high boots. I had worn it a lot when we were dating, had barely touched it in the months since our wedding.

I called Mom to see if she'd sit with Tiff. She wasn't very happy about the reason for her services, but she agreed to take her for the night.

So we returned to the restaurant where we'd staged our fight two months before, this time staging another scene: that of a happy, crazy-in-love young couple. Ruth was there, and whenever Vic saw her, he pulled me close and whispered nonsense into my ear. He touched me more than was his habit, held my hand across the table, slipped his arm over my shoulder, caressed my wrist as he glanced surreptitiously around the room. Once again he pulled out the chair for me, graciously opened the door as we entered and finally left. I didn't mind. It was as I always imagined it would be.

Vic surprised me by taking me to the county fair afterwards. He was terrific at the games. By the time we left, we were both struggling over the stuffed animals he had won by pitching baseballs, throwing darts, and shooting ducks. It was almost as if the months had vanished, and we were teenagers again. Almost.

Part II
San Remos

Chapter 13

"Call me Uncle! Uncle Vic! Never call me Daddy! Do you understand?"

"M-huh." She nodded shakily, her two-year-old fuzz of blonde hair waving at the crown of her head.

"Say 'Yes, Uncle Vic.' Say it!" His voice grated like gravel; the words clipped off at the ends so tightly that spittle flew. I cowered at the other end of the room. I waited for her little bones to snap under the pressure of his callused hands. I cried, ashamed of my fear, afraid he would return his attentions to me if I made the mistake of emitting a sound. *Please, Tiff,* I prayed, *Please just do as he says.*

"Yes, Uncle Vic." Her child's voice held no fear, only a surprising defiance, an I-know-better-but-I'll-do-it-because-you-forced-me quality. But Tiffany was that way. She refused to cry when spanked: instead she stubbornly gritted her teeth and smiled when it was over. She was showing that stubbornness now, in the face of her father's barely controlled rage.

I trembled, relief weakening my ever-constant guard.

July 1968. Vic and I had been married two years. You'd think I would be used to it by now. Used to the fabric of lies this hid our secrets. The mercurial temper of my husband. The tension. You'd think I would have learned to accept the sacrifices an agent's family has to make.

The divorce that never happened prefaced a period of near normalcy in our lives, at least what I thought was normal. It was a period when the ties between Vic and me were strengthened by the illusion that our love, which had never died, would stand the tests of time. His job didn't change, or the routine of secrecy to which I had become accustomed. But our marriage resumed, picked up, began again almost as if the two-month "separation" had never happened. For all intents and purposes, we were a happily married couple. At least, there were no more lies about that.

Vic's explanation to my hesitant query about the divorce was just a simple, "They changed their minds. We did the job without finding it necessary." Further explanation was unnecessary, and would not have been forthcoming anyway. I was lucky he said even that much; I was so thankful to remain his helpmate I didn't pressure for more.

But there were still the nights without him, the lies when he was gone for days, the coded telephone calls and knocks on the door. I was ever aware of my "bodyguards" and the other pair of ears listening on the phone.

I was lulled into a sense of security by the routine of it all. The cover stories became second nature, and the worry faded into occasional headaches which were treated with steady doses of aspirin. I did what I was told, and I was proud that I was such a perfect wife.

I didn't make it to college. Somehow, even though we got a loan for the first year, I never got past the first day. Vic complained that my schedule would interfere with his, that we couldn't afford a sitter for Tiff, that he needed to know I was safe in the house. Instead, he got me a part-time job as a dishwasher at Winkler's, told me he felt better with me close by, said I needed to learn how to take care of myself. He had an obsession with the idea that I should know what to do in case "something happened" to him. We used the money from the loan to pay bills. He arranged for a neighbor—a friendly mother of five—to care for Tiffany without charging us.

In 1967 I met Vic's parents and younger siblings, when they moved back to the States for a brief period. While his mother completely intimidated me, I respected his stepfather. His brothers seemed to accept me. But it was his younger sister Candy who made me feel welcome, made us a family. Just a year or so younger than I, Candy treated me like a big sister, confided in me, teased me about Vic. I helped her dress her hair for the Prom, listened to her boy problems, and shared teenage confidences. The time I spent with her was especially precious, since, with her, I could almost forget who I was, who her brother was. But I could never share the secrets I kept about her brother's double life.

Early in 1968 US military activity in North Viet Nam escalated, and, for the first time in years, America resumed the draft. I had not given politics a single thought, despite Vic's profession: I thought about his involvement only as it affected our life together. Patriotism was a very broad concept in my mind. Yes, I believed that citizens should be willing to die for our country. Yes, I was proud of my own indirect involvement in our nation's safety. Yes, I would do whatever it took to allow my husband to do his job. But accepting his job as an agent was a whole lot easier, for me, as long as the "enemy" was faceless, an abstract idea, an unknown source.

But suddenly, the enemy had a face. Victor was drafted.

"There's been a mistake of some kind, Steph," he said, "I can't be drafted. I'm the head of a household. I have a wife and daughter to support." He looked at me with uncharacteristic bewilderment, the official notice from the draft board in his hand.

"I don't understand. How can you be drafted anyway? Aren't you already serving?"

He rolled his eyes. "Nobody knows that. I'm strictly classified! For chrissake, do I have to explain everything to you?" I slumped back, still confused, still misunderstanding. Didn't the Army even know whom the CIA employed? "It's just a mistake, that's all. You can't trust paper pushers to do anything right." He was silent for a few seconds. "If you were pregnant, they couldn't take me."

"Pregnant? You want another baby?" The suggestion surprised me. Fatherhood hadn't affected Vic's life: he took little interest in his tiny daughter, asking only that I keep her quiet when he was home, and that the time she required didn't interfere with his routine.

But I was also pleased. It was time. I'd always wanted a large family. Tiff needed a sibling. In my enthusiasm, I waived the reason behind the suggestion, buried my questions and confusion—my mind immediately shifted to the possibilities.

"Yeah, I want another baby," Vic replied. "I think it's time Tiffany got a brother. We can get started right away." He might have been talking about adding a new bathroom. His expression was thoughtful, his opaque eyes glittering in contemplation.

"But what about the draft board? Will they believe you?" The notice fluttered in his hand. "What if I don't get pregnant that fast?"

"Don't worry about them, Steph. I'll take care of it. I'm not going to end up in some swamp in Nam. I've got a job to do here." And as he spoke, he crumpled the little slip of white paper until it was no more than the size of a dime.

The plan went into immediate action. I went off the pill and dropped a few hints to our families. Vic even told his best buddy that he was going to be a father again. By the time the review came up, the "new baby" was an accepted part of our life, even though I had not yet conceived. And of course, Vic was excused. Free to continue his work.

This was my training ground, the proving ground for my love. I, who valued honesty above all else, learned to lie. I lied to my parents, my friends, strangers.

Most of the lies were inconsequential, involving Vic's cover. Nobody's business. I didn't always understand the lies or the intricate reasons for them, but I didn't have to. They saved our lives.

There was more. I learned to obey without question, to react without thinking. I molded myself to fit the image of the wife he needed. I became an intensely private person, unwilling and, ultimately unable, to share my thoughts or feelings with others.

Then Vic lost his job at Winkler's. He was set up, of course. Vic had no reason to steal cartons of eggs and loaves of bread. We had, by that time, our own chickens, and I baked bread every Monday. But the evidence was found buried under garbage lying in the bed of his pickup. Twice. In our world, the world of undercover operations, suspicion, and constant danger, small things took on immense proportions. Everyone was under suspicion. But who? And why? It must be his credibility, I decided. Someone wants to cast suspicion on his character.

Someone wanted him discredited, gone, out of town. Someone would, perhaps, take more serious measures.

Conferences were called, late-night meetings with The Boys. The decision was reached: we would have to move.

In a matter of days, everything was set: Vic had a job waiting for him in San Remos, a town some 300 miles away. A coastal town. Closer to the seaports and the city of San Francisco. A cousin of mine lived there. Karen. Maybe we could get reacquainted.

Vic stayed in San Remos to begin his job and find us a house while I made all the arrangements back at Woodsville. We had furniture to move, of course, and some things to dispose of. The weeks seemed an eternity, but were also surprisingly relaxed. I found that, even though I worried about my husband, the tension which was a part of our daily routine lessened. My entire family—my parents, Travis, and Brandy, along with Brandy's husband Greg—helped me pack, sell the chickens, discard unwanted items.

One night near the end of the second week, the telephone rang. I waited. It was late, nearly ten o'clock. Vic should be calling about now, I worried. My body ached with the tiredness that comes from long hours of physical exertion. Greg had just left. He'd been helping me carry boxes into the U-Haul truck I'd rented for the long drive to San Remos. Hesitantly, I picked up the receiver. "Hello?"

"It hasn't rung four times!" The voice on the other end could belong to no one else but Victor.

"I know, but it's late—"

"All the more reason to use the code! I can't trust you to do anything, can I!"

"Vic, I'm sorry, I just didn't think—"

"Right. You didn't think. Now listen. I don't want you having any visitors while I'm gone."

"Visitors?"

"Yeah, visitors. Like Greg."

"Greg? He was helping me—"

"Look, you never know what kind of gossip is being spread around town. I won't have my wife talked about like some slut in the streets. Understand?"

"Yes, I understand."

"Good. You know you can't hide anything from me."

"I know," I said softly, my breath catching.

"Do you remember an old tramp saying hello to you yesterday?"

"What?"

"A guy with a stocking cap and an old raincoat. Remember him?"

"No. Why would he say hello to me?"

"Because that was me."

Bewildered, I listened in silence.

"I was there yesterday. On business. That was a disguise. Just so you know I never leave you alone. There's someone watching you right now." I glanced toward the open window. "That's right," he said, as if he saw my furtive glance, "I know your every move. And don't forget—the phone is bugged. So behave yourself."

"Vic—"

But there was silence at the other end. Trembling, I went over to the window and closed it, pulling the shades down. Eyes. Always prying eyes. No wonder I had nightmares.

I ended up driving the moving truck by myself, discouraging my family from any further help. I certainly didn't want them to see Vic after his phone call. *Maybe being away from the family will help*, I thought, grinding gears in the old rental. *We can start a new life here, where no one knows us.* Mentally I crossed my long-lost cousin off my list of things to do, people to see. She would have to be kept out of my life, this life where there was no room for sentiment, no room for family.

Six hours later, Vic met me at the door of our new home, angry and accusing.

Together, we unloaded the U-Haul, silently tramping back and forth from the moving truck to the house. I didn't have time for first impressions; I lifted boxes and chairs and baby toys until my arms burned with fatigue. Some men helped us, heaving and huffing with Vic over the larger items. Neighbors, I assumed. I was thankful for their help and their presence; Vic hadn't spoken one word of greeting.

The neighbors finally left. Tiffany slept peacefully in her new bedroom. The U-Haul remained parked in front, ominously empty. Its cavernous box looked bleak and lonely without our household goods stacked inside. I closed the front door of my new home and turned to begin the task of putting things in order.

Vic, slouched in his easy chair, held a revolver.

It was the .22 pistol I had bought him for his birthday two years ago, bought with pennies painstakingly saved from my grocery budget. Now it was pointed straight at my heart.

My hand, still on the doorknob, tightened convulsively. My feet were cemented to the brick-design linoleum.

"I told you I didn't want you talked about," he said, his voice belying the casual handling of the gun in his hands. "I told you to be careful."

Stay calm! my head screamed. I couldn't take my eyes off the weapon. He broke it, funneled bullets into the chamber, closed it. "I don't know what you're talking about," I said, hearing and hating the tremor in my voice. "I haven't done anything wrong."

"You call entertaining men 'right'?" The gun lifted, swiveled toward me again. I could see the black hole of its barrel, the tunnel through which my life could end.

"I haven't entertained any men. I honestly don't know what you're talking about."

"Greg! Your sister's husband! Greg was at our house half the night. Wasn't he?"

"I told you, I told you he was there. But not half the night. He'd gone before you called. Remember? That was only ten o'clock. You know that." My lips felt so dry, I couldn't swallow, couldn't get anything inside to work. I was dead. I knew I was going to die here. Before I'd even seen my new home. I dared to raise my eyes, to meet his in a helpless plea.

His gaze was not on me, but somewhere beyond me, over my shoulder. The gun remained steady, pointed at my chest.

"I know everything," he said, grinding the words out with brittle precision. "My loving wife has been carrying on with my brother-in-law! Nobody cheats on me! Nobody!" And the gun barrel stretched until I could see the blackness, like the iris of a cold, steel grey eye staring down my throat.

"Vic, you have to believe me," I panted. "I would never cheat on you! I love you!"

"I don't believe your lies. You little slut!" I saw the tension in his face, his shoulders, and his hands, and the fingertips tightening...

The solid barrier of the door behind me prevented me from falling, somehow gave me strength, strength to argue for my life. "You're wrong, Vic! I wouldn't cheat on you! My God, how can you even think that, after all I've been through for you! I love you, Vic! Please, you've got to believe me." The words ended abruptly as I choked on them. The sudden silence stretched, time stopped as I watched him, afraid to speak, afraid to move.

The gun turned, swung slowly around until it pointed directly at his temple. "Then I guess I'm the one who should die. I've put you through such hell," he said, his voice now monotone, all anger gone, evaporated. The emphasis on the word "hell" was the only familiar sound, as the word was ripped from him, as if hell was a very familiar place.

And now I begged for his life even harder than I had for mine. "No! No, Vic, please. Please, listen to me. It's all right, I want to be a help to you. I don't mind the hurt. Please, oh God, please, Vic…" Sobbing, horrified and feeling somehow guilty for putting him in this position, somehow causing this distrust and despair, I released my hold on the doorknob and stepped toward him, my arms reaching. "Please, honey, put the gun down. It'll never happen again, I promise. I'll never see him again. Please."

The gun shifted, once again pointed in my direction. I caught my breath, my chest tightening painfully. But it continued to drop, until it finally rested on the little table beside him. His eyes cleared.

The breath left my body, and with it, the tension that had held me upright. I wilted, exhausted, into the nearest chair.

"You'd better see if we've got anything for supper," he said.

So began our life in San Remos. And in the months that followed, I learned that what had happened was not as bad as what was possible.

Our new home was a two-bedroom duplex, situated in a half-square of identical duplexes, all of which faced an inner parking area. The back windows looked out over a well-kept, fenced back yard, beyond which lay the street. The yard was communal; it contained a swing set, a sand box, and plenty of cool green grass.

We settled into routine—Vic went to work, as usual, to his cover job at Sandy's Restaurant, a fast-growing chain, while I plunged into the challenge of making a home for us. We made a token visit to my cousin Karen, just to satisfy family requests. I knew that we would never be able to resume our old friendship, but I told myself that it was for the best. No one could know me, no one could enter the space in which I lived. I enjoyed having immediate neighbors, although I was careful to keep an appropriate distance from them. It wouldn't do to let anyone become familiar with our routine or with details of our family life. We must appear to be like any young couple in America. I could almost forget, sometimes for hours, that we were not. We had a Mission.

I was as much a part of that mission as was Vic: the only difference was that my orders came from my husband.

We had been ensconced in our new home for perhaps two weeks when Vic once again told me I would have to get a job. "You've got to learn how to take care of yourself, Stephani," he said, over and over. "I won't be able to take care of you forever." I'd never had to actually apply for a job before; the thought of being appraised for my abilities, and judged for the lack of them, was deeply intimidating. After several attempts at various businesses, Vic told me to go to Sandy's. "It's all set," he said. "The manager knows you're coming."

Vic offered to watch Tiffany while I drove to meet my new employer. But when I got there, Tom Savatini appeared ignorant of the scheme. He took my application, noted the little experience I'd acquired at Winkler's, and sent me on my way. His wife stared at me closely, her forehead frowning in concentration, but when she remained silent, I shrugged off her scrutiny as mere curiosity. Disheartened, I turned the car toward home, practicing, under my breath, just how I was going to tell my husband I'd been turned down by his own Boys.

I stopped once on the way home, forestalling the inevitable by checking in with the doctor I had seen a few days before. I hoped he would have some good news for us.

After Vic's draft status had been cleared back in Woodsville, I had plunged forward with our plans to have another child. I'd dragged Tiffany's crib from the storage shed and repainted it, hunted for blankets and layette items, looked for bottles and sterilizer and other equipment among the cast-offs in the shed. Vic had not mentioned the "new baby" again, but most of the people we knew had already been informed that I was pregnant, and I began to feel the excitement of anticipation. This pregnancy would be different, I thought. This pregnancy would be shared by the two of us. I imagined the various stages, the tenderness between us, the secret smiles, the sounding of baby names. This child would give us even more to live for, more to fight for, I thought.

It was only as I was leaving Doctor Banlen's office that I realized a pregnancy might change Vic's plans about me working. But it was too late for second thoughts: I had finally conceived.

ASK ME NO QUESTIONS

"Honey, I'm pregnant! You're going to be a father again!" My voice shimmered with excitement and not a little trepidation. He hadn't mentioned the "baby" since our move...*Please, please be happy.* "Maybe this time we'll have a son," I said, hoping to bring about a smile.

Silence.

Where is he? Wandering through the living room, I entered the bedroom. Tiffany was playing safely in the tiny yard behind our duplex. "Honey, did you hear me?"

I found him in the bathroom, combing his hair into a high wave, Elvis style.

"Hon? Vic? Did you hear me? I'm pregnant."

Brushing past me, he reached into the closet, dropping discarded shirts on the floor. I watched, the anxiety growing.

Examining a pink long-sleeved cotton shirt, Vic ignored me as he buttoned it on, dropping the hanger where he stood.

"Vic? What's the matter?"

"Why should something be wrong?" The Victor voice, detached, preoccupied.

"Vic, I just told you that we're going to have another baby. Isn't that wonderful?"

"I suppose, if you like babies." He continued to dress, selecting a tie and then a sweater to create the "Ivy League" look.

"But—this is the one we planned. This is what we wanted."

"We? I don't recall planning to have another child. When did this conversation occur?" His distant, impersonal tone frightened me. I couldn't find my husband, couldn't get inside that cold facade, when Victor-the-agent spoke.

"A couple of months ago. Before we moved here. You said that if we had another baby, they wouldn't induct you into the army. You said Tiffany needed a brother. Remember?"

"They couldn't induct me anyway, Stephani. I had already served. I was 4F because of my eye. You've got it all mixed up."

"But you said..."

"Get this straight, Stephani. No amount of kids is going to change my life. I'm not going to leave the Company. If you don't like it, I can always leave." As if to emphasize his words, he brushed past me, our shoulders connecting briefly in the space of the doorway; he slammed the front door behind him.

Sinking into the sofa, I fought the sense of unreality whirling about me. The failure to get a job—even my great "news"—diminished in importance as I tried to recall that conversation of three months ago. Vic's voice echoed in my mind,

I saw once again his look of helplessness as he held the draft notice in his hand... *"If you were pregnant, they couldn't take me, Steph..."* Had it all been a game? Part of his job? A ploy by the Company? Or a cruel joke?

There was so much about our life that confused me, so much I didn't understand. I lived in virtual silence, never sharing chitchat with neighbors, never confiding in friends or family, never speaking to my husband unless first spoken to. I lived in a constant state of bewilderment, obeying "orders" which frequently contradicted, trying to piece snippets of "monversations"—those monologues in which Vic told me what to do, gave a condensed, need-to-know reason for the order, and waited for a nod or other sign of acknowledgement that I'd heard—as if, somehow, seeing the "big picture" would give me some clue as to the direction in which we were moving. I lived in reaction, my only source of proactivity lying in the form of our daughter, Tiffany. And now, the baby. Which Vic didn't remember planning, talking about, spreading the news even before it was conceived.

Of course, he had so much on his mind...and it probably wasn't such a great idea, the way we had to live. I guess I thought we could have a normal life once we moved. I guess I hoped we could just be a family. I should have known better.

He was right. I had married him knowing what he did. I had married him for better or worse, with faith that our love was strong enough to face all obstacles. It was too late to complain. I would not become a burden; I would not be known as a whiner, a nag, a quitter. There was only one possible path for the wife of a hero—that of undying support. That was all I could give him, all I could offer.

It would just be up to me to have the baby and take care of him—it had to be a son—until he could really know his father.

The decision was made: I squared my shoulders, so to speak, shook off the demons of insecurity, and accepted what I could not understand. That much I could do. The CIA worked in mysterious ways. Who was I to question them?

Chapter 14

"I need your help on this one, Steph," he confided late one night. We were lying side by side on the floor in front of the TV, the sounds of the midnight TV huckster competing with our conversation. "I have to hold some meetings here, some top secret meetings. People will be coming and going."

"What do you want me to do?"

"I need you to leave."

"What?"

"I'm going to send you to your grandmother's. She'd appreciate a visit anyway, wouldn't she?"

"I suppose. It's been awhile since I've seen her. How long?"

"I don't know for sure. A few weeks. Maybe a couple of months. We have to set up this operation. It will take some time."

I was silent, my eyes watching the screen in front of us but seeing the past weeks of job hunting, setting up a new house, and preparing for the new baby. Weeks of becoming familiar with the neighborhood, the route to the grocery store, the faces that belonged here and those that didn't. I played a game whenever I walked along the busy streets: I would look closely at the people nearby and try to guess whether I had seen them before. The man reading the newspaper so handily in the park, the bum leaning against the corner of the grocery store, the woman driving past in the light blue Ford. Had I seen them before? Was he my bodyguard? Was she? I would stop suddenly while walking, glance behind me as if I could catch one of them following me from a safe distance. My ears were constantly on the alert.

But they were too good. I could never tell who followed me, who watched over me. It comforted me to know that someone was there.

"There have been a lot of developments since I got here," Vic resumed. "My partner is a guy named Jerry. Sometimes he has to disguise himself as a woman. If you ever see us together, don't let on that you know me."

"If I see you?"

"It could happen. You'd laugh, Steph. You really can't tell that he's a man. He hates that disguise." My husband chuckled softly, the vision before his eyes obviously that of his luckless partner. "My code name is R.J. I'm not supposed to tell you that. But you might hear someone mention me. I don't want you asking any questions. If you ever hear the name R.J., don't even think about it. You'll know it's me."

I listened intently, as if by memorizing what he said I would see beyond the words, beyond the sketchy puzzle, into the picture beyond. Besides that, I didn't want to forget anything, in case some piece of this puzzle would be needed later. Vic frequently accused me of forgetting things, or worse yet, remembering them wrong. I closed my eyes, visualizing his words imprinted on my brain. I would never forget them.

I fell asleep on the floor not long after that, as Vic became interested in the rerun on television and his voice stopped. It was unthinkable that I would go to bed without him. I had long ago become used to curling up and sleeping whenever my eyes became too heavy to keep open.

I awoke to feel his weight crushing me to the hardwood floor, his hands pulling at my waistband. My breasts were tender with the sensitivity of pregnancy; his touch, never gentle, was painful now. "Vic, stop," I whispered, adjusting my body on the floor. He appeared not to have heard, his legs were moving mine apart. "Wait a minute, honey. The floor hurts my back." Still he did not respond. I flinched as his fingers tightened on me, then he began to move and the pressure of his body seemed to drive me into the floorboards. I forced myself to relax, forced my back to become one with the floor, to mold itself into the shape beneath me, on top of me. He held my wrists, held them to the floor as he supported himself above me. The TV glared before my eyes.

He finished, and immediately stood up and went to bed. I followed him there. It was bedtime.

Two days later Tiffany and I boarded the bus for my grandmother's house, some one hundred miles to the north. "You'll have to tell her I'm training for a management position in Santa Barbara," Vic instructed. "I don't want to leave you alone in your condition." I nodded, absorbing the words.

Our new baby was due in December, five months ahead. Although my doctor had expressed some concern over the uncertainty of the length of our visit to Nanna's—I was seeing him weekly—I really had no choice. I would just have to take care of myself.

ASK ME NO QUESTIONS

The ride to the northern California coast was uneventful. I wrote a letter to Vic, a letter that would never be mailed. "As we travel away from you, mile after mile, my love stays with you," I wrote, "and I am continually amazed at the strength of it. You are my life, and I am so proud, so humbly proud, to be your wife."

I thought about him, this enigma I had married, and I marveled at his singularity of purpose, his ability to shut out everything and everyone in order to do his job. My heart went out to him, and to his daughter, who might never, ever know him, and to his unborn child, who might not even know he existed except in my memory. I thought about all these things, and I resolved to be strong. For them. For him.

The bus groaned to a halt, brakes hissing. I reached for my daughter, grasping air. "Tiffany? Tiff! Where are you?" I looked around frantically, eyes searching for a twenty-five pound bundle of blonde fluff. She was so small...she could be picked up by anyone!

"Tiffany!" My voice rose in fear, nearly shrieking in sudden terror. "Tiffany, where are you!" Dropping my travel bag, I pushed through the standing passengers, stepped over bags and feet and—the tall man stood, immovable. Beside him, her tiny, fragile hand clutched in his, stood my little girl.

"Let her go," I gasped, fear choking the breath from my lungs. "Tiffany, come here. Come to Mama." Silently the big hand led the little one forward, forward to safety. I nearly gagged with relief. "I'm sorry," I said, my voice strained, "I thought—" *what, that you were the enemy? Sure, Steph. Tell him that you think he's a drug dealer, a Communist, whatever the "enemy" is these days. Tell him he thought he was going to kidnap your daughter so he could get at your husband.* "—never mind. Thank you."

He smiled as I led my little girl away, a polite, impersonal smile. It could have meant anything.

Stepping from the bus, I spied my grandmother waiting beside a small sedan. I rushed over to her as quickly as I could, bags and toys and baby all akimbo. "Nanna! Oh, Nanna, it's so good to see you!" Hugging the tiny woman, I tried to quell my trembling. Relief poured out of me as I heard the bus start up again, begin to move along its way. Pressing Nanna to me, I silently thanked God we were safe.

And as I turned to the car to load our possessions inside, I glimpsed the bus station in the reflection of the window. A tall figure stood in front of the building. His eyes, shaded by dark glasses, seemed to be directed my way.

The visit turned out to be a nightmare of renewing old acquaintances and hiding that now constant companion, anxiety. Nanna, my mother's mother, was a formidable authoritarian whose word was never crossed. A widow of some ten years, Nanna had not retired to spend her days in doleful mourning. A staunch Christian, her good works kept her body active and her mind sharp. She made up in will what she lacked in height; barely five feet tall, she ruled her home with more taut authority than our legendary Viking ancestor ran his ship.

My days were planned. There were myriad relatives to visit, relatives I hadn't seen or thought of in years.

There were the cousins, of course, children for whom I had babysat not too many years past. Five of them. Stalwart Scandinavians, the four boys ranged in age from eleven to three, while the one girl in the family was nine. Too young to have anything in common with me.

Then there were the elders, the nine brothers and sisters in Nanna's family, as well as a few of my dad's. The only person close to my age was my cousin, Leah, a newlywed herself. Perhaps I would see her on this visit.

Nanna had it all planned, each day, each meal, each visit.

I listened to the chatter, the insignificance of it washing over me as I wondered for the thousandth time, Where is he now? Is he safe? Are the meetings going well? *Oh God, please let him be all right.* It was only with tremendous effort that I replied to the inane questions: How are you doing in your new home? Do you like it? Have you seen your cousin Karen yet? You know, she has a little one, too. A boy, I think. Do you live close to her?

I replied with nods and vague smiles, my eyes always on Tiffany. Mustn't let those little fingers knock over a precious vase, or sticky up a TV screen.

"Yvette, have you seen Yvette? She's got herself a real nice husband now. They manage a restaurant. You know, one of those chain things. Let's see...the name escapes me." *Are you thinking of me? Do you miss your family?* "Sanders I think, or Sandy's, something like that..."

"What? Sandy's?" Suddenly my attention was fully in the present. Aunt Matilda had said something that made my skin prickle..."Did you say Sandy's?"

"Yes, I think that's it," the old lady repeated. "I have her last letter right here," she fumbled around on the cluttered coffee table. "Here it is...Read it for yourself. Do you know Sandy's?"

Suddenly, the day was cold. Sandy's Restaurant, the letter read. Vic's cover. My fingers twisted the letter. I remembered Yvette, the manager's wife, and her husband Tom. Recalling the woman's long scrutiny at that meeting, I wondered.

It couldn't be...my cousin? How was that possible? She had looked vaguely familiar, but surely I would remember my own cousin!

"How long has it been since you've seen Yvette, Stephani?" Aunt Matilda's voice brought me back to the homey kitchen and the steaming fresh coffee.

"Hm-mm? Oh gee, I don't know. Years. I think I was about—nine, maybe. Maybe younger. I don't remember." *God! It can't be!*

"Well, you'll have to be sure and look her up. Doesn't your husband work in a restaurant? They should have a lot in common."

The reedy voice continued, but I didn't hear it. *How am I going to handle this? I can't let the family know what's going on. Vic will kill me when he finds out. I have to warn him!* By the time Nanna turned the old Studebaker home, I had worked my worry into full-blown, throat-aching, head-splitting anxiety.

It was surely one of life's jests that I would be met at every turn by someone who could blow our cover. The life I had chosen to lead was lonely, wrought with crisis after crisis, a fragile strand of livable moments strung out between heartbreaks. I could count the happy times on the fingers of one hand; yet I could not let go of the only love I knew. Somehow, I would warn him. Somehow, we would get through this, too.

It was two days before the telephone rang and Nanna called out that it was for me.

"Vic! Vic, how are you? Is everything okay? I'm so glad you called—"

"Calm down. Get it together. This is going to be short." The brief commands indicated the importance of listening, of taking great care, of giving the right responses. This was not the time for "love," "I miss you," or any other endearing phrase. Just listen.

"Are you there?"

"Yes, I'm here. I'm sorry," was my muffled reply. *Can't let Nanna see my reaction. Must maintain the charade of a loving couple.*

"Good. Listen. The Company isn't very pleased with your progress. You haven't let go. You're not strong enough. You've got to stop leaning on me so much."

"What? I don't know what you're talking about. What do you mean?" Once again, I forgot. I reacted. Felt instead of thought, reacted instead of reasoned. Heard the accusation in his voice instead of the caution. Proved his point.

"Your letters," he resumed. "They're too much. They say too much. Don't you know they're read before they get to me? They don't like what they're reading."

"They're what? Vic, what—"

"You can't keep calling me 'darling' and all that stuff. You've got to let go."

"My letters are read before they get to you? They're censored?" *Oops. Lower your voice! Nanna is right there!* "Vic," I struggled for control. My tone changed, became quieter, more businesslike. "I don't understand. I write you to tell you how I feel. My letters are to you, not to the Company. Why do they read them?"

"For the same reason they listen to our phone conversations." The warning was unmistakable. "To make sure you are a safe risk. To insure the safety of the team. If you're not ready for this, there is only one thing left to do." *And you know what that is,* I heard the silent admonishment.

"Yes, Vic. I understand. I'll be fine. Do what you have to do." *I love you!* The line went dead. *Wait! I didn't tell you about Yvette!*

"How is he?" Nanna chirped cheerfully. "You didn't sound very happy." Her bright little bird's eyes glittered with curiosity.

"Oh, he's just working hard," I countered, a smile forcing my lips apart. "He gets a little testy without me around. You know how men are." *You're not strong enough...you haven't progressed far enough...you're not a safe risk.* I returned to the chore at hand, cooking dinner, while the events of the day receded into vague autopilot, mechanical motion requiring no thought. Reality was the rhythm in my brain, repeating the refrain over and over again.

Finally, I was alone. The day had ended. No more chitchat to force myself through. No more dangerous ground to cover of relatives lost and found. Somewhere in the midst of my thoughts I realized I hadn't mentioned cousin Yvette to Vic. Just one more mistake. One more piece of evidence that Vic was right. I wasn't thinking clearly.

By bedtime, I was exhausted. Tiffany slept guilelessly beside me. I watched her for many minutes, wondering what her future would be. *Will you ever have a father?* I asked myself. *Will you ever know a real family?* The baby fluttered inside me, reminding me of another subject I wanted to avoid.

"What do you think it will be this time, Steph?" they asked. "A boy?" "You don't eat enough, Stephani," they said. "You're eating for two, remember." "You're gaining a little weight, aren't you, dear?" they probed. "You want to be careful, you know. Easier gained than lost." And the worst: "Is Vic excited about the new baby?" Is Vic excited? I responded inwardly; Vic doesn't want it. Vic doesn't think of anything except his company. *No, no, mustn't say that! Vic loves me. Vic wants this baby. He just can't let it affect his work. He loves us, really. Deep down...*

I awoke with tears slick on my cheeks. The lace curtains moved slightly with the midnight breezes. Tiffany breathed deeply beside me, little baby breaths filling her small lungs. Had I left the window open? I jumped up to close it, lock it. Holding my breath, I scanned the shadows in the room, the image of the man at the bus station leaping into my mind. I watched for movement, listened for footsteps. Finally, satisfied no one lurked in the darkness, I turned the bedside lamp on, pulled out my notebook and began to write.

"September 18, 1968

"You said I haven't progressed far enough yet, that I am still not strong enough. What did you expect, an overnight miracle the moment we left you? I think I have come very far.

"I have learned what it is like to live without you, isn't that what you wanted? I know what it's like to live a lie, to tell people what they're supposed to hear when inside I know it is just the opposite. I know what it's like to smile when I am really holding back tears. I've learned what it is to go to bed at night and wake up every few minutes because I think I hear the telephone ring; or awaken, expecting to find you beside me, and realize I am alone. I know what it's like to try to sleep, but instead lie awake, wondering where you are, how you are, if you still love me, if all those happy days of our courtship and early marriage really happened; I know what it's like to wonder if you are still alive.

"I know what it's like to feel my whole body actually hurt with loneliness; to hold back the tears until my throat aches and my head aches, and every fiber in my body aches with the strain; to get up in the morning and push my feeling aside in the daily routine of living; to suddenly sicken of a television program or a favorite book because it's all nonsense, I don't believe in happy endings anymore. I know what it's like to act normal and smile when my heart is breaking. I know how it feels to talk to myself and pretend it's you, and wonder if I'll ever have that pleasure again, and wonder how you will act toward me if you do see me; to feel our baby kick inside of me and cut off that first instinctive pleasure because I know the dreams I had will never come to be.

"And now I know what it's like to ask myself if my dreams will ever be fulfilled, or if it's worth it to dream at all. I think I have learned my lessons very well.

"I know what it is to believe when there is no evidence; to trust when a life is being torn apart; to hope when everything is negative; to love when it seems I have lost.

"I know what it is to summon courage when at my weakest; to pray when God seems to have left; to be patient when there is nothing for which to wait but discouragement.

"And through it all, I know I cannot have you on any terms but your own, nor would I want you in any other way."

These words summed up my life and all that I believed. But I would never be able to share them with the one man who needed to hear them. They would be forever locked away in the pages of my journal.

Chapter 15

The afternoon was bright, the mist retreating in the face of a September sun. Packed and ready, I awaited Vic's arrival. The day had come, it was time to go home...Home. What is home? *I wish I knew*, I thought, watching Tiffany pile wooden blocks on top of each other. *Maybe I'll never know. It's supposed to be something secure, something safe. Today I'm going home, and I'm scared. I have no idea what I'm going to meet at home. Surely not safety, not security. I just have to believe. I have to believe that it will all be worth the sacrifice.* Gritting my teeth, I joined Tiffany as she played on the floor. Together we waited for Vic to arrive.

When I heard the sound of his car roaring down the long tree-lined driveway, my senses sharpened, my focus changed. Life began. "Tiffany," I called, "Daddy's here! Come on, honey, let's go say hello!" Trying to remain calm, I forced myself to walk, slowly, to him. *One step at a time, Stephani. The picture of a mature, strong, woman, not an excited teenager. Mustn't give him anything to worry about. They're watching you!* "Hello, honey. You're a little late—did you have any problems?" *Surely I can call you 'honey' here—we're supposed to be happily married.* I kept my smile composed, just a slight show of teeth, nothing too radical. No wide grins. No hello kiss. What Vic would call "mature."

"No problems," he answered, smiling. "Hi, Tiff! How's my little punkin?" His voice warmed as Nanna walked up behind me, her old-fashioned heels clumping along the redwood block path. Vic saw her coming. "How's my favorite grandma?" he said, "I hope my wife's been keeping you out of trouble." Overpowering the tiny woman with a bear hug, Vic turned on his charm. He had a special regard for elderly women.

Smiling up at him, she scolded him good-naturedly. "You're going to stay for supper, aren't you? We've been waiting for you."

"Oh, I wish I could, Nanna. I hate to miss your cooking. You taught my wife something while she was here, didn't you?" Wrapping his arm around her shoulders, he began walking with her toward the house. "I'll never forget that cake you made the last time we were here. Man, that was so good my mouth waters just thinking about it."

I trailed along behind them, carrying Tiffany. The ache began way back in my throat as I watched them walking so closely together. I struggled to keep my composure. *My time will come,* I thought. *It's ridiculous to be jealous of my grandmother! Come on, Steph, show him how strong you are.*

Nanna talked Vic into staying after all, just a quick meal, thank you. Afterwards, I settled Tiffany into the car while Vic hugged my grandmother goodbye. Then it was my turn.

"Thank you so much, Nanna," I said. "I'll write, I promise." *I don't know what about, though. I'll guess I'll have to make something up.* I held her for a long minute, feeling her warmth and her love. Then I let her go and stepped into the car, holding Tiffany beside me.

As we sped away from my grandmother's house, the visit was immediately forgotten, past, over. I was transposed instantly into the present, with the man behind the wheel. My nerves tingled with the need to sit close against him, to draw from his body the love I knew was there. But I remained on the passenger side, quietly tending to my wriggling daughter. Vic hadn't even mentioned the change in me, the evidence of our new baby growing inside of me. It didn't matter. Only the mission mattered. I waited.

For many minutes, the only sounds were Tiffany's chatter and the radio blasting Elvis' latest record. "Suspicion torments my heart. Suspicion keeps us apart. Suspicion…" The winding road eventually lulled Tiffany to sleep, although I was hard put to keep her still while Vic took the turns at his usual NASCAR speed. I clung to Tiffany and the car door in an effort to remain upright, biting my lips to keep from asking him to slow down. He loved to drive fast.

Fifty miles sped under us; the country road became a highway. Picking up even more speed, Vic at last broke the silence.

"Remember Vanessa, the agent I told you about?"

"Vanessa?" I repeated. "I thought his name was Jerry." *Your partner, a man disguised as a woman.*

"No, Steph, Vanessa. My new partner."

"Oh. Vanessa." *What happened to Jerry?*

"I'm working with her very closely now. She's my cover at the restaurant. We're supposed to be going out. In fact, I have to go through an entire courtship with her, pretend to be in love with her. You'll have to stay away from Sandy's altogether. We can't be seen together."

As he spoke, I reached back into my mind, tried to remember his words of a month ago. *You can't really tell he's a man…*

"Of course, Vanessa will be acting like she loves me, too. We'll be spending a lot of time together, when she's home."

"Home? I thought she worked in the restaurant with you."

"She did, but she's in Stanford now. College. That's where we're working, down in the city. So I'll have to be gone a lot."

"Oh." *What happened to Jerry? Will you be home when your son is born? How long will I have to share you with Vanessa?*

"I want you to know that I love you, Steph," his voice softened, became the Vic I knew. "I have never stopped loving you. I never will. I just have to do this. I have to stop those bastards who are ruining our country with their drugs, their lies. I'm sorry if this hurts you." Reaching across Tiffany's slumbering body, he touched my hand, briefly, a whispering breeze across my fingertips. The puzzle of Jerry/Vanessa's identity receded. I must have forgotten. Or he forgot to tell me. It didn't matter, wasn't worth quibbling over. Vanessa was his new partner, a college student who worked in the restaurant with him. *Got it.*

"I know it's hard. But I think in the long run, it will make a woman out of you."

Woman? This will make a woman out of me? What does that mean? I glanced over at him in disbelief. But his tenderness held me captive, steadied me. I nodded, those traitorous thoughts cloaked behind my smile. "I'll be fine, Vic, as long as I know you love me. That's all that matters."

"I do. No matter what it looks like, I love you. Always remember that."

"I will."

"This operation may take a little time," he continued, as if the tender moment had never happened, "You'll have to be my sister until it's over. It could be three years. I'll have to leave you for awhile, until it's safe again."

"Leave me? When?"

"I don't know yet. They'll tell me. Don't worry, they'll take care of you. I'll be able to stay in touch. We'll get back together when it's over."

Struggling to remain calm, to hide the panic in my eyes, I looked from my husband to the road ahead of us. Thinking, while my heart pounded in my ears, *Not again! I don't want to go through this again!*

Vic saw my struggle.

"Whatever it takes." The voice was no longer tender. "'No mission too difficult.' I'll do whatever it takes. Remember that."

"Yes, Vic, I'll remember." I hastened to reassure him, the lines of our motto registering in my brain. 'No mission too difficult, no sacrifice too great. Duty first.' Duty first. Duty to country. Duty to God. *Is this what You want, God? For our children to have no father?* We rode on, the sound of the wind rushing past the open window.

I didn't realize how much our lifestyle had become a part of me, of the woman I would one day be. I had learned to listen to his words, his instructions and explanations, and hear to the tone of his voice, the underlying emotions. The words didn't matter, only the feelings mattered. I would do anything as long as he loved me. That was what I listened for.

Upon reaching San Remos, Vic took us out to a small diner as a treat. "How'd you like to go out to dinner?" he'd asked when we reached the outskirts of the city.

"Oh, could we?" I cried, surprised.

"Sure. We'll just have to be careful, that's all. We'll go someplace where nobody will recognize us."

So we stopped at a little greasy spoon and enjoyed a trucker-sized hamburger. For awhile I felt young again, like a teenager out on a date. The stolen moments would stay with me for weeks. They would have to.

It was while we lingered over our last cup of coffee that I remembered to tell him about Yvette and Tom. He listened intently, told me not to worry and thanked me for warning him. My heart swelled with pride and relief. I had helped him.

Later, after an hour of small talk and relative relaxation, we stepped into the small duplex we called home. Familiar smells assailed me. Cigarette smoke. The linoleum. Something else…dirty dishes. Unwashed linens.

Vic turned the lights on. The little living room was strewn with ash trays, cigarette butts and ashes spilled onto the floor. The kitchen sink was piled high with dishes and glasses, some food caked on them, some with remains of meals congealed into a slimy mass. The coffee pot contained cold coffee, grounds spilled beside it. I had been gone a month: every day of my absence was written within the walls of this house. Vic certainly hadn't made any attempt to keep it clean while I was gone.

Putting Tiffany to bed, I stepped into the bedroom to unpack. It was a mess. Dirty clothes were piled on the floor, the bed linens hadn't been changed. The bed, unmade, was a tangled mass of sheets. I sighed, the thought of cleaning pushing the happy dinner far back in my mind. I bent to strip the sheets from the bed.

ASK ME NO QUESTIONS

Hands encircled me, pulled at my clothes, pulled me against him. His lips nuzzled my neck. Turning me around, he pushed me down on the bed, stripping me as I fell to the tangled sheets. For a moment my apprehension over the new mission, the disappointment at the messy house, left me. This was my husband. My love. The reason for my existence. I was home.

Chapter 16

"You've got to stop her," Vic said. "She could get us all killed."

"How? She's only a baby! What could she do to us?"

"They could get to me through her. Do you think I wouldn't gladly trade my life for hers? She's got to be stopped! She can't call me Dad. No one must know I'm her father. No one must know we're married."

Home. There are so many cliches about that place: home is where the heart is, you can't go home again, there's no place like home. Home for me was a man, a man I had vowed to love, to support, to cherish, until death do us part. I took that vow very seriously, perhaps because, for us, the chance of that parting was better than in most marriages.

By the time I returned home that summer, the chill of coastal fall was already in the air: I was nearly six months pregnant with my second child, a child who might never know his father. Tiffany was two-and-a-half years old, a blonde bundle of dynamite exploding every hour with questions, demands, challenges. And Vic/Victor, my love and my life, was an enigma I thought I knew as I knew my own soul.

I plunged into the perimeter of Victor's activities immediately upon returning to San Remos. Every day he came home from work at Sandy's, quickly changed his clothes, and left again, to return late, late at night.

I lived for his return. That was when he confided in me. He talked about Vanessa, the current mission, even, at times, asked my opinion of how best to deal with his new partner. He was in a tricky spot, having to act as if he loved someone with whom he had just a business relationship. I wanted to help him, wanted to understand.

And when he was gone, I wrote down his words, wrote in the journal which became my only confidante. The secrets hidden there could have destroyed us all.

ASK ME NO QUESTIONS

A few weeks after my return from Nanna's, Vic told me of my next challenge: I was to meet Vanessa. "You have to do this, Stephani," he said. "She doesn't know who you are, of course. She's been told only what she needs to know—that you're my sister."

I was silent as I absorbed his instructions. The test had come. How good an actress was I after all? I would soon find out.

"This is the story: your husband is missing in Viet Nam, and as your loving brother, I am taking care of you until he's found, or you get on your feet."

"How long has he been gone?" I asked, resting my hand on the mound of my stomach. I had gained eleven pounds while visiting Nanna. She believed in the old adage, "eating for two."

"Whatever it takes. Details aren't important. You don't really have to discuss it with anybody, anyway. Just pretend you're too upset to talk about it. You can do that, can't you?"

"Of course, I just wanted to be sure my story was the same as yours."

"Well, that's all that needs to be said. Nobody's going to press you for details."

There was silence as I digested the information. It wasn't too different, really, from playing a character on the stage. It shouldn't be too hard. After all, I only had to meet this woman. I didn't have to become her friend.

"When is this event going to take place?"

"This weekend. I'm bringing her over here on Saturday. We'll play pinochle or something after dinner. She doesn't know that you know she's an agent, so don't make any slips. I could get in big trouble if the boys knew I tell you so much. To you, Vanessa's my girlfriend."

The word "girlfriend" suddenly loomed before me: I hadn't thought about that aspect of this dinner. "You mean I have to watch you holding hands, watch her fawn over you?"

"Yeah. She'll be putting on an act, too."

It seemed ironic. It seemed like something that, if I approached it from the right angle, could be funny. A story to tell my son someday, about when his mom and dad fooled this world in order to protect him. "No problem," I said. "What do you want for dinner?"

So I became Mrs. Frank Michael Brian, Army wife, possible widow. I kept the family surname long before that trend became fashionable, just in case verification was ever needed that required my last name. And a two-year-old child began to call her own daddy "Uncle," beginning another trend, a trend of lying and loss of identity, an insecurity which would haunt her for decades.

On Saturday I gave the house a good cleaning before they arrived, my "big brother" and his girl. Tiffany kept an early bedtime, so I didn't need to deal with her. I was worried about her making a slip and calling Vic "Daddy." I wanted everything to be perfect.

Then they arrived, and it was too late to worry.

Vanessa was not at all what I expected in an agent. But then, that was their gift. They could blend into a crowd, be different people at different times.

She was everything I was not—brunette, with deep brown eyes and slender lips. Chiseled cheekbones, a square little face. Although she stood head to head with me, she had a cheerleader's figure, curvy in all the right places. I felt my ungainly shape grow even larger the moment I saw her step from Vic's car.

Apparently Vic had filled her in about my "tragic" life, for she asked no personal questions, giving me a sympathetic glance before she asked if she could help with anything in the kitchen.

"No, everything's ready," I replied cheerfully, "Just make yourself at home."

Somehow I got through the long evening...after dinner, Vic suggested we play three-handed pinochle. Vanessa was just learning the game; I, of course, had been taught right after Vic and I were married.

Vic always played as if his life depended on winning. Once, long ago, we had played a two-handed tournament that had ended with Vic throwing the cards on the table in disgust because I was in the midst of a lucky streak. After sweeping the offending bits of plastic onto the floor, he'd stomped away, his erratic temper barely in check. I seldom won a game after that day; I wondered, how would Vanessa fare?

Despite his temper, Vic was an expert at the game. That Saturday night Vanessa and I were quiet, I lost in my thoughts as the challenge of my husband's "girlfriend" presented itself; Vanessa undoubtedly going through a similar process...we were playing both ends against the middle.

The clock had ticked into a new day when Vic finally escorted the sexy brunette into his car. I waved goodnight, secretly hoping I never had to see her again as I watched their silhouettes nearly merge in the darkness. I remembered, vividly, when I had sat so close to Vic that we were almost one...I crept into bed, the double bed that so often now bore the impression of only one body.

When Vic returned he warned again about Tiffany. "She's got to be watched.," he cautioned. "She could be in danger. We have to make sure nobody knows we're married."

"Well, I'm not telling anybody. I haven't even seen my cousin Karen since we came back from Nanna's."

"I know, Steph, but Tiffany could break our cover. You've got to be careful."

"What do you want me to do?"

"You can't let her keep calling me 'Daddy.' She's got to remember I'm 'Uncle Vic.'"

"How can I do that? You're her father, that's how she knows you."

"You have to do it, that's all. We can't take the risk of anybody knowing. They could get to me through her, or through you."

"Oh."

But Tiffany resisted our attempts to change her Daddy into someone else, resolutely refusing to obey our instructions.

In the midst of the infamous "terrible two's," Tiffany was especially stubborn and rebellious. At times there was no controlling her. It was as if she, too, had secrets she didn't share, knew things I didn't, and couldn't help but best me at every opportunity. I put her temperament down to her stage of life and the lack of a father, and focused all my energy into mothering her.

I developed a life of my own, of sorts. Since Vic was gone so much, I began to attend a nearby church, finding comfort in the music and the familiar religious dogma. It was hard when people asked me questions about myself, for I had no answers. I told the lies; I burned inside. *Forgive me, Father*, I would pray. *You know I must protect Vic.* And there was no need to pretend sorrow over my "missing husband," for that part was the truth. For all intents and purposes, I had no husband.

Chapter 17

Sunday, October 13, 1968

"Something has gone wrong. Vic is in trouble in the city; two men are trailing him and he can't shake them. Also—Yvette and her husband Tom have found out who I am—Tom called me tonight. It's all crumbling apart. What am I supposed to do?"

My hands trembled as I wrote. The pages filled rapidly with evidence of my fear. It was late, the house tomblike in its silence. I was alone in the bedroom, the bedside light casting long shadows against the walls.

The conversation with Tom Savatini had been short. "What kind of game are you playing?" he'd demanded. "I see Vic with Vanessa Cain all the time, then I discover you're married to him! And you're Yvette's cousin? I'm telling you, you'd better have an explanation for this! This company isn't supporting shenanigans like this! You tell Vic he'd better call me before he comes in tomorrow!"

I had no reply for him; I'd had no preparation, no training in how to deal with a blown cover. Instead, I merely acquiesced, agreed to let Vic handle it, and was relieved when Tom hung up.

Later the phone rang again. I waited this time, counting four rings, a silence, another shrill ring.

"Vic?"

"They're after me," he hissed, his voice low and flat, metallic through the instrument held against his mouth. "They've been on my tail all day."

"Vic," I interrupted. "Tom's found out. He knows Yvette's my cousin. He's really mad, wants you to call him before you go to work." The words rushed from my mouth without a breath between the phrases. I had to warn him! *Who is after you? Where are you? Tell me you'll be all right!*

"Listen—we'll take care of Tom—we've been prepared for this—don't say anything to him. I'll be there—afterwards."

"Yes…I understand. Are you all right?"

He didn't answer immediately. For the space of a heartbeat I waited, straining in the silence to hear, to force my mind's eye see what was happening. Then he mumbled, "The story we've taped should convince them—otherwise we'll go to Plan B." And he was gone.

"Plan B" meant one thing: divorce. It had become a familiar phrase over the years, his way of reminding me what he was sacrificing to allow me in his life. I don't believe he knew what that reminder did to me, no matter how often I heard it. It was an insult to the vows we'd made, a wound torn open so often it had no chance to heal. It left me frantically renewing my efforts to live up to his expectations. I would do anything, right or wrong, to support him.

Dawn was creeping into the room when he got home. Although I had fallen into a fitful doze, my ears picked up the click of the lock as he opened the front door.

"Vic?" I slid from the bed, groping toward the hallway in the semidarkness. "Vic, are you okay?" His arms were around me, holding me steady. I didn't cry. I just let him love me, memorizing each touch, each feeling in preparation for the day when he wouldn't return at all. I knew that day would come.

He hadn't touched me since my return from Nanna's weeks ago. Explaining that it was part of the need to distance himself from his family emotionally, he'd kept his distance physically, too.

But that morning, Vic loved me.

The sun was sneaking weak rays of warmth through the thin curtains when he began to talk.

"I have some good news," he said, lighting a cigarette as he spoke.

"Oh? Did everything turn out well last night?"

"I lost them, if that's what you mean. The good news is that the Company's moved my orders back—I can stay with you until the baby's born."

"You can stay? Our baby will see his father?"

"Uncle—never forget! Uncle! Yes, I'll be there at least until then. But you'll have to plan on making your own decisions after that."

"We'll be fine." I asserted. Hope surged through my body. I felt almost giddy with the release. *He'll be here to see his son's birth!*

He left, leaving me with a rare embrace and reassurance, and I didn't see him again for three days. He called occasionally, the phone shrilling its allotted four times, followed by a silence, then one ring. His voice was almost always hushed, flat, and hurried.

One such call drew my attention to the newspaper. "Did you see the article?" he asked. At my negative reply, he pointed out a minor front-page article recounting the events leading up to a major drug bust in the city. There had been an explosion, a rescue, an arrest. An agent had nearly lost his life. "That's where I was the other night," he said. "That's what I do."

That same day I got a note from Tom Savatini; Tom said he was sorry for the "misunderstanding," asked how I felt, and offered me a job after the baby was born. He said he'd tried to call, but no one answered: he said he would be glad to help if help were ever needed. I didn't reply. A few days later, Tom and Yvette were transferred and I never saw them again.

My departed cousin was, I'm afraid, low on the scale of priorities. My emotions were too uncertain to concentrate on anything beyond my husband's safety. He was playing a dangerous game, his life was too complex for me to keep up with its constantly changing developments. His relationship with Vicki filled my mind with fantasies. *What are they doing now? Are they safe? Will she be able to play her part convincingly?*

I never doubted Vanessa's role: she was an agent, working undercover with my husband. That was all there was to it. The part she played was dangerous, just as dangerous as his role. But he had a wife, a child, a baby on the way. She was free to do her job. His burden was greater. I could lighten his burden, I thought. I could make it easier for him. But I didn't have the courage to leave him. Not yet.

In mid-November Vanessa came to visit again. This time dinner was more casual, the house less sparkling. Tiffany stayed up awhile, her innocent baby eyes reprimanding as she observed her "uncle" and his "girlfriend."

"Daddy," she said once, clearly, unmistakably, "who that?" Her pointed finger seemed deliberate, accusing.

"Tiff," I admonished, quickly inserting myself between my daughter and the object of her curiosity. "It's not polite to point. I told you, remember? This is Vanessa, your Uncle Vic's friend." I glared at her, my expression protected from the "friend" by the back of my head. "Now, come on, say 'hello.' And be nice!"

"'Lo," she mimicked, her eyes on Vanessa's face, searching, perhaps, for a clue amidst the puzzle. Her eyes left the woman standing beside her father, rested upon him. She frowned, a baby frown, complete and unhidden. "Un-cle?" she said, the word coming out split, as her psyche must be. I couldn't watch anymore.

"Come on, Tiff," I said, taking her hand, "let's go get a cookie." Breaking my own before-dinner rule, I picked her up to allow her access to the cookie jar, held her while she plunged her hand into its ceramic mouth. I held her a little too tight, a little too long; she squiggled from my arms, the cookie brandished like a trophy in her pudgy baby hand.

"She doesn't remember her father," I said to the woman watching us. "She's always called Vic 'Daddy.' He's the only one she's ever had."

Vanessa smiled politely, her bottomless brown eyes unreadable. "That's okay," she said soberly. "I understand."

We eyed each other carefully, the toddler standing between us a barrier to any relationship we might have had. In another life, perhaps. Another time. She played her part of the devoted girlfriend very well.

I hid my pain well, too, I thought, as I watched the quiet repartee between Vic and Vanessa. I smiled, thinking, *but I know the truth*, and served dinner armed with my own secret thoughts. It gave me a sense of power to know that only I knew the real truth, only I knew that she was just a tool in Vic's game, while I was part of his life.

But I had to choke back tears when Vanessa followed my husband to our bedroom while I was banished to Tiffany's. I don't think they need to carry the game quite so far, I thought, the armor of my trust suddenly feeling very heavy. Vic gave me a silencing glare over Vanessa's head; I clamped my mouth shut, my eyes stinging.

Lying in my daughter's bed, I fought the depression that threatened to engulf me. *It's his job*, I repeated to myself, *it doesn't mean anything. They're not doing anything anyway—they're just playing the game.* But my spirit dipped into the hole of despair despite my frantic self-assurances. I didn't care anymore, couldn't feel anything, was lost in a limbo of vanishing hope and shattered dreams. I accepted the game as gospel—this was my life, this nether world of distorted reality. In a city of some 50,000 souls, I was alone, living in a vacuum of unreality. My only purpose was to serve as Victor's credibility, his backup.

As Thanksgiving approached, I tried to think about all my blessings. Childlike, I counted them one by one: my husband. His love for me. Tiffany. The baby. Overall health. God. His love for us. The times Vic and I had shared, both good and bad. His devotion to his country. His life. His idealism. His purpose. Vic. Victor. My love. *Thank you, God. Thank you for him in my life. Even if it's only for a while.*

The prayer accomplished its purpose. Peace was attained, at least for the moment. I found I could face another hour, another evening, even perhaps another night before resorting to the ritual again.

And then Christmas came, and I spent the long day staring at a sorry pine tree that blinked and twinkled frantically in an effort to be merry. Vic was, of course, with Vanessa. The presents under the tree did little to brighten my mood, although I smiled over Tiffany's toddler excitement and shared Christmas songs with her. Just the two of us: a bright-haired little girl and her very pregnant mother. I wanted to be brave, for Vic. I felt anything but brave. I felt alone, forgotten, and unloved.

But my self-pity disappeared when, at four o'clock on Christmas Day evening, a bouquet of white carnations arrived with my name attached. Immediately contrite, I set the arrangement on the coffee table in front of the little tree and begged God for forgiveness for my lack of faith. He had remembered me after all.

In fact, Vic remembered his real family enough to come home shortly after Tiffany's bedtime, get her up, and spend an hour putting her little bookcase-toy chest together, a gift from "Santa." He even brought a gift for me—a new bathrobe for my pending hospital stay. That terry bathrobe became my blanket of security, his acknowledgement of love for me. The hour or so of figuring out instructions for Tiffany's toy was a bright light in an otherwise very bleak existence for Tiffany and me—I could only hope she would remember this instead of the days and weeks without her father's presence. I clung to those moments: they were my lifeline.

It was very late by the time we all finally retired. I entered our bedroom quietly, hoping my husband hadn't heard the verbal battle I'd had with our toddler. She was too excited to go back to sleep; it had taken precious minutes of persuasion, and finally the "voice of authority" to convince her to go to bed. Vic didn't believe in reasoning with a child. He said they understood only commands. Maybe he was right.

The glow of the cigarette was the only light in the bedroom. Sliding my new robe off my shoulders, I crept in beside him.

"I don't think this is going to work," he said, his words clipping all the Christmas joy right out of my body. I held my breath, afraid to ask what "this" was.

"I think I'm just too determined to do my job. I've got to finish this, no matter who gets hurt. I can't let anybody get in the way."

I let the sound sink into the darkness. *What do you mean? What are you talking about?* He had explained everything to me already—what more was there to say? I knew the plan: I knew he was going to leave me as soon as the baby was born, leave for an indefinite period of time, probably years. But he had always reassured me that we would be together when it was over. *Who's getting in the way?*

The cigarette disappeared. I heard him snuff the butt in the ashtray next to him. I held myself tight, not daring to move, even to breathe, as he turned over on his side. Waiting for more, for something more, I let my breath out as slowly as I could, my lungs aching for relief. *Tell me what you mean!* I wanted to scream. *Tell me what you're thinking! Tell me what to do!* But I knew better than to ask the questions that reverberated in my mind. My job was to listen, to obey. That was the bargain we had made.

As his breathing became steady in sleep, I carefully moved to a more comfortable position, maintaining the inches of distance between us. There would be no unexpected touching in the night.

The new year arrived, and with it an increase of activity away from home. Vanessa was nearly always in the picture now, a constant companion.

The couple had gone skiing after Christmas, taking the youth group from Vanessa's church on a weekend excursion to Lake Tahoe. It was such irony that Vanessa was a religious woman. I remembered when Vic went to church with me, during those months before we were married. He had been involved in the youth group then, too. He could always quote verses from the Bible from memory, using them to prove his point. Now he was co-advising this group, with Vanessa.

Maybe the mission involved some of the college kids in the church.

I watched the dawn of 1969 alone, resolving to be a better wife, a better mother. I vowed to devote my life to his children, to keep his memory alive to them. *I will not give you reason to leave me,* I promised. *I will not bring you shame.*

The days crept on, as grey inside as the rainy skies outdoors.

On Sunday, January 19, 1969, Vic returned from church early in the afternoon, without his teammate. He slammed into the house, breathing heavily, fire in his eyes. His lips were set in that now familiar line, his teeth ground together in an effort to control himself. I had taken a step toward him; now I took a step back.

Stomping into the bedroom, he threw his Sunday clothes on the floor, whipped out a tee shirt and jeans. "I need to be alone!" he shouted raggedly, his eyes glinting. He slammed the door; the frame shook. "Stay out of here!"

I stood, stared at that door, expecting it to continue its sweep, expecting the frame to splinter. I had never seen him this angry.

The phone rang. Before I could turn toward the sound, that door opened with a whoosh! of air, and Vic pushed me aside to get to it. "Go into the bedroom!" he ordered, countering his first command.

The door closed once more, this time gently, softly, as I pushed against it. My heartbeat was loud. I sat gingerly on the side of the bed, ignoring the tumbled clothing and cigarette resting on the ashtray. My ears strained to pick up any clues in the monologue outside. I was never allowed to hear the telephone conversations in my house—this time I determined to eavesdrop.

I needn't have tried so hard. The telephone table crashed to the floor. "What? They can't!" The bedroom door swung open of its own accord. I watched my agent/husband jump up and down in frustrated rage, resembling a monstrous Rumplestiltskin. He punched the wall, growled and snarled. His eyes were glazed, unfocused. My breath caught in my throat as I watched.

"No!" He screamed, slamming the telephone receiver to its cradle. It slid to the floor, joining the toppled table. "No!" Jumping once more, he turned to me, his fists flailing the air. "What are you doing?" he screamed. "Get into bed!" And as I obeyed, trembling, he leaped into the room, crashed onto the bed, and fell upon me. The bed collapsed in a heap of broken slats.

His hands pulled me, tore at my clothes, pushed me in unfocused frenzy. This was the madness I sensed lurking behind the charming smile and smoothly uttered words. This was the pain I had always known would be my destiny. Still it surprised me.

And then it was over, and sanity returned as suddenly as the sun peaking from behind storm clouds. He pushed himself off me, off the broken bed, looked around, and started laughing. "I think we need to fix this," he chuckled, as he lifted the blankets to observe the damage. I stooped to help, staying away from him as I stripped the bed in silence. My body convulsed in cramps from my stomach to my ankles. Bruises popped up black against the whiteness of my skin. I tried not to look, tried not to think. Didn't want to ask the questions that lurked, unformed, in the caverns of my mind.

Upon removing the mattress, Vic saw that the damage beneath was easily repaired, and it wasn't long before we once more had a bed. He lay back down when it was made, sucking on a cigarette in contemplation. At his gesture, I joined him immediately, watching his eyes, sitting carefully on my side of the bed, my back propped against the pillows.

I had not spoken since he walked in the front door.

"Vanessa told her parents," he said. "She said that after church today, she felt that God wanted her to be open with them about our work. So she broke silence."

Listening to this turn of events, I wondered what it would mean for their plans. Would Vanessa's parents disappear, as had Tom and Yvette?

"They don't believe her, don't believe she's an agent. They think she really loves me, of course, but they think I'm 'taking her for a ride.' Their words. So they've forbidden me to see her or talk to her for one month." There was more. "They're transferring her to Wheatland College, in Chicago. She leaves on Monday."

Hope shimmered, unbidden, through my body. *Oh, God,* I thought, *maybe You don't want us to separate, either!* But almost immediately, guilt chased the hope away. *This is his job, his life. Our country's safety.* My hands tightened over the knot of my stomach, where our baby was still curled into a tight ball after the assault of the past hour. *I'm sorry,* I thought. *But someday it will all be right.*

"During the next month, I have to prove to Mr. and Mrs. Cain that I love their daughter." Vic resumed his monologue, speaking as if I weren't even there, as if he was merely thinking out loud. I thought he had forgotten my presence altogether. "That's where you come in."

Me? What do I have to do?

"You have to write the letters," he instructed, uninterrupted by my quick glance. "You can say all those things that lovers say in ways I could never dream of. But you have to code them, too. I'll tell you what needs to be said. You just say it in a way that will be convincing. They'll be read, of course, before they get to Vanessa."

Of course. All correspondence was read before it went anywhere. Just like the telephone was tapped, and I was followed, and "they" always knew what I was doing. I understood that. Accepted it.

"The Cains might call you, ask you questions. About me. We'd better be sure we've got the story straight." We rehearsed our cover, then, the story of my MIA "husband" and how my "brother" Vic had taken me in. "Now, there's one more thing," he said. "We've been saying that your husband has been missing for more than two years—has never seen his daughter, Tiffany. Your baby can't possibly be his, can it?"

"No, I guess not," I whispered. I hadn't thought—had never dreamed he wouldn't claim his son—now what? How do we explain my pregnancy? "You were raped," he said. "We never talk about it, naturally. The Cains probably won't even ask you about the baby. They're more interested in me. They don't want to embarrass you. Just tell them you can't talk about it. But tell them in a way that won't make them suspicious about us. You can do it."

"Sure, ho-Vic. I can do it. It's no problem." And so, smiling, I assured him I could lie with the best of them. I pushed back the memory of the rage and the fear, and the bewildering attack just minutes before. He was upset, his life was at stake. Our country's future hung in the balance. It was natural that he would lose it sometimes. I could take the hurt, I could take the loneliness. I was strong.

I never thought that what he had done to me moments before was exactly what we had decided would explain my pregnancy: rape. Back then, marriage automatically indicated consent. A husband should never have to force himself upon a wife, anyway. That was what we believed.

He left then, went out the door in his usual brisk fashion, screeching tires as he sped down the street. Guiltily, I went to Tiffany's door, wondering how much of the noise she had heard.

Peeking into her room, I spied her sitting on the floor in the midst of all her toys, which were scattered all over her room. She looked up at me with adult eyes, eyes that deepened into pools of secret knowledge, accusing eyes. I smiled. "How about a jammy snack?" I invited. She gravely reached out her arms and we walked into the kitchen together.

It was a long time until evening. I waited for the telephone to ring, for the lies to come out of my mouth, but the only sounds in the night were the television and Tiffany. I headed for bed around ten o'clock. It wasn't until I began to undress that I noticed the blood. It wasn't much, just smears of red-brown stains on my thighs. I sat in the bathtub, unmoving, until they soaked off my skin.

Chapter 18

February 1. Tomorrow would be Groundhog's Day. I sat in my favorite chair in the living room, watching the television newscaster speculate on Mr. Groundhog's prediction. "The weather forecast is sunny, which means six more weeks of winter," he grinned, his straightened, brightened, and otherwise cosmetically enhanced teeth flashing under his television-trained smile.

The sun may have been shining back there in Groundhog land, but in sunny California, the fog obliterated everything beyond twenty feet. Visibility was nil. Tiffany played quietly in her room, and I wondered if my baby was ever going to be born. It almost didn't matter anymore—the child we had planned that age ago would be an orphan, a fatherless casualty of CIA imperatives. Two days ago, Vic had told me that the clincher in their cover was that Vic's name could not be on our child's birth certificate. I was horrified, but Vic assured me that his "boys" would take care of things, correcting the official record when no eyes were watching. "Don't worry," he soothed, "They'll make sure I'm on there. But you have to fill out the papers according to our cover. We don't know who works at the hospital—it could be an informant for the enemy. If it's known that I have a wife and children, we could all be in danger." That was the key, of course. I just couldn't jeopardize the Mission. The "we" Victor spoke of was not necessarily his family, but his team. "No sacrifice too great" was the order of the day.

Worrying about the future did me no good, nor did wondering where he was at the moment. So I did what amounted to my best contribution these days—I waited.

The grey day melted into a charcoal night. Tiffany ate her supper and went to bed: I sat in my chair, standing every now and then to stretch and change position.

A nagging restlessness began to pervade my mind, driving me from the chair and into the rooms of the tiny house. Thoughtlessly I dusted this and put that away, finally running a bath in an effort to relax. I was bored, that was it. Even tension and worry eventually become monotonous when they are the sum and total of your life. I wanted to see the sun, to step out of my prison for just a little while.

But that was not to be. As I lay in the warm water, the ceramic bed seemed harder than before, the weight of my baby pressed me against the bottom of the tub. He was surprisingly still tonight, no kicking out my ribs or karate chops in my kidneys. Which was just fine, since I was tired of carrying his load as well as my own.

I stepped from the tub just as the first sharp pain cramped my belly, shooting up my spine in a brief knife-jab. I stopped toweling, surprised at the force of the cramp, then resumed when it seemed to die away.

A few minutes later it jabbed me again, this blade of agony, and I thought that perhaps I had better try to find Vic. He had given me one telephone number to call in an emergency—I prayed that he was at the other end.

A woman answered, an unfamiliar voice. Asking for "RJ" as I had been instructed, I held my breath as yet another cramp engulfed me, this one remaining a second longer than those before. "I think it's time," I gasped, trying to remain calm. "Can you come right away?"

"Hang on," he replied. "I'll be there as soon as I finish up here."

"Okay. Thanks." *Thanks? Thank God you were there.*

I made it to the bedroom where my suitcase lay ready, took it to the front door, and paced the floor while I waited. It was just a matter of minutes before my husband drove up and walked me to the car in a businesslike way. He must not have been very far away.

"Tiffany," I asked.

"I'll get her," he replied.

At the hospital, I was wheeled away while Vic struggled with the paperwork. A brief examination was all it took to convince Dr. Banlen that my reservation for the delivery room would be taken up immediately; in less time than it took us to get to the hospital, our new daughter was born.

Dana Catlin was a pink and black vision of newborn beauty; her glowing pink complexion was enhanced by a crown of thick black curls and long, curling black lashes. Her rosebud of a mouth could have made any Ivory baby envious, and her perfect little fingers already grasped my own with a determined power surprising in a body so small. My disappointment over her sex was brief—I had been so sure she was a boy—and my only concern was Vic's reaction.

ASK ME NO QUESTIONS

I needn't have worried. Other than a single rose awaiting me upon my introduction to my temporary room, Vic was absent from his daughter's first hours. The card read, "I love you." I held it to my heart and thanked God for his safety, as well as Cat's. Then I filled out her birth certificate with the names he had chosen for his daughter and those I had chosen for my absent "husband."

A surprise showed up on my second day in the hospital—Mom appeared beside my bed. "I'm going to take you home," she said, "and make sure you get some rest."

It was fortunate that Vanessa was gone during those brief, hectic days. The "rest" that I was going to get was interrupted by our move into a larger apartment. Vic had found it while I was still in the hospital, signed the agreement and paid the rent. It was a surprise, a larger home for the four of us.

My job—and Mom's—was to pack the boxes, while Vic put everything into the car and drove it to the new place. Mom tried, kept reminding me to take it easy, not to lift, to get some rest. But Vic was in a hurry, emptying the car before we could get the next load ready. He needed help with the furniture. Our new home was on the second story—one flight of stairs, one dozen steps—and a jumble of boxes, clothing, and kitchen utensils greeted me at the end of the day. The beds were set up in the right rooms, the new crib closest to the master bedroom across the hall. It was a standard rental, all Navajo White and tan, with carpets that would show every drop of Kool-aid, every speck of mud.

Mom's visit forced a facade of normalcy into our lives. Sleeping in the baby's room, she was there for Cat's first night-time feedings, allowing me to slumber through. At first, her presence seemed a Godsend, for the lifting and packing had taken its toll, and I began to bleed heavily as labor-intensive cramps struck with crippling force. That first evening I took up a position on the couch, breathing slowly, deep, deep breaths, willing the bleeding to stop before anyone noticed. Personal intimacies were not discussed in our family; I had had little in the way of woman-to-woman heart-to-hearts to prepare me for these embarrassing problems. The entire subject disgusted Vic. I doubt he even noticed when or if I was in the midst of my monthly flow. This river coming out of me would not be mentioned. I suffered in silence, moving only to change the soaked pads and discard them in the plastic bag I kept hidden under the bathroom sink.

We retired early that first night in our new home; Vic's solicitous aid as he helped me undress in the semi-darkness sparked the embers of hope for the future. He was not one for chivalry, believing every woman had to be strong enough to take care of herself. I was almost arrogant in my pride that I was strong enough to take care, not only of myself, but also of him and our children.

When it became obvious that his actions had a motive that had nothing to do with husbandly concern, I did not protest. I was weak with fatigue, barely able to stay awake, much less start what would surely be an argument. I didn't want Mom to hear us argue, didn't want her to think that my marriage was less than perfect, didn't want to see her knowing look the next morning. I was quiet as his body drove into mine, tearing stitches and tissue. When it was over, I slipped into the bathroom to clean myself and examine the extent of the damage. Then I got back into bed, careful not to disturb my sleeping husband.

The week after Catlin's birth was a reprieve, a paradoxical semblance of normalcy that nearly drove me out of my mind. Constantly on guard in case I should slip, I nevertheless managed to keep my wits close enough without falling over the edge. Inside, I could call Vic "honey," and give him a smooch without being scolded, although he would glare at me, his back to Mom so she wouldn't see. He would kiss me back, tease me affectionately, hold Tiffany briefly when Cat demanded my attention. I thanked God that Tiff had been so stubborn about the "Uncle Vic" issue; she seemed happy, now, to snuggle against her Daddy whenever her baby sister cried. When Vic was at work, Mom and I did what women do in normal homes: went shopping, washed laundry, cared for the children, talked. Tried to re-establish a relationship which had been torn apart by my insistence in going my own way.

It was hard to know what "normal" was, after three years as a spy wife. But I did my best to inject some warmth and humor into our daily routine. By the time Mom returned to her own home, I just about had the hang of it. When I kissed her goodbye on the seventh day, my heart protested her leaving. The shadow of the future wrapped its tentacles about me, pulling me back into reality.

Catlin was a colicky baby, crying at all times of the day or night, but she was so beautiful I didn't mind. I could never get the hang of calling her "Dana K," as Vic wanted, she was just my little Cat. Vic had already objected to the way I had spelled her name on the birth certificate, insisting that "Catlin" should have started with a "K," followed by "a-i"—"Kaitlin." He said it was part of the Brian family history, and I had ruined the tradition by changing it. But it was on her birth certificate, right next to "father's name: Frank Michael Brian," and there was no fixing that. I asked Vic if his team had made the switch in the records department; he told me it was all taken care of.

Cat showed a remarkable strength at the early age of three days by raising up off her stomach, her tiny arms and shoulders pushing, head held high and steady.

I knew then that she was a very special baby. I promised her I would always be there for her.

Tiffany was not pleased at the attention her new sister received, and immediately displayed her jealousy. She began to throw temper tantrums whenever Cat was in my arms, howling like a wounded calf for all the world to hear. It was utterly amazing that a twenty-five pound bit of fluff could produce that much noise, but she did.

Except when Vic was home. As soon as Mom left, Vic's affectionate display ended, and Tiffany was told to "sit down and behave" whenever she ran to her father. So she contained her anger within the walls of her room, tearing up toys and clothes and furniture in enraged silence.

And then it was mandatory that I find a job, for my time as Vic's protected sister was running out.

Chapter 19

Vanessa,
"I love you. How many times have I pronounced that since we first met? Still more, how much have I thought it, lived and breathed it? You may never know how great this thing is within me...God sent me a woman, one woman for eternity, and I had to choose between my life and my love. Both are monumental in their importance to me, I could do without neither. Yet when I travailed against this love you personify, I could not struggle resolutely. It was too great a price to pay for my life; the price of my soul..."

I wrote as Vic dictated, letters from a love-smitten young man to his sweetheart; letters that were at times overly florid with four-syllable adjectives but which contained secret messages within those syllables. As I wrote, I knew the message was really for me. I was the woman, his love. I was the heart of his choice. It was as if he talked to me through those coded messages, assured me of his love, confided in me of his struggle.

"Eventually, my love, all those in the organization who are married must give up their wives and families...they all have to select either their lives or their loves, and I can see the result. You cannot comprehend what they have to experience, those wives..."

I can. I know what we experience, what we sacrifice. I live with this pain every moment of my existence. As I wrote of his "love" for Vanessa, I vowed I would not be the cause of his sacrifice. I would be strong, for him. I swallowed the bitter pill of his professed "love" for this woman, this pretend-love, and imagined that he spoke those words aloud to me.

"I am hopelessly, irrevocably lost to this love. I desire only a life with you, built on a foundation of trust, respect, and understanding."

Trust. That's what our love is based on. We trust each other with our lives, and with our secrets.

ASK ME NO QUESTIONS

Everyone in my world now knew me as Victor Charles Brian's sister, the wife/widow who had lost her husband in Viet Nam. From our landlady to Vic's employers, everyone saw and heard what they were supposed to, the world the Company had engineered. I played my part well, displaying just the right amount of melancholy at just the right times. No one dared ask me about my husband, or the circumstances of Catlin's conception. *It doesn't matter what they think; all that matters is the mission.*

It was with this conviction that I resolutely enclosed my loneliness within my heart and carried on the next step in the plan: a job.

I began the hunt with fantasies of rising above the world of fast food and french fries. Despite the offer at Sandy's, which the new managers had reiterated, I could not bring myself to work in the same proximity as Vic, and possibly Vanessa. I couldn't imagine being forced to watch them every day and pretend he was my brother.

The days became weeks; February brightened into March, and no word came from the various agencies through which I sought employment. I had taken typing tests, filled out a dozen applications, talked to numerous personnel "counselors." No one wanted to hire an unskilled, uneducated, inexperienced new mother. As March warmed toward April, the optimism with which I began cooled into frustration, became anxiety, until finally I was fighting the edges of panic. Vanessa would be home soon, and with her return would come the end of my marriage.

One day as I struggled with a heavy sack of groceries, balancing Cat on one arm, the bag on the other, a voice hailed me.

"Hi!"

Glancing up, I searched the area for a body behind the voice. The apartment complex formed the shape of an elongated "U," the base comprised of four apartments on each of two stories, with one unit on either end. As I was already nearing the stairway that led to our upstairs end unit, my searching took in only that part of the building. I spied an open door, first floor, second apartment, just parallel to the stairway. In the doorway stood a woman, a dark-haired, somewhat heavyset woman with deep brown eyes and a square jaw. She carried her weight well on a tall—five-foot-ten-inches or so—frame designed for strength rather than fat. She had a wide mouth and perfect teeth, and she smiled at me in neighborly invitation.

"Care for a cup of coffee?"

I looked up toward my home, hesitated. Should I? Vic was at the restaurant. It was just a cup of coffee—nothing to get excited about. What could it hurt?

Besides, my "bodyguards" would surely know where I had gone. I glanced around, searching for an inconspicuous gardener, an innocent-looking maintenance man. No one lurked about. They were really good, these guys. Why not?

"Sure," I replied, hefting Cat and the groceries, "just let me put these down." I knew they had to be out there somewhere.

But once I was within the safety of my apartment, I began to have second thoughts. *What if they're not close enough to see where I've gone? By the time Vic gets home, the girls and I could be long gone. I don't know this person—she could be a plant, someone placed here to watch my every move.* Cat was nodding sleepily, Tiffany playing quietly with her crayons. *Maybe I'd better not. Maybe—*

"I thought I'd bring you a cup—you look kind of all in."

She was there, standing at my door, which I'd foolishly left open. A cup in each hand left a trail of steam in the cool air; the aroma of freshly brewed coffee drifted toward me.

"Come on in," I stammered. Glancing outside, I shut the door. *I hope Vic's men are out there.* "Would you like some peanut butter fudge?"

"No, but thanks," she laughed. "I'm still trying to get rid of my Christmas overkill." Handing me a mug, she said, "I didn't put anything in it. I'm Carol Nokes, welcome to our humble homes." Her smile was contagious, and as I cautiously accepted her extended hand, some of my reservations faded. Surely everyone in the world wasn't on the other side? Her remark about not putting anything in the coffee felt particularly ironic, considering my thoughts just before she came over, and I wished I could have shared them with her.

As I stirred in a teaspoon of sugar and a dash of milk, I realized that she was the first person, outside of family, I had actually talked to, conversationally, in over three years.

After the introductions, in which I briefly stated my relationship with Vic and my uncertain marital status, Carol told me all about life in these apartments, giving me a rundown of all the tenants and their foibles. She was a nurse at Charity hospital, she said, so everyone came to her for their aches and pains. It was kind of fun, since she knew everyone "inside and out," literally. I laughed, my mouth stretching in unaccustomed levity.

An hour passed, an hour of such strange lightheartedness that I was almost relieved when Carol said she had to get home. "Tony will be ransacking the refrigerator if I don't start supper," she said, "and *that* I don't want to deal with. Between him and the boys"—she had two, ages five and eight—"they could clean me out. And I've already spent my allowance for the month."

We stood, and as I handed her back her mug, she said, "By the way, they're starting a nurse's aide class next week at the hospital. There's room for more, if you're interested."

She filled me in on the details: a six-week class, with "lab time" in the hospital, all of it paid. Certification at the end, and guaranteed employment. Excitement bubbled up within me—I had a feeling, a conviction, this was what I had been looking for. God was speaking to me, telling me He hadn't deserted me.

I didn't mention Carol's visit to Vic—I figured his men would tell him anyway. The years of asking no questions had trained me to silence; silence about my thoughts, my feelings, my ideas. Vic always knew what I did. He had more important things to worry about than my bit of news. He couldn't be distracted by my worries, my fears, or my dreams.

And maybe, just maybe, I didn't want him to know that I'd accomplished my assignment. He would leave me as soon as I had a job.

Carol arranged to get the application for me, and all I had to do was wait in suspense while the papers were processed. Somehow, I was accepted. Vic took the news calmly, showing less enthusiasm than I had anticipated. *But it's bittersweet for him, too,* I thought. *Now he has no excuse to stay with me.*

The rest of the week I was occupied as I arranged for a babysitter and shopped for the appropriate uniform. Being busy helped me to cope with Vic's eminent departure: although I struggled to face a life without him, the reality stared at me like a yawning hole, a black void in which I could see no hope, no life. I hid the despair from him, told myself to be strong. At least I had a job. And a friend.

Then Vanessa came home.

Chapter 20

It's just for spring break, I thought. *Just a week in which to reunite with Vic and plead their cause further with her parents. Then she'll go back to Chicago to finish the term.* So I thought.

Vanessa's return pumped new energy into Vic's activities. For more than two months, he had been morose, moody, short-tempered. Despite the resumption of their relationship, it was long-distance; it wasn't the same as working together, in proximity of each other. Vanessa was working on her parents, Vic said, but they were reluctant to allow her to return home again. At least, not before the school term ended for the summer. Vanessa had promised them she would continue her education, regardless of her love for Vic or her "real" work. He didn't tell me much; I knew the questions that popped up inside my head would always be unanswered. I told myself to be happy she was gone, be glad I had my husband all to myself.

And I was happy during her absence, for despite the strain, despite his reluctance to talk about their work, Vic was once again talking to me about our lives after the mission, using my writing skills to communicate to his partner, and was generally more aware of my existence. With her return, that tenuous camaraderie disappeared.

As if we were following a script written by the fickle gods of chance, Vanessa's spring break coincided with Easter, and Easter that year fell on my birthday. My twenty-first birthday. By now, I had been attending church regularly, even singing in the choir. On this particular day, we were to sing a cantata as well as hold the regular Sunday service.

And in another church in another neighborhood, my husband was to be the "layman preacher," the guest speaker representing the youth group. In Vanessa's church, Victor was known as a deeply religious young man.

ASK ME NO QUESTIONS

How ironic life is, I thought, as I watched him button his white shirt and knot the navy blue tie. *You haven't been to church with me since our wedding, and here you are preaching a sermon at Vanessa's church, in the service of the CIA. I'm sure you'll be wonderful.*

I watched him go, tried not to imagine him with his other family, and left soon for my own church. I thought, briefly, about another birthday, in another town. The birthday he had stood me up, the day Ruth had gotten tortured. Was it only four years ago? *Please keep him safe*, I prayed, my eyes on the stained-glass scenery inside the hallowed walls.

When I returned from the service, I changed clothes, put the girls down for a nap, and baked a cake, carefully frosting it with white topping. Then I wrote "Happy Birthday" with blue icing, adding a big "21" in the center. "Happy birthday, Stephani," I said aloud. "Do you think he'll remember?"

I knew it was foolish, I knew I was selfish, but I wanted him to think of me. I wanted a real birthday, with a present, and maybe dinner out, and a legal glass of wine. If we'd lived near Reno still, we would have gone to the casinos, I could have walked in with my driver's license at the ready...

Suddenly the silence of the house rose up to swallow me, and within the silence I heard the voices of my past. *Do you, Stephani, take Vic as your lawfully wedded husband, to cherish and obey, for better or worse, for richer or poorer, in sickness and health, as long as you both shall live?...To cherish and obey, as long as you both shall live?...To obey as long as you live? As long as you live?* "Yes! Yes, I do! As long as I live!"

The voices stopped. The house was dead calm, as if all the voices within its walls were stilled. Rising from the chair, I went to Cat's room, scooped her up, then woke Tiffany, dragging her along behind me. With the toddler in tow, and my baby in my arms, I stumbled to the parking lot, where I'd parked our old Chevy truck, and, shoving the children inside, I slammed the door and started the engine.

"Where are we going, Mommy?" Tiffany rubbed her eyes, still sleepy from the swift awakening. "Is Daddy coming with us?"

"No, honey," I said, my voice trembling with the effort to sound calm. "Daddy's not coming with us. We're just going for a drive."

Barely able to see the road through the tears, I wound in and out of traffic, aimlessly driving, the words still resounding inside my skull. *As long as you live. As long as you live.*

So much pain was building up inside me that it was hard to concentrate on driving, hard to hear Tiff as she prattled on. I found that I was on the freeway, headed for the coast, and I pressed my foot down hard on the accelerator.

Forty minutes later, we were high above the ocean, following the highway as it wound about the cliffs overlooking the grey-green sea.

"Where are we going, Mommy? Are we going to see Grandma?"

"No, honey. We're just going…for a ride."

As long as you live.

But I don't want to live like this! The inner voice screamed, my head was a battlefield for conflicting forces, it wasn't possible that Tiffany couldn't hear the war going on. *I don't want to live like this!* There was a turn up ahead, a sharp turn with a wide pullout just above the sea.

I shot across the road, forgetting to look for oncoming traffic. But no one was coming. No one would be there to stop me.

Pulling to the edge of the road, I turned off the ignition and watched the waves smashing against the rocks far below. The flimsy guardrail served merely as a warning, a reminder of what was beyond. Clutching the steering wheel in both hands, I watched the waves, mesmerized by their power. I didn't want to live like this anymore. I wanted a normal life, a husband at home, children who could know their father. Was that too much to ask?

"Help me. Please, Father, help me! I can't take it anymore." Turning the key, I started the truck, letting it idle while the power grew. I stared at the ocean, the grey waves, the whitecaps, barely seeing them, seeing only the infinity inside their depths.

I can't do it anymore, God! I can't! I felt the pedal beneath my foot, felt the old truck tremble as the power grew. I felt it begin to move. The waves rolled toward me, their rhythm inviting, their pull irresistible.

And then a car pulled up beside me, a car full of children in their Sunday dress. The man waved at me, smiling, while he cautioned his kids to stay back from the railing, and he put his arms over their shoulders while he pointed at the horizon. The woman joined him, careful of her stockings as she knelt to lift a little boy. Together they watched. "Look, Mommy," Tiffany pointed, too. "There's water coming up out of the ocean! What is it?" And focusing my teary eyes, I squinted into the sun and saw a large shadow on the water just as a spurt of water shot into the air. A moment later, the grey whale rose from the sea in a graceful arc, disappearing with a flap of his huge tail.

"Look, Mommy! Did you see it? What was that big fish, Mommy? Can we see it again? How can it stay afloat in the water? Was it magic?"

"Yes, Tiff, it's magic," I murmured, caught up in the beauty and excitement of the whale's emergence. I listened to Tiffany, heard the wonder in her voice, the awe over something so natural, and I knew I had to go on. There was still much to enjoy, much to treasure.

And I had made a promise I could not break.

Turning the truck around, I drove back to the apartment, back to the life I had chosen.

The cake was still on the table, the house still silent. Yet I knew Vic was there, for I had seen his car in the parking lot. When he didn't appear immediately, I began to walk down the hallway toward our bedroom. Perhaps he was asleep. With his schizophrenic schedule, he often took a nap when he was home.

Then I saw Vanessa's purse, and her white gloves, and her jacket. They were at the end of the couch, neatly set, with the gloves lying over the purse, which in turn rested against the arm, its handle turned down as if it was going to stay awhile. The jacket was folded over the back of the couch, touching the other objects as if they were a unit, inseparable. I stopped, letting the implications of their presence sink in. Then I walked into the kitchen and put on a pot of coffee. Doubtless, they would want some refreshment after their reconnaissance. Reconnaissance? I would not think about the implications. Vic had told me the need for privacy, the absolute necessity for being completely sequestered. Besides, she was supposed to be his fiancée.

The afternoon shadows lengthened. I watched the news on television, gave Tiff her dinner, and was just beginning to feed Cat when Victor emerged from the bedroom, his eyes red-rimmed with sleep.

"Where were you?" he demanded. "I was worried sick about you."

I replied calmly, "I just took the girls for a ride. We saw a grey whale."

He raised his index finger toward my nose. "Don't ever go anywhere without telling me. You know that. Don't ever do that again."

"I won't. I'm sorry that I worried you."

Vanessa appeared, her eyes questioning. Vic smiled, ignored the silent question, grasped her arm, and escorted her out the door. I stared at the sorry birthday cake sitting alone in the center of the kitchen table and took a deep breath. Then I pulled it toward me, toward my two-month-old baby, and watched as she demolished it with her flailing fingers.

Returning to work the next day, I was soon caught up in the hospital routine. I forgot my self-pity of the day before and concentrated on my studies. *What's the big deal, anyway?* I thought. *Everybody turns 21 sometime. Such a to-do over trivialities!*

Vic's work was about important things. He didn't have time for a stupid birthday.

Anyway, with only three more weeks of class, I was excited about the next step, when I would be a Certified Nurse's Aide, making the princely sum of $350 a month. Enough to support my daughters and me while Victor was gone. He hadn't mentioned a date yet, but I knew it had to be soon. The Company had already given him an extended deadline because of me. I didn't think they would be understanding for too much longer.

The day of graduation arrived. There wouldn't be a formal ceremony, just the presentation of certificates and refreshments afterwards. Following that, we would each be given our floor assignments and first week's work schedule. We would be on duty six days a week, followed by two days off, so that we would have a weekend off every six weeks. I would be working the swing shift, 3:30 to 11:00 p.m.

I looked smart in my crisp white uniform, I thought, admiring myself in the mirror. I had lost what little weight Cat had added to my frame. The years of eating sparingly, one meal a day, kept my weight at a slender 110 pounds. I was proud of that fact, proud that I gained next to nothing during my pregnancies, proud that I could control something in my life.

I twisted my long hair into a French knot, adding years and severity to my face. I touched my eyelashes with mascara, hoping Vic wouldn't notice this new vanity. Vic hated makeup.

My shoes were sparkling white, the unfamiliar nylon stockings swishing as I walked. It was a big day.

At Charity, the atmosphere was decidedly cheery. The graduating students struggled to keep their pride in hand, their faces radiant, their hands twisting nervously in their laps. Sitting on metal folding chairs while we listened to the administrator's formal speech, we all tried hard to keep our breathing at a normal level. Several students tapped their feet in their eagerness to go on. Some had brought family members to share the celebration.

Finally it was over. Since I could not participate in the celebration afterwards—even though I was sure no one here could be an enemy—I hurried home, where I faced a different kind of surprise.

Chapter 21

I opened the door to the apartment and stepped into a different world. This was home, this was familiar; yet it was an alien life. For a while, at the hospital, I could be me, Stephani Jean Brian. A new me, someone who was liked and respected for my intelligence and ability. A professional. No one ever asked me personal questions, no one wanted to know about my real life. It was, "How are you, Stephani?" and "How ya doin', Steph?" Surface stuff. Once I stepped through this door, though, I was no longer just an ordinary person. I was the wife of a CIA agent. Here I must cloak what I say, how I feel, the very expression on my face. Here I must guard my words, move with caution, follow Vic's lead.

And never more so than today.

"Hi, Steph," greeted Vic, Cat in one arm and Tiffany hanging on the other. "How was class?"

"Hi," I replied, my tone light but not intimate, pleasant but not too cozy. *Wait, my mind cautioned. Something's up.* Hiding my expression behind the act of putting my jacket in the closet, I said cautiously, "Class was great. I graduated today." Carefully neutral. No traces of accusation, no "where were you?" in my voice, no hurt feelings. I would never be called a bitchy wife.

"Graduated? Why didn't you tell me? We would have come and watched. Here," he said, handing the baby over to me, "I think she's wet."

Cradling Catlin, I gave her a kiss, hid my confusion. *We? Who're we?* Then Vic said, "Remember my brother Sean? He came to see Vanessa and me off—he's consented to be my best man."

I glanced up then, a smile ready to burst into panic on my face. My heart was running as fast as it could, *getaway, getaway, getaway* in double time. "Sean? Of course I remember. How nice of you to come." *Best man?* He was sitting on the sofa, hidden until Vic moved aside. He looked the same as he had when I met him several years ago, tall, husky, with football shoulders and a farmer's open face. He and I were the same age, and although we'd never had more than an introduction, I had felt safe with him. He looked slightly uncomfortable now.

"Well, Sean and I are going to go to the restaurant," Vic said. "You've had a big day. We'll eat there."

"Oh. Okay." *Wait! Why's Sean here? Whose best man is he?*

And they left, the sunlight streaming in the door for just a sliver in time as it opened and closed once again.

My panic continued. Automatically I changed Cat's diapers, fixed Tiffany her dinner, washed up, picked up, wiped up, my hands moving fast in an effort to stay ahead of my mind. *Keep calm,* I told my head. *He'll tell you what you need to know when you need to know it. You knew it was coming. You're prepared. Be strong. Help him.* By ten o'clock I had cleaned the apartment as much as humanly possible, and my internal clock was beginning to wind down. Yet I couldn't relax. I didn't know what my part was. I hadn't been shown the script.

At 10:05 the telephone rang: four rings, silence, one more ring. I picked it up, trembling.

"I'll explain later," he said without preamble. "Sleep in the baby's room tonight. Sean will sleep on the couch."

I prepared our guest's bed, then retired to my own "guest" bed. "He'll fill you in when he can. Just take your cue from him," I said to no one in particular, "You can do it. You're an actress." I heard them come in, listened to them talk in that brotherly way, knew when my husband went to bed and when he turned over in his sleep. I heard Sean get up in the night and use the bathroom and Vic's alarm ring at 4:30 a.m. Cat awoke at 6:00 and Tiffany at 7:30. I left for work at 2:30, my first day on the job. When I returned home at 11:30 p.m., the house was quiet. I paid Nancy, the sitter, and retired to the bed next to Cat. I was asleep almost immediately.

With the morning came all the usual chores. I noticed the couch was unoccupied, so we three female members of the family ate our breakfasts and prepared for the day ahead. I wondered briefly where my brother-in-law was, but didn't care to spend a lot of time worrying about it. Vic would tell me when it was time. *This is just another lesson in the school of life,* I told myself. *"This, too, will pass." Look to the future.* And I did. I thought about the time when we would be a real family, after Vic's work was over. The fantasies helped to dim reality's pain.

I realize now that I was holding the questions at bay, refusing to think about the incongruities in my life just in case I would have to face something I couldn't comprehend. Perhaps I knew instinctively there would be no answers to those questions. I heard Vic turn on the shower, and made sure there was fresh coffee in the pot.

Five minutes later, the bathroom door opened, steam rolling out into the hallway. I loved the feeling of a steamy bathroom, the heat dissipating into the air, the smell of soap and shaving lather. Following its trail down the hallway, I went into the master bedroom, the fresh cup of coffee warming my hands.

"Good morning," I chirped, a sunny smile pasted on my lips. "I didn't hear you come in last night. You must have worked late."

"Yeah, we were really busy. Did a nine-hundred-dollar night."

"Great! How's Sean doing? He looks the same as I remember."

"He's fine. He's going to stand up with Vanessa and me. We're going to Tahoe in a couple of days."

"Oh." I blanched, felt the blood leave my head. *Careful, careful,* I told myself. *Let him tell you.* " Vanessa's parents came around, then, did they?"

"Oh, yeah. They don't know we're getting married now, though. She's not coming home from Wheatland for good until June. Hey, it won't be a real marriage. Won't even be legal. But we'll be working together for a long time. It'll be better if we're together. Then no one will suspect. You know that."

"Yes, I know. It's just hard—I'll miss you." Biting my lip, I could have chewed off my tongue. *No sentiment! Be strong!* "Besides," I added with as much lightness as I could muster, "I'm sure Vanessa isn't going to get you fresh coffee every morning."

The lightness was lost on him. Gulping the hot brew, he sat on the bed to pull on socks and shoes. "That's probably true," he said seriously. "She's more concerned with getting the job done. She can be a real witch at times, too."

Then, changing the subject, he filled me in on the plan. "I told Sean we're already divorced. He met the Cains, which helped convince them we're on the level. He thought it was kind of strange we're still living together," he stopped his grooming long enough to flash me a conspiratorial grin, "but I told him we're still friends, and you needed to get on your feet."

"I'm sure he loved that explanation," I said as lightly as I could. "He's always disliked me, anyway. Thought I trapped you into marriage, didn't he?"

"Yeah, I guess he did." He kissed me, then, a real kiss with passion and love and understanding behind it. I responded hesitantly, giving back a measured acceptance of his offering. Vic didn't like aggressive women. He was the hunter, he'd often said. So I controlled my responses to his lovemaking just as I controlled them in our life, taking my cues from his actions.

"Vic, the door. Tiffany's up."

The door was promptly closed.

When he left thirty minutes later, my fears were gone. He loved me. I just had to get through the next few years without him. What were a few years in a lifetime?

Vanessa arrived on schedule, and the two took off in Vic's shiny Chevy, just washed and waxed for the occasion. Sean would meet them in Reno. They were eloping, the Cains none the wiser. Apparently Vanessa's parents' consent to allow the couple to see each other was conditioned: they could become engaged, but could not marry for a year. They were only following Company orders by "eloping" now. Sometimes even the CIA had problems in messing with other peoples' lives.

Vic had explained it all to me, of course. The marriage would be a farce, performed by another agent. It wouldn't even be on the records. Sean, as best man, would be the witness for the world, to validate and corroborate should there be any questions. Vanessa wouldn't tell her parents until it became necessary for them to live together. In the meantime, Vic would still be around for me and the children. At least for a little while.

But I would have to be doubly careful about Tiffany. She could be a problem, with her stubbornness and her child's insistence on voicing the truth. Sometimes I thought she said things just to provoke trouble. She seemed to delight in causing scenes, her angel blue eyes belying the precocious little mind under that cap of blond hair. I protected her as much as I could, but she had to sense the awkwardness that ruled our lives.

The newlyweds returned two days later, Vanessa flashing her bright ring at me for a minute before they disappeared again. She played her part well, holding on to Vic's arm with just a touch of familiarity, throwing loving glances his way while she gave me a quick rundown on the weather and the drive. I knew she kept it brief out of consideration for my own plight: I played the role of welcoming sister-still-mourning-MIA wife to the hilt. It helped, that role. It protected me from the truth. It gave me permission to feel the pain while at the same time allowing me a secret triumph in knowing that it wasn't true. My husband was alive. My husband was not hers.

"And look what Vic gave me for my birthday," she exclaimed. I looked at Vic, a silent question. She extended her arm. Wrapped around her slender wrist was a thin gold bracelet, a lover's knot tying the two ends together. It looked very fragile. "We celebrated my twenty-first birthday on our wedding day. Vic was so sweet. He even had champagne waiting in our room." I fought to stay focused on her words. *You remembered her birthday!* my brain screamed.

ASK ME NO QUESTIONS

"Come on, Vanessa, we've got to get going," my husband urged. "You've got a plane to catch." And with a last glance over his shoulder, he propelled her out the door.

I stood, staring at the closed door, seeing not her shiny wedding ring, but the gleaming gold bracelet encircling her wrist. A birthday gift.

The children's voices brought me back, forced me to think about their immediate needs. But the bracelet remained a solid reminder of his priorities.

I had just another month to get through, another four weeks to survive before Vanessa returned for good. In my new environment at the hospital, I began to expand my horizons, learning procedures and techniques that made me feel needed and useful. Only once was my story questioned, and that once came from Mrs. Cain, as she did, indeed, call and question Catlin's paternity.

The telephone rang while I was at Charity; the head nurse summoned me to the phone, giving me a stern reprimand for receiving a personal call. When I heard the strange voice—very blue-blood, mind you—I began to tremble, praying that I responded as I should.

"What is your relationship to Victor?"

"He's my brother."

"Where's your husband?"

"Missing in action."

"How long has he been away?"

"Three years."

"How is it that you have an infant daughter, when your husband is gone?"

"I was raped."

Simple. Three words. Shaking humiliation in the execution of them. A sigh of relief when they were out.

"Thank you. I'm sorry, dear. I had to ask."

"It's all right. I understand."

I returned to my station, gulping in huge breaths of air.

Chapter 22

Vic's "wife" came home from exile, and I saw very little of him. Despite his frequent absence, I began to half believe that he would never leave us, after all. The summer was marching on, and still he hadn't been told a specific date, a deadline. "We have to play it one day at a time," he'd said once, when Vanessa had just returned from Chicago. "We're in a crucial stage of the operation. Just sit tight. And be prepared."

I did that—"sat tight"—awakening every day with the thought that this could be the day. I would go through the motions of living—feed the girls, clean the house, shop, wash, work, etc.—and, somewhere in the middle of the day, the simple routine lulled my fears into little more than a nagging thought in the back of my mind; something like the string tied around your finger, put there as a reminder of something important, but you're able to think about other things because of the string. Eventually, the intensity of the fear lessened, became habit, and I was able to ignore the increasing distance between Vic and his family.

I was on an island, the black waters eating at the bit of solid ground beneath my feet, until, one day, there would be nothing left on which to stand. That day was approaching faster than I knew.

I didn't understand the delay. I just accepted the reprieve. We moved again, this time to a brand new duplex just outside of town. It was more private, allowing Vic more freedom to come and go without suspicious glances from neighbors. Besides, the other unit wasn't occupied yet. A two-bedroom, it proved rather awkward during the times I had to spend in the children's bedroom, but I squeezed the twin beds in beside Cat's crib and made do.

Life was quiet. Working the p.m. shift at Charity allowed me all day with Tiffany and Cat. I took them on trips to the coast, spent hours at the beach, found a quiet spot near the river, where we paddled and played, away from the worry of everyday life. It was, if not "good," as near to it as I thought possible. I was grateful.

ASK ME NO QUESTIONS

Then one day in late July, this surreal serenity vanished, and the fates tugged at the invisible string on my finger.

Vanessa and I were sitting outside on the sparse lawn in front of my home, watching Tiffany pull Cat in her wagon, when Vanessa suddenly blurted, "I was wondering, Steph, if you'd be one of my bridesmaids? I'd really like you to be part of the wedding."

Keeping my eyes glued to my children, I swallowed, taking a deep breath before I answered. "I don't know, Vanessa. I don't know if I can handle weddings yet." *How could he? I can't do this!*

"It's been nearly four years, Stephani. Don't you think it's time you started living again?" Her voice was soft, gentle, concerned. She wanted to be my friend.

"As far as I'm concerned, the war will never be over, not until my husband comes home. I just can't let him go." *I'll never let him go!*

"It would make Vic so happy to have you stand up with us. Think about him, won't you? He worries about you."

"I—I don't know. I'll think about it." *I don't have to think about it! I won't do this!*

"Thanks, Steph. I really appreciate it."

There was silence then, a silence laden with lies and deception. We were both playing the game, each believing the other was someone we were not. Only I thought I knew the whole truth. I thought she played the game too well. *I don't need your pity!*

"Vanessa? When's the wedding?"

"Vic hasn't told you?" *Incredible*, her expression read.

"I really haven't seen much of him lately. I work at night, you know. He's not here during the day." *He's with you. He's always with you.*

"Oh, gosh, I'm sorry! We set the date for early September. September 12. My parents want us to have a church wedding, even though we're already married. They didn't think much of our May elopement."

"You told them?"

"I had to, Steph. I've always been honest with them. It was really hard to lie. But once I told them Vic and I were already married, they immediately began to make plans for a big wedding. That's why Vic and I aren't living together yet. I promised I'd wait until we were sanctioned in the church."

"Oh. Vic didn't tell me." *September 12. The end of my life.*

The silence was uncomfortable now, heavy with good-byes. *You're really going to do it, Vic. You're really leaving me.*

Vanessa got up then, brushing the grass from her shorts as she stood. "I have to go, Stephani. Please think about the wedding. I know how close you and Vic are."

"Sure," I choked. "I'll think about it."

"I can't do this, Vic, I just can't do it! Please don't ask me to be in your wedding!"

He was pacing the floor, covering the length of the living room with long, impatient strides, his fingers ruffling the hair at the back of his head as he walked. Two weeks had passed since Vanessa's painful request, two weeks in which I had thought about little else. Every time I thought about the two of them, the crowds of well-wishers, the minister blessing their "union," tears would begin their silent journey, brimming over my eyes despite my attempts to be strong. This was against everything I believed in. This was real.

"Vic," I asked tentatively, "How can this be happening? How can you have a real wedding? In front of all those people?"

"It won't be real! Don't worry, it's all arranged." But he didn't stop pacing.

"Vic, her family is going to be there! I can't lie in front of all those people. I couldn't make it through the ceremony!"

He stopped his silent marching, came to me and wrapped his arms around my shoulders, pulling me to him. "You won't have to, Steph. It'll be all right. You don't even have to come."

Relief poured through me. Leaning within that rare embrace, I silently thanked God for watching over me. Vic kissed me, a passionless kiss of promise. "Don't worry," he repeated. "Don't worry about anything. I won't let anything hurt you. I'll always be here for you."

He left shortly after that, slightly distracted, silent. But it was not an ominous silence, as I was by now so accustomed to. Instead, it held a hint of understanding, a spark of regret.

Now my time with him was even more precious than before. I had dinner with him once, just after midnight, at Sandy's, a daring and dangerous thing to do. I sat at the counter, watched him work between gulps of coffee and long drags on his cigarette. He sat beside me for minutes at a time, talking low, his voice for my ears alone. I memorized his every movement, every nuance.

At home, he seemed more careful about how he spoke to me, forcing himself to slow down, to see how his words affected me. Unlike the years just gone by, instead of the familiar reminders of "Plan B," he spoke of the years ahead, when we'd be back together. "I won't be far away," he'd say. "I'll take care of you."

ASK ME NO QUESTIONS

It was in that kinder, warmer atmosphere that our world disintegrated, and all the careful planning, all the secrets, shattered.

The night was dark, for the sun had hours before it would begin its ascent into the coastal sky. Vic and I were asleep, together on the double bed that so seldom held the two of us anymore. I didn't awaken at the sound: it came from the edges of the mists, a distant thud that was out of context with my dreamless sleep.

Suddenly Vic threw off the blankets, hurling himself out of bed as the pounding grew louder. "Get up, Steph!" he growled, his voice low but penetrating. "Somebody's here! Get into the other room!"

I obeyed automatically, whisking into the girls' room in the still-dark house. There, I crouched behind the door, my ear pressed to the wood.

"Where is she? We've come to get her out of here."

"Dad!" Vic cried. "What are you doing here?"

"We're going to take Stephanie home with us," my father yelled. "She's lived in this devil's den long enough!"

"Stephanie, it's your father," Vic called. "Come out here!"

Oh, God, I thought. *How did they get involved in this?* Upon reaching the living room, I faced both my parents as they stood over Vic, Dad taller by four inches and fit as only an outdoorsman could be. Mom hung back a little, bristling in her outrage. "What's going on?" I cried, rubbing my eyes and gathering my thoughts. "What are you doing here in the middle of the night?"

"We know all about this scam you're in," Dad said, his voice as authoritative as if I still was his little girl. "We're going to take you and the girls out of here."

"And if you won't come, we're taking the kids anyway," Mom spoke up. Her eyes glistened with unshed tears.

"Why? What are you talking about?" Shakily I wrapped the ends of my robe about me. *Think, Stephanie, think. What do they know?* Vic was just standing in the middle of the room, his face as white as the quarter moon in the black sky. "Why don't we sit down and talk about this?"

"Why don't you go down to the restaurant, have a cup of coffee, and give us a chance to get dressed," Vic said in his most cajoling tone. "You look all done in after your drive here. Have some breakfast...on me. We'll answer all your questions. Just give us a chance to wake up."

They hesitated, their anger dying as they took in our dishabille. Dad glanced at Mom; she looked at me and said, "You'd better be here when we get back."

"I'll be here, Mom," I replied, "I'm really happy to see you."

They were ushered out the door with assurances of our presence two hours hence. Once gone, Vic began to pace, his hands at his head.

"What the fuck is going on," he muttered. "What do they know? We've got to figure this out." He stopped pacing, headed for the bedroom, pulled on clothes and shoes. Clutching his car keys, he admonished me, "We may have to leave. You'd better get my suitcase packed. We'll only be able to take the car." Then he walked out the door. "I'll be back," he said, his voice muffled as he threw the words over his shoulder. "Just be ready."

As I dressed, I thought of the operation, the mission. Was it jeopardized now? What did my parents think they knew? I started a pot of coffee, gathered up Vic's clothes, stuffed them into our biggest travel bag. Then I began to put Cat's necessities together, and some things for Tiffany. As morning dawned and the summer sun illuminated the little house, I could think only of Vic. *Where is he?*

Six-thirty arrived. Mom and Dad would be here in another thirty minutes. What was I going to say to them? *The truth, of course. At least as much of it as possible.* Where was Vic? A car turned into the drive. *Good. Now we can plan together.*

He came in, breathing as if he had been chased by the demons of hell. Perhaps he had. Grasping my shoulders, he explained what we must do.

"Look," he said. "You've got to appeal to your father. You've always been his little doll, now use that to convince him that whatever he thinks is wrong. We can't let them destroy what has taken so long to build! A year, Steph! An entire year's work down the drain! You will have to convince him. We have to salvage the mission."

"I can do it, Vic," I told him, calm now that I knew my role. "Just tell me what I'm supposed to say."

"Tell him that you can't divulge the details, and he'll have to promise to keep it secret, but that my marriage to Vanessa is not real, that I work for the government. Tell them you'll reveal the whole story some day, but that now they'll just have to trust you. Tell him you love him."

"All right. Don't worry, he'll believe me." He would, too. I knew my father would take my word for anything, because I was not a liar. Not really. I wouldn't be involved in anything illegal. I was his baby, his doll. Once he knew that I was working for the good of my country, he would be proud of me. So I told myself.

They returned, then, to the little house, just as they had promised. I took my dad aside while Vic sat in the living room with Mom, neither of them speaking. Vic offered her a cup of coffee, which she refused.

In the kitchen, I stood before my father, begging our case. They had gone to see Vanessa's parents, Mr. and Mrs. Cain, he said. They had found out that Vic was going to marry Vanessa in a few weeks. They came to rescue me, to take me away from this "den of iniquity." My father looked at me with pity in his eyes. I could feel his disappointment in me. Again.

"It's not really like that, Dad," I pleaded. "It's not what it looks like. Vic works for the government. Of course, the Cains don't know it. Please believe me. Nothing is what it seems. He's not really going to marry Vanessa, it's part of the operation. I can't explain it all to you. But I love him, Dad, and he's a good man. Better than you know. I can't desert him now."

Once again I saw defeat in my father's eyes, the same look of failure that I had seen years before, when I had begged him to accept Vic as his son-in-law. Once again I felt the pain, and the joy, of knowing that love would be the victor. Silently, he nodded his head. "If that's what you want."

They left for the second time, silent as they closed the door behind them. My heart went with them—but only for a moment. Then my attention was on my husband. "What do we do now?" I asked.

Part III
Flight

Chapter 23

Reno, 1980

"Come on, baby, you can do it. You don't want to be late for work." The voice reached me from a far distance, resounding through the fog of my mind like an echo from a far shore. I felt his hand on my elbow, the other supported my back as he led me to the bathroom. He turned on the shower and helped me in.

It was cold. A thousand needles pricked me, stung me, shocked me into feeling. I shivered, hunched away from that assault, jerked in involuntary spasms as I gasped and, head down, held my body tight against the knifelike jabs.

"Come on, Steph, you've got to get cleaned up. Today's a work day. No more laying around. At least, not until tonight. Then we can return to our little love nest."

Grabbing a washcloth, he held it out to me, the picture of patient husbandly concern. I reached for it, all my reflexes on automatic.

"That's right. Now be a good girl and get ready for work. I'll be waiting."

The curtain closed, isolating me within the chamber, the water now warming up to the point of creating steam, the steam as foggy as my mind.

"You'll be my wife until you die! You'll never leave me!"

Yes, Vic. Until I die. I'll never leave you.

The hands began to scrub, lathering up the soap until my body was covered with white foam.

* * * * *

September 1969

Reno. Eugene and Portland, Oregon. Salt Lake City. Paducah, Kentucky. Chicago, Springfield, and Taylorville, Illinois. Kansas City, Omaha, Fargo. The towns and cities across the United States began to blur, to look the same no matter what their size, population, or location. Amidst the sea of strangers, I thought I glimpsed a familiar face now and then, a face I knew would follow me to the ends of the earth. My bodyguards. Reminders of the ever-present danger in living the life of a spy.

We left San Remos, California, just hours after my parents' unexpected visit. Vic had followed Mom and Dad out the door nearly on their heels, leaving me terse instructions to pack what I could into the car and "be prepared." He would call as soon as he had his orders.

The car didn't hold much; there had to be room left for a six-month-old baby and a three-year-old. Vic's clothing, guns, and personal items went first, then as many baby items as I could jam into the trunk. Tiffany and I were last, with Tiffany faring only a little better than me. By the time I stuffed my things in, there was room for only a few necessities. I couldn't put much on the seats, since I had to make it all look ordinary, like a family just going about their business. No one could know we were leaving. No one could be given the opportunity to try to stop us. I covered the sweaters and underwear with one of Cat's blankets. Her baby seat would have to go on top of the clothes.

Vic's first call came; I was to terminate my job at the hospital, collect my check, and await further orders. At Charity Hospital, I hastily explained to my surprised supervisor that I had a "family emergency" and didn't know when I would be back. She was sympathetic and sorry to see me go.

I cashed my check and returned home to pace the floor, wondering where Vic was and if I would see him again. "If they don't like the way this is going, you might never see me again," he'd said before he left. And how could the Company "like" any of this? The entire mission was ruined. If we left San Remos, what would happen to Vanessa? *None of your business*, I told myself. *She's an agent. She'll land on her feet.*

The telephone rang, its shrillness deafening in the silent house. By now I was so focused on him, on this crisis, that all the normal sounds of living had receded into the distance. Everything came to me through a fog.

Except the telephone. Four rings, silence, one more ring—I grabbed the receiver. "Yes?"

"Here's the deal," Vic said. "I'll be at a motel just outside town, you know where the old road meets the highway?"

"Yes, I know."

"Go there in exactly one hour. If I can leave, I'll be waiting outside. If they have other plans for me, you keep going." My heart thundered, my ears strained. There was a lot of noise at the other end of the line. "If I'm not there, go to the

ASK ME NO QUESTIONS

Travel Inn in Napa. Wait there for my call. If I call you, I will be using my code name. Got that?"

"Yes. RJ."

The silence was sudden as he hung up. *What if Mom and Dad come back? Force me to go with them? What if they don't believe me?* The doubts assailed me, seemed to float in from the other side of the closed front door. I stared at it, seeing my parents, seeing them crash through it, watched them pick up my children and carry them outside. I saw the Cains behind them, waving their arms, hands pointing, accusing, judging. *What if they bring the police?*

I couldn't wait there. Impatiently I gathered the children, locked the house, and left San Remos.

I drove aimlessly for a while, then headed for the appointed spot in order to be there at the appointed time. Slowing the car as we neared the motel, I strained my eyes for sight of Vic. I was nearly past before he emerged from the trees near the entrance. I stopped quickly and pulled over to the side of the road as he jumped in beside me. "Keep going," he said, and the car shot forward as I pressed on the gas.

He was silent for most of the drive to Reno, Nevada, alternately sleeping and giving me directions. When we reached the summit of Donner Pass, he told me to pull over so we could switch places. Then he drove on into the Biggest Little City in the World.

It was strange to be in this place after so long—I recalled that long-ago day with Beth and the man beside me. Where was she now, that best friend of my childhood? Where were the aspirations of that young actress? *Tomorrow is ours.* Beth's voice echoed in the heavens. *No, Beth,* I thought. *Today is all we have.*

I would not be allowed to call Beth even had I wanted to. No one must know we had fled here. That was one of the purposes in our coming: to hide, to mingle with the transient population of this gambling town. To become anonymous.

Our stay in the famed fun city was relatively short. The brevity of our visit was of little importance, for this first stop set the pattern for all of our subsequent moves, all of the visits in the nineteen states and faceless towns we would pass through together.

There would be the sudden order, the hasty packing of essentials, a long drive and lots of phone calls. The journey would terminate at a restaurant, usually a Sandy's. Sometimes we stayed in motels until the next hurried, frantic move; sometimes we rented a house or apartment and pretended the traveling was over. I guess I always hoped it was.

In Reno, Vic immediately began work at one of the local Sandy's Restaurants, using his experience to advantage. Good cooks were always in demand. His "boys" were all avoiding him: he was left in the dark, without contacts, until the situation in San Remos cooled down. He was restless, spent his free time nervously pacing the motel room or roaming the casinos. When he went outside, he constantly searched the crowds for signs of familiar faces, listened for a softly spoken word which would give him direction.

Finally, it came.

"Stephani! Where are you? Come here for a minute!" His voice was jubilant, carrying the buoyancy of a lifetime long past.

"What is it? I'm bathing the babies. In the bathroom."

He came to me, grabbed me in a quick, hard hug. "It's all right. We can be married again!"

I turned into his arms, surprised, overwhelmed, grateful. I could be Mrs. Victor Charles Brian! No more pretence! No more holding back the intimate smiles, the touches, the secret language of married people. I sank against him in relief.

"And you can go to work with me," he continued, switching his attention to Cat and Tiffany in the shallow tub. "We can be together all day."

"Work? You mean at Sandy's?"

"Yeah. Come in later today, this afternoon. Bring the girls. I want everybody to meet my beautiful women."

And so it happened that I began a new career and ended up in the fast food business after all. There was an underlying motivation to my new job: "This way I can keep an eye on you," Vic said, only half teasing. "The boys deserve a break now and then." But at least we could work together, at last we could be husband and wife in public as well as at home. It was the beginning of a new era.

My career in the food business began on the eve of deer hunting season. The restaurant was packed from midnight to seven a.m. with hunters heading out to their favorite spots. I hadn't so much as ordered from a Sandy's menu for the past year; now I was expected to know the dishes, and their prices and appropriate abbreviations, before I hung the ticket on the cook's line.

As the newcomer, I was assigned the area least likely to fill up—the dining room—and a paltry four booths. Either someone had forgotten the season, or this was a unique way to separate the waitresses from the busboys. Along about one a.m. my four paltry booths were supplying a steady stream of khaki-clad rednecks, and my fifteen-table dining room might just as well have been a convention.

ASK ME NO QUESTIONS

Thanks to the new night cook, I was able to serve them all—haphazardly—within a reasonable time frame while he priced and totaled the tickets. Never had I been so grateful for Vic's presence, nor so proud to be able to call him my husband. For eight hours I was able to glimpse the Vic I knew and loved so many years ago—the playful, teasing, flirting young man who was also a whiz at flipping pancakes. He created a rhythm to the job that was nearly audible; he helped the illusion along by drumming on the hidden counter, spatula in hand, while he scanned the orders. The customers enjoyed the show as much as I enjoyed playing in it.

An unexpected bonus of this job was the sudden acquisition of ready cash. Besides my paycheck, I carried home pockets full money, the change bulging in the bottom of my uniform pocket, the dollar bills squashed together en masse. The importance of that money was not apparent then, but it was a comfort to feel the weight of it there in my pocket each day.

The restaurant became my link to the outside. Unlike the hospital, which was an entity, a world, unto itself, working in the restaurant exposed me to life. Through it passed people, people with normal, everyday concerns. Happy people. Sad people. The mediocrity of it all was exciting, even overwhelming at first. "Normal" people leading normal lives were nearly incomprehensible to me.

"Hi, Stephani! What's special today? You're lookin' good!" "Hey girlie, how about a refill? I'm in a hurry!" "Hel-lo, beautiful! What're ya doin' after work?"

I heard it all. Some of it embarrassed me, some confused me, some even horrified me, but I reveled in it, the glory of human voices.

Trained by now to silence, I didn't say much. I listened. I smiled. I served people their meals, refilled their coffee cups, cleaned up after them. And I learned a trade, counting my tips in the morning with newfound relish. This is *my* money, I thought, clinking the coins together, laying the bills out straight and neat. I did this myself!

Of course the money wasn't really mine. Not to keep. No, as soon as Vic got home he took care of it, stacking the coins and wrapping them, sometimes buying them from the till for change at the restaurant. I never saw the money once he pocketed it. But that didn't matter. I was contributing to our well-being. I was sharing in the responsibilities of our marriage. And I had found something I could do well. Something Vic was proud of.

We rented a dilapidated two-bedroom trailer house in Reno's sprawling suburbs, a building that served as little more than four walls and a roof over our heads. It was not a home, would never become home. We were in transit.

Three weeks after we had arrived in Reno, Vic rushed into Sandy's, his face a grim mask barely hiding the panic in his eyes. I was working a morning shift that day, after having already worked the usual graveyard, because the a.m. waitress had called in sick and no replacement had been found.

Noting Vic's expression, I immediately walked over to where he sat down and poured him a cup of coffee. "What's the matter?"

"We've got to leave," he said.

"Leave? You mean now?"

"Yes. Now. Clock out. I'll square it with Steve." Steve was the restaurant manager.

I turned around, set the coffee pot back on the warmer, picked up my purse and sweater, and punched the time clock. As we walked out, I felt the eyes of my customers following me. Some of them hadn't even received their food.

"What's going on?" I dared to ask as we got into the car.

"Your dad is in Harrah's. I think he saw me."

"Oh."

That was it. Once again we threw our things into the car, packed up the babies, and drove away.

"Where are we going?"

"Eugene."

"Oregon?"

"Yeah."

We lapsed into silence. Vic didn't explain; he didn't need to. Once again we were on the run; once again I tacitly accepted the blame. It was my parents who had innocently intervened in San Remos. It was my parents who were about to interfere in Reno. Innocent, ignorant, and probably righteously indignant. I knew they loved me, but my loyalty belonged to my husband. Somehow, their mistakes became my fault. Just the fact that I was their daughter condemned me. *I'm lucky Vic doesn't just up and leave me behind*, I thought miserably. *I deserve it.*

But my husband wasn't one to hold grudges. His mind was focused on the future, never the past. His job—his real job—was at stake, and the lives of countless, faceless others. How would this flight affect his career? Would the "boys" be so forgiving a second time? I didn't know. I didn't know anything.

The drive to Eugene was quick and quiet. The children slept much of the way; I had learned to keep my tongue still while Vic worked out a plan. His mouth pursed in concentration, his eyes were never still. He stopped once to grab a cup of coffee, but otherwise drove steadily, relentlessly. I watched him drive, wondering, for five hundred miles, what was going to happen next.

ASK ME NO QUESTIONS

In Eugene we went to work at a Sandy's located near the University of Oregon, again on the night shift. Once again Vic began the tedious task of setting up a cover, establishing a network of informants. He left me alone during the days, catching only two or three hours of sleep in the afternoons. There had been no contact with my parents, no further word to them. Our life—my life—was filled with the tasks of moving into an apartment, renting furniture, sorting clothes, finding a sitter, and going to work. I didn't have time to think. I didn't want to think. I lived on a "need to know" basis; I knew nothing.

We were there barely two weeks when Vic collapsed behind the grill during his shift.

An ambulance took him to the hospital, where he was diagnosed with acute hepatitis. The doctor recommended that I send the babies somewhere for a few weeks, somewhere they would be safe from the contagious disease. Then I would have to sterilize everything Vic had touched. When he came home from the hospital, his utensils, his linens, everything he used would have to be separated and sterilized until he was well. Reluctantly I called my mother, the only person in the world who could help me. "No," she said, her voice cold and distant through the line. "I'm sorry, but I can't help you."

The break was complete. I was alone.

Chapter 24

In the weeks that followed, a renewed sense of isolation enveloped me, cushioned me from the pain of losing my parents. In the back of my mind I had always thought, I suppose, that I could turn to them if I needed them. We wrote to each other regularly, kept in touch at least in a cursory attempt to remain informed as to each other's lives. My letters were shams, of course, mere outlines of activities and events. Chit-chat letters, I called them. "Vic is so busy, he's doing well in the restaurant business. The children are growing. The weather is fine." Always optimistic, always upbeat. Praise for my husband, the man they never liked. Please-approve, please-like-me letters that never spoke of the loneliness, the uncertainty, the confusion.

Now there would not be even that link. Mom's words rang over and over in my mind as I sterilized and sorted and separated and sterilized again, careful to keep Vic's utensils away from those the children used, paranoid about infecting them with the disease. *"No, we can't help you."* Their rejection reinforced my sense of fate. I had to be strong; I was the only one who could take care of my children, the only one who cared about my husband. Once again, prayer sustained me, maintained my strength. I don't know what I would have done without God.

I prayed continuously, it seemed, for days. *Please protect my children, Lord, please keep them safe from harm. Please bless my husband, Lord, please keep him safe from harm. And please forgive me, Lord, for the pain that I have caused. Help my parents understand. Help them forgive me. Please keep us safe and able to continue to do Your work.*

I didn't know how to face a future without Vic.

My prayers were answered; God was still listening. Vic recovered, but the weeks of illness cost him his job. We moved on to Portland, Oregon, where it seemed the Sandy's was expecting us. Apparently the "boys" hadn't deserted us altogether.

ASK ME NO QUESTIONS

Portland proved to be a wonderful place for us. Our apartment was on the edges of the big city park, so it was easy to take the girls there to play on nice days. The children remained healthy despite their close proximity to their father during his illness, and they thrived in the cool, damp air of the seaside city. Vic took me out to dinner frequently, and we explored the variety of restaurants available. I tasted German food, Chinese, Italian, and his favorite, New York steaks.

It seemed that we were, at last, rewarded for the difficult years, the sacrifices we had made. Vic was promoted to assistant manager of the restaurant shortly after our arrival; I rewarded him with the news that I was pregnant with our third child. Maybe this one would be a boy. A son. I loved my job, loved providing for my family and being part of a team. Vic handled the finances in his usual totalitarian manner; I emptied my pockets automatically after a day's work, leaving the details of paying bills and managing the money to him. We never lacked for material enjoyment. The CIA and its clandestine influence in our life faded to a manageable background. There were times I could even pretend it didn't exist.

But the calm couldn't last. Early one morning in January, 1970, during a particularly hectic breakfast rush, our past walked right in the front door of Sandy's as if she had never left. I was finishing my shift, serving the last of my orders, when I glanced up at the trio just entering the dining area. In an instant I recognized the swinging seal-colored hair, the shining brown eyes, the petite figure.

Vanessa. Only the training of past years prevented me from dropping the plates where I stood. Instead, I served the food with a smile pasted on my face, refilled the endless coffee cups of the patrons in my station, and kept track of the newcomers out of the corner of my eye. The Cains had been directed into the dining room. Vic was due to walk in any moment. I couldn't let him stride into an ambush. Finishing up as quickly as possible, I began to wipe down the counter nearest the door, watching for my husband. He entered, pushing the double doors open with a little difficulty against the blustery winter wind. I caught his eye, began to walk toward him.

"Coffee, miss?" A customer asked, holding up his cup.

"Wha-sure," I said, continuing toward my husband. "Just a moment."

Approaching Vic, I pulled him out of the line of vision from the dining room. "Vanessa's here," I hissed. He stopped, his face blanching. "In the dining room. I think her parents are with her."

He slid into the office, where I assumed he would speak with Bill Nestle, the manager, before coming out onto the floor. Moments later, a waitress knocked on that door, poked her head in, and came out with Vic on her heels. He disappeared into the enemy camp.

I gave my morning replacement an update on the section and clocked out, my mind reeling with possibilities. What should I do? What would Vic want me to do?

As I passed the dining room entryway on my way out, I searched for my husband in the crowded room. He was easy to find: Vic was standing beside their table, calmly listening to the three visitors. In fact, he was smiling, at ease. It was Vanessa who seemed edgy. Her lovely face was flushed, her hands moved constantly as she talked. The other two people sat quietly, one hand of each resting on Vanessa's chair. Moral support. I had to get home, I couldn't leave the girls alone. I left, my stomach churning.

Vic arrived home an hour or so later, brusquely brushing away any problems the new arrivals portended. "It's nothing," he said. "Vanessa's just pissed because of the way it ended and screwed up her explanation to her parents. We were supposed to have had a fight, call off the wedding, and I would have just disappeared. But she told them we were married in Reno, so now they're ready to sue me for bigamy."

"Bigamy? How? How could they do that? You weren't really married! How did they know about us? She didn't even know about us!"

"Yeah, well, she found out. The guy who started the whole mess, Tim Eldredge, blabbed all over the restaurant that he knew us, asked about you. It all got back to Vanessa. She forgot all about the mission, all about her vow of secrecy. She told her parents. So now they want revenge." The smoke from his cigarette floated in the air above him, the misty spirals seeming significantly mysterious in the afternoon sunlight, a symbol of the maze that was my life. Tim Eldredge was a former high school classmate. He'd recognized Vic when he stopped at the restaurant as he was passing through San Remos. His friendly greeting to Vic had developed into the snafu which followed. *Thanks, Tim. A year's work down the drain. Your country thanks you, too.* "So what's going to happen? Are they going to take us to jail?"

"Sure," Vic grinned, taking my hand and pulling me toward him, his eyes glinting golden with mischievous glee. "They're going to throw us in the caboose and toss away the key. But we'll be in there together. Forever. Just you and me in the dark, with only a cement floor for a bed." His intention to distract me from the Cains was too obvious, even for me, and I refused to allow him to draw me away from them. "But Vic," I said, as he nuzzled my ear, "what are they going to do? Can't the Company do something? She could ruin our lives!"

ASK ME NO QUESTIONS

"No," he said abruptly. "No, the Company can't do anything. You get into trouble, you're on your own. So don't expect any help from them. The calvary doesn't charge in."

Stubbing out the cigarette, he drew another from his shirt pocket. "Anyway, it doesn't matter. The Cains aren't going to do anything."

The sharp smell of sulfur filled the room as he struck a match. The end of the filter tip glowed as it caught fire.

"Why? I don't understand. They came all this way, and now they're not going to press charges?"

"Because of you." The words were spoken softly, so quiet in the stillness that I nearly missed them, blending with the smoke to disappear in empty air.

"Me?"

"You."

It didn't appear that he was going to explain. I looked at him in confusion, the questions written on my face. He smiled that secret smile, making rings out of the smoke issuing from his mouth. "Vanessa saw you working, and decided she didn't want to hurt you. So she's filing for an annulment." He chuckled, his arm encircling my waist. He patted my protruding stomach, where our child hid beneath the taut, smooth skin. "Seems you have some usefulness, after all."

In the ensuing moments, I forgot about my unanswered question—the question about Vic and Vanessa's "marriage." There wouldn't be a record of it, since the whole thing was a sham. There couldn't be any charges at all, since they were merely acting out their orders.

It was much later that afternoon when he told me the rest. "She wants to see you," he said nonchalantly, combing his hair in preparation for the "evening shift," that nightly routine that had never changed.

"See me? Why?"

"She wants to tell you what a bad doobie I am, that you're making the mistake of your life by staying with me." The smile was there, reflected in the bathroom mirror, but I felt his eyes following me as I picked up about the room. Leaning against the doorframe, I asked again, "What kind of mistake could I be making?"

For just a breath in time the query hung there, as the smoke had hung before, a mist which seemed to hold secrets which I couldn't grasp. But the moment passed, and my husband simply smiled, beginning to erase the shadow of scraggly growth on his chin with a straight razor.

"Do you think I should see her?" I asked.

"It's up to you," he shrugged. "I'm not going to tell you what to do." The shaving cream covered half his face, the sound of scraping metal against skin enhanced the irony in this conversation. I hadn't made an independent decision in four years.

"Well then, I will see her. I'll tell her what a mistake she's making." A sense of righteous indignation straightened my back to the task.

Wiping his chin with a towel, Vic put his shaving implements in the cabinet behind the mirror before he turned to face me. "Just remember," he cautioned, "we are all still employees of the Company. You can't say anything which will endanger our position."

"I won't," I assured him. "I just don't understand why she's doing this. Surely she's not blaming you for what happened. You were only following orders!"

"Well, honey," he said gently, compassionately, "you can't be angry with her. She wasn't supposed to fall in love with me."

"She fell in love with you? Really in love?" My heart wrenched for her pain, for his predicament.

He merely nodded in reply, obviously embarrassed. "I'm really sorry," I said quietly. "But she must not love you very much, if she wants to hurt you now."

He kissed my forehead, his fingers caressing my hair. "Not everybody loves like you do," he said. "That's why you're so special."

We stood like that for several minutes, close in spirit as well as body. In that moment, I was sure that I would never know another like him. My love for him welled up inside me.

I dialed the number where Vanessa was staying, my hands trembling with the need to assure her she was wrong about him. But the voice on the other end of the line told me that the Cains had checked out: I had missed my opportunity. We never heard from Vanessa again.

We stayed in Portland a total of nine months: our third daughter was born there. Deanna was three weeks overdue when I fell from the second floor landing of our old apartment, ending upside down at the bottom of the twenty-three steps leading to Tiffany's bedroom. Ironically, I was preparing to go to the doctor's office for my weekly checkup when I walked to the top of the stairs to see if Tiffany was ready. At her ready answer to my call, I stepped back just one foot length, balancing my ungainly bulk by touching the wall nearest me.

I awoke seconds later, lying on my back at the bottom of those twenty-three steps.

Stunned, I blinked my eyelids several times in an effort to clear the screen before me; I saw stars, all right, and blackness, a yawning black hole which invited me inside, away from the pain which would surely begin if I moved.

ASK ME NO QUESTIONS

"Are you all right? What happened?" Hands pulled at me, tugged at my armpits, willing me to sit upright. The face of my neighbor, a large young woman with straight long blond hair, occupied the screen directly in front of me. I blinked the stars away, forcing my eyes to focus. "I fell down the stairs," I said stupidly.

"I can see that," she replied. "Are you all right? Can you move?"

"I don't know." I began the task of curling my legs, which were sprawled straight out in front of me, underneath my trunk, and with her insistent hands tugging at my underarms, was able to set my feet on the floor. It was more to her credit than mine that I was able to shakily straighten my limbs again, and she then helped me to my bedside, where I sat surveying the damage.

My entire left side, from shoulder to ankle, was scraped and scratched; the bruises were beginning to color in between the red spots. My back and head felt like the center of my heartbeat, thudding in rhythm to that organ now as feeling began to return. My head had withstood the worst of the fall, and it throbbed sullenly in angry protest. But I was fine. Of more importance was the child residing within me. The baby had not moved.

Reassuring the nameless neighbor, I rose from the bed, put on my shoes, gathered up a petrified Tiffany and drowsy Cat, and calmly drove to my appointed meeting with my obstetrician. He in turn sent me scurrying back home to collect my bag and go on to the hospital.

Vic was on duty at the restaurant. He'd been waiting for my call for weeks, so it was no trouble to take time off to drive me to the hospital. After checking me in, he left with the girls and a promise to come back to see me the next day. We were on our own in this city: just us and our children. Other people could indulge in family support and the trust of friends. We had only each other.

Deanna emerged with little fanfare, although the nurses were on the edge of panic when she threatened to arrive before Dr. Ross made his appearance. As it was, I interrupted his supper, thereby earning his ire for the remainder of my time under his care. At least, I think that's what happened, for I can find no other explanation for his studious ignorance of my injuries. He entered the delivery room like a spectre, his sterile gown flapping behind him while he pulled on his gloves. "Clean up this mess!" he barked, as he positioned himself at the end of the table. "I can't work in all this blood!" The delivery nurse flinched and placed her hands on either side of my face, almost as if she were protecting me, and then they all settled down to work. I couldn't feel anything below my waist, thanks to the anesthesia, and I was furious. This wasn't anything like the births of my other babies. *Why do women want this?* I thought. *I can't feel anything!*

Actually, I did feel the tugs—without the pain—of the snips as Dr. Ross prepared the opening through which Deanna slid. And I felt those same tugs—without pain—as he sewed up the incision. But my legs were dead sticks that wouldn't obey my direction, and my womb may as well have been a test tube. I craned my neck to watch the birth as it was reflected in the little mirror the nurse placed near my right cheek, but I couldn't see a thing. I may as well have been back in my room, back in my apartment.

But my anger concealed the pain emanating from the fall—the raw skin on my back and shoulders, the bruises on my arms, the goose-egg on my head; the ensuing headaches and stiffness and stabs of pain between my shoulder blades. The cuts and bruises went untended, as did the fractured vertebra at the base of my neck. This little piece of unmended bone would serve as a reminder of that day for the rest of my life.

That night as I lay in my bed, I smoothed some of the cream I found in my bedside cabinet over my arms, but it stung and I hastily wiped it away. I asked the night nurse for something to relieve the pain, and she told me I wasn't "due for any pain medication for another hour." The next morning, the day shift awakened me with their bustling energy, and my nurse helped me off the bed and into the shower. "What happened to you?" she asked when she saw my back. "I fell down some stairs," I replied. "You're lucky you weren't killed," she tisked, and she closed the door.

I let the water spray over me, relished the warmth and the silence. The stinging of my scratches ceased after a few minutes, and I felt the newer, fresher wounds of delivery. My body was empty now, empty of the life it had carried and protected. Deanna was alive and healthy, with no ill effects from the fall down the stairs. For that, I was grateful. I couldn't have borne it if she'd been hurt. For that, I thanked God. My body would mend.

Ten days later I was back at work, hawking hamburgers to the steady stream of tourists passing through the beautiful Rose City. The Oregon summer was literally in full bloom, with the scent of hundreds of varieties of flowers drifting down to the apartment from the park.

I asked Dr. Ross to check the area of my neck that was still bothering me from the fall when I saw him for my six-week checkup. I'd been experiencing pain along my right arm, and I'd dropped plates from a sudden numbness during work. He felt along my spine and declined giving me an x-ray, assuring me that if I was "really hurt," I'd feel more than those sporadic, shooting pains. The headaches I was experiencing, he explained, were a normal result of the spinal I'd been given. "They'll go away in time, he said. "Don't worry."

ASK ME NO QUESTIONS

And so I tried to believe him, and I shoved the pain and the accidents to the back of my mind. There were too many real worries for me to think about.

Vic had already moved on, this time leaving me behind to pack and make all the appropriate explanations. His new assignment was in Salt Lake City, Utah. And it was there, in the town founded by a prophet, that our odyssey became a frantic attempt to escape from the demons that haunted Victor Charles Brian, agent for the CIA.

Chapter 25

"We have a unique program designed for him," Bob Towers, VP of Operations, explained. "He's the only person in the Sandy's Corporation with such a program." He gestured to a chair, and I perched on the edge of it, listening with trepidation. Vic had disappeared for several days, gone with just a few words of rare explanation. There'd been tension at the restaurant ever since I arrived, tension which seemed to emanate from all the employees. I'd grown accustomed to the casual rapport in most waitress-busboy-cook relationships; this tension was unusual. They all seemed to watch us, Vic and me, as if we had come from another planet. Of course, we weren't Mormons, but I didn't believe that had anything to do with the way we were treated. It wasn't an obvious cold shoulder, it was more that something was slightly "off." I'd begun to watch my tables more closely, looking for missing tips. It didn't help that my husband seemed as tense as everyone else.

Then, four days ago, Vic had come into Sandy's while I was working, signaled me to his place at the counter, and muttered, "I've got to go to headquarters. A meeting. I'll be gone a few days." His expression brooked no questions. I nodded, smiling while I poured coffee into the mug before him. "Don't worry," I said. "we'll be okay." He dipped his head in a brief nod. I continued on, checking on my other customers. When I glanced back toward his seat, it was empty.

He'd returned late last night. This morning, a tall, husky man had appeared from the manager's office. He watched me, seemed to scrutinize my work for five long minutes. Then, when there was a lull in the line of orders and all my customers were served, he approached me.

"Stephani Brian?"

"Yes." I looked straight at him, curious. I didn't know who he was, had never met him. The fact that he'd come from the manager's office was enough to intimidate me. Was he going to fire me? Did I do something wrong?

ASK ME NO QUESTIONS

"Bob Towers," he said easily, extending his hand. "Do you have a minute?"

Managers didn't ask that question unless they knew the answer. I walked beside him toward the back, my apprehension growing.

"I want to assure you that we are all aware of the problems you're having here," Mr. Towers said. I stopped in midstride, glanced up at his face so far above my own. Bob Towers lived up to his name, at least in height. "Yes," he continued without returning my look, "we know there's been some difficulty."

We walked in silence, the clamor from the dining and dishwashing areas diminishing. We reached the office doorway; Towers gestured me inside.

"Vic is in a unique program," he said, "and we want him to continue." Was the "we" the Company, or the Corporation? Was Towers one of the "boys" or merely a Sandy's executive? I assumed he was a Company man, since Vic would never go to all this trouble just to keep a job at a restaurant. Towers' comments confirmed my belief.

"He's doing a good job for us. With this position, he can be mobile immediately. We send him where he's needed the most. And he has your full support, doesn't he?"

I nodded, my heart pounding. *Of course he does*, I thought. *I'll do whatever he needs. Always.*

"Well, then, I guess I don't need to say any more. We're very proud of Vic. I know you are, too." I nodded once more. Bob Towers shook my hand for the second time. "Thank you, Stephani," he said gravely. "I know it isn't always easy."

He ushered me out of the office, closing the door behind him. Like so many of the people in our life, that was the only time I ever saw Bob Towers.

The mysterious tension continued, but I ignored the undercurrent, memorizing Towers' words. One night just three weeks after arriving in Salt Lake, Vic stormed into the restaurant and disappeared into the office. Moments later the door slammed open and my husband stalked out the front door. *What's going on?* I thought. *What's happening now?* Vic's face was thunderous, his mouth set in a grim line. I continued working, my eyes constantly flitting from the front entrance to the manager's office. An hour later, Vic once again came in, this time carrying the little sack that held my week's accumulation of tips. *That's mine!* I shouted silently, protesting this violation of my handwork, this negation of my toil. *You can't take what's mine!* But the words were unspoken, they merely echoed in my brain as I watched the tarnished coins disappear into the cubbyhole with Vic and the boss. Later my husband emerged with a wry smile, but I never saw my money again.

We left that night for Paducah, Kentucky. The mysterious ailment followed us, and we were sent to Chicago, Illinois. Three months in Chicago proved no cure, so we trekked to Springfield, then Taylorsville, then Kansas City, where we spent the summer crammed into a tiny motel room. We moved on to Omaha, Nebraska, finding a miniscule two-story, two-bedroom shoebox just days before Tiffany began kindergarten.

The scope of my life changed as my children entered into it: while Vic held my heart, three little girls with dusty blonde hair gripped my soul. We were so alone, together. Our lives revolved around their father's coming and going, moving and moving some more. Material possessions meant nothing, as furniture and appliances were acquired and discarded. Whatever would fit into whatever size U-Haul we could afford was what we took. If Vic packed, which was rare, prized possessions and necessary household staples would inadvertently be left behind. I became a packing expert, sorting necessaries from expendables with determined dispassion.

The disease that followed and found us at every turn was that of distrust. Not within me—I trusted him with all our lives. No, the distrust was emanating from the Sandy's corporation itself. Perhaps the trainee-managers were jealous of Vic's unique position, created for him by the head office; perhaps there really were discrepancies in the monies counted each night. Perhaps it was all a plot set up by the Company to give Vic an excuse to travel from one city to another, a plan that in some way gave him a cover. I would never know. I just had to believe in God and the system.

But I cried when it happened again in Paducah, even spoke to the manager myself. He merely shook his head with obvious reluctance to change the course of events. In Taylorsville the manager took me aside to ask questions about the amount of business during my shift. I swallowed the indignation that threatened to spill out from my mouth as Vic and I were escorted to the door for the last time. It was anger I felt, anger that this man, this silent man who had sacrificed everything in his belief, in his country's honor, would be so humiliated. But I kept silent, as he did, suffering the ostracism and the judgment with righteous scorn. Someday, they would know the truth. *Someday they will all know the truth,* I vowed. He deserved laurels.

I don't remember when the first whisper of doubt crept into my heart, or when the fear for his life began to twist into a fear for my own. It wasn't in Omaha, where he was arrested and taken through the mockery of a trial over the supposed rape of an employee. The woman was under age. Her father pressed charges, and since the alleged crime was perpetrated with the girl's consent, all he could produce was a statutory rape claim. I sat in the courtroom behind Vic, dressed in my best emerald green dress, my hair carefully brushed to a glossy halo, my eyes shining in trust and love at the innocent man before me. It was a civil court, therefore no jury stared in reprimand or sympathy, just the judge behind his altar, nodding or shaking his head at the testimony presented him.

The girl, whose name was Emma, was a brunette, with a healthy ruddiness to her complexion and a hint of fat in her tall frame. Vic hated fat. "She's lost a lot of weight," he whispered to me, "She was a lot bigger than that. Ugly." Emma gave her testimony with a degree of hesitation and a glimpse of tears, describing the criminal act as it allegedly took place. "He called me into his office," she said timidly, eyes downcast, "and then he touched me."

"Where did he touch you?" the prosecutor queried.

"Near my waist," she whispered.

"You must be specific, Emma," he pressed. And so with sheepish glances toward her former employer, my husband, she described a scene that could have been taken from prime-time TV. In fact, it probably was, although in 1971 those kinds of issues were still pretty rare.

"Did you tell him to stop, Emma?" Now Vic's lawyer stood before her.

"No, I was afraid," she said. "He was my boss. I was embarrassed."

"Did you protest in any way?"

"No."

"Did he, in fact, have intercourse with you?" I watched her face, watched the lies come to her lips. I saw a hint of a smile in her eyes behind the tears.

"Yes." Damning words. Damn woman. Vic had told me about her pursuit of him, her constant flirting. He had told me how she'd attempted, not once but several times, to "talk" to him when he was in the office doing the books. He'd laughed at her, told her he was happily married, even showed her a picture of me, but that hadn't stopped her. How she could sit there in front of him—and me—and lie; it made me ill. I rested my hand on Vic's shoulder. Let the judge see my support of my husband. Let him see that Vic had no reason to seek sex outside of his home.

I was not called to testify, nor was Vic. The judge's decision was against us.

I have never understood the workings of our country's legal system; I knew less about it then. I was twenty-three years old, the mother of three children, the wife of a hard-working, honest man who had no time, much less inclination, to dally with other women. I had never denied Vic his marital privileges even when it was not particularly convenient or even comfortable, at times, for me. It was one of the vows I had made to myself on our wedding day. If these charges were not so serious, the situation would have been ridiculous. And now, although he was judged "guilty" by the man sitting up there on his throne, Vic walked out of the courtroom and went home with me, an appeal date set.

The second trial took place months later, after we had moved to Fargo, North Dakota. I did not accompany him that time, and he came home a free man.

"They threw it out," he said. "The judge dismissed the charges altogether."

My faith in our system was restored.

But it was in Fargo that the first telephone call came, a call in which a stranger asked if this was the residence of one J.R. O'Keith. A chill streaked down my back when I heard the name of Vic's alter ego.

J.R O'Keith was one of the names he used in the service of his country.

"Excuse me?" I choked, not knowing how to answer, my mind racing. Vic hadn't warned me, hadn't said this would happen! "Who's calling, please," I asked, trembling.

"This is the operator," the voice replied. "Mr. O'Keith is making a call to St. Paul, Minnesota, and charging it to this number. Is that all right?"

"Oh. Yes," I answered, relief pouring through me. *But why? Why is he calling St. Paul? And where is he calling from?* I couldn't ask the forbidden questions. I had to wait for unasked-for replies. Replies that never came.

It was in Fargo that a motel receipt fell out of his pocket as I was preparing to do the laundry, a motel receipt naming a date that was impossible for Vic to have used. He had been at work that night; it was one of those long shifts when a cook hadn't shown up so Vic had covered for him, working a total of twenty-eight hours before finally getting a relief cook in. He had called me from the restaurant twice. I checked the date repeatedly, carefully folding the receipt and hiding it in my journal while the questions flooded my mind. How could he have used this? How did it get in his pocket? Where was this motel? *St. Paul*, this ticket said. *St. Paul.*

Vic was "let go" once again. This time the manager and his wife gave me short shrift too, telling me to get out without any signs of sympathy or understanding. "They were jealous," Vic said. "Renee was so jealous of you she used to complain to me all the time."

"Jealous? Of me? Why?" I asked, remembering the anniversary party Vic and I had arranged for them, the cake I had baked, laboring over the decorations. "I thought they were our friends."

"We don't have any friends. Remember that, Stephani. There is no such thing as a friend to the Company." Bob Towers' words resounded in my mind, but now there was little comfort in them. What did it matter that someone knew the truth if we lost our jobs, our self-respect?

And it was just a few weeks later, when the girls and I had been moved to an isolated cabin hidden deep in the Minnesota countryside, that Vic had wrapped his fingers around my wrists and dragged me into the house, his rage overwhelming in its fury. I was terrified, shaken by his strength and by the wildness in his eyes. It was the same unfocused look as that day Vicki told him they couldn't see each other anymore, the day he broke the bed. The day he took me so violently I could barely walk for hours afterward. Maybe the fear had begun then, three years before. Or perhaps it started even before then, on the day he pointed the pistol toward me in cold deliberation, its blue-black barrel an impersonal reminder of the fragility of life.

Perhaps I had always been a little afraid of him, subconsciously recognizing that opaque barrier in his eyes for what it was—a refusal to see that part of himself, an effort to hide the madness which threatened to leap out at unexpected moments.

And perhaps the doubt and fear combined to magnify in that lonely little house in the woods, fed by isolation and sparked by years of anxiety.

"Vic, let go! You're hurting me!" I cried, pulling against him as my feet left the ground a second time. In answer, my husband pulled a little harder, stumbling up the steps at the back door. Light from the kitchen slashed over his face, bounced from the glitter of his golden eyes.

"Daddy! Daddy, you're home!" The kitchen suddenly filled with the sounds of the children, their small bodies squeezing into the space as they clamored for attention. The interruption broke the frenzied wildness of Vic's temper; he changed before my eyes into a playful, loving father. My skin tingled from his grip, my shoulder sockets ached. But the man standing before me was the picture of a family man.

Had those moments out in the dark really happened? Moving around the foursome now wrestling on the living room floor, I stepped into our bedroom to remove my coat. Yes, there was a small tear in the seam under the arm; the skin around my wrists was mottled pink, with an angry purple beginning to surface in fingerprint shapes. I hadn't imagined it.

Retracing the past quarter hour in my mind, I strained to remember what I had said, what I had done to cause the incident. It was a blank, a hole in my memory as black as the night sky.

And then the pattern resumed, that pattern of lies and secrets that was such an integral part of our lives.

I was serving dinners now at a steakhouse, the new restaurant we were moved to. Not part of the Sandy's chain, it was only one of several changes in the usual routine. There were times when the work took Vic outside the areas in which there were Sandy's "stores"; during these times a different restaurant was always waiting for him.

The Wrangler was a step up from the pancake house, serving steaks and seafood, along with the famous Minnesota walleye and bass. It opened in the mornings for traditional breakfast, and stayed open late for the dinner crowd. I had begun working the breakfast shift, but was suddenly moved to evenings "because they need the best help at night," according to Vic.

Camille was one of the morning waitresses, a slender blonde with soft cheeks and chin, square shoulders and sturdy, shapely legs. I had only just met her before my transfer to nights, but had liked the sparkle in her cool blue eyes and the smile on her thin lips. She was working this night because someone else had called in sick: in the world of waitresses, you are always on call.

"Hello, Camille," I greeted her, balancing a heavy tray on my shoulder. "How has the morning been? Everyone still enjoying the tourist season?"

"Yes, we're still pretty busy. I guess you probably know that, though. Your brother must tell you all the gossip."

"My brother?" I repeated, the words coming out in a rush.

"Yeah, Vic. You still live with him, don't you?"

"Oh. Sure." I recovered, hiding my surprise and retreating into the world of the Company. *I should have known*, I thought. *Vic's on a mission. Why didn't he fill me in? I could have blown everything.* "I don't actually see much of him, though," I continued in a breezy you-know-how-brothers-are confidence, my voice lowered to include only Camille in the conversation. "He goes his way, I go mine. You probably see more of him than I do."

"Maybe," she smiled. "We've been able to get in a little sun. He sure does like to fish! I don't do much more than hold the pole out over the water. But it's fun. Oops, I see my table is ready to order. See you later!"

Jealousy shot through me, waves of pure green rage rippled through my body like an electric shock. *Camille! Why another female agent, why not Jerry, his partner from way back? Is every woman in America going into the spy business?* Following on the heels of that inward outburst was guilt, guilt that I could even think such a thing. Camille was just doing her job, as Vic was. I had no right to take out my insecurities on her. She looked awfully young—must have just gotten out of spy school. Of course, I'd never be able to ask her.

At home the following morning, Vic told me he had to go to a survival camp for a few days. Extensive training, he said. Actually, he was furious about it—he had been through survival training years before. "They want to test me," he fumed, packing a very few pieces of clothing into his sleeping bag. "Me! Five days in the wilderness, with nothing but my knife. They think my reflexes need sharpening, that I'm getting too old."

"Sure," I grinned, trying to cheer him up. "You're an old man at twenty-eight. I'll bet you can't even catch me." I darted past him toward the bedroom door, hoping he would take the bait and follow. I had to distract him, make him forget his anger.

The trick worked. In minutes he was smiling again, telling me how much he hated going away from me, from us, how he would be back in a week.

But while he was gone, the summer sun seemed too hot, the shadows too ominous, my thoughts too scattered to concentrate on everyday routine. Pieces of long-dead conversations filtered into my mind, until it seemed a pattern formed. It seemed that we moved in a circle, the circumference of which took two years to travel. The first mission, 1966, in Woodsville. Two years later, San Remos. Then Chicago, in 1970. Now in Detroit Lakes, Minnesota. The absences, the mission, the lies.

More than that. "A friend of mine is in trouble…" "Is it dangerous for a pregnant woman to do things like ride a horse, do strenuous exercises?" "This friend's girlfriend…she might be pregnant." "Is it possible to have a miscarriage just because of making love? If it was…really wild?" "This friend of mine…she's pregnant." "How does a woman have a spontaneous abortion?" "What are the months when it would most likely happen?" "What causes it?" "I have a friend…"

With too much time to think, the voices formed a pattern, too. Always women agents, always the pretense between us of brother and sister. And the loving times, the in-between times when we could really be husband and wife in fact as well as name, were almost always between cases. Vic said that he could not be distracted when he was working, had even told me the Company gave him a drug which curtailed any temptation he might feel to make love to his wife…

A certainty took hold of me, took hold and would not let go. Vic was involved with Camille. I knew it. Deep in my soul, I knew it. Whether or not she was an agent didn't matter. He wasn't supposed to be involved. He was supposed to remain detached. It was my turn for anger, my turn to storm about the house, searching for clues, fuming at the injustice of it all. What was I going to do? What could I do?

The week crept by, slowly, slowly. I went to work each afternoon, the rage in my heart carrying me through the hours. There was only one question that kept running through my head—why? He had always known that he could have his freedom any time he wanted it. I loved him too much to trap him in a loveless marriage. I trusted him, because all he had to do was say he wanted out.

But the anger died, couldn't last the hundred-plus hours of his absence. Doubt turned against me, as I remembered also moments of happiness, stolen moments when he begged me to remember he loved me, only me. Indecision tormented me. What do I do? *Remember Camille*, my brain hissed. *Remember your promise*, thudded my heart.

No questions. No regrets. I tossed in the night, seeing Vic's face before me, pleading with me to stand by him. I worked during the day, seeing her in every waitress uniform.

The turmoil within wore me down. There was no room for anger, no room for doubt. Out of the dying battle came a resolution, a resolution to set him free, to give him free rein to pursue his dreams, to work as he should be working—alone, able to give his entire heart and mind and soul to his country. No distractions. No wife and family to worry about. Finally I was at peace. I knew what I had to do.

He returned, his body dragging with fatigue. "I've had it," he said wearily. "I passed, the sons-of-bitches, I passed—as number three! Damn them! Damn them for putting me through this!—Don't touch that! It's got classified information in it."

My hand snapped back from the overnight case, the small bag he had dropped in the living room on his way to the shower. But it was too late. I was closing the case, not opening it, when he saw me—and I had seen the forbidden. Pictures of Camille. Camille and Vic. Dressed in flannel shirts and jeans and tennis shoes, proudly exhibiting their catch of trout. The woods behind them. The campfire nearby. Smiling, happy. Who had held the camera? All the determination fled, all the doubts returned.

Shaking, I followed my husband into the bathroom, where the steam from the shower already filled the room with mist. "Vic," I shouted over the water sounds, "Where were you, really? Who were you with?" I couldn't let him know I had seen the pictures, had disobeyed him. I wasn't brave enough, or foolish enough to confront him with what I thought was proof of infidelity.

ASK ME NO QUESTIONS

Just doubt, just suspicion.

The shower stopped. "What are you talking about?" he screamed. "What do you mean, 'where was I'? I told you! How dare you question me! How can you doubt me? I love you! I love you so much I can't give you up, even though the Company wants me to! And this is what I get? Doubt? Questions? I should have left you when they ordered me to, if this is my reward! My god, to think I trusted you, told you secrets no one is supposed to know about—you could have me killed, for chrissake!"

"Killed? How could I have you killed? I just—I just wanted to know—Camille said—"

"Camille has nothing to do with this. Camille's just my partner. Haven't you learned anything? Do you think I would go through all this—" he flung his arm out to include the cabin, the isolation, the staying together no matter what—"if I didn't love you?" He exhaled, his anger gone as quickly as it had appeared. "I just don't know you, do I? I really don't know who you are." The bathroom door closed; Vic turned from me and closed it in my face.

I stood, exhausted, my eyes glazed with tears. The old green paint of the door was beginning to peel in the middle of the panel. Like my marriage. "Oh, God, I'm sorry, Vic. I'm sorry. I didn't really distrust you, I just..." *God, how can you be so stupid!* The words hurled at me, my brain turning against me, the same mind that had started the questions. *He loves you, and you repay his trust with accusations! Stupid girl! Stupid!* Weakly, I attempted to speak to him, to touch him through the barrier of the door. To take back the words which betrayed my suspicions. "I'm sorry, Vic, I didn't know...I didn't mean to question...Vic, I'm sorry." The tears streamed down my face, too late, too late to retract the words, take back the doubt. *How could I do this to him, how could I...*

I heard the front door open. The girls, coming in from playing in the summer sun. Quickly I wiped the tears from my cheeks. Cat and Deanna shrieked delight at their father's homecoming, always a cause for rejoicing. Tiffany yelled too, determined to be leader of the group, although she squirmed away when Vic, emerging from the bedroom, dressed and refreshed, attempted to crush her, along with the two little ones, in a giant bear hug. Shrugging past me, Vic herded his children outdoors, becoming a child as instantly as he could become a brother, a husband, an agent...*a lover*? No I would not think that. I'd betrayed him with my thoughts, my accusations. He needed my loyalty. No questions. Never, ever again. Never ask questions. *You could get me killed.*

The day continued as if we had not lived the previous hour. Vic put up a rope swing in the back yard, which Cat immediately climbed, hand over hand, until she waved to us from a height of twenty feet. Tiffany then had to try her hand at it, mimicking her younger sister's movements until she, too, laughed at us from far above our heads.

Two-year-old Deanna had no athletic skill, contenting herself to cheering the other two on. And Vic displayed a congenial smile the entire time. A smile that didn't quite reach past his lips.

It was only a little later that he grimly filled me in on the plan for the coming months, a plan I had heard before. This time there was to be no missing husband, just a dead one. I also had to change jobs. I was to go to the little hospital in Detroit Lakes and apply there as a nurse's aid. Vic didn't say why this was necessary, but then he never explained. The Company wanted it. That was enough.

"There's one more thing," Vic stated matter-of-factly. "I will be working in the Fargo store most of the time. They're moving me over tomorrow."

Carefully I controlled my dismay, carefully I hid behind a business-like facade. "I'll need to pack for you then. Which shirts do you want?"

"Better give me half a dozen. And my blue slacks. The Fargo Wrangler is much fancier than the one here."

So I folded underwear and several pairs of trousers into the bag, keeping the shirts on hangers. This was my punishment. Retribution was swift in the Company.

He left the next morning, before the children awoke for their breakfast. He left with a parting peck on my mouth and not a glance back.

Chapter 26

There. It was there again. Right by the window. No, it's gone.
"I saw you, you know. I know you're here."

Silence. My eyelids closed once more, unable to fight the weariness. I was so tired...But there. Again. A shadow without substance, a dark Angel hovering near the bed.

"Go away!" I shouted, but the words sounded weak, a mere whisper in the night. The Angel of Death. She was here, in my room.

It was hot, so hot. The quilt was so heavy...Tossing it aside, I crawled to the window, opening it...*no, can't do that, she'll come back*...pushing on the old pane with all my strength, I attempted to close the window. It wouldn't budge. But it was cool, the snow felt good...I stumbled back to bed, shivering.

The Angel didn't return, but I felt her presence. I knew she had come to warn me. *Vic? Is Vic in danger? The girls. Maybe they are the ones she's after.* I tossed the blankets off, feeling the chill immediately on my body. I was slippery with sweat. I couldn't walk, couldn't make my legs move. I fell, my hands grasping at the covers before I hit the floor...*The girls, where are the girls? They're sick, I need to get them their medicine...*

"Steph? Stephani, are you alright?" A cool hand stroked my cheek. A weight was resting beside me, tipping the mattress slightly to the right. Lazily I fought my way to the light, out of the depths of whatever hell I had been visiting.

"Hmmmh? Vic?"

"No, it's Lori. How are you feeling?"

"Lori...Is the Angel here?"

"Angel? Are you dreaming? Sleep awhile longer. I'll be here."

When I awoke to full consciousness, it was nearly noon. I could hear my daughters playing in the living room, chattering and scuffling.

Other voices penetrated the room. Carol and Wendy, Lori's teenage daughters. The aroma of fresh coffee wafted through the door Lori had left cracked open.

"Ready for some breakfast?" My friend came in, her hands laden with a tray on which rested a coffee cup, complete with steaming brew, and two pieces of buttered wheat toast. I tried to swallow some coffee, but gagged on it almost instantly; the toast was better, staying down when I took tiny bites.

"You've been a pretty sick lady," Lori said softly, watching me. "Why didn't you call?"

Leaning back on the pillows piled behind my head, I just looked at her, bewildered. "I didn't even think of it. I was fine, I was a little tired, maybe, but I didn't feel sick. The girls had the flu, I took care of them. I wouldn't bother you, Lori. You have your own family to look after. I'm supposed to take care of my children."

She was silent, staring at me in puzzlement. Finally she lowered her eyes, began to pick up the dishes. "I thought we were friends," she said, her voice very low. "I thought we could trust each other."

"Lori, wait! I do trust you! We are friends!" I grabbed at her, upsetting the coffee mug in the process. "Please, Lori. I'm sorry…please don't go." I fell back against the pillows, my body trembling with exhaustion. "Please believe me, Lori. You are my only friend."

She stopped, ignoring the coffee slopped onto the bedclothes, and looked at me again, a long, searching look. "Please," I whispered.

She sat down again, avoiding the wet spot on the spread.

"Stephani," she said, "you've been very sick. What would have happened if I hadn't come by to check on you? You've missed work, the girls haven't been to school, the house was freezing when I got here. You could have all died in this place, and no one would even have known. And you didn't think to call for help?"

Now it was my turn to stare. "How long?" I asked. "How long have you been here?"

"Two days," she answered. "I've been here for two days, and God knows how long you were out before that. I came by because I thought you might want a ride into work on Monday. You were lying on the floor."

Her words shocked me into wakefulness. "The girls? Are they okay? I heard them playing in the living room."

"They're fine. They were nearly well when I found you."

ASK ME NO QUESTIONS

"I'm so sorry, Lori. What would I do without you?" Tears of shame began to fill my eyes. How could I lie to this woman? How could I repay her kindness with deceit?

"It doesn't matter now," she said. "But where is Vic? Why didn't you call him?"

"I couldn't," I said. "I don't call Vic. He calls me." But he hadn't, not lately. Vic didn't call me anymore. The price of distrust.

Lori shook her head, not understanding. But I couldn't tell her any more. I couldn't risk Vic's anger.

She stayed with me the rest of the day, going home only once she was satisfied that I was able to function. The virus had hit me harder than most, but now that it was gone, I recovered rapidly. But I didn't forget the dark Angel I had seen, nor the love that Lori had given.

Both experiences were new to me: both opened my eyes to the world about me in a way not previously appreciated. The Angel, real or imagined, made me aware that forces other than the material operated on this plane. She had appeared before me three times that night. I interpreted her appearance as a warning, a warning to Vic. Somehow, she was trying to tell me Vic was in danger. Immediate danger. The illness had somehow heightened my senses, opened my mind to the paranormal. Or sent me over the edge of sanity. I didn't tell Lori or anyone else about her. She was just one more secret in a life of secrets.

But I believed that I had truly seen her, and I hugged the knowledge to my heart. Always a sensitive, I believed that God had sent this Messenger into my life. All the years of imagining, waiting to be told that my husband was dead, or wounded, or captured, culminated into that moment in a dark, cold bedroom. I was warned. I prepared myself for the inevitable.

The advent of a friend at just that time in my life only confirmed my belief. God wouldn't let me go through this alone. He'd sent someone to help me. Lori. Her love made me realize how small was my world, this gilded cage in which I had been imprisoned.

I'd met Lori Brown at Detroit Lakes Community Hospital two months before, where I had gone, at Vic's direction, to apply for a job. Of course, I'd gotten the position. I'd never doubted that possibility. We always had a job waiting for us, whenever the Company or Fate decreed a change in our lives. The hospital was a return to familiarity, a return to what had once been a fulfilling role. This time, in addition to my care duties as a nurse's aide, I was also trained to serve as a unit secretary, transcribing doctors' orders onto patient charts for the nurses.

I loved the responsibility, loved making people well. This world was so removed from that other, so full of important decisions and warm, caring people.

It was almost a new life for me, since Vic came to the little house in the woods only on weekends, and sometimes not then. I was to learn how to live on my own, my punishment for doubting him. Of course, "on my own" simply meant that I was to walk the thin line of "acceptable behavior" as the sister of a spy, and to follow orders to the letter. I was to attract no attention to myself, make no alliances with the locals, and keep the little house safe for Victor, a sanctuary where he could rest and retreat from the eyes of his world.

I did not know how to be a person in my own right. I felt abandoned, lost. I needed the sense of order the Company gave me, the purpose in the lies. But I was alone. There were everyday decisions I had to make. Almost against my own will, I began to enjoy making those small decisions, began to feel a confidence in making them that I had not felt in many years. I found a wonderful, reliable sitter for Cat and Deanna. Tiffany began the first grade. I pretended we were the same as everyone else, pretended our life was normal.

And for the first time in over six years, I made a friend. Lori Brown was the unit secretary on the third floor, about ten years older than I. We discovered in our first conversation that she lived just a mile or so away from me, on the same county road that led to the little town of Detroit Lakes. She and her husband owned a few acres, which they hobby-farmed, and had two daughters. Tim, Lori's husband, was "a little slow" in the head, the result of an accident years before. Nonetheless, he held down a full-time job and did his best to keep up with his teenage children.

But his handicap was a strain on their relationship, as there were times when his wife worried over his tardiness at night, or his ability to drive through the icy roads, and even in the fact that she was an intelligent woman with many interests which her husband couldn't share, because he just couldn't keep up. I could tell she needed a friend, too, for she bore her burdens with a silent strength which belied the sorrows beneath her heart.

The couple designated themselves my guardian angels during the harsh Minnesota winter: I could never have made it without them.

As occasionally happens between two lonely people, Lori and I became very close, as close as our secrets would allow. She never complained about her lot in life, nor did I. But there was one secret I found impossible to keep from her—the secret of my marriage.

It happened so quickly, I wasn't even sure that she had guessed. Vic was home, had arrived on Saturday with his laundry and his perpetual weariness. Despite the distance between us, the impersonal relationship he maintained, my heart went out to him. He looked drained. He slept through the day, played with the girls for awhile Saturday evening, and slept soundly all night. Sunday morning he lingered over breakfast, asked how things were, and prepared to leave again. I was hungry for a sign, a gesture, a touch, anything that would assure me he still loved me. I missed the days long past—had they ever existed, or was my memory somehow skewed?—when he would confide in me, tell me how it was going. But that was long over.

"Honey," I called out as he opened the door, "you forgot your coat, it's beginning to cool down at night." And as I handed it to him, I tiptoed up to his mouth and planted a kiss on those cool lips, determined to break through the business-like barrier he had shown me since his transfer.

He slipped his arm around my waist and pulled me—for just a second—close to him. "Don't worry," he murmured. "It will be all right." And he kissed me quickly and quietly. My heart thudded in my chest.

We turned together to go outside. That's when we saw Lori, watching us with her mouth gaping open.

Vic walked calmly, purposefully to his truck, never missing a step. "Take care of yourself, Sis," he said, and waved goodbye.

"Hi, Lori," I stammered, wondering how long she had been standing there. "Come on in." *God, what did she see? I've got to explain. Got to cover up.*

I reached for a couple of mugs and poured out coffee, my hands trembling. Lori said nothing to break the silence, just sat down with an inquiring look in her trusting blue eyes. Lori had the biggest, clearest eyes I had ever seen, as wide and innocent as a baby's. She was as honest a person as I'd ever known, with a heart that reached out and gathered you in without question. I knew she wouldn't ask the obvious. I knew I had to say something.

"You know," I stated, my voice low and intimate. She just looked at me, her eyes filling with compassion as well as questions.

"Lori, I—I don't know what to say," I searched for a way out of this, a way to explain those spousely kisses between siblings. I couldn't bear for her, my friend, to think the worst.

"You don't have to say anything, Stephani," she said. "I never really believed he was the children's uncle, anyway."

"But I want you to understand. It's not like it appears. We just can't let anybody know we're married."

"I won't tell, if that's what you're worried about."

My own eyes filled with tears. I reached out to her, touching her hand on the table. "Thank you, Lori. I wish I could explain. It's not anything illegal, or bad. I just can't tell you…"

"It's okay, Stephani. I'm here for you. Don't worry." And the bond between us grew, as Lori became an integral part of my life.

I trusted her instinctively, knowing she would never betray us. I'd never experienced such friendship before, nor have I since. I've come to believe that she and the Angel were inexplicably linked, part of that dark winter in the woods.

Vic continued to treat me with ambivalence, coming home on the weekends with little communication during the week. He bought an old red Chevy pickup, the second in a series of three red trucks, leaving me with our reliable Oldsmobile. The truck's heater didn't work, nor did the windshield wipers, but he said he would fix them when he had time.

As the winter snows approached, I thought of him driving out there alone on the highway with nothing to keep him warm. I did not doubt, would not allow myself to think that he was anything but alone. I had learned my lesson; I wouldn't, couldn't think otherwise. I prayed for his safekeeping, prayed he would always come home to us.

And now, since I'd seen the Angel, I knew that God had not abandoned me. I hadn't even had a warning that I was getting sick that weekend. I never got sick, hardly ever even caught a cold. But Tiffany had once had a bout of rheumatic fever, and her tonsils bothered her every winter. Cat and Deanna were prone to catch the sore throats from Tiff. I doctored them and fretted over them until they recovered, but it wasn't anything unusual. Vic didn't believe in seeing a doctor unless you were on death's door, so I never mentioned such mundane things to him. The children were my responsibility, anyway. He didn't have time.

Thank God for Lori, I told myself. *Thank You, God, for Lori*, I repeated to the deity. *And thank you for the Angel.*

I returned to work, shaken by the knowledge of our isolation. Until now, I had felt there was a purpose for this madness, a reason for the sacrifice. I had vowed to be strong, to help my husband, and, in the process, help my country. The years had crept by, almost unnoticed. Now I asked, are the sacrifices worth the price? Will our children ever know their father? Or will he die before we ever have a chance for a normal life?

There was no one to ask these questions. I had only God, God and the Angel, to look to. But she didn't come back, and God was silent. I had to stay alert, by myself, to danger.

ASK ME NO QUESTIONS

It was a bright day in November, when the leaves were orange and red and brown and the chill of fall had not yet turned into the frigid cold of winter, that I had another glimpse into the forbidden.

He had arrived home with the usual load of laundry and red-lined eyes: I thought I would surprise him by cleaning his Chevy while he slept. Vic had never been a neat person, always leaving his tools just as he discarded his clothing. The cab of the truck reflected that habit, with mail and bills and dirty rags lying about on the seat and floor. After collecting and sorting everything, I opened the glove compartment to leave some of the mail inside—Vic didn't like me to handle any of it, had never let me become involved in household budgeting. As I slipped the wad of envelopes into the box, I noticed more junk inside. Torn papers. Blue. Like a greeting card. I put the handful of mail on the seat, reached in to gather up these bits of scrap, and that's when the words caught my eye:

craving for peanut butter, so the baby

this little guy, he's getting bigger

my mother, so you can come

A knot formed fast in my stomach, clutching at my innards until I felt as if a giant tong had reached out to squeeze my body into a tight ball. Carefully I searched for the pieces, finding scraps of blue paper under screwdrivers and old rent receipts, until I had a mound of ragged two-inch squares across which floated the damning words I did not want to read. But read them I did, piecing them together until the whole sordid story poured out before me. It gave me little real information; it was a love letter, full of pat phrases and smooshy words that implied a relationship I did not want to acknowledge. Never once was his name mentioned, never once did it say "your baby" but I knew. I knew what I did not want to know.

She didn't sign her name, just some idiot nickname I had never heard. The envelope was gone, there was no return address. Yet it had to be Camille. It had to be Vic. Why else would it be in this truck? *Wait, Stephani! Slow down. Breathe. Think. Whatever it looks like, whatever it says, it could be something else. It's probably in code. Yes! Remember, the letters you used to write, the love letters to Vicki? Remember? That's what this is, that's what this has to be! Trust. That's what it's all about, Stephani. Trust. Love is trust.*

Ashamed of my thoughts, ashamed of my doubt, terrified of the truth, I put the pieces back in the box and closed the door on them. He would never know I saw them.

Winter closed upon us. Christmas slipped by, with Vic making an obligatory appearance late on the twenty-fifth. Despite his hasty assurance months before that "it will be all right," he had continued to be distant and aloof. Occasionally he'd reach for me in the darkness of our bedroom; otherwise, he was a stranger. I fought to maintain my strength, struggled to remember words of love spoken so long ago, prayed and straightened my back literally and figuratively, and prayed some more.

At Christmas, the children shrieked with pleasure when their father opened the door, his arms laden with boxes and bags. "Ho, ho, ho!" he huffed, dropping the gifts as the girls launched into him. I let them have their Christmas, let the excitement flow into the little house, remaining on the sidelines as I watched Santa Claus charm three little girls with the wonder of Christmas. Too late for dinner, he played with them for a very few minutes, tucked them into bed, and left, his old truck protesting as he drove off in minus-fifty-degree weather. Briefly, the shadow of the Angel flirted into my mind: I whispered a prayer and began to clean up the remnants of wrapping paper, shopping bags, and cardboard boxes.

A piece of shopping bag floated into view: "St. Pa," I read. I searched for the rest of the bag, the fragment clutched in my hand. St. Paul. Had Vic gone shopping in St. Paul? Why? What would he have been doing 250 miles away?

But even if I found the rest of the bag, what would be the point? What would it tell me? I gave up finally and went to bed. But I did not sleep.

I was working on a patient chart on a sub-zero afternoon in January when my fears returned to plague me full force.

I looked up from the charts to see Lori walking toward me; the whisper of her uniform had alerted me to her approach. The carpet may have muffled her footsteps, but I sensed a wariness in her stride that was unusual. In that instant, I knew the Angel had reached out to slap me into reality.

"What is it?" I asked.

Her face was solemn, the sparkle in her blue eyes dimmed. "There's been an accident," she said. "Vic's downstairs in Emergency."

The silence of the surgical wing swooshed in about my ears.

"Is he all right?" I asked as calmly as I could, the words barely rising above the quiet. I watched her eyes as she answered.

"There's been some injury to his head. They're not sure how serious yet."

Taking a deep, slow breath, I averted my eyes to the paperwork in front of me. What do I do now? What is "proper" for a sister to do in a situation like this? *Not too much emotion...some, but not too much.* "Can I go down and see him?" I asked.

"Come down with me," Lori replied. "I'll take you."

ASK ME NO QUESTIONS

Gratefully I left my desk, letting Sherry, the charge nurse, know that my "brother" was being treated downstairs. Frowning, Sherry nodded curtly. "Hope he's okay," she called after me.

The swish of two uniforms moving in unison was all I heard as Lori and I walked to the elevator. The unspoken secret lay between us. *Vic is my husband!* I cried. *I know,* she replied. Our minds melded, uncannily, as they so often did during our short friendship. No words were needed. She knew.

Reaching the emergency room, Lori directed me toward the gurney on which Vic lay.

He looked dead.

His fair skin had not lost all color, but it was grey, with the veins in his forehead casting a bluish haze beneath the epidermal layers. So seldom was he still, so seldom in repose, it was as if I was viewing the body of a stranger. Without the vitality of his personality, he was just—a body.

"Vic," I whispered, not daring to touch him. I wanted to touch him! I wanted to feel his pulse beneath that grey skin. Was it cold? Would I feel warmth? I wanted to know that he was alive.

"Excuse us, miss." The x-ray technician brushed me aside, taking the head of the gurney as another technician moved to the foot. Together they wheeled my husband away.

"Where are you taking him?" I called. "Where are you going?"

"Just to x-ray," the head man replied. "We'll be back shortly. You'll have to talk to his doctor."

I felt a hand on my shoulder. "Come on," Lori said, her fingers squeezing in encouragement." Let's go get a cup of coffee."

"But Sherry—"

"Sherry can wait a few minutes. Let's go."

Numbly I followed her, my mind screaming questions. *What am I going to tell them? They'll want information. They'll want to know more than I can tell them. Can they find out? Can they discover the truth?*

The coffee was black and strong. I smelled its strength, I felt its heat. But it had no taste in my mouth. It burned, but it didn't have any flavor.

"Steph?"

I heard her voice; I had an obligation to answer her, to respond. She was my friend. "Sorry," I said. "Guess I spaced out." I felt my mouth stretch into a weak smile.

"It's okay. He's going to be all right. Hang in there."

Tears began to well up in my eyes. I couldn't face a life without him. Blinking fiercely, I forced the panic down, swallowed it hard as I fought for control. "He's got to be all right."

Reaching over the table, my friend grasped my hand. She felt warm. Was Vic warm? "Pull yourself together, Steph," she cautioned. "I don't know what's going on, but I know you have to be strong. I'm here for you. Tim's here, too." The pressure of her hand was reassuring.

"Thanks, Lori." Again I smiled, mustering enough courage to look at the worry in her eyes. "I'll be all right. Thanks for being my friend."

We rose together, tossing the styrofoam cups in the garbage and returning to our respective floors. Vic was in God's hands now. He had to be okay.

They sent my husband to Fargo for further treatment, his head injury requiring the skills of a neurologist. As the next of kin, I was allowed to call and visit, allowed to express the proper concern and be told the appropriate information concerning his treatment. But I could not tell him I loved him. I could not hold him in my arms and feel the comfort of his body, nor give him the strength of mine. *I'm sorry*, I cried, *sorry for doubting you. I promise, I promise! I'll never doubt you again!* Alone, more alone than ever before, I held my children, let them see the smile that hid the tears, and prayed—I begged—for his recovery. And the Angel haunted me, for I knew now that it was the Angel of Death.

But it was not yet time for Death to win. God had plans for us still: a week after the accident, Vic returned home, bandages around his head and weakness slowing his body. But he was alive, he would heal. His mind was intact.

I, however, had to save my relief and joy for another day. I had other worries. On the very day that Vic returned home, I was called into the hospital administrator's office.

Donald Farrell was a young man, a barely-into-his-thirties success story. Detroit Lakes Community was his first hospital. He was tall, fair-haired, blue-eyed, and known for his fair dealings with employees. I had always felt nothing but support from him, had even thought that, since he gave me the job, he was somehow connected to the Company. It never occurred to me that I'd been hired on my own merits.

"Come in, Stephani," he invited cordially as I stood outside his office door. He sat behind the desk, gesturing to a seat directly across from it.

As I sat on the edge of the straight-back chair, I felt all the questions rising within me. *What do you know? Are you a part of the team? Were you told to give me the job? What am I supposed to tell you?* Farrell was staring rather perplexedly at the view outside his window, his hands steepled together in concentration. I waited.

ASK ME NO QUESTIONS

Silence pervaded the cubbyhole of a room he called an office. I clasped my hands together in my lap, the knuckles gleaming white.

"You've been a good employee, Stephani. I hope we can continue to expect the best from you."

"Of course," I replied. What's coming next? I wondered. I'd missed very little work while Vic was in the hospital. I'd remained calm when people asked about my "brother."

"I need to know why you lied to me."

"Lied?" My heart leaped to my throat.

"I understand that Victor Brian is your husband." His eyes remained on my face.

My cheeks grew hot as the flush rose from my chest, spread to my neck, and burned its way to my forehead. *How can I to bluff my way through this? Maybe it's a trick. Maybe he's testing me. Oh, God, help me! What am I supposed to say?*

"National security is one thing," Donald continued, "but lying to your employer is a serious offence. You could have taken me into your confidence."

"I don't know what you're talking about," I heard myself saying. Strangely, my voice sounded calm. "I don't have anything to confide."

Donald Farrell continued his assault on my nerves with a steady, calculating stare. Suddenly he rose, strode to the door and threw it open. "Get back to work," he barked, dismissing me curtly. And I exited as bewildered as I had entered, getting no satisfaction when I sought an answer in his eyes. He was not going to tell me what he intended to do, if anything. I just had to sweat it out.

Of course I didn't know that whether I was married to Vic or not had no relevance to my employment. I lived in a world in which fear of discovery, fear of making a mistake, fear of Vic's anger, ruled my every thought and action. I thought that perhaps Donald Farrel was an "enemy," one of "them." When he didn't do anything after our interview, I thought that perhaps he had been asked by the Company to "cooperate." The Company, after all, held my life in its hands, mine and Vic's and three innocent little girls'. I lived from one crisis to another, constantly defending my family from harm. How was I to know what was Company business and what was merely life? It was all the same to me. Everyone was an enemy.

Chapter 27

Spring began to thaw the winter's cold. No longer did we need to plug our cars in at night to keep the oil from freezing: no more did I worry that Vic would plunge headlong over the icy roads to his death. Nor did I think about St. Paul or Camille or babies or love letters. Vic was alive, he was home with his family. The spectre of the Angel began to fade, and I adjusted to warmer days, a busy ward, and the juggling of babysitters. Donald Farrell didn't fire me, didn't bring retribution for my lies. Vic's job at the Wrangler was over; there would be a new assignment once he was fully recovered.

He began to reacquaint himself with his children. Tiffany was a lively first-grader, a tall, bony little sprite with flying strands of white-blonde hair. Cat, at three-going-on-four, was impossible to keep corralled. One day I would find her at the top of the oak tree in our front yard, the next day she would be in the midst of the pine trees in the back. Deanna tried to keep up with her siblings, her sturdy two-year-old legs propelling her as fast as she could move them, but most often she would end up far behind, her howls of anguish ignored. On warm days Vic took them fishing with him, otherwise he left them to their own devices. One day I came home to find he had given them all haircuts, little bowl-cuts with ragged edges that made them look like the orphans they were.

We moved from the snug little cottage at the end of a lane to a big box farmhouse, a two-story monstrosity that had no electricity or indoor plumbing. But it was on a hundred acres of rolling Minnesota hills, and when the sun rose over the eastern side and shone on the house, it lit the yard like a halo, making each little blade of grass stand at attention and sing "Hallelujah!"

And it had a barn.

One day Vic came home with a horse, an albino mare named Jezebel. She wasn't much to look at, but she was gentle enough for the girls to ride three at a time. Soon another horse joined our stables, a Shetland pony heavy with foal, followed by a Welsh pony stallion, and then a two-year-old Moroccan Arabian, also a stallion. I don't know how Vic paid for these animals, or how much, if anything at all. He had a way of acquiring things that required no cash, and I knew better than to ask. I just enjoyed them as I had not enjoyed anything since the first year of our marriage.

It was good that I had them, for there was little else for me to enjoy. My relationship with my boss was still tenuous, Lori was strangely distant, and Vic's convalescence began to erode an already strained relationship.

Vic's idea of parenthood differed vastly from mine. With Vic there were no in-betweens: there was right and wrong, black and white, play and rest. At home he mostly played, and as long as he was having fun, the children were allowed to have fun right along with him. But when he was tired, they were supposed to be quiet, to stay out of his way and let him rest. They could do whatever they wanted, as long as they left him alone.

I returned from work to a daily sight of unwashed dishes, food left on the table, clothes tossed on furniture or the floor, and general pandemonium. The girls may or may not be within earshot, and Vic was usually taking a nap. Outside was no less self-defeating. Vic had decided to raise chickens and had bought 200 chicks, which he'd put in one of the outbuildings. The dogs, of which we had ten—our black lab bitch had whelped—had discovered what great sport chasing chickens could be, and spent their days digging holes under the fence surrounding the shed. Once a dog tastes the delight of young chicken bones, there is no stopping them. It fell to me to fix the fence, punish the dogs, and clean up the mess. None of which was my forte.

The spark of confidence I'd begun to feel diminished as the need to make small decisions was usurped by my omniscient husband. Each day I left a world in which I was given a modicum of respect by my peers, and entered into a world in which I commanded not even a token nod of it. The confidence was replaced by a growing confusion as I waited for Vic to heal and to forgive me—for what?—and to become once again the man I'd fallen in love with.

I was little more than a drudge, a slave to the house and the children and the man I'd sworn to love. I see that now. But then—well, then I was too tired, most of the time, to think clearly. Too frightened to question. Too confused to do anything to change the course of our lives. Vic's commitment to his country—my country—overshadowed any thoughts of personal happiness. In my mind, my husband was making the biggest sacrifice, while I at least had my children, a job, a chance to touch normality. I counted my blessings.

The horses were my escape, my attempt to recapture the sense of belonging in a world I'd lost years before. I took my painted stallion into the hills and gave myself up to the sights and sounds of nature around me: the steady beat of Meshak's hooves on the ground, the wind's whisper through the long grass, the birds talking to each other in the treetops. Peace. Reality. Contact with all I had meant to be and all that I had lost. And then, rejuvenated, I would return home.

Vic did not like my absences. Suspicious by nature, he accused me of meeting someone out there in the hills, leaving my children to fall into danger while I played, conscienceless, with my lover. I had long since learned that no amount of logic would sway him, no tears would soften his heart. Stoically I accepted his judgment, and silence would be my sentence. Days of silence. Nights in which he would turn to my body and take what was his without one endearment or one gentle touch.

Finally I abandoned my rides on Meshak, concentrating instead on the Welsh stallion. I broke him in the paddock near the house, in sight of Vic should he care to watch. The horse's wildness matched my mood, his desperate attempts to unseat me a challenge I could meet. I rode bareback, having no tack but a halter and a rope with which to guide him. Together we fought the demons that raged within.

When Vic decided that my punishment for imagined transgressions had the desired effect, life returned to normal.

"Normal" was confusion.

Vic was not used to idleness: as he regained his energy, his frustration grew. The Company had not yet reassigned him, so the absence of the "boys" was a point of frustration, too. Our status as brother and sister was technically on hold, but we could not suddenly emerge as husband and wife. In short, we were in limbo, trying to assume a normalcy neither one of us could comprehend. Our life had never been "normal."

The waiting began to pull us apart.

"Can't you do anything right?" he yelled, his voice loud enough to drown out the squeals emanating from the yard where the girls swung on their tire swings. "I told you to have lunch ready when I got home!" The trout hanging on the line were flung into the kitchen sink. Some of them flopped frantically as they gasped their final breaths.

"I'm sorry, Vic, I just had to fix the chicken fence before the dogs got in," I said, dodging past him toward the stove as I recognized the beginnings of another raging verbal storm.

I didn't make it.

ASK ME NO QUESTIONS

"Why do you always have excuses?" He growled in my face, his hand gripping my arm as he swung me toward him. "No matter what I tell you to do, you always have an excuse."

"I'm sorry, Vic! The dogs were getting into the chicken pen. Do you want them all killed?"

"That's not the question! The question is, 'Why isn't lunch ready?' God, I work my butt off so you can have food on the table, and you can't even have a decent meal waiting for me when I get home!"

The incongruity of the question didn't enter my mind: I was the one working while he went fishing. He didn't even like fish all that much, and usually gave it all away. And I had no idea when he would return home, so how could I know when to have lunch ready? But this was not the time to think. This was the time to appease.

"I'll get it right away. What do you want? The fish?"

"No, I don't want the fish. Fix something with that beef roast. God, do I have to cook, too?"

He dropped my arm, and I held my breath as he stomped into the bedroom, throwing his tee shirt on the floor on his way. I could always follow the trail of Vic's path through the house by picking up his clothes.

But I didn't pick them up now. As he flopped onto the bed with a cigarette dangling from his lips, I dared to rub my arm, the arm which carried his fingerprints in mottled blue skin, and slowly expelled my breath. In a few minutes I had the fire stoked in the stove and the meat browning in a pan.

After lunch, I set the dishes in the sink, heated water for the girls to wash the dishes, and, after getting Tiffany started on the chore, went outside to feed Meshak and the others. It was still early in the afternoon, the sun high in the west, but I needed the distraction, and Vic was napping.

The Shetland mare was lying in the straw in one of the big stalls, a tiny bundle of long, delicate legs visible beside her. "Oh, Holly," I whispered excitedly. "You've had your baby!" The little mare looked at me contentedly as her long tongue gently washed her foal.

I had to get the girls. They had to see this.

I whirled and ran toward the big barn doors, stumbling in the dim light as I hurried to get the children. They had to see the miracle! "Girls, come here!" I ran, the barn as familiar to me as my kitchen. Except that I didn't realize the barn beams were so low. As I raced toward the door, a slender beam of light showing the way, I cracked my head full force on one of those beams.

It dropped me where I stood.

I awoke, dazed, the sounds in the barn muffled as they filtered through the numbness in my skull. How long had I been unconscious? Moments or hours? My head roared with pain just above my right ear. Clamping my teeth together, I found the floorboards with my hands and pushed against them. *Up. Have to get up.* My legs obeyed sluggishly. Nausea and dizziness fought against me, my body a thing apart from my limbs. Gritting harder, I pushed again, inhaling deeply as I fought my way to a standing position. *There. I can do this.*

Slowly moving toward the filtered light threading through the door, I staggered to the opening, fighting the pain and the nausea with every step. When I reached the door, I stood with my hands on the rough boards for minutes while I steadied myself. The nausea receded, dulling to a manageable level. The whirling slowed.

It seemed strange to walk into the afternoon sunlight, to see that the world hadn't changed in the last few minutes. My world seemed different, as if a lifetime had passed in those seconds while I lay on the floor of the barn. But everything outside continued as before. The children were in the house, finishing the noontime dishes. Vic was inside also, napping. The fish were still on the counter in a cold bucket, awaiting cleaning. Nothing had changed.

Slowly I made my way to the bucket of fish, grabbed a knife from the drawer and headed back out the door. "When you've finished cleaning up, I have a surprise for you," I told my daughters. Three eager faces turned toward me, eyes begging for more. "I'll tell you when you're done," I said. I couldn't trust my voice yet; it hurt to talk, hurt to breathe, hurt to keep my eyes open. But the nausea was diminishing. I went back into the sunshine listening to the excited whispers behind me. They would be out in seconds, wanting to know the surprise. Meanwhile, I cleaned the fish, fighting the nausea and the lights that twinkled in front of my eyes. My chore was interrupted within minutes, as my children rushed out to see the surprise. The pony foal was promptly named "Hoss" by Deanna, who plopped down beside the baby and wrapped her chubby arms about its neck, momma looking on indulgently. I snapped a picture of the event and cautioned the girls to beware the protective instincts of the new mother, although she seemed to enjoy their excitement as much as the rest of the herd did.

I left them to finish cleaning the fish, the picture of their wonder a balm to my mother's heart. *Life is made up of moments,* I thought. *Little moments that make everything else worth the pain.* I carried that picture with me for many months, returning to it whenever the current moment became unbearable.

The sun was setting behind the westward hills that evening when the dizziness returned. It was nearly imperceptible, so slowly did it overcome me. I was working in the yard beside the house, pulling the weeds from around the fragile stems of flowers I had planted weeks before. The sun felt warm at my back. The pain had dulled to a steady throb above my right ear, knifing occasionally behind my eyes but generally bearable. Vic had napped throughout the afternoon and the children played near Hoss, his newness a magnet to their innocent delight in the miracle of birth. It was so peaceful, so unlike my life. Perhaps the bump on my head really did change things. Perhaps I had entered a twilight world, an alternate reality…

I awoke to noise, noisy voices calling out orders and noisy wheels as gurneys and wheelchairs squeaked by me. Noise that felt familiar and unwelcome. Clanging as someone bumped the side of a medicine cart against the wall close by my head. Noise that almost overpowered the sound of my heart beating in my brain.

"Stephani?"

A light burned on the other side of my eyelids. A rocket burst behind my eyes, the pain bouncing off my skull.

"Go away," I said, my voice reverberating through the chambers in my head. My body lay like lead, heavy and inert, lifeless.

"Stephani, open your eyes."

"Go away," I repeated.

Suddenly there were fingers on my eyelids, prying them open. The light increased.

"Go away!" I said again, flopping hands flapping at the light. "That hurts!"

"Stay awake, Stephani." The voice encouraged. "We're taking you in for x-rays."

I felt the jerking beneath me as the gurney upon which I lay began to move. The floor of the hospital was smooth, yet I could feel the wheels as they moved over it. *Curious*, I thought. *Like the Indians with their ears to the ground.* Then the feeling and the sound faded, and the pain receded.

The concussion was termed "mild" but was serious enough for them to keep me abed for a week. It was strange to be a patient in the same hospital where I worked, embarrassing to have the doctor for whom I charted orders poke and prod, and the nurses with whom I transcribed those orders record my most intimate bodily functions.

I had never been so pampered. I was very proud of my self-reliance: my previous visits to hospital were merely for the births of my children, brief journeys through labor and delivery rooms and on home again. My longest stay for childbirth had been a total of thirty-two hours; this week was a retreat from everyday cares I could easily get used to.

I especially relished the showers. Since we had no running water in our house, the simple task of showering was a luxury. I lingered over this morning routine as long as I dared, standing in the hot water until my body fell with ease into total relaxation. I had never felt so clean.

Vic visited once, bringing in a bouquet of spring flowers and kissing me nervously while he kept one eye on the door. Hospitals made him nervous. Upon my release, he waited in the car at the hospital entrance and drove me home hurriedly, as if escaping a prison camp.

I was remanded to his care with guarded instructions. "No work for two more weeks," Dr. Campbell warned. "You are to stay in bed and rest. You'll have to have someone help you with the chores and the children." He shook his finger in my face. "I mean it, young lady. No work."

I nodded, wondering how I was to follow his orders once I was beyond his watchful eye.

"Come on, Stephani," Vic said the next morning. "I need to get going. Eat your breakfast and I'll take the plate away. Do you want another cup of coffee?"

"No, honey, thanks. I'm floating now. Where are you headed today?"

"I have a meeting," he said hurriedly. From his tone I knew it was Company business and I'd better not ask. "Will you be alright?"

"Sure," I answered, happy to be home with my family. "Tiffany's off to school, isn't she?"

"Yeah, she nearly missed the bus. You have to get on that girl. I can't handle her." Taking the half-empty plate from my lap, he gave me a peck on the cheek and turned to go. "See you later, babe. Take it easy today."

I heard him close the door on his way out, heard the sputter of his red pickup as he started it and drove down the drive. In another few minutes, the sounds of Cat and Deanna playing upstairs reached my ears as their feet thumped on the floorboards above my head.

I was home, safely ensconced in my own bed. It didn't matter that I would not get to stay there, as Dr. Campbell had ordered. The throbbing had diminished, I had pills for the pain, and the dizziness occurred only when I moved quickly. I could handle it.

I lounged for some fifteen or so minutes more, sipping my warm coffee and relishing the feeling of staying in bed without feeling guilty. But in too short a time

ASK ME NO QUESTIONS

I felt the need to find the outhouse, and I slipped out of bed and made my way into the morning sun.

By the end of the day I was more than a little worn out and a lot resentful at Vic's absence. I had taken it as easy as I could, pacing my energy throughout the day, alternating between simple household chores and children. We always needed water in the house, so the five-gallon buckets had to be filled from the well. Though we needed just two buckets, this job took me nearly an hour, as the well was down behind the barn. My head throbbed and the dizziness returned while I performed the task.

The horses had to be fed and watered: Jezebel, the albino mare, had surprised us with a foal while I was in the hospital. It was a gangly white colt that we named Abednego. Unlike Hoss, "Abby" kept his distance, running from the children when they attempted to make friends.

I left the weeding for later, as well as any chores concerning the chickens. They were Vic's project, after all. He should have taken care of them before he left. Neither did I make the trip upstairs to face the girls' rooms. I knew they would be a mess.

By dinnertime I had the house nearly shipshape and a load of clothes on the line. It was overwhelming what a week away did to a house.

Vic returned late in the evening, long after Deanna and Cat were in bed. Tiffany was mulling over homework in the living room, and I had collapsed into an easy chair near the front window. My head whirled with exhaustion.

I heard the sounds of my husband open the front door, heard him walk past the living room into our bedroom. I kept my eyes closed, unwilling to make the effort to either open my lids or get out of the chair.

"Hi, Daddy," I heard Tiffany say solemnly. She was always on uncertain ground with her father, had been since the years in San Remos when she had been told he was her uncle. Poor little girl, no wonder she was a problem. She had lost her identity when she lost her father.

"Hi, Tiff," I heard him reply. He sounded preoccupied. *Oh, well,* I thought. *His focus on the Company will keep him off Tiffany's back for a while. She can slip off to bed unnoticed.*

"Stephani?" he called.

Unwillingly, I raised my voice in reply. "Hi, honey," I answered. "Would you like some dinner?"

"No," he said shortly. "I would like you to come here."

Groaning inwardly, I delayed moving. It was so nice to just…sit. My head was thumping with every heartbeat, the squish-squish of my lifeblood flowing through that muscle magnified inside my cranial cavity. The bed in the next room squeaked as my husband lay down upon it.

"Stephani."

"Coming."

I touched my daughter gently as I passed her, kissed her softly and said, "Don't you think it's time you went to bed, too?"

She turned her sky-blue eyes upon me, wrapped her bony arms about my neck, and squeezed hard. "Goodnight, Mommy," she said. "I hope you feel better tomorrow." My skull pounded, the pressure rising as she pulled on my neck in a fierce hug. I braced my hand against the back of her chair as I fought the pain, kissed her again, and bid her goodnight. She scrambled from the chair, leaving her notebook on it as she headed up the stairs. Blowing out the lantern, I joined my husband in the dark bedroom.

Chapter 28

"We're going back to the West."

The words were blunt, the tone determined. Vic sat at the kitchen table, picking at the remains of the evening meal. He'd just returned from a week's absence, a meeting with his team. He was nearly well: it was time to go back to work.

The bucket I held over the sink jerked as his words brought me short. Hot water splashed back at me. "When do you want to be ready?" The sink once again began to fill as I poured the water, heated on the wood stove, in preparation for washing the dishes.

"As soon as possible. You can give notice at the hospital to coincide with the end of your sick leave."

"That's just two weeks."

"Yeah, that's about right." Vic reached for the last of the potatoes, cleaning out the bowl.

I thought of all that would need to be done…the horses and chickens, the packing…it wouldn't be easy to get ready in such a short time.

"We'll sell the horses," he stated, as if he had read my mind. "And we can butcher the chickens and sell them too. I'll put the word out at the store." The "store" was the Country Crossroads cafe and grocery store, a vital link between neighbors in the rural community. The Crossroads grapevine substituted for a newspaper. Whenever anyone wanted to know anything, they would just go to the Crossroads.

"Where are we going?" I asked nervously.

Vic didn't answer. Ignoring me, he finished his dinner, got up from the table, and walked out the front door.

Later, I asked again, trying a different tack.

"It'll be nice to have running water again," I said, as I settled next to him in the double bed. "And spring is a good time to move. Maybe the girls will have a chance to see their grandparents." My parents had moved to Arizona, to an area I had not yet seen. We'd kept in touch over the years—sporadic, no-nonsense, notes that told the bare essentials and left all the important things unsaid—but our relationship had never really recovered from the estrangement our secrets had created. "Maybe we can stop and visit them on our way."

"We'll do more than that," Vic replied. "We're going to be living real close. We're going to the same area."

"Oh, Vic, that's wonderful! I'll get started right away."

"Get your letter in to the hospital tomorrow. You'll have to butcher the chickens. I'll be busy."

The next few days were a blur of packing, telephoning and thinking ahead to all the possibilities. With the excitement came the doubts, the worry over a myriad of niggling thoughts. *Will Mom and Dad still accept us? How will we be able to live close to them and still keep our secret?* How could I cover for Vic's absences, his unpredictable life? Of course, they knew something was out of the ordinary, they had been told part of the story back in San Remos, but had they forgiven me for deceiving them?

A few days later I whispered goodbye to Meshak, hugging him with a last, lingering caress before the buyers came to pick him up. There had been no question about taking him with me. *Just like my piano,* I thought as I released him to the new owners. *I'm always saying goodbye.* This was the second time I'd had to leave horses behind; I'd left two pianos over the years. Refusing to let tears betray my feelings, I forced a smile as Hoss, Holly, Abby, Jezebel, Red and Meshak were herded into a trailer and pulled away behind a big blue truck.

The chickens were the hardest to get rid of. I began the chore of feather-plucking immediately, and with the long days of my recuperation in front of me, killed, plucked and cleaned over 200 of the squawking fowl by the deadline Vic had set.

Lori had all but deserted me since Vic's accident. Despite several attempts to talk with her, I could not find out why my friend was so cool. She just wouldn't talk. We left Minnesota without even a goodbye to the woman who had saved my life. I'd attended my exit interview with Mr. Farrell feeling as though I was under a cloud, a cloud of distrust and suspicion. But there were no answers.

Once again we were running, although whether running to or from I no longer knew. I had to assume the order to move had come from Vic's superiors.

We treated the trip West as a vacation, a short reprieve from the tensions in our life. We meandered across the Midwest, going south from Minnesota through the Indian country of the Dakotas, then west through Nebraska. Vic had relatives in southwestern Nebraska, dairy farmers whom he hadn't seen for over a decade. The visit was pleasant and uneventful, but Vic's delight in "Cornhusker" country gave me several anxious days. He strutted around the elder Brian's home, basking in the false joy that such reunions often bring. I reminded him as discreetly as I could that we were on our way home, for that's how I thought about this coming reunion of my own. Home was family. My family. I wanted to see them more than ever. I wanted to feel loved again.

We left Nebraska at last, driving in a southerly direction, cutting through Kansas, Oklahoma, and Texas. At Amarillo we turned west, enjoying the heat in scenic New Mexico. Unlike the roads that had steadily taken us eastward, this trip simmered with happiness, with hope and high spirits. Vic was light-hearted and carefree; the years seemed to melt from his face as the miles sped by. I put the years behind me, too, the years of fear and worry and confusion. Doubt and suspicion and resentment were cast aside consciously and deliberately as I embraced the newness of this journey, determined to hang on to this joy. I would not question the happiness I felt then. I would just bask in it for whatever time we had together.

Finally we reached central Arizona, where my parents had established a new home shortly after the San Remos debacle. We arrived, travel-weary but joyous, anticipating a renewed relationship with my parents and young brother. In a matter of days, Vic began working at his new job in the resort town of Sedona, about sixty miles from my parents' home in Prescott.

I had a new job, too. Vic offered my services to his boss, the owner of Jake's, a kind of jack-of-all-trades job involving waiting on tables, bookkeeping, and hostessing. My pay was in tips; my hours were long. Jake's opened its doors at 6 a.m. and didn't close them until 10 p.m. But I didn't mind, not the hours or the lack of pay, for I was working with Vic. We were once again husband and wife. We were close to my family. The sun shone. I didn't question our good fortune, I just accepted it. The tension and confusion I'd felt in Minnesota dissipated as I threw myself into our new life.

Like most euphoria, it didn't last very long.

We moved to Sedona in June: by September the glow was already wearing off. The summer had been rejuvenating, with picnics and camp-outs as we joined my parents for a number of outings. But once school began and we were more restricted, the bubble began to fizzle. That little bit of independence I'd experienced in Minnesota raised its ugly head, and I found myself resenting the autocratic way in which my husband ordered my life. My children were beginning to act out their frustrations, too. The school called to report that

Tiffany was a problem child. I discovered that she was Seanping classes and lying about it. She was also neglecting her homework and mouthing off to the teacher. After a consultation with the principal, another with Tiff, I began to spend more time with my daughter. All of my children were feeling neglected, all a little confused about our new surroundings.

But Vic didn't like the attention I gave our children. More and more, he called me in to work whenever I was supposed to be at home. I couldn't please him, no matter what I did.

While I felt these things, these conflicting emotions in which I tried to hold on to the love we'd shared while holding down the resentment, I went about the days without voicing my feelings. With Vic, there was never any discussion, not just about feelings, but about anything. He was a man of action, not words. He lived on a "need-to-know" basis; consequently, so did I. Unfortunately, our personal life was conducted just as was his business life: impersonally. He gave the orders, I carried them out. Occasionally, we managed to reach beyond the daily order of business and actually touch each other's heart. It was those moments for which I lived. Moments in a lifetime awash with business as usual.

Thanksgiving approached, our first Thanksgiving with family. The restaurant closed for three days during the holiday, so we were free to go to my parents'. While there, Vic surprised me with a real holiday—a trip to Las Vegas. We left the girls with their grandparents and took off, pretending to be, once again, young lovers.

Las Vegas was fun, but it was the return trip I would remember. A blizzard impeded our travel as we drove toward Prescott. We decided to grab a motel room for the night, rather than be caught on the highway in the snow, so Vic called the owner of Jake's to report our delay. We were both due at work the following morning. "What?" I heard him say, his voice rising as it did when he became agitated. "When?"

I listened, curious, dreading the outcome. I'd heard so many such one-sided conversations. "We'll be there tomorrow," he concluded, hanging up.

"What was that all about?" I asked.

"Jake's was robbed during Thanksgiving," he replied, his voice thoughtful.

"What? Robbed? But how could that be? You don't keep money in the till when it's closed."

"They found the bank deposit sack I'd hidden," he said, as he switched on the television.

"You hid a bank deposit? Why? How did they find it?"

ASK ME NO QUESTIONS

"I put it there for Tom," he explained impatiently, his voice slowing in that I've-got-to-explain-everything-to-you tone. Tom Bolen was the owner of Jake's. "He was going to open today. I had to leave him money for the drawer." He flopped down on the bed, obviously exasperated with my stupidity. "The bank was closed for the holiday, remember?"

"Oh. Right. Where did you hide it?"

"I don't want to talk about it, Stephani. Let's just relax and enjoy one more night of our vacation."

I called my parents to let them know we were not out in the snowstorm and tried to put the robbery out of my mind. Vic was not about to share any more information with me.

The robbery became the focus of our attention for the following weeks. The police questioned Vic, but, curiously, not me. The cafe was abuzz with gossip, rumor, and speculation. Who did it? How had they known where to find the money? Vic had hidden it inside the milk machine, one of those monstrous metal tanks that held several gallons of milk. The robbers had apparently gotten in the building through a small window in the back of the kitchen. There was too much evidence that suggested someone familiar with the lay of the restaurant, the routine. Vic was asked to take a polygraph, which he passed. Eventually the police moved on to more recent crimes, more solvable puzzles. They never found the thief.

While all of the excitement was taking place, Vic's youngest brother George joined us. He appeared one day without warning and insinuated himself into our lives as if he belonged. He stayed in our house for a short time, but, thankfully, found his own place before he became a nuisance—which was fortunate, for Vic's schedule was becoming increasingly frantic.

I was so used to his comings and goings that I almost forgot the Company owned him. Months went by with no comment on his current assignment. What Vic did while I gave him a break from the Kitchen in the afternoons was a mystery to me. I was busy dealing with other problems, problems with the children and problems with their uncle.

George's invasion in our life was just one more complication I could easily do without. Not unexpectedly, Vic spent more time with him than he did with me. They took several trips to Las Vegas together, weekend jaunts in which they gambled and relaxed and did whatever guys do when they're away from the women in their lives. I didn't know how either of them could afford these trips: I'd never dealt with the bills, had no voice in our budget, so I really couldn't comprehend our financial situation, but I knew, from Vic's grip on household expenses, that money was tight. I'd gotten a call from the utilities company, and I'd put them off. When I told Vic they'd called, he'd said they could go "screw themselves," and assured me the check had been mailed.

George worked at Jake's, too, but he couldn't make much money. I suspected from conversations I'd overheard that George was not the most honest person I'd ever met. Not that he was a thief. I wouldn't go that far, but he was casual about other people's property, lived beyond his means, and laughed about his ability to con his acquaintances. And he took total advantage of his brother's absences.

By the time Christmas approached, I saw so little of my husband that I could not have told anyone where he was at any given time. He worked at the restaurant during the morning hours, took off in the afternoons for what I assumed was Company business, worked the evenings until closing, and disappeared for most of the night. It was during these nights that George would come over and keep me company for a while. The girls, especially Cat, loved "Uncle Georgie" and nearly always were rewarded with a raucous pillow fight or game of hide-and-seek.

Vic was less thrilled with his brother's visits.

"I don't want another man in my house, with my wife, when I'm not here!" he stormed.

"But he's your brother," I protested. "Your brother! What could you possibly object to?"

"He came in here the other night and you were in your nightgown. You didn't even bother to cover up!"

"He came in because you let him in. I didn't have time to cover up!"

Vic's hands closed on my arms as he shook me. "I want to know what's going on," he said, grinding the words from behind clenched teeth, "and I want to know now."

"Nothing! Nothing is going on! I don't even like your brother," I whimpered, the dread smothering me as I collapsed against his hands. "There's nothing going on."

"There'd better not be," he threw me from him. "There'd better never be."

He left then, and I remained slumped against the wall where I'd stumbled. I stayed there until the trembling stopped, and I wondered, as I did so many times, if my daughters had heard, if they were asleep and safely ignorant.

The next day George came over early in the morning, and he and Vic talked and joked and puttered with the cars as if they were the best of friends. How could Vic accuse me without also accusing his brother, I asked myself. How could he be so friendly with George and so hostile to me?

But I soon had other, more important things to worry about, for the disease which had stalked us all across America had followed us to Sedona; once again Vic was fired from his job. Accused by Tom Bolen of embezzling, less politely called "skimming," he was let go with neither notice nor cause. No one spoke to me about it. I heard only Vic's ravings at the injustice of it all and the pitying assurances of a customer who had, during the weeks since Thanksgiving, become first a "regular," then an almost-friend.

Masculine friends were always to be avoided, looked upon with suspicion. Kept at a distance. They only wanted one thing, as Vic constantly warned me. And I'd better not be giving it to them.

But Wayne Childress was gently persistent. Older than I by a generation, I believed he looked at me with a father's gentle eye. He knocked on my door the first day after I, along with my husband, became unemployed, and offered his support and friendship. And a loan.

"If you need anything, anything at all, please tell me," he said. "I want you to know I don't believe the stories."

"Thank you," I replied as I nervously handed him a cup of freshly brewed coffee. "I just can't believe anybody would even think such a thing." The memory of the Thanksgiving robbery skipped through my brain.

"I hope this doesn't embarrass you," Wayne was saying, "but things might be kind of tight for awhile…if you need a loan to tide you over…"

I flushed, the heat erupting as I suddenly saw myself through his eyes. "Oh, no," I said hastily, "we're fine. Really. Thank you, though."

We sipped our coffee in awkward silence, then Wayne stood up to leave. "I mean it," he said as he handed me his half-full cup. "If you need anything, let me know."

"Thanks. Thank you so much. I will."

"Don't let them get you down," he said as he stepped outside.

"I won't. Thank you."

He left, and I knew I'd never see him again.

I was alone in my misery. Sedona was a small town then, little more than a village. Hollywood megastars owned fancy homes hidden out in the red hills. Tourists passed through on their way to Phoenix or Flagstaff. Indian artifacts and New Age seminars gave the area a quirky mystique. My family and I were merely another story for the grist of gossip circulating through the stores strung along the highway, if we rated even that. We were newcomers, after all. No one really knew us. No one cared.

It seems unbelievable now that I couldn't hear the clamoring in my subconscious. Year after year, job after job, town after town, the pattern repeated. The fear and confusion slowly evolved into doubt and suspicion. The doubt came unreasonably, on the heels of fear. The development of suspicion was slow, interminably slow. I trusted him, had always trusted him, believed what he told me because I'd never had reason to disbelieve. And I had to have reason. I had to have proof. Whatever I doubted, Vic brandished proof. Whenever I questioned, he waved loyalty. Wherever I looked, there Vic resided. He was my life.

I could not believe he was a thief, this man who gripped my heart. He had no reason to steal. If we were ever truly short of money, surely he could dip into his savings from his Company employment. Surely, if we really needed money, there was enough in that bank in San Francisco to keep us happy for as long as was needed. Surely his pride would not keep him from telling me. And if Tom Bolen thought Vic was robbing him, why didn't he bring charges against him?

I need not have worried. Vic was rarely unemployed for more than a week. And now, now he got another job, as I knew he would.

"This gives me more mobility," he explained when he drove the delivery van—a bread delivery service, of all things—into the driveway. "I go all over Central Arizona. I've got specific people I'm supposed to keep an eye on."

I eyed the bread truck doubtfully. This was certainly a departure from managing a restaurant. But with the Company, you do as you're told. We both knew that.

We remained in Sedona only for only a few more weeks; Vic had found a lovely little ranch house situated on eleven acres in the valley near Cottonwood. George had rushed out of our lives one day in February, the Arizona State Police hot on his tail. They caught up with him at the Nevada-Arizona border, his truck filled with stolen goods. Unbeknownst to me, there was also a shed full of hot stuff just behind my garage…I let the police take whatever they wanted. At least they didn't think I was an accomplice.

We moved to the ranch in late February. I was grateful for the cool isolation of the place, thankful to put the shadow of Sedona behind us, even though Vic delivered bread to many of the same people we'd served as customers at Jake's. He didn't mind the talk, the rumors, the cool reception. He just shrugged it off as part of the job, part of life. Besides, most people didn't believe the gossip. Vic was too charming, too personable, too unassuming. No one could see him calmly pocketing money from the cash register. Perhaps no one gave him credit for having the brains to ring up a ticket and somehow lose the money without throwing the till off. He didn't come across that way. Only I had ever seen the cold-blooded stranger that lurked behind those golden eyes. And I couldn't even imagine him robbing his own employer. It would be like robbing himself.

The move seemed to lighten Vic's entire demeanor, as moving almost always did. He loved coming home now, loved working outdoors on the ranch. Soon we had collected three horses, and the girls were jostling about on Toby, an old grey mustang who had the patience to endure their wild urges while giving them a placid pace. I was presented with an elegant black mare Vic swore was an Arabian but who trotted like a pacer. And he rode Red, a muscular Appaloosa whose color announced his name.

The ranch was actually a campground; the acreage ran along the Cottonwood River, where small picnic areas had been gracefully insinuated into the landscape. During the summer months, these campsites were rented to church groups and clubs. Part of our rental contract was an agreement to manage and maintain the campgrounds. There was also an artesian spring which had been widened and lined with river rock to form a lovely, natural swimming pool, which we all used nearly every day. The pasture that held and fed the horses consisted of some five acres, off limits to the campers.

It seemed an ideal situation. Here, maybe we could heal. Maybe we could forget Sedona. Here, our new baby would be born, and we could be a family, shutting out the world beyond, shutting out the CIA and the enemy, and everybody else, too. It would be our own private oasis.

I was experiencing a difficult pregnancy. Unlike the previous three, this time I'd known I was pregnant almost immediately. One day I'd thought I was dying from the pain in my stomach, and I'd gone, unknown to Vic, to the doctor. He gave me the news of my pregnancy and then told me I had to change my diet if I wanted to deliver a healthy baby. "No salt," he said. "None. You have a toxic reaction to it. You'll lose the baby if you're not careful." So I knew I was pregnant, and I told Vic about it, hoping he would be happy. He still hoped for a son. This time, I told him. This time it'll be your son.

I prepared all my own food, unsalted, and I maintained a rigorous routine with the horses and the upkeep of the ranch.

It was June before the idyll became a nightmare. In June, Vic brought a woman home one day, a young, pretty brunette with sharp black eyes and a tentative smile. Her name was Vicky: and, like Vanessa of the past, she was working with my husband.

It started when Vic went to Flagstaff for the annual Pow-Wow. He needed to meet someone there, someone the Company was tracking down. Vic had been meeting with the guy for a month or more, working undercover, getting his confidence. The Pow-Wow, with all its attendant excitement, was an excellent background for the meeting. He was supposed to be gone for the afternoon—he was away for three days. There was no word from him, no coded phone calls, no messages delivered by a stranger. Nothing.

I was stiff with worry. I couldn't call the police for a Missing Persons report: I couldn't call attention to Vic. I couldn't tell anyone, if there had been anyone to tell. The girls didn't question their father's absence.

I stayed in the house near the phone, praying and weeping and wiping the tears surreptitiously when the girls were nearby. They couldn't know that something was wrong. I couldn't allow them to worry.

On the third day, Vic rolled into the long driveway, his shoulders drooping with exhaustion.

"Vic!" I ran to him, my six-months-pregnant body as yet no hindrance. I barely showed. "I was so worried! Are you all right?" I looked at him, stared at his face as if he'd been gone years instead of days. I saw the exhaustion written in the lines of his face.

"I'm fine," he said, leaning into me a little. "I'm just so tired."

We walked to the house together, our arms supporting each other. He headed for the bedroom, where he collapsed on the bed.

I began to untie his shoes, slipped them off his feet. "God, I can't remember," he mumbled.

"What? Can't remember what?" I asked.

"I don't know what happened," he muttered. "One minute I was in the crowd. I'd met with the guy. The next minute I'm in a car in the middle of nowhere. " His eyes searched mine. "I don't know where my pickup is. I don't know how I got in that car." He gestured toward the driveway, toward the car he'd driven home. It was a late-model two-door Cadillac, the kind of car I'd never dreamed of seeing in my driveway.

"You don't know how you got that car?" I asked incredulously.

"No…I can't remember anything. Three days are gone…I have to get back to Flagstaff," he said abruptly. He sat up, and as suddenly fell back on the pillows. "God, my head hurts."

"You need to rest before you go flying back up there," I said. "Take a nap, get a shower, I'll fix you something to eat. You're not strong enough to go back there now."

ASK ME NO QUESTIONS

He rested, taking my advice for once, and then he insisted I close the door and join him, and, finally after a few hours in bed and a meal, he was able to walk steadily, and he headed back out to find the pickup.

I was bruised and sore after he left. It seemed that, the further along this pregnancy progressed, the more Vic needed me, the more difficult it was to find the peace our lovemaking used to bring him. He needed my assurance, needed me to give without reservation, and while I was healthy and strong, I found his sexual advances intimidating. He was unknowingly rough with me, unaware that his heavier weight and passionate abandonment hurt me. *As long as we don't hurt the baby, I will abide,* I thought frequently. As long as our child was all right, I could bear any amount of pain. But I could not tell him how to love me, I was so grateful that he did love me. I could not worry him with needless concerns. I would abide. My body would heal.

He returned late that night with his pickup; I never learned what he did with the Cadillac. He was on a mission. No questions could be asked.

A few days later, he told me he would be bringing his partner by to meet me. "Her name is Vicky," he said, a smile twisting his lips. "Isn't that ironic? Vic and Vicky."

"Yes," I said. "It is." My eyes searched his, but there was no guile hidden there, and I prepared myself to once again play the part of his sister. Once again, his pregnant sister. What story this time?

This time there was no story, at least not that I was aware. Vicky stayed only for the evening, shared only a few minutes' conversation before she and Vic strolled down to the pool to swim in the dark. The girls had been put to bed. I watched the lantern swing from the branch near the pool, and I wondered what they talked about, but I didn't pursue the suspicious thoughts to their conclusion. I would not go there tonight.

And in the weeks that followed, I tried to ignore my brain, tried in vain to ignore the jealous accusations that followed them as they met by the river, out of sight for hours. I kept out of their way as they came and left and returned again.

Twice I mounted Ebony, my black mare, and tried to find them, following the trail along the river until the rocks blocked my path. Twice we swam the river, using the heat as an excuse to cool off, but I did not find them. I followed them and berated myself for my suspicions, and rode Ebony over the slippery rocks as I flogged my mind for its jealousy. But I could not find them, could not find proof for my suspicions.

Vic said they would be gone for several days. They had to transport a prisoner—presumably, the man he'd met in Flagstaff—to the Federal Marshall's office or some such thing. I barely listened, I was so filled with anguish. I didn't want to believe my heart, didn't want to listen to the voices that told me he and Vicky were lovers, but they wouldn't keep still. They filled my mind, and I didn't hear what he told me.

He made love to me before they left, and when he was gone I remained in bed and waited for the pain to die. But when I could move again, it was still there. It was part of me.

And then it ended, as they all ended. Suddenly the mission was over, his job done. Vicky disappeared from his life, and we moved on as if nothing had happened.

But something had. I had changed. I no longer believed with my whole heart. I no longer obeyed unquestioningly. I no longer gave freely, or in totality. I no longer knew whom to trust or believe. But I had no proof of any wrongdoing, and I could not take back my life.

Part IV
Awakening

Chapter 29

Nebraska. I hated it. It was flat, windy, and empty. But it was a new start for us—another—a renewing of our vows and our marriage. Here, Vic promised, we would be husband and wife.

"I've told the Company I've had enough," he said to me. "I won't do it anymore if it's going to hurt you."

We'd left Arizona suddenly, inexplicably. In one sense, I suppose I was happy to have Vicky out of our life, relieved to think we could be a normal, un-CIA-related family. But another, secret part of me resented the move again, away from family and anything familiar. I had loved the ranch, loved the horses, loved the availability of a daily swim. Tiffany had finally settled into a routine at the tiny country school, had joined the Blue Birds and was beginning to learn social skills. Cat took to the country life like a barn kitten in the midst of mouse heaven; Deanna was growing sturdy and strong in the haven of the country. Why couldn't we have stayed? Why couldn't he have left the Company and remained where we were happy?

Why couldn't we at least have waited one more month, when the baby would arrive?

But Vic had become enamored of Cornhusker Country during that brief visit the year before, and there was no dissuading him. As it was, there was never a discussion about the move; as usual, he merely informed me of the decision after it had been made. And, as usual, I smiled—halfheartedly, doubtfully, suspiciously—and nodded and began packing, while Vic disposed of the horses.

We found a small two-bedroom house near the edge of town and parked the U-Haul in the back. I began the task of unloading boxes, careful to balance their weight with my legs and keep the strain from my back and my overdue baby. Vic began negotiations to buy the town's only restaurant. His relationship with one of the oldest families in the area gave him a credibility even the CIA couldn't match, and in just a few days we were the proud owners of Vic's Cafe.

It seemed an incredible turnaround, this new life. *Maybe,* I thought, *maybe it will be all right after all. Maybe we will be a real family.* "Goodbye, CIA," I said out loud, "Goodbye, J.R. Goodbye R.J. Goodbye Vanessa, and Vicky, and every one of you 'boys.' May you rest in peace." I threw myself into the tasks of creating a home, a business, a life: I put the Company out of my mind.

Big mistake.

The town of Granston was comprised of less than three hundred people, boasting a service station, a variety store, a grocery store, a beauty salon, three churches, a bar, a grammar school, a bank, and Vic's Cafe.

The cafe was an important piece of the town's center of commerce. The farmers met for early morning coffee, their first break in a long day. The businessmen met there for breakfast. The housewives came in for lunch, combining their trip into town with an opportunity to socialize. The kids came in after school, buying french fries and ice cream cones.

The familiarity with which the townspeople treated each other was like the summer sun after a long, cold winter. A thawing of the human spirit. I distrusted it, knowing as I did the secrets people hid beneath their social masks, but it was interesting to watch. "Hey, John! How's that brand new baby boy!" the banker would yell to the service station attendant. "Is he changing oil yet?" "More like John's doin' the changin'," the owner of the bar would inject. "John" would take it all in with a self-conscious grin, his pride in his small family evident.

It was that way with everyone. Half the town was related, anyway, and the other half were sure to be entwined somewhere in the back of the family tree.

We established a routine very quickly: Vic left the house at five in the morning to get the grills hot and prepare the special for the day. I joined him as soon as the girls were up and dressed. We'd all four walk the few blocks to Vic's Cafe, where I would give Tiff and Cat their breakfast before sending them on to school. Cat began kindergarten that year, while Tiffany was in third grade. Deanna stayed in the kitchen with her father, who proceeded to pay her more attention than he'd shown any us for seven years. "You're my special girl," he'd croon, letting her stir the pancake batter while he poured water into the huge bowl. "You're Daddy's girl, aren't you?" Deanna would nod happily, enjoying the limelight while her sisters were gone.

But the attention would be temporary: as soon as a customer hailed the new restaurateur, he would be out in the big dining room, gossiping with the other men. Deanna sometimes pouted silently, snitching tastes of batter. More often she'd turn to me, and I would have to settle her into a game in the back room, where we'd set up a little television and a box of toys.

ASK ME NO QUESTIONS

Vic and I worked together rather well, I thought, as he played the part of a successful businessman and I that of his "better half." Like normal people. Maybe the demons that had chased us across America would finally come to rest.

During those first days in Granston, I left the cafe in the afternoon when school let out and went home to housewifely chores. Since I was due to deliver any time, I wanted to get our new home in order before I had to go to the hospital, which was in a neighboring town about fifteen miles away.

But after a few weeks, I found myself returning to Vic's Cafe more and more often, to bring something to Vic that he needed, to join him for dinner, and finally to give him some hours off. We'd hired a young woman named Marsha to wait tables in the evenings, and an elderly lady, Sarah, washed dishes and clucked her tongue over me all day. Once or twice I called home to ask Vic something, and he didn't answer the phone…he said he was napping.

By the time Jasmine, our fourth daughter, came into the world, we'd established a fairly predictable routine. I expected, once the new baby took over residence, that my own hours would be cut back a bit. That was why Vic spent so much time away from the Cafe, after all—to make sure everything was settled down when I took time off.

Jas entered into our lives at 4:45 a.m. on a Monday morning, September 24, 1974, after fifteen minutes of good, gut-wrenching labor. I'd been admitted the night before in anticipation of an induced labor, but Jas refused to cooperate, an indication of the challenges which lie ahead. I expected to go home that same day, as I had done three times previously, but Dr. Givens smiled kindly and shook his head. "We'll see," he said, while he read my chart and scribbled illegible orders on it. Then he left my room with a last admonition to "rest."

My doctor was an institution. The walls of his office, which was in his home, were covered with photographs of the babies he'd delivered over the course of thirty or more years.

"What can I do for you?" he'd asked the first time I saw him.

"I'm pregnant," I'd replied, surprised. When Vic's cousin Sharon had talked to Dr. Givens, she'd told him the reason for the visit. "I'm due any day now."

He gave me the once-over, shook his head, and pointed to the examining table. After a cursory examination, he shook his head once more and said, "Well, it's in position, but I don't think you're ready yet. You don't look near close enough."

"I am. In fact, I think I'm overdue."

For answer, he frowned and wagged his head yet again. I was beginning to feel as though I had said something awfully stupid. Didn't I know my own due date? "Come back in a week or so," he said.

At Dr. Givens', you didn't make an appointment. You merely went to his house and sat on the porch-now-waiting-room until he poked his head through the door. "Next," he'd bark, and the person who'd been waiting the longest would go into his office. It sure simplified the process. If an emergency came in, he'd take it ahead of everyone else, and we'd all wait even longer. But no one seemed to mind.

So I began to see him on a weekly basis: I saw him twice more before Jasmine was born.

Now, Dr.Givens' retreating back was replaced by the sight of my new daughter as she was carried in for her morning visit. I held her tightly, smelled her new baby smell, hugged her soft cheek next to mine. "Your life is going to be different," I promised. "You're going to have a family. A real family."

I watched other new mothers come and go during my unprecedented four-day stay at the hospital. After the first day, when Vic poked his head in the door briefly, he just called to see when I was coming home. Finally the news was what he wanted to hear: Dr. Givens signed the release forms on Thursday. "I hope you enjoyed your rest," he said kindly, shaking his head at me. I will always remember him that way, his head shagging solemnly from side to side. He was always so serious, always questioning my replies to his queries.

"Sure," I replied, unable to tell him that I only wanted to go home. I wondered how the girls were faring at Cousin Sharon's, whether Tiffany was missing much school, if Deanna was eating anything but her favorite snacks, if Cat had managed to get through four days without falling from a tree or some other daring-height object. Vic reported cheerfully that they were all fine, everything was fine, I just needed to get home.

And so when Dr. Givens released me, I expected to go straight home, straight to my own kitchen, where I wouldn't have to eat lukewarm, tasteless food and where no one asked four times a day if I'd had a bowel movement. When Vic stopped at the Cafe I expected that he was just checking in.

But he came around to open the door for me, motioning for me to get out, and, carrying Jas, I followed him inside.

We were greeted with big Midwestern smiles—lips stretched cautiously over clamped-together teeth—heads bobbing nearly in unison as we were honored with grave nods, then everyone went back to their business. Midwesterners are notoriously private.

ASK ME NO QUESTIONS

Sarah, our dishwasher, was a little more vocal, clucking her tongue when Vic told me to get to work and flashing her dark eyes in disapproval when Vic settled Jas in an empty bus tub.

Marsha, our part-timer, had quit, Vic said, and he'd been running the cafe alone all week. It had been really hard, waiting tables and cooking, but Dr. Givens hadn't been cooperative at all. "I told him I really needed you, Steph, but he ignored me. Too bad he's the only doctor for fifty miles around."

This wasn't exactly the homecoming I envisioned. Still, he couldn't do it all by himself, could he? But the questions hammered at me in spite of my attempt to sympathize. *It seems awfully strange that Marsha quit just when I was gone,* I thought.

She didn't seem like the kind of person to take advantage like that. She knew I was going in to the hospital.

But the habit of a decade kept my lips clamped together. I found an order pad and went through the swinging doors to the dining room.

By eight o'clock I was ready to collapse. Our customers persuaded Vic that I should be home in bed, and he bundled Jas and me up and swept us out the door in a picture of husbandly concern. The two-block drive home was quick, with my loving husband barely setting my bags on the floor before turning right around to spend the last hours at the cafe.

I stood just inside the doorway, facing the silent house, my sense of relief dissipating as the condition of the house rose up to meet me.

It smelled.

It smelled of dirty dishes, dirty laundry, and that closed-in musty smell old houses get. I knew without taking another step that there would be caked-on food on the dishes, there would be molding leftovers in the garbage can and discarded clothing on the floor in our bedroom. But the sight that discouraged me the most was the waist-high pile of soiled little girls' clothes in the middle of their bedroom. Hadn't they stayed at Sharon's for the last four days? I turned my back on that pile; there would be time to deal with it tomorrow.

Jas slept through the first few hours, the hours that I cleaned the kitchen and my bedroom. I was just putting her back to bed after her eleven o'clock feeding when Vic came in.

"Ah, God," he sighed. "It's so good to have you home." I felt his hands encircle my waist. "Vic," I said, determined to keep him at a distance for at least a few nights. "I'm really beat. And I'm awfully sore. Let me just get the baby put down for the night."

"Come on, baby, I'll rub your back. The baby looks fine. You need a little TLC."

Guiltily, I shoved the resentful thoughts back into my head, gratefully I followed him through our bedroom door. As he unbuttoned my blouse and turned me around, I sighed with relief. His hands began to knead my shoulders.

I was nearly asleep, his ministrations lulling me into a dreamless swoon, when I felt the weight of his body on mine, his bigger size pushing me into the soft mattress. I was naked except for the pad soaking up the blood still seeping from between my thighs. The September heat made everything sticky.

It had been so comfortable, so wonderful to be cared for, to feel those work-roughened hands massaging my aching muscles. Even though Vic never knew his own strength, even though his rare backrubs were just a little too hard, I welcomed the thoughtfulness behind the action. Why did it have to stop? For a few minutes I'd thought he really was thinking of me.

His hands were on my hips, those work-roughened hands that had felt so good a few minutes before were hurting me now. He was pushing the pad away and I was fighting to wake up when I felt the first stab of pain. My body was being ripped apart, my face was smashed into the pillow, and I couldn't move my arms, couldn't breathe, couldn't bear the pain. And then I was outside myself looking down and I knew I didn't have to feel anything anymore. I could just leave, at least in my mind.... I didn't have to feel, or to think, or to know anything. I could be safe.

It was over in seconds. Vic rolled off me and I swooped back inside my skull, and I watched him light a cigarette as he stretched out in the dark. My body remained still though, still and silent, the stickiness of the hot night flowing into the wetness beneath the juncture of my legs, my abdomen cramping in sharp, short pains that brought my knees up to my waist in gasps of breathlessness.

But that pain was bearable. That pain was microscopic compared to the voice that forced itself into my brain. *It's never going to change. It's never going to be any different.* But I pushed that voice back where it belonged, somewhere far away, and drifted, away from the pain, away from the voice. Vic loved me. That was all that mattered.

By the weekend I was seeing spots in front of my eyes, bright red spots that flashed at me throughout the day. I was sweating despite the fact that I felt cold, despite the air conditioner running full blast in the cafe. Sarah did her best to help me, but what could an eighty-year-old woman do to help? I could barely help myself.

ASK ME NO QUESTIONS

But Vic got a lot of ribbing from his customers about working his wife to death, and by two o'clock Saturday afternoon the cafe was empty.

"I'm taking you home," he announced suddenly. "You can take the weekend off, spend it in bed." Ushering me to the stationwagon, he locked up and drove me home.

Once again I was lulled into thinking, *He really does think about me. He does know how tired I am.*

We arrived at the house, and as I deposited Jas in her bassinet, he kissed me briefly on the cheek, told me to get some rest, and turned back to the door. "Where are you going?" I asked.

"I'm going to spend some time with the kids," he replied. "We're going to go bird-hunting. Sharon's roasting a chicken for dinner. I'll bring you some. But don't you even think about us. Go to bed and rest."

Sure. Rest, I thought. *I've got a baby to care for. How can I rest? I thought you would be here to help me.*

But I did go to bed, snuggling Jasmine next to me. The spots blinked on and off even when I closed my eyes, and my forehead was so hot it hurt. But I fell into an exhausted slumber anyway, awakening only when Jasmine cried out for her dinner.

This is good. The house was quiet. I moved about it slowly, putting baby things away, arranging bottles and sterilizer in the tiny kitchen. The floor needed vacuuming, but I ignored that, preferring to accomplish simple tasks that avoided strain on my aching body. I felt so weak, I tired so easily, it was an effort to pick up the dust cloth and shine up the buffet in the dining room. But it was peaceful. The only demands were from a tiny five-day-old mite who didn't know anything but love.

I knew then that Jasmine was a blessing. She was mine. The first child I named, even though Vic had insisted on her middle name—Morgan, after his uncle. Vic had named Jas's sisters.

Jas became more and more my child as the months wore on. Something was beginning to grow within me, a stubbornness born of despair. For the first time I brought the baby into bed with me, to play with or to feed. Not in the night, when Vic was home, but during the day I would take her in to our bedroom, lie down with her, and sing to her while she had her bottle. I could never nurse our children; Vic thought breast-feeding was gross. He thought of my breasts as his.

But I was beginning to care less about what Vic thought.

The weekend of rest helped revive me; by Monday the fever had died and I was nearly back to my normal energetic health. Monday also saw a new change in routine, for Vic had to go to North Platte, fifty miles away, for supplies, leaving me in charge at the Cafe all afternoon. Once again I was waiting tables and cooking, with Sarah clucking her tongue and shaking her head. Her eyes flashed at me once, when I was up on a ladder fixing a broken curtain rod. "I don't think you should be doing all this," she said disapprovingly. She stood at the bottom of the ladder until I was safely down, then stayed in the kitchen until I sent her home after the dinner rush.

The trips to North Platte and sometimes Ogallala became routine. I knew the need for "supplies" was a ruse, no one could need that many supplies, not when the suppliers came to us regularly. No, I knew Vic had to be working undercover. The Company must have put some pressure on him.

I was used to this routine, used to Vic's absences and the caring for the children and the business by myself. Sometimes I did resent it, but I reminded myself that I had made the bargain when I consented to marry an agent. It was just...God, how many years, how long did I have to wait for a normal life? The feeling of noble sacrifice had died a long, slow death.

The reality was that this life consisted of loneliness, hardship, and too many unanswered questions. I didn't mind the hardship, didn't mind working for no pay, ever, didn't even mind not knowing where he was or when he would be home. I could adjust to all those things.

But I hated his lack of interest in his children, our own on-again-off-again relationship, the constant need to lie, lie, lie. The motto we lived by—No mission is impossible, No sacrifice too great; Duty first—had become a burden, an incredibly heavy yoke that weighed down on my shoulders until I felt my spine would be forever crooked, hunched over in absolute defeat. I had made the supreme sacrifice, although I was unaware of it then. I had sacrificed my children and myself.

I should be happy I'm his wife, at least, I told myself. *I should be grateful we don't have to be brother and sister here.*

And I did have his relatives to talk to, his aunt and uncle and cousins. They all seemed so friendly, so accepting of us. But other than children and business, what topics of discussion could we cover? What is your life like, I wanted to ask. Does your husband tell you what to do and when to do it? Do you have any money of your own? How does a normal person live?

I observed as much as I could, listened all the time.

ASK ME NO QUESTIONS

But when Vic's sister Candy came to live with us, I didn't want to listen at all. I didn't want to know.

"What are you doing?" she demanded that first week. "You just let him tell you what to do, you don't ask him what he's doing, do you really think he's getting supplies?"

The questions came in a torrent. Candy had been with us just over a week, a week in which she watched her brother come and go, leaving the business in our hands.

She was here at his request, I discovered. After Marsha had quit, while I was still in the hospital, Vic had talked to his mother, found out that Candy was at loose ends, and paid for her plane fare to Nebraska. She was going to give me a break, he said, help out at the cafe and watch the girls when I worked.

Her presence seemed to give him more time to disappear each afternoon. His explanation didn't impress her.

"You've changed, Stephani," Candy accused. "You're not the same person I knew seven years ago. You're a wimp. You let him walk all over you." And she tossed her head, her black eyes spitting derision and her ebony hair flying.

Her words hurt. "You don't understand! It's not what it looks like!" I defended. Candy had been a friend seven years ago. The only person in Vic's family who had anything in common with me, the only one who tried to get to know me when they all returned from overseas to meet Vic's bride. She had been a junior in high school and we had spent hours together experimenting with hairstyles and makeup, talking about men. Of course, she didn't know that even then I had secrets bearing down on my shoulders. But I was younger then, so much younger. Had it only been seven years? It seemed like decades.

"No, it's you who doesn't understand," she tossed over her shoulder. Slamming through the front door, she sat down on the porch, elbows on knees, head propped up by her hands resting on her chin.

Warily I followed her, Jas in my arms. "There's a lot you don't know," I said, sorting in my head what I could say, what I couldn't say. "It's not what it looks like. Honest. He's really working on something, something I can't talk about."

"Yeah, I'll bet. Do you know about the women he's bragged to me about just since I've been here? Do you think he hasn't told me what a fool you are, how he can make you do whatever he wants?"

"He's just telling you those things so he can explain his actions. He has to say something, and he can't tell you what he's really doing. I shouldn't even be saying this," I stopped, chastising myself. Blabberer! You have to take it. You have to listen to her berate you for an idiot! Shut up!

Candy turned her head, looking at me with something like pity in her eyes. "Don't you think I know what he tells you? I've heard him talking to Dad. I know he tells you he's in the CIA. He isn't. He can't even get security clearance. Dad's checked for him."

I stared at her, my mind refusing to grasp what she was telling me. When did Vic discuss any of this with his stepfather? When did he even talk to Jorge? We didn't keep in touch. But Candy continued.

"Vic's marriage to Vicki was annulled because her parents talked to Mom and Dad, Stephani. She didn't press charges for bigamy because she felt sorry for you, and also because my parents didn't want a scandal like that in the family. The Cains came to Woodsville and saw us. I met them."

"Their marriage was never real," I interjected. *Stop this! Stop it!*

"Sure it was. Vic was really scared, too. It wasn't the only time. There was that girl in Minnesota, too. The one who had his baby. Dad had to pay for her delivery. Can't you see what he's done to you?"

"Camille? Camille had his baby?" Fragments of a letter appeared in my mind. Fragments I had found in his pickup...

"He's no more a CIA agent than I am. How could he even get in? They want college graduates, or at least Army Intelligence. Vic's never even been in the Army."

"Yes, he was. He was a mess sergeant. He was discharged because of his eye, when he got shrapnel in it."

"What are you talking about? He ran away from home when he was sixteen and joined the Coast Guard. Then he went AWOL from that. He's never been in the service."

"But he was drafted, that first year after you moved back, don't you remember? He went down to talk to them, because they had his records mixed up. Remember?"

"He got out of that because of you. You were pregnant with Cat. Don't you remember? Come on, Steph! Get real!" She was running out of patience fast. But I couldn't face it, couldn't take it all in. The lies...oh, God! The lies...*how could I know? How could I find out the truth?*

"The marriage license."

"What marriage license?" Candy turned away again, disgusted with what must appear to be my stupidity.

"His and Vicki's. It shouldn't be there. It shouldn't be on record, if it was a fake marriage."

"That's easy to find out," she said. "Just call the county records."

Shaking, praying, I went into the house, Candy right on my heels. I dialed the operator, got the number for the Washoe County records, and asked. "Do you have the marriage license for Victor Charles Brian and Victoria Cain?" I asked, pushing the air through my vocal cords, forcing my voice through the wire. I could barely speak.

"Social Security number?"

I gave the clerk Vic's number, then the date of the wedding. "Just a moment."

It was only a moment. Then she gave a number. "Ju-just a minute," I said as shock bolted through my brain. *It was real! Their marriage was real!* Candy handed me a pencil and I wrote the number on a scrap of paper, my fingers shaking so badly I could hardly grasp the pencil. "Thank you," I whispered into the phone, setting it on the cradle.

"Wait a minute," I told Candy, and I rushed into the bedroom where I kept all our family records. Digging Cat's birth certificate out, I then returned to the phone and called the hospital in San Remos. After connecting with the proper person in that county's records department, I was told I could get a copy of Cat's birth registration by sending in three dollars. "It will be changed," I told Candy. "It will have Vic's name on it. This one"—I waved the hospital copy in front of her—"was just for then, just to cover us so Vic wouldn't be in danger. He was undercover then."

Candy's reply was a look of disgust. "Do you realize how silly you sound, Steph? How could you believe any of this? Where's your brain?" And she left me, heading out the front door and stalking off down the street.

"No, no, no!" I yelled at her retreating back. "You're wrong!" The tears started then, those damned tears that seemed to be such a part of my life…. I slid to the floor, letting the screen door close before me. "Oh, please be wrong," I whispered, the ache in my throat making the words little more than a croak.

Vic was late that night. I felt him crawl into bed long after midnight, felt him stretch out on his side and settle into a softly snoring sleep. Candy had not returned, but was in her apartment, a tiny one-room studio Vic had rented for her. My head throbbed from the hours of crying, the years lost. It couldn't be true. It couldn't be true! Eight years of loneliness, eight years of sacrificing my life for his made it impossible.

It took more than a week for the birth registration to get to me. During that week I waited, doing what I had always done, acting as I had acted for eight years. I was an actress, wasn't I? I couldn't bear Vic's touch, his lovemaking made me sick, but I forced my body to lie still, I forced a response, a smile, a reply.

When I saw the names on Catlin's official birth registration, something inside me died. After the "Father's name" it said "Frank Michael Brian."

"Did you get it yet?" Candy asked. "Am I right? It doesn't matter anyway. You know he can't be an agent. You know that, Stephani."

"It hasn't come," I lied. "They said it could take several weeks. You know how the government is."

"You have to confront him, Steph. You have to do something. You can't let him get away with this."

She wouldn't let up. Day after day she harangued me, keeping the horror alive while I tried to assimilate it in my brain. *It's all a lie,* my head screamed. *No, it can't be!* answered my heart. I loved him. Why would he lie to me?

But everything was falling apart. Sarah had finally given up on me and gave notice at the cafe. I missed her comforting presence in the afternoons when I worked alone. Candy worked at night and during the noon hour rush. Vic disappeared as soon as the rush hour was over, now to play cards with the boys at the bar next door. I went home most nights, leaving Vic and his sister to work together. His weekly trips to North Platte continued. There was no family, no unity, no purpose for my existence.

Business remained stable, but Vic was restless, and was working on acquiring another restaurant in the neighboring town of Ellensburg. This had a bar, too, so he would have the liquor business as well.

A week or so after I got the birth registration in the mail, I told Candy I was ready to confront Vic.

"Good," she asserted. "I'll be with you. Don't worry. He can't get away with this."

We picked Sunday night for the big event. Vic's Cafe was closed on Sunday, so it gave me all day to work up my courage. I put the children to bed, hugging them more closely than usual. When Vic got back from his cousin Sharon's where he regularly visited, Candy and I were waiting.

"We need to talk to you, Vic," I said, my voice trembling. "Could you come here for a few minutes?"

"What is it," he asked, "Do you have another complaint? Am I doing something else for you to nag about?"

Glancing at Candy, I continued. "No, I don't have anything to nag about. I have something to tell you."

Plopping down on the sofa, he faced both of us suspiciously. "I know when I'm being ganged up on," he said. "Do you need more money, Candy? Don't I pay you enough?" Candy's black eyes flashed dangerously, but she held still. Vic wasn't paying her anything, unless you counted room and board. He felt that paying her rent and supplying her groceries was enough, despite his agreement to pay her a salary, too. She was always in need of money.

"No," she said, her beautiful mouth turning down. "You don't pay me anything. But that's not what this is about."

"Oh. Then what's up? I need to take a shower. What's on your mind?"

Candy turned her eyes to me. "It's now or never," they seemed to say. "Stephani has something she wants to tell you."

It was here. The moment of truth, as it's called. Both of them looked at me, brother and sister, so similar yet so different. His opaque stare held a touch of madness, his square jaw thrust forward in gritty determination. I could never get inside Victor Charles Brian. I could never read him.

Candy was softer, younger, but just as stubborn, just as determined, and clearly sane. Intelligence sparkled in her eyes, intelligence and sympathy and love. She was an open book, all her emotions shimmering on the surface of her face, her hands expressive in their communication. "Don't you, Steph," she urged.

"I don't believe you're a CIA agent," I blurted.

We waited, the silence growing. My heartbeat was so loud, I knew Vic could hear it. I knew he knew I was scared. *I'm sorry!* I called to him. *I don't want to hurt you!* I couldn't breathe, my heart filled my chest with its pounding.

"You don't know what you're talking about," he said quietly. Too quietly.

I glanced at Candy. "I know about the marriage to Vicki," I continued. "I know you were really married to her."

"You put her up to this," he said, his eyes swinging to his sister.

"She deserves to know the truth," Candy told him, meeting his stare defiantly. "You can't keep lying to her."

"How do you know I'm lying. You don't know anything."

"Come on, Vic, I was there when the Cains came to see us. I know about the marriage, the conversation you had with Dad about Camille, all the women you've bragged about over the years. You've never even been in the Army, how can you be an agent for the CIA? You know it's a lie."

The conversation quickly became a shouting match between Candy and Vic, and I, thankfully, was forgotten. Then he turned his gaze to me.

"You believe all of this?" he asked harshly, his voice reminding me of the little boy that hid somewhere deep inside him.

"Yes," I answered, wavering under his stare.

"Then I guess that's all there is to it. I'll pack my things. You won't ever have to see me again."

He walked out the door a few minutes later, one suitcase in his hand. He drove our stationwagon off with a typical spinout, throwing dust and gravel at the door.

I looked at Candy, bewildered. Now what? I had no transportation, no money, no husband. But my life was shattered anyway. Somehow I would have to pick up the pieces.

"Well, that was easier than I thought it would be," she commented. "He'll probably be back. Don't worry, he won't go far."

"Won't go far? I thought the idea was to leave him. I thought once we proved he was lying, I would have a new life."

"Well, that's up to you. I would say that now he knows you don't believe him, he'll behave. You just need to forgive him, start over. Give him a second chance. He does love you, after all." She left then, her duty done. I stood in the doorway of a silent house and watched her stride down the block with confident steps. Where did all that "give him a second chance" come from? I thought she was backing me up, making me face reality. I thought she was my friend. Instead, her loyalty seemed to switch to her brother. I was more confused than ever.

He did return. I hadn't gone into the cafe to work on Monday, so I was unaware of what transpired there, but in the evening he came to the front door with tears in his eyes, begging me for that second chance. He didn't mention the conversation of the day before, nor did I bring it up again. "I love you," he said. "I just want to be your husband. Someday you'll know the truth."

Chapter 30

Vic bought the restaurant/bar in Ellensburg, leasing Vic's Cafe to another entrepreneur. The deal in Ellensburg included a box-square two-story farmhouse on two acres, so we made preparations to move there. We were in just after Christmas, beginning the new year in another "new" home and job; 1975 arrived amidst a gloomy, drizzly cold rain and no hope for the future. I was deadlocked.

After Vic's return and apology, Candy supported him as much as she had harangued me before. "He's said he was sorry," she told me. "You should accept it. If you love him, you'll stay with him." But she pressed to take the "victory" and negotiate for some concessions. "Tell him what you want, Stephani. He's in a position to concede." So together Candy and I worked out a deal, a plan for our new career. We made Vic hire us as the entertainment in his new lounge.

We named ourselves "Salt and Pepper" because of the contrast in our looks and personality. She was "Pepper," of course, all fire and brilliance; I was "Salt," the stable one, the mainstay. She sang most of the leads, her fingers flying over her twelve-string guitar, while I learned to beat out the rhythm on a tambourine and blend my voice in harmony. We learned 75 songs for our opening night, four hours of singing in a smoky bar with cowboys twirling their women around and farmers bringing their wives in for steak dinners. It was a dream come true, finally. A chance for me to shine.

Vic stayed close to home, now, the bar/restaurant occupying all his time. Perhaps Candy was right. Perhaps, from now on, he would "behave." In another month he had transformed a small building on the property into a grocery store, with a little fresh meat counter along one side. He was thriving as only Vic could, enjoying the attention of being the new businessman in town, the thrill of having the only retail outlet in a thirty-mile radius.

He listened to Candy and I sing our songs, watched the whirling cowboy dancers with amusement at first, but by the third weekend, he was stepping up to the small stage and cracking jokes during our breaks. Some of the jokes were about us, and while they may have been funny in a negative sort of way, they were not necessarily in good taste. The fourth weekend nearly killed us altogether; Vic was more intent upon being the comedian than the cook. On the fifth weekend, Candy didn't show up. Since I couldn't play an instrument, our act was dead.

"I can't take him anymore, Steph," she told me. "He isn't paying me for my work, other than the gigs on weekends. But twenty-five dollars doesn't go very far. He won't stay out of our act. He tells me what to do, how to live my life. I've had it." There was more to it, of course. Candy had found a cowboy, someone who was funny and sincere and good, someone solid with whom she could spend her life. She wasn't interested in her brother and his problems.

I felt betrayed. As far as I was concerned, Candy had deserted me twice. First, when she had pushed me into confronting Vic, only to tell me I should take him back, now in pushing him to make one grand concession, only to leave me without a partner. I was devastated.

With the absence of my ally, life quickly regressed to a state of undeclared war between Vic and I. Somehow he felt he had to punish me for doubting him, for humiliating him in front of his sister. Vic had to be everybody's hero…I had diminished him to a fool. There was nothing I could do which pleased him.

So began a new dimension of loneliness, a new heartache. For nearly a decade I had had a noble cause to comfort me, a reason for the insanity of my life. Now, with the doubt, the near certainty that he was, after all, not an agent for the CIA, there was no anchor. The entire purpose of my life was gone.

But the habits of years were too hard to break. I had the one concession, the single drive that kept me going: my singing. I tried vainly to find another partner. Customers, who were evolving into acquaintances approaching friendship, told me about this girl or that man who played a guitar, had a "real country voice," could really "wail out a song." Vic had other performers come to the saloon during the weekends; I always asked them if I could sing a song or two with them. They always agreed readily. But my confidence was gone. Without Candy's encouraging presence to buoy my spirit, I couldn't find my voice.

I wrote, on the days when I could think, trying furiously to analyze and adjust and bring some semblance of sanity into my life.

"I feel like I am going stark raving mad. My existence, such as it is, is just that— an existence. I am not a calm, placid person who is content to daily tend my housework like an obedient slave. I would like to be that, since that is so obviously what he wants and needs. But I'm not like that. Perhaps this ambition of mine is what is destroying our relationship, but it wouldn't need to be destroyed if he cooperated with my needs as I once cooperated with his. I don't expect him to make me happy. Each person has that responsibility unto himself. But to be blocked in every way—no, I cannot say that. He has promised not to block me in my quest for a little independence. But I have no way to get anywhere, no telephone to call anybody, and no one to talk to.

"I have discovered after ten years that I am a person who has been lied to, cheated on, and robbed of my personality. At least I believe he lied to me. There is no proof that he hasn't, and unaccountable circumstantial evidence that he has. Therefore I do not believe anything he has to say and I find it very hard to respond to him in any way. Although my mind keeps saying I love him, I don't know if that is true or if I love only what I thought he was. I can't leave him. Why? Any self-respecting woman would have left years ago. When I first began to doubt, I should have had the guts to question him. To demand answers. Will it forever be an unsolved issue? Can I live this way without losing my mind? When it started up again last summer and I saw so many incongruities in what he said and what I saw, I should have questioned him. WHY DO I TAKE IT?? What is there about me that can accept something so monstrous and yet go on living with it??? I am hurting myself, him, and our children.

"On the surface everything is normal. He appears to be a loving husband and a doting father. And I think he is trying to be just that. So why can't I forget the past and live in the present? Because he is still doing things that I think are wrong, mostly concerning Candy. I have helped him hurt many people. I have to accept that responsibility. Will his desire to change right all that has been wrong? Dear God, what can I do? If I leave him he will fall apart. That much I know. He will revert to the person he was on the way to becoming when I met him. Can I live with that? Either way, there is so much wrong, so much guilt I have to accept. Have I become so afraid of life that I will let these things go on without rectifying them? Oh, how I would like to talk to Vicki, to Camille, to find out what really went on. But that is over. What concerns me now is here. I am lying more now than I ever did for him; every day is a lie when I want to be somewhere else, doing something else. Who am I and what have I become?"

There were no answers. The struggle was internal. Outwardly, I performed all the duties I had been taught, calmly keeping house, minding children, waiting tables at night and dreaming of becoming a singer every second. I could not tell anyone—ever—what I had discovered. I had been stupidly, foolishly blind. Now I must pay the consequences.

The betrayal I felt was more than that of my husband to me. I had been betrayed by the society in which I lived. Taught to sacrifice self for my brother,

I had indeed sacrificed my life for that of my countrymen. Taught to submit to my husband, I had obeyed him in every instance. Taught to turn the other cheek, not once but "seventy times seven," I had looked the other way while the man I loved beat me at every turn; psychologically, emotionally, physically. These lessons are ingrained in our society. These, and the ideal of romantic love, were my undoing. I had nowhere to go, no one to turn to. So I wrote, pouring my confusion into words on blank pages.

"October 19, 1975
"I don't know where I'm going or what I'm going to do. My marriage is in big trouble because I won't conform to what my husband wants me to be, and I don't know if I will be able to stick to my guns and be what I need to be. Right now I see myself as a bitchy, unhappy wife and a poor mother, a terrible housekeeper and an all-around selfish person. Selfish because I'm trying to satisfy my needs too, because I'm confused and have to figure out who I am. But to concentrate on self is wrong, we're told, happiness only comes from giving all of ourselves to others. Well, I tried that route, I thought only of my husband and family for the first ten years. I suppressed all thoughts of self and ignored frustrations even when those needs were denied. All it brought me was more frustrations, and guilt that seems insurmountable. I'm damned if I do and double damned if I don't...I can't give up! I guess it's fight or die, die little by little, day by day. If only I weren't so unsure! I have no self-confidence, I don't trust my own decisions or my wants or needs. I used to know who I was. But all that was built on a lie..."

On and on it went, the days melting into nights and the circle becoming more blurred. I painted murals on the walls of the girls' bedrooms, pounded frantically on the piano Vic had traded for a bar bill, kneaded bread dough furiously and smiled and laughed and chatted with an endless parade of customers.

Vic never noticed my confusion. I was too good at hiding my feelings, too uncertain to let anything seep through the cracks in my personality. I let him buy me things I didn't want, trinkets that began to fill the house with useless charm. For Christmas he gave me twenty-four different candles, "home accessories" he had bought from a home party saleslady. And a three-foot-tall Wile E. Coyote, its golden eyes reminding me curiously of my husband. Useless gifts for a useless person. I hated myself.

In January Vic's parents visited us, the first visit they had ever paid us. I know now that they stopped in to see us only because they were visiting Candy, who had married her cowboy, but at the time I thought it was especially nice of them to take an interest in their son and his family.

Vic had another opinion about it.

"She just wants to gloat," he muttered, stuffing spaghetti in his mouth. "Wait and see. She'll tell me everything that's wrong with the business. She won't have one good word to say about it."

I had not seen the venerable Ruby since 1967, nine years before. While a bit dominating, she seemed to be a decent, emotional woman who appreciated hard work. But Vic had told me how she had abused him as a child, how he was always the butt of her anger. His stepfather, Jorge Mendigurian, had been a lifesaver in many ways, giving Vic the stability of a family with a father role model, as well as saving him from his mother's wrath. Jorge was a man to be respected; although he had never finished high school, he had worked himself into a top-secret position as a missiles expert, a civilian working for the military. I felt it was this role model that affected Vic the most, for it was Jorge's example that gave Vic the aspiration to be his country's unsung hero.

The visit was short. Ruby and Jorge spent most of their time with Candy and their new son-in-law, even though they slept at our house. On the third night, I was serving dinner when the tension, which had been building for three days, broke with an explosion. Vic left the house in a fury, heading for the bar in tight-lipped silence. That was when Ruby turned to me.

"I don't know how you can stand it, Stephani," she said in her assured way. "I would have left him years ago." While I shook my head and shrugged in a well-that's-the-way-it-is kind of shrug, she came up to me, put her hand on my shoulder in the only affectionate gesture I was ever to receive from her, and said, "If you ever decide you've had enough, I'll help you. Whatever you need. If you want to go back to school, or need help with the kids, whatever it is, I'll help you. All right?"

I nodded, tucking those words back into my head to recall time and time again. I was not alone after all. His own mother offered her help.

The Mendigurians returned to their home in Woodsville, California, the next week: when I saw my mother-in-law again, I would be very close to asking her for that help she promised.

But in Ellensburg, Nebraska, in 1976, I was not yet ready. My only help, my only solace, was God. Surely, He knew the purpose for this time of confusion. Surely, He knew where I was supposed to be, and surely, if I waited upon Him, I would hear the message. In the meantime, I prayed, and I strained to hear His answer, and I waited.

There were several couples in that small town who became good acquaintances, people with whom Vic and I shared the after-midnight hours. Usually they would all come to our house after the bar closed on Saturday, for a breakfast of scrambled eggs, hash browns, and sausage or bacon. The weekend's entertainment often came with them, for any entertainer would be unable to sleep after a four-hour gig, and this was a way of unwinding. I tried to talk to these people, these wandering minstrels who did what I wanted so desperately to do. But they were all men; not once did Vic hire a woman to entertain the cowboy crowds. They called me "hon," "sweetheart," and even "gal," appreciated my cooking. But none gave me advice on achieving my dream. Sometimes, one would become overly friendly and make suggestive innuendoes, even touch me briefly, while I searched nervously for Vic's ever-present eye. They were harmless flirts, which didn't matter as far as my husband was concerned. Vic frowned whenever one or the other showed me any attention, and I knew I would pay for my indiscretions later, when we were alone.

After one of these nights, Vic would be especially amorous, as if he had to wipe out the memory of those other men who found me attractive. Since the bar didn't open until noon on Sunday, he could spend the morning in bed. He kept his arm flung over me, effectively blocking any thought I might have of escaping. The girls had to fend for themselves on Sunday, getting cold cereal and watching cartoons on TV until I could escape.

Escape was the word for those mornings. Despite Vic's apologies, the pall of distrust had not dissipated. I had lived a lie; I could not erase it or remake it. The guilt of my own participation in those lies hung over me like a shroud. Apathy was my only defense, my only protection. But I was not yet ready to give up my love for him. I could not face the enormity of the lie. I clung to my faith in a higher power.

However confused I was mentally, my body seemed to be sending a message of its own. It cringed at his touch. There were times, on those Sundays mornings, when I forced the bile back down my throat, when I gagged as he sought my mouth in a wet kiss. The smell of tobacco on his breath, something he had always had and which I identified as "his" odor, was enough to shut down my sense of smell; my nasal passages closed and I held my breath until the kiss ended.

Vic had never been a considerate lover, taking what was "his" without giving anything of himself. For me, there had never been pleasure in our lovemaking; more and more often now, there was only pain. There was, after all, only one objective; the man's privilege to exert his power over his woman. "Good" women didn't enjoy the sex act, anyway.

ASK ME NO QUESTIONS

And I would never deny him his conjugal rights, for I feared his anger even more than I dreaded his love.

March was windy and cold that year, the wind whipping through the vast empty plains like a banshee, howling as it swept through the eaves of the house, into the chimney and through the cracks in the window sills. One Saturday afternoon, Vic drove to the house during the afternoon lull and insisted that I come on down to the bar to help him. Reluctantly I allowed him to hustle me into the car, leaving instructions to Tiff to watch her sisters. At almost-ten, she was a tall slender girl with too-serious eyes and an impish smile. "I'll be back in just a little while," I told her. "Be sure you all stay inside."

We got to the saloon, and I walked into the building, head down against the wind.

"Surprise!" "Surprise!" Looking up, I saw our friends and regulars, gifts and decorations. It was a surprise party. For us. It was our tenth anniversary.

That night the celebration continued. Heartened by his attention, I dressed carefully, putting on the minidress with the wide sleeves and scooped neck that Vic liked. I made up with equal care, wanting to hide the wan color of my skin with a touch of blush, a hint of lipstick. I added eye shadow and mascara, blending the brown and green on my lids so they dramatized my green eyes. My hair was still long; I curled it, teased it a little, and gave it a spritz so it would hold up for the night. Saturday nights were always busy anyway, and tonight we would be especially busy with our anniversary celebration.

Manny "The Crooner" Kunz was our entertainer, and as he held the audience in thrall, I watched for newcomers and refills and took dinner orders. During the second set, Manny asked me to join him, so I sang harmonies to popular country songs. As I left the stage area to resume my working duties, Vic caught my eye and motioned me beside him. "What is it, honey?" I asked, slipping my hand through his arm. "Is everybody okay?"

"You look like a whore," he replied, deliberately disengaging his arm from mine. He walked away, joining the group who had surprised me that afternoon with a party. In a moment he was smiling and laughing with them, his eyes never flicking my way.

"We have the honor tonight of wishing our hosts a happy anniversary," Manny announced just then. "Stephani, Stephani, do you have a special song you'd like to hear?"

"Yaah!" "Happy anniversary!" "AH-ha!" Shouts and whistles filled the room as our customers joined in the congratulatory calls. Manny waited, his hand holding the noise down. "What will it be?" he repeated.

"'Help Me Make It Through the Night,'" I replied, tears stinging my eyes.

Vic shot a look of venom my way, hiding it with a smile stretched over his lips. "Come on over, Stephani!" the group called. "Let's make a toast! Ten years!" "A toast to the Brians! May they have many more just like the first!" "To the Brians. A decade of marital bliss!" The laughing increased, the jokes got rowdy. Vic sipped his Cold Duck, laughing with them, matching joke for joke. I was forced to sit beside him, forced to pretend I, too, drank and joked and laughed. But inside my heart was breaking. Inside, I was dying.

The tenuous hold Vic had on his temper began to slip increasingly often. It was not uncommon for him to grab me, pin my arms at my sides while he shouted obscenities in my face, or throw things at me. One afternoon he lifted the end of the kitchen table and shoved it toward me, dishes and food all sliding to the floor. Before I could escape the prison of the fallen table, he had hold of me, his fingers bruising my wrists while he dragged me over the furniture, into our bedroom. Throwing me onto the bed, he turned abruptly and left the room, slamming the door behind him. I was unhurt, but his anger terrified me. I huddled on the bed, hoping he had left the house, hoping he had gone for a drive as he so often did, whipping the stationwagon around the turns of the dirt roads that crisscrossed the countryside.

I heard a pop! in the distance, recognizing it for sound of a gun. "Tiffany!" I screamed, scrambling over the bed to the door, rushing into the living room in search of my children. "Tiffany! Cat! Where are you?"

"Up here, Mom," they answered in unison. Running up the stairs to their rooms, I saw my children cradling each other in their arms, Jasmine hunched in the center. Deanna clung to Tiffany, Catlin clutched the baby, and they were all together in a tight circle of arms, their backs to the world.

"Oh, God, are you all right?"

"Yes, Momma. How come Daddy has a gun? Is he gonna shoot us?"

"No, no honey," I assured Cat, gathering the four of them to me. "He's just target practicing." I held them for a minute, my mind racing to the sound of the gun. "Stay here. Just stay in here for awhile, okay?" I gave them an encouraging— I hoped—smile, hugged them once more, and retreated back down the stairs, heading for the gunshots.

The sound came from the outbuildings, what used to be the chicken coops. Cautiously I approached the door. A shot rang out, the bullet whining through the air before it chunked into the wall beside me. My heart raced, thudding so loudly I couldn't hear anything else. I stopped, listening, pushing my heart back to a quieter beat, breathing so shallowly that I could not discern my breaths from the breeze. Hesitantly I opened the door.

"Vic?" I called. Please don't shoot me, I prayed. "Vic, are you in there?"

"Go away," he replied, his voice brutally clear. "Get out of here."

"Honey, I just wanted to see if you were all right." I saw him then, crouching in the dimness of the corner, his back against the wall. The building was old; cracks in the walls allowed the light in, missing boards in the ceiling gave me enough light to see him clearly. His eyes glittered. "What are you doing?" I asked foolishly, feeling the stupidity of the question even as I voiced it. "You might hurt somebody."

"Good. I want to hurt somebody," he said, pointing the revolver toward me. "Maybe I should just shoot you now and get it over with." He cocked the trigger, the click! reaching my ears over my erratic heartbeat.

"You don't really want to hurt me, Vic," I said, keeping my voice steady. *Please don't shoot!* I prayed. I stepped into the dim light, ducking my head into the darkness. "Come on, Vic, let's go back into the house." *Away from the gun*, I continued silently...*Leave the gun here.*

"Get out of here."

I saw the determination in his eyes, heard the flatness of his voice. Memories of San Remos flashed into my brain. His finger moved slightly on the trigger. The gun jumped a little in his hand. I turned and ran.

The girls spent the afternoon in their rooms, I cleaned house furiously, my mind on the man outside. Would he come into the house? Would he kill himself? The shots sang out sporadically, distant popping sounds that startled me with crisp awareness of our isolation. Finally the time between shots lengthened until an hour or more had passed since the last round. I heard the stationwagon leave our driveway, and I ran to the window. Vic was driving, his profile unmistakable in the afternoon sunlight. The ordeal was over.

I crept back out to the chicken coops, my heart in my throat. I had seen him leave, I knew I'd seen him go, but with every step I expected to hear another shot, to feel the bullet cachunk! into me. I peered into the gloom of the building. It was empty.

Chapter 31

Home! We were going home again. *You can't go home again, Steph.* We are going home! I ignored the voice inside that wanted to quell the bubble of hope, the excitement at moving back to what I considered my part of the country. Reno. We were going to Reno.

The days following Vic's shooting spree had been tight with tension. The tension spiraled into dread and, ultimately, a terror that drove me into a strange twilight world where shapes and sounds were mere echoes of reality. I walked around my husband, avoiding him as much as possible without appearing to avoid him. I became a yes-man, a brown-noser; a robot programmed to obey. I hated myself for my inability to defy him.

Vic put the restaurant and all its adjunct properties up for sale. I began packing. We pretended to discuss the move and all it would mean to us; I prayed we would live long enough to reach the Sierras far to the west.

The restaurant never sold, so Vic turned it back to the man from whom he bought it. The country store went to him also. It was Vic's defeat, but my victory. We were leaving. That's all that mattered.

Vic never was one to hang onto a loss. We jammed our personal belongings into a small U-Haul and headed back West. If I had a map of the United States, our route would have criss-crossed half a dozen times. But it didn't matter. We were going Home.

The trip took about a week, with stops at motels along the way. Once again we treated it as a vacation, especially me, since I didn't have to cook or clean, and I could spend a little money on clothes for the girls. While we were in Cheyenne, Wyoming, I went to the local K-Mart. Piled high on my cart were summer outfits, swimsuits, and shorts in various sizes. The bill came to eighty dollars. I presented the MasterCard to the clerk. She handed it back to me. "Sorry, it's been denied." Shrugging to hide my embarrassment, I reached into my purse where

ASK ME NO QUESTIONS

I had smuggled two hundred dollars. My wallet was empty. I left the clothes in the cart and pulled the girls after me to the car.

I told Vic about the strange denial of our charge card; he shrugged and told me not to worry about it. I asked him about the money, to which he casually replied, "You probably misplaced it, Stephani. You know how forgetful you are."

But I hadn't misplaced it. I remembered putting it in my wallet before we left Elsie. It was money I had saved from tips I'd earned waitressing. What had happened to it?

I mentioned the money again, when we were a little further down the road. "I'll help you look for it," Vic offered. "When we get to the next motel. We'll go through everything."

That night we began the search. I was standing between the beds, opening a suitcase, when I happened to glance up. From my position, I could see Vic in the mirror of the bathroom. He was reaching into his pocket. I watched as he opened his palm, saw the wad of bills he held in his hand, saw him open the drawer in the bathroom vanity and place the bills in my zippered makeup case.

"What's this?" I heard him say. Then, "Stephani, I found the money." He came out of the bathroom with the case in his hands, the bills sticking out of it. "You put it in your makeup case," he said in that know-it-all tolerant tone a man saves for his wife. "You must have forgotten what you did with it."

I grabbed the case from his hands, but he took the money and slipped it into his pocket. "I'll keep this for you," he said. "You'd forget your head if it wasn't tied on."

I hadn't forgotten it. I knew I hadn't forgotten it! As the miles slipped behind us, I retraced my movements concerning that wad of bills; over and over, I retraced my steps. I saw myself waiting for my husband's absence from the house, watched myself take the money from its hiding place behind the baking tins on the lowest shelf in the cupboard, reach into the jar in the corner, and withdraw my secret hoard. This was the money with which I bought gifts for my family, or for Vic. I'd never liked asking him for money for presents, especially those I bought for him. It was like using his money to buy his own gifts. I thought I could use it during our trip for treats, or for spontaneous fripperies that Vic might object to. I might even need it once we reached Reno, if we were low on funds. Vic would be so surprised. He never credited me with any money sense. I'm sure Vic didn't know about it. When did he take it from my purse? I never left my purse. Maybe I did misplace it. Maybe Vic was right. But I'd seen him take it from his pocket! Hadn't I?

We reached the "Biggest Little City in the World" just before our funds ran out. Even that two hundred dollars. If only I'd taken better care of it…but I hadn't.

Fortunately, Vic began working almost immediately, and we were able to rent a big house close to the downtown. We had no furniture, but that didn't matter; we'd been in that predicament before. Furniture would come. I threw myself into moving in, getting acquainted with the town, and shedding the last remnants of the past two years. The atmosphere in Reno was so different than that in the Midwest. Freer, more open. Familiar. Maybe I could put it all behind me, after all.

We'd been in Reno about a week when the car broke down, and I was forced to look for a job. I immediately sought out my old territory, Sandy's. For once I felt absolutely confident, and I was hired.

So began a familiar routine. My shift was 6 a.m. to 2 p.m., so I arose early, before the girls were up. Vic was supposed to watch them; he didn't go to work until evening. But after a few days, I realized that the children were left alone nearly all day, while my husband took in the pleasure of the Reno gambling halls.

Ever since I discovered my husband with the money I had so carefully saved, ever since he took that money away from me with the easy confidence of one who always has his way, I hid the earnings I brought home every day. This was money to be used for living, not gambling, I told myself.

He found my hiding places. There was never any discussion about the money, it was just gone. I would get home from work, pay off the sitter, and change my clothes, taking the wads of bills and handfuls of coins from the uniform pockets and placing them in the middle of the bed. Then I would count it all, separating the coins so I could wrap them, enjoying the pride of acquisition. I made good money as a waitress, averaging ten dollars an hour in tips sometimes.

And every day it disappeared.

Vic didn't say anything about it, but I knew he was taking it. Sometimes he would come home, always in the early hours of the morning, jubilant. "I won a hundred dollars at black jack last night," he'd say. Then he would pull me toward him as if I were the prize for his winnings.

Other mornings he'd sneak in silently, slip in beside me, and roll over to his side of the bed.

One day I returned from work to find him methodically tearing the bedroom apart. "All right, where'd you put it?" he asked me.

"What?"

"The money. Where'd you put it this time?"

Good. He hadn't found my new hiding place. Maybe I could salvage some of it. "I don't know what you're talking about," I replied, turning away from him to hide the trembling in my knees. Unzipping my Sandy's uniform, I began to change.

"Don't lie to me, Stephani. You know I'll find it eventually."

"Why?" I asked, suddenly tired of the games we played. "Why do you have to take it? It's money for our bills, for groceries."

"What do you do with all our money?"

"That's for me to know and you to find out," he smiled grimly. "Now hand it over."

"No," I replied, trembling. "I want to get the girls some new school clothes. I need to save a little before school starts." The coins in my uniform pocket clinked as I let the dress slip off my shoulders to the floor. My back was to Vic; I could hear him breathing. My jaw was clenched tight with the fear I fought to hide. What would he do?

As I stepped out of the uniform, he grabbed it, flinging it on the bed. Dumping the pockets onto the bedspread, he rifled through the bills. "Don't think you can hide anything from me, Stephani. I'm the reason for your existence." The words were spoken without expression, as if Vic was reading an interesting item in the newspaper. Expelling a long breath, I awaited the explosion. But he swept out of the room, the look in his eye enough to quell any thoughts of rebellion.

Soon after that, Vic also began to work at Sandy's, as the weekend assistant manager. Keeping his job at Harold's Club, he came into my workplace during the Saturday morning rush, overseeing my work as well as the rest of the crew for the remainder of the day. It was during this time, the first weekend he worked, that a new waitress was hired.

Typical of the restaurant business, there was a fast turnover. Applicants came in regularly on the off chance there would be an opening. Vic interviewed several prospects that first afternoon. I watched them come in and leave, some with a smile,

some not so happy. The blonde had been one I saw come out with a smile. She had even, white teeth that sparkled. Her eyes were a deep brown; her blonde hair was long and wavy and shining. About the same height as me, she wore her well-proportioned figure with a confidence I could never emulate.

A week later, I saw the same young woman walk toward me, a Sandy's uniform smoothly covering the voluptuous curves, emphasizing their fullness while maintaining a modesty that belied her engaging smile. "Hi," she said in greeting. "I'm Melissa. I guess Vic told you I'd be starting today."

"No, actually, he didn't mention it, but that's pretty normal," I replied. "Come on, I'll show you where everything is."

We spent a few minutes while Melissa became familiar with the layout of the waitress station, where the condiments and supplies were kept, and the general routine. She was friendly without being overbearing, quick on her feet and efficient, and I felt she would be a good working companion. She didn't mention Vic again, and I accepted her as part of the team at Sandy's.

Working in a restaurant requires a flexibility that is unlike nearly any other profession—especially for servers, since the work schedules are usually made out weekly and may vary from week to week. There are usually a few service people who are fortunate to have the same schedule every week: generally 6a.m.-2p.m., 2p.m.-10p.m., and 10p.m.-6a.m. if the restaurant stays open all night. Then there are the in-between shifts: 7a.m.-3p.m., 5p.m. to midnight, for instance, and also part-time shifts, which cover the rush times only, or weekends only. Melissa had a different schedule every week, so I did not become well acquainted with her. Usually she came in during my shift and worked later; sometimes she came in an hour or two before my shift was over, so our time just overlapped. There was never time for more than salutations and a few perfunctory remarks while we worked.

One afternoon about three weeks after she started, Melissa arrived at work, her eyes pink with unshed tears. It was early afternoon, during the lull before dinner. I was getting ready to go off shift. Noticing Melissa's rueful expression, I asked her if everything was all right.

"It's your brother!" she burst out, "He won't leave me alone!"

Suddenly the bright summer evening turned cold. "My brother?" I asked, my lips stiffly forming the words. I shivered as I heard her reply.

"Yes, Vic. He's driving me crazy. I'm really scared."

"Why don't we take a break," I said, my voice sounding very strange—high and thin, like the wail my heart was keening—and I led her into the back employee's table. The restaurant was nearly empty anyway. The cook would tell us if a customer came in.

"Now tell me. What is Vic doing?"

"Well," she began, drawing in her breath and blinking her eyes to keep the tears from smearing her mascara, "we've been seeing each other for about a month. Just a few dates, really. About two weeks ago I told him I didn't want to see him anymore, and he just went nuts. Jumped all over me, told me he couldn't live without me, calls me all the time. I can't take it anymore! He sends me flowers every day. Roses! I don't know what to do!"

The tears had begun despite her attempts to keep them back. I had to overcome my own panic while I pretended to comfort her. "I don't know what to say," I commented, my hand touching her shoulder briefly. *He's doing it again! I thought. The same story! The same game! Has it always been just this—just a game to get women?* "I'll talk to him, Melissa. I'm sorry he's doing this to you." Then, taking a deep breath, I made a decision. "But there is something I think you ought to know," I plunged on, "Vic's not my brother. He's my husband."

"Oh, my god!" she exclaimed. "I'm sorry. Your husband? Vic is your husband?" She looked at me with guilty eyes.

"Yes. My husband."

Melissa touched my hand, then, her expression one of compassion. "I'm so sorry. I didn't know, honest to God. He said you were his sister, that he was helping you-"

"I know the story," I said. "It's not your fault."

"He's not going to get away with this," she said angrily, her eyes deepening to nearly black. "I'm not going to put up with it." Her tears dried up faster than my own heart slowed to a normal rhythm, and as I watched, her face became set in a determined scowl. "Don't worry, Stephani. I'll take care of it."

That night I waited for Vic to come home. His shift at Harold's Club ended at 1a.m.; I passed the time by practicing what I was going to say.

I needn't have bothered. Vic burst into the dark house in a rage, slamming the front door so loudly I thought the girls might awaken upstairs. He came into the bedroom, his mouth drawn down into a familiar frown, his teeth clenched, his eyes blazing, glittering with a familiar glaze. Turning out the overhead light, he undressed in the darkness and flopped onto the bed.

"Vic?" I said tentatively. I wanted to turn over and go to sleep, to escape his attention. I wanted to avoid a confrontation. I wanted to be safe, to return to the warm cocoon of ignorance I'd enjoyed for so many years.

But I owed it to Melissa to confront him—to Melissa and to myself. "Vic, can we talk?"

"Go to sleep," he growled, his voice muffled by the pillows. "Talk in the morning. I'm tired."

My brief moment of determination dissipated, any courage I might have drawn from Melissa died. Sliding down into the covers, I turned onto my side, away from my husband, and closed my eyes.

He's driving me crazy. Your brother. I can't get rid of him. He scares me. He's driving me crazy...Your brother.

The words reverberated behind my eyelids, pounded into my temple. Who are you? Tinker, sailor, doctor, spy...Vic had never actually denied working for the CIA. He'd just told me to believe whatever I chose. He'd been so hurt, so angry when Candy and I had accused him of deceit. But why did he need to lie about our relationship? To protect me, he'd always said. To protect our children and me. Maybe Melissa was just a ruse, a cover. Maybe she was one of Them, an enemy. No, that's too ridiculous. She was just an innocent bystander, a victim of his schemes.

I slept, the images and the questions whirling in chaotic revel through my brain.

I awoke in the middle of the night with a heavy weight on my chest. I couldn't breathe. I had been dreaming, I thought, the shadows of the dream still in my head. It was Vic I dreamt about, Vic was chasing me, hurting me, yelling at me. There was a struggle...and as my brain began to shift through the shadows, the weight lifted. But instead of relief, I felt my body jerk in fear, freeze in anticipation. Then the pain came, and I awoke.

Vic was on top of me, penetrating me in short, deep thrusts that tore my insides apart. Oblivious to my pain, he grunted as his hips slapped against my pelvis, his breath coming in sharp gasps beside my ear. Then he rolled off me and sprawled onto his stomach on the other side of the bed.

This was not a new experience. There had been a time when I welcomed his loving, was even grateful for it. But increasingly, Vic's "lovemaking" brought only pain, as he seemed to enjoy a rough form of "play" that hurt me, leaving bruises and bloodstains. I accepted it with the same stoic acceptance as everything else in my life, shoving the confusion and the humiliation far down into the dark corners of my mind. If I protested, Vic accused me of being frigid and unfeeling.

Besides, he'd told me shortly after our wedding that men liked to be the aggressor, that a woman's body did not respond to passion the same way a man's did. A Good woman pleasured her husband by accepting and complying with his demands: only Bad women actually enjoyed the passionate foreplay and varying positions the entertainment world seemed to portray as normal.

I'd never questioned his knowledge. He had been experienced, I had been a virgin. What did I know of sex? Thus there had never been any kissing, fondling, or caressing, at least not for me. Occasionally Vic wanted to be touched, and he would direct my hands to the appropriate places and instruct me in the proper movements. But even those times were rare. Our lovemaking served one purpose, just as our life together had but one reason: to please Vic.

This night was no different.

But the dreams were becoming an integral part of my life. Even on those nights when Vic was away, the dreams disturbed my sleep, and it was becoming more and more difficult to close my eyes at the end of the day.

I reneged on my vow to confront him about Melissa. The wounds were too raw; it was difficult to move without thinking about the night. And the pain in my heart was dulled by too many years of tension, uncertainty, and confusion. I just didn't have the energy to fight him.

It didn't matter anyway, for whatever the plucky waitress had said to him must have finally worked, for the next time I saw her, she told me he was no longer a problem.

But my problem remained. What could I do? I was paralyzed. I could not move forward, and I could not regain my belief in my husband. But I could not go on like this, either.

Chapter 32

"It happened so long ago...I was just a teenager, just a stupid, dumb kid. I ran into a guy on a motorcycle and killed him. God, I was ruined! My life was ruined! Can you understand?"

I looked across the table at the man to whom I had been married for thirteen years. Thirteen. Was this going to be an unlucky year? I was not superstitious, but somehow his words, linked to that mythical number, made my skin crawl.

"Steph? Do you understand?" He pleaded with me, his hands holding onto mine as if they were his lifeline. I looked at those hands as if they belonged to someone else. *This is it,* I thought. *It's now or never.*

Vic and I were sitting at a booth in a seedy coffee shop, the kind of place in which he appeared to feel so comfortable, so at home. I was growing more cynical every day, listening to the words as they issued from his mouth, all the while listening for the underlying meaning behind those words. I had learned that what was said was never—never—what was actually meant. Vic spoke in a kind of code, just as he lived for a "code" that only he understood. If he said, "I love you," what he meant was "I possess you." If he said, "I'll be home late," he meant "I'll be home when I feel like it." Could be later today, could be tomorrow, could be next week. The fact that he told me he'd be late was enough explanation. A simple "When?" in response to his statement would be met with silence. "When" was a question, and questions were absolutely forbidden.

We'd been in Reno nearly three years. Three stagnant years. We'd moved four times, were now living in the twin city of Sparks, a street's-width away from the famed gambling town. Vic had jumped from job to job just as easily, from the casinos and restaurants to a home milk delivery route. I, too, had changed jobs, moving from the familiarity of waitressing to the pulsating world of newspapers. I sold classified advertising space for the Reno Gazette-Journal, a daily newspaper with a circulation of nearly one hundred thousand. It was a job for which I'd discovered I had a surprising aptitude. I was a now a "professional."

ASK ME NO QUESTIONS

But our life was a maze of lies and half-truths. Too many inexplicable things continued to happen, things that Vic insisted were a result of his position in the CIA. He never talked about "missions" anymore, never took me into his confidence, but made innuendoes, implications, and occasionally veiled threats of what would happen to him if I didn't act "appropriately."

"Appropriate" behavior translated into keeping his secrets, asking no questions, and obeying him implicitly. Although I was allowed to go to church, even sing in a gospel group, I never spoke about him, our marriage, or our life in general. I could talk about our children in general terms, but I couldn't show their pictures, or give specific information, such as age, name, school they attended, etc. It would be too easy for "the enemy" to kidnap them.

I accepted these conditions because I didn't know how else to appease him. And appeasing him was what my life was all about.

I listened to him now, this enigma I had married. Listened and watched. Vic's hands were tense, their tightness communicating through his fingers into mine as he grasped my hands. His eyes wandered off, as they always did when he talked to me, off somewhere in the distance above my head. His eyes were one of the features that had fascinated me in the beginning, his curious opaque eyes that had no depth. You looked into them and met a wall. Coyote eyes. I thought these things as I listened to his words.

"I was young, I was in a strange town, and I was going to be ruined. The boy was dead. I couldn't do anything to change that." His hands were clammy; they began to slide over mine, feeling like grease in my palms. "I was desperate, I admit that. I didn't know what to do." Now his eyes met mine in a plea for understanding, the first time he looked at me, really looked at me, since entering this fine establishment. *What do you see?* I wondered. *I'm not the same little girl you married. I'm older now, not so easily taken in.* I stared back at him dispassionately.

"I was approached by some guys who saw the accident," he continued, his eyes now upon our hands. "I didn't know it then, but they were from the Mob. They paid off the parents of the boy, so they wouldn't press charges against me. That's when it started."

"What started?" I asked, stiffening against the tingling at the back of my neck. *Don't listen to him! Don't believe him!* The tingling continued until its tendrils touched the length of my spine.

"The work I do for them. The Mob. I'm in their debt for that accident. I've been working it off all these years, doing things for them." His voice lowered; I had to strain to hear him. His eyes were still on our hands, his thumbs rubbing against my palm.

The tingling in my back had stopped, giving way to an icy stillness that enveloped my entire body. The Mob. *Don't believe him!* The Mob. "What 'things' have you done?" I choked.

His eyes flashed at me, swerved up to that nebulous area above my head. "Things like beating people up. Enforcing. I've even killed a guy." His hands clenched mine. "I had to do it. I owe them."

Silence grew between us then. I had no reply, no words of encouragement or denial. My mind was whirling as all my determination left me. "I've even killed a guy" hung over the table like a tunnel of black smoke, a tornado of memories that were snaking toward me, threatening to engulf me in the void. I sat still, stunned, shocked, and scared. His fingers bruised my hands.

I couldn't see any confirmation in his face, couldn't tell whether truth or fiction lodged behind his eyes. He looked the same as he always had, yet nothing was the same. Something had, almost imperceptibly, changed.

"I'm asking you to forgive me, Steph. I know I've lied to you, but I couldn't tell you the truth. I couldn't. And I've only got a year to go. Just one more year, and I'll have paid my debt."

"A year? You never get out from under the Mob," I hissed, finding little breath to support my voice. For a moment I disbelieved him. For one second, I retaliated, feeling the lie.

"That's just movie stuff," he said, cracking a crooked smile. "That's not real life. In a year I'll be free." He looked at me again, right into my eyes. "Can't you give me a year? That's all I ask. One year."

"I've already given you thirteen years!" I could feel the fear rising, feel the tornado getting closer, its mouth yawning before me.

"I know. I don't deserve a chance. I know I've hurt you." His hands clenched tighter, holding me to the table, holding me. "But I promise you I will change. We'll have all we ever dreamed of. I promise. Please. Give me a year."

A year, just one more year. What did it matter? I'd told him I wanted a divorce, but I had no idea what to do with my life without him, however unbearable living with him was. I had nowhere to go, no one to turn to. I couldn't deny him, couldn't break the bonds that held me. The tornado whirled, spinning, taking me with it. "All right," I nodded. "One year. I guess I can give you that."

I returned to my desk at Gannett, dazed, exhausted. My co-workers looked at me, curious, but kept their comments to themselves. They were used to my silences. I was not a part of the office banter that lightened the work days. But my friend—my secret friend—Elizabeth noticed my pallor when she stopped by later, and asked me what was going on. "You look terrible," she said in her usual forthright way. "What's the matter? Has Vic done something?" I shook my head, unable to speak about it. "Let's go to my office," she directed. "We can talk in private there."

I had met Elizabeth Bramford during a brief fling as an Avon Lady. She was my boss then, and had taken a special interest in me. When she'd moved to Gannett, she'd paved the way for me to follow her. I owed her. She'd shown me the possibilities.

A half-dozen years older than I, Elizabeth was married to a very successful lawyer and believed in "giving back," as she called it, to the less fortunate. Apparently I fit into that category. But Elizabeth never made me feel obligated, or less than she was. She lifted me up.

Meekly I followed her to the Ladies' room, Elizabeth's "office" away from her desk. Seeing it was unoccupied, she turned and looked me in the eye. "Now, what's happened? You look like you're scared out of your mind."

"Oh, God," I whispered, beginning to wilt as the tension eased from my shoulders. "I am. I don't know what to think, or what to do, Elizabeth, I'm so confused! I don't know what to believe."

"Tell me," she urged. "I know you're under a lot of stress. What is the matter? What's happened?"

Indecision washed over me. Elizabeth knew as much as anybody, which was nothing. The gospel group of which we were both a part knew only what they could surmise from my behavior. I never shared womanly secrets about my life. Only someone as perceptive as Elizabeth, who had been the closest thing to a friend I'd known since Lori, would even think to suspect Vic was behind my bewildered state.

So I thought, anyway. I was so sure that I hid everything from the world, it would never occur to me that someone—anyone—would think I was anything but a happily married woman.

"Stephani, come on! Can I help you? What do you need? What can I do?"

"Oh, Elizabeth," I gulped, "I just don't know what to do."

Pushing me gently onto the couch in the tiny lounge, Elizabeth gave me her most businesslike expression, her eyes logical, clear, and very, very determined. "Look. I won't tell anyone. You know that. Whatever you say won't go beyond this room. But you obviously need to talk to somebody. What is it?"

Gulping in a breath of air, I looked at her, seeing the openness, the honesty that was so much lacking in my life. She was normal, for God's sake! How could she help? How could she understand? "I can't tell you, Elizabeth. I just can't tell anybody. It's too terrible."

"Okay. Ask yourself this: what's the worst that could happen if you told me? I would know your deep, dark secret. Only me. You could unload all that guilt and fear I see in your face. You could get back in there and go to work, relieved. I could go back to work, not worrying about you because I know—I know—you're strong enough to deal with this. Does that sound so bad?" She smiled, her well-cared-for teeth even and white beneath her glistening pink lips. Her perfume was subtle, understated, expensive. She was my friend. My own friend.

I smiled back at her, a watery, shaky smile that took all my remaining strength. "It's so silly, Liz, I feel embarrassed to even tell you. I'm sorry I worried you."

"It's okay, Steph," she assured me. "I won't force you. But I want you to know I'm here if you ever need me. Ever. And if you need legal advice, you know Reed would help you." Reed was her husband, a very prominent attorney. "So, feel better? You still haven't told me, you know."

"I know. But it's okay, really. You just put everything into perspective for me. Thanks."

Elizabeth hugged me, her expensive perfume wafting over me in delicious escape. I closed my eyes, breathing in the aroma and letting myself feel her solid strength. She was small-boned, trim, and tough as nails, running miles every morning and working out every evening. She had a gym in her house, right next to the hot tub. She lived in a different world than I could even imagine.

Exiting the "office," Elizabeth gave me a reassuring goodbye pat and we separated, each to our own desks. I felt considerably better, knowing Elizabeth and Reed were in my corner. Tucking that bit of knowledge into a corner of my mind, I picked up the earphones at my desk. "Gazette-Journal," I said to the waiting customer.

A year. What was one year in the course of a lifetime? Nothing. What was one star in the heavens? A mere speck. Squaring my shoulders as I left the newspaper office, I tried to think. *A year.* The prospect of any amount of time spent as a repetition of the past thirteen was incomprehensible. Yet, making a decision was equally daunting. *What do I do? What can I do?* I asked over and over again on that short walk to the car. Waiting for a sign from God, a visible message that would be incontrovertible, I squinted in the brightness of the setting sun. Nothing happened, no one answered.

At home I repeated the actions of thirteen years of domesticity, listening to the children with one ear tuned to the heavens, awaiting a Message that would change my life. After dinner, Vic retired, as he had to get up in the early morning hours to run his milk route. He gestured to me to join him. Reluctantly, I obeyed, made a stop in the bathroom and prayed, my sense of bewilderment growing. *What should I do? Is he lying or telling the truth? God, tell me!* But nothing happened. No One intervened.

The next day the first arrangement of flowers arrived at the office. "Wow, Steph! Who's your secret admirer?" Work stopped when the bouquet was delivered. I was suddenly the center of attention, the target of envious glances and gleeful gossip.

"They're just from my husband," I protested mildly.

"Wish mine would send me something like this," somebody said.

"You can have these," I offered. The flowers made me apprehensive. They looked surprisingly like a funeral arrangement. I moved them to the counter where their colorful mixture could be seen and enjoyed by everyone.

The deliveries continued, a new arrangement every week, reminding me of my promise. One year.

How could I commit to another year?

Yet there were practical considerations, too. My take-home pay was one hundred thirty dollars a week, plus a monthly bonus that ranged around five or six hundred dollars. Our house payment was eight hundred dollars. An apartment large enough for all of us wouldn't be much less. How could I even begin to make ends meet, should I leave Vic? Utilities ran to nearly three hundred a month, food would be out of the question. *Get another job,* I told myself. *Work as a waitress on the weekends.* Do something! *Not yet, not yet,* I cautioned myself. *See what happens first.*

"See if God will intervene" is what I really meant. "Ask and ye shall receive." Isn't that what the scriptures said? *Oh, tell me, tell me, God. What should I do?*

I made an appointment with the minister at my church, deciding that professional counseling would give me some answers. Charles Goodwin was a warm, approachable man, a preacher who smiled from the pulpit, talked about love and forgiveness, healing, and living as a child of God in a world filled with opportunities for growth. Positive aspects of the Christian life. He was easy to talk to, and as I stammered out my confession of confusion that first afternoon, he was gentle, listening with a slight smile of encouragement of his round, bespeckled face, his brown eyes kind.

I couldn't tell him anything about our life, of course. Just my feelings. Just theological and spiritual questions, like, for instance, God's viewpoint of divorce.

"Of course, marriage vows are to be taken seriously," Pastor Goodwin told me, "but God doesn't mean for anyone to live in unhappiness, either. All avenues for reconciliation should be explored, every effort given to fulfill the promise of marriage. But I can also tell you," he smiled, emphasizing the serious nature of the discussion, "that it seldom works out if just one of the partners is trying. Have you tried talking to Vic about this?"

Heat swept up my neck to my cheeks. "No," I said, shaking my head as my fingers twisted in my lap. "He doesn't know I'm having these problems. I don't know how I could even approach him about them."

"Would he be willing to come in with you and talk to me?"

I chuckled, a wry chuckle that caught in my throat. "No, he wouldn't. That much I know."

Pastor Goodwin shook his head, a frown pursing his lips for the first time in an hour. "Well, I don't know then, Stephani. What would you like to do?"

"I would like to be happy, Pastor Goodwin. I would like to know if I'm doing the right thing. I just feel so torn."

He patted me on the shoulder sympathetically. "I'm sure that God will help you. Would you like to pray with me right now?"

I nodded, thinking, perhaps, that he might have a little better connection than I did. Maybe God would tell him what I should do. Dutifully bowing my head, I held his hands gratefully in my own, their warmth comforting me.

Vic began to "drop by" the office, sometimes taking me out to lunch, sometimes just to chat for a second. The lunches became excursions into the hills outlying Reno—long, meandering trips that somehow never included the consumption of food. Vic would talk during the entire trip, his words wandering as much as the road. "God wants us to be together," he'd say, "we were meant to be together forever." And the unfocused glaze of his eyes terrorized me, for they were a signal of danger. His foot became an anchor weight on the gas pedal, pushing the car faster and faster on the dirt road, until we were spinning around curves and thumping over the ruts made by logging trucks. "I know you love me, Stephani, I know you don't want to leave me. We're always going to be together."

By the time he stopped the car, my heart would be racing, thumping in harmony to the bumps on the road, and I would be wondering frantically, Is he going to kill me here? Am I ever going to get back to civilization?

But after ten or fifteen minutes of sitting in the hills, hidden by the tall pine trees, Vic would reach over and kiss me, promise to love me forever, and turn the car around to head back. By the time we reached my office, he would be as calm as the agent he'd always professed to be. "Someday you'll know the truth, Stephani," he'd say. "Someday you'll understand everything."

ASK ME NO QUESTIONS

The truth eluded me. In the days after Vic's "confession" about his relationship with the underworld, he became obsessed with the idea that I would leave him. He seemed to have forgotten the Mob story altogether, reverting once more to the Company as the flame that drove him. "You'll understand," he said, over and over. "One day I'll be able to tell you everything, and you'll be glad you stuck it out."

But my fear of him grew.

The counseling sessions with Pastor Goodwin stopped in midsummer; there was so little I could tell him, so much I had to tell. He gave me no answers, no direction, just encouraged me to find "happiness" and prayed a lot. Well, I prayed a lot, too, but God was talking to Vic. Every day.

Vic's refusal to give up on our marriage gave me some bargaining power; I pressed for an opportunity to go to college, and he grudgingly allowed me to enroll at UNR, for one class. I couldn't quit my job, of course; we needed my income, but I eagerly anticipated the challenge of college coursework. The evening class also gave me a legitimate excuse to be away from home and my increasingly scary husband.

Our house was so different from every other home I knew that it was becoming increasingly difficult to return to it every day. The instances of normalcy I glimpsed in acquaintances' homes—church members, Elizabeth's, a neighborhood Bible study group—were such a revelation to me I could barely comprehend the difference. But I liked what I saw in those places. I liked the warmth, the sense of ease, that most of these people experienced with each other. It was so different from my home, where words were so carefully chosen, where everyone tiptoed around Vic, where tension ruled.

Vic had changed jobs again, becoming an independent woodcutter. He had a big, old one-ton Chevy truck that constantly needed repairs; he'd come back from the mountains swearing at the brakes, repeating harrowing stories of near-death escapes as he rolled down the logging roads with a load full of wood. I prayed, God forgive me, that he would crash and my problems would be over. But it never happened: he always returned.

I had to take some decisive action, do something that would move my life forward, take it out of the maze of lies, questions, doubts and indecision. Upon the recommendation of my supervisor, I called the Washoe County Mental Health Department and made an appointment with a psychiatrist there. Since God wasn't talking to me, I thought that maybe a shrink could tell me what to do.

Dr. Marriet Hanley sat before me, her pencil poised. "Just what do you want to get out of counseling?" she asked. She waited intently while I tried to formulate an answer, her brown eyes hidden behind fashionable glasses, her auburn hair curled and cut and teased until it resembled a bird's nest on her head, with tendrils carefully hanging in wisps over her ears and forehead.

What do I want out of this? I asked myself. *I want to know what to do with my life! I want to be able to discern the truth! I need to know! Is he an agent for the CIA or an enforcer for the Mafia?* But those were questions she couldn't answer. "I want to be able to make a decision, and stand by it," I said slowly, the words hanging low in the space between us, nearly disappearing into the air over her wide desk. "I want to decide what to do with my life and not let anyone change my mind."

Dr. Hanley watched me as I spoke, her pencil scratching notes on the yellow pad on her desk. "What kinds of decisions? What is it you want to decide?"

"Whether or not to stay married." There. The words were out, I had said them aloud. I waited expectantly, my hands twisting in my lap. My face burned with embarrassment.

"Tell me about your marriage."

It was an open question. I couldn't answer open questions. I had forgotten how to think, how to formulate reasoned dissertations: I knew only how to respond to direct orders or specific questions demanding specific replies.

Dr. Hanley waited.

My hands twisted.

The minutes ticked.

Finally she broke the silence. "How long have you been married?" she prodded.

"Thirteen years."

"How old were you?"

"Sixteen."

Again she waited, eyes gently encouraging, pencil poised. I looked at her helplessly. "I can't help you unless I know what the problem is," she said.

I sat, unable to voice my fears, my suspicions, my broken dreams. I didn't know where to start, and I didn't know whom to trust. I couldn't tell her anything about Vic's undercover activities—real or imagined—and that was the basis for everything. I couldn't tell her that I was afraid of my husband, that he had taken away my identity, brutalized me emotionally and physically since our wedding day until I no longer knew who or what I was. I couldn't tell her those things because I didn't yet fully recognize them as brutality or abuse or the systematic rape of my being that they were. I only knew that I was afraid, and the fear was so deep that I couldn't let it out: it would overcome me.

So I sat, twisting my hands and sweating with the effort to put my thoughts into some kind of order. Anything. Say anything.

"I just want to change my life," I said.

"How?"

"I want to be happy."

"What do you need to be happy?"

"I don't know...I need to be strong enough to make a decision. I want to decide for myself what I want, and I want to stick to it."

Dr. Hanley watched me while I spoke, and continued to look at me after I finished. "I want you to go to our group sessions, if you can. They meet once a week, and last for six weeks. Can you do that?"

I nodded, relieved that the interrogation was over.

Vic made no objection to my counseling sessions, other than cautioning me about the need for secrecy. "A shrink might do you some good," he said. "You've sure been acting crazy lately. I'm afraid to leave you alone with the kids half the time. Maybe she'll straighten you out."

So I began the sessions with a group of other crazy people and two therapists, and I spent two hours once a week listening to intimate details of other people's lives. My contribution was nil, though, as they spent a lot of time talking about their sex lives. When the therapist, a man, looked pointedly at me, and asked if I had anything to share, I could only shake my head, my lips glued together. I couldn't talk about sex. No way.

"Does your husband treat you good, then?" a "patient" asked.

"Yes, Stephani, tell us. It's okay," another person encouraged.

They were all looking at me expectantly, their eyes eager, their bodies leaning forward in anticipation.

"He gets all he wants," I stammered, fear lacing through me. Would he find out? What would he do?

"So do you get all you want?" someone said, not unkindly.

"I don't get anything I want," I heard myself say.

"Do you mean he takes you against your will?" They were all looking at me, waiting, encouraging smiles like pumpkins heads, all looking at me.

I nodded slowly. "Well, not exactly," I said, contradicting myself. "I'm his wife. I would never deny him his rights."

"What about your rights?" the therapist joined in.

I stared at him in confusion. My rights? "I'm his wife," I said. "I take my wedding vows very seriously."

"So you have sex even when you don't want to."

"You're a fucking machine."

"A fucking machine. Is that what you are, Stephani?" Voices came at me all at once, the phrase reverberating inside my head. I was a fucking machine. How appropriate. I had sacrificed my life, my dreams, my ambitions and talents, to become an object, not even of desire, but of simple animal instinct. The shockwaves echoed through my body.

"I am a fucking machine," I repeated.

"A what?" they asked.

"A fucking machine. I am a fucking machine!" I shouted, tears squirting from my eyes.

"Good," they said, nodding in appreciation of my acknowledgement. In another moment, the group had moved on, someone else began to share his story. Meanwhile, the phrase—I am a fucking machine—rolled over and over in my mind, a tape on "play" that wouldn't stop.

The end of my six weeks approached rapidly. Dr. Hanley interviewed me as the last session closed. "I would like to see you and your husband before we do anything else," she said. "An associate of mine, Dr. Chung, will join us. Do you think Vic will come in?"

"I don't know," I replied. What about me? I asked silently. What about my decision to leave him? I could feel the walls closing about me once again. I was not going to be allowed to make a decision.

Reluctantly, I asked Vic if he would see the two psychiatrists. "Why?" he said, "You're the problem. I don't have any problems."

"Because they want to see us together. To make an evaluation, I guess."

Surprisingly, he agreed.

The interview with Drs. Hanley and Chung was a step backward. Together, they asked Vic and me to describe our relationship, then to demonstrate what the word "marriage" meant. I stood beside Vic, took his hand, and we faced the world together; Vic took me by the shoulders, placed me in the corner, and stood in front of me, his arms outspread. No more words were needed.

Then my counselor said, "I'd like you both to attend a six-week group therapy, a couples group. Could you do that?"

I didn't need to reply, for Vic answered for both of us. "Sure," he said. What about me? I screamed inside. I want to leave! I want a divorce! I don't need any more therapy sessions! I was betrayed, double-crossed by my own psychologist. Vic would convince them all that I was crazy, that I needed "help." He would be the winner. He was always the winner.

I suppose I needn't have worried: Vic never intended to follow through with the sessions. He simply didn't go, and told me to stay away from "them" too. "We don't need them, Stephani," he assured me. "I'll take care of you."

But a week or so later, I discovered that Dr. Hanley had become a customer of Vic's; he was seeing her outside the auspices of the Mental Health Clinic offices, "delivering wood" to her house. Her betrayal was complete. So much for professional counseling.

Chapter 33

The failure of my counseling sessions was a distinct victory for Vic. Somehow, the fact that my weeks with a psychologist did nothing to loosen his hold on me gave him a sense of power that was beyond anything he had experienced before. He gloated over Dr. Hanley's recommendation, which was that I should stay with him until further counseling, or treatment, was completed. That recommendation seemed to prove to my husband that all the problems were in my head: it gave him the confidence that nothing else would stand in his way. He began to accompany me everywhere, insisted upon driving me to work and home again, to the grocery store and any other place I might want to go. I was away from him only when I was at work or at church activities, or when he himself was working.

Vic's woodcutting business gave him a flexibility of schedule which allowed him to do whatever he wanted. Some days he didn't even work, depending on the weather. But he was also gone on May weekend days, and I could enjoy the time without him. I would work on my homework assignments from UNR, take the girls on outings, or just clean house without Vic overseeing the entire process.

One day in late October, he came back and reported that a big fire was raging in the mountains he'd just left. In fact, he'd had a hard time getting out. He'd cut some trees with Forestry markers on them and had given the emblems to Deanna for a souvenir. I retrieved those emblems and hid them among other "evidence" I'd begun collecting. Evidence of what I didn't know, but I needed proof, proof of anything, one way or the other. Maybe the Forestry markers would come in handy someday.

A week later a Forestry agent knocked on our door, explained that he was investigating the fire, and had tracked Vic's truck down through various acquaintances and leads. He pointed out the broken window and scratched paint on the truck and took a scraping of that paint back with him.

ASK ME NO QUESTIONS

Vic was livid. When the agent left, my husband turned to me, grabbed my arm, and shoved me into the bedroom, slamming the door behind him. "How dare they question me?" he raged, his hold on me tightening. "Do they know who they're dealing with?" His eyes were glazed; he was out of control, and I knew there was nothing I could do to stop the assault which followed.

Winter settled upon us, and with the death of summer sunshine, so followed my hopes of resurrecting my belief in my husband. Despite the doubting of my doubts, the confusion over what was truth and what was fantastic, unbelievable falsehood, I could not feel love. Daily I prayed for a miracle, a sign from God that would wipe away all fears, all doubt, all despair. But the miracle never happened.

By then, the winter of 1979, I had become ensconced in my church, an American Baptist affiliate, and made tentative friendships with normal people. People whose lives weren't directed by the CIA or the Mafia. People to whom my husband was a faceless name, a man they knew only through my steadfast excuses as to why Vic could never attend services. "He works on Sunday," I said, over and over again. Perhaps they were used to unsaved souls whose spirits were in the shaking hands of hopeful spouses. They never pressed.

The holiday season approached, and with it the most dreaded time of year. Christmas. I hated Christmas. For me, it was the loneliest day of the year, for we were a "family" who never seemed to be able to catch the spirit of it all. If we remained at home, just the six of us, we had the rituals to relive each year, the waiting until the children brought us coffee in bed, then, before that first cup was drained, we would allow the stockings to be raided. Of course, Santa had left gifts out, unwrapped, for the girls to discover. These they could enjoy until after breakfast, when the presents could be unwrapped in earnest. Always, one of the children was appointed Santa's helper, the chosen one who presented the gifts, one at a time, to waiting hands. Then each gift would be opened quickly, the ripping and tearing an accepted—encouraged, even—part of the ritual. Everyone had to watch while the gifts were exposed.

And each year, I had to express my surprise, my delight, in the gifts Vic bought me. They were terrible things, cheap, gaudy baubles that took up a lot of room but had no value, either monetarily or sentimentally. One year he had done all his shopping at a home decorating party. Of course, he hadn't gone to the party, but the distributor had brought him a catalogue, and he chose my gifts from the slick paper pictures. That was the year of the candles. At least a dozen of them—squat fat scented candles and tall, slender ones, with gaudy glass and plastic greenery holding them captive.

The children's gifts were no better: hundreds of sticks or logs or puzzle pieces, tiny little parts to put together and to lose before the end of the day. Vic could never see the sense in getting children anything but cheap toys. Perhaps that was all the child in him, all that he knew of family.

That Christmas was different. We were going to visit my parents in Arizona, which meant the gifts would probably be bought at the last minute, at places which stayed open late. Of all the Christmas rituals we had, family visits were the worst. There would be the days of reminiscing, catching up, and looking ahead. Questions. "What are you doing now?" "Do you like your new job?" "Does Vic like his?" "Are you going to stay in Reno for awhile?" I hope you don't move anymore. It's bad for the girls." "I hope you keep this job. It sounds like you could get ahead there." I hated all the questions. I knew that all my answers were lies, made up replies to satisfy their curiosity. I don't know! I wanted to scream at them. I don't even know what tomorrow will bring! But I smiled and let the lies trip off my tongue.

And then we would have to go home, and that was worst of all. When we entered the door of our current domicile, the trappings of politeness and familial love slid off as if they were intrinsic in the coats we wore. The children disappeared into their rooms to play with their new toys, Vic disappeared into the living room to watch TV, and I disappeared altogether. In my house, I did not exist. Only the spectre of my hopes and dreams survived, only the shell of my body moved to the tune of my husband's desires. I lived only to serve him.

That year, 1979, the Christmas visit was preceded by another event, an event of minor importance in the overall scheme of things, but one which, nevertheless, I remember as monumental.

My church choir, of which I was a part, gave a Christmas cantata the Sunday before the great holiday. I had one of the solo parts, a small section of one song belonging to me, only me. Amazingly, I still dreamed of singing, really singing, and had performed numerous times in this small church as well as with a gospel sextet. Vic allowed me this one frivolity, this single joy. The night of the cantata, I dressed carefully in my best holiday apparel, a long, blue dress with yards and yards of skirt falling, billowing from my waist. Over the dress I placed my most prized garment, a crushed velvet cape made by my own hands. Falling to the floor, the deep green velvet glistened when it caught the light. Inside, I had lined it with silk. It had a hood for protection against the elements, and slits for my hands to slip through if I chose. Now, though, I just let the cape rest on my shoulders, drawing comfort in its warmth. I felt like a princess.

ASK ME NO QUESTIONS

"Where do you think you're going?" Vic's voice was low, a growl in the quiet of the evening. The girls were in their rooms, having been fed and settled with homework or toys.

"The cantata is tonight," I replied breathlessly, my stomach tightening anxiously.

"I didn't say you could go," he contended, his eyes glancing over me derisively.

"Yes, you did, you told me it would be okay. Remember? I asked you weeks ago. We've been practicing for two months." I stood at the bottom of the stairs, my hand tight on the railing. He stood just in front of me, his face level with mine.

"I've changed my mind. You don't need to go anywhere tonight. Now go change your clothes." He didn't shout or yell, his voice was still quiet. I stood my ground, trembling.

"I can't, Vic. I have a solo part! They're depending on me to be there!"

"I said you don't need to go! Now go take that—rag—off!" His voice was louder now, raised to a roar above my plea. He raised his hand to pull at the buttons that clasped my cape at my neck.

"Vic, listen to me! You said I could go! They're counting on me. I can't let them down. I can't just not go!"

My pleas were useless, of course. He shouted at me even as I protested, his face inches from mine.

Something snapped inside me. I could not, would not let him stop me this time. He had to listen! He had to! "Vic!" I yelled, attempting to drown out his voice with my own. "Stop yelling at me! Listen to me, why won't you listen to me!"

But he kept on shouting, his breath in my face, his finger poking me in the chest in an emphatic order. Before I knew what had happened, I slapped him.

But the sound of that slap was immediately drowned out by the ringing in my ears as he responded in kind. I didn't feel it, not right away. No, I heard the echo of its impact as my head cracked against the wall beside me, and, grabbing the railing, I caught myself, hung on to my balance in a shaky attempt to stay on my feet.

"You slapped me first," he said. "Just remember that."

Evidently he thought that was the end of the argument. Surely, he had no reason to believe I would disobey. Hadn't I always obeyed? I knew that vow well, perhaps the best of them all. Love, honor, and obey. And if you cannot do the first of these three, then remember the last, remember to obey!

I watched him retreat, followed him with my smarting eyes, until he disappeared from view in the living room. I waited until the TV was turned up, waited until I knew he would not be alert to my movements. Then, picking my purse up from the floor, I sneaked out the front door. I had to sing in the cantata.

It was dark when I returned, dark and wet with winter snow. I approached the house warily, my cheek still sore from the slap he'd delivered hours before. There had been questioning glances at church, a single, "Is everything okay, Stephani?" but that was all. A repair of makeup in the bathroom and no one could tell. But my head still ached, whether from the slap itself or the breaking of my heart I didn't know. My life was over, as far as I was concerned. It didn't matter anymore whether he was an agent for the CIA or not. I could not live in constant terror of the man who held my life.

Brave thoughts. Desperate thoughts, coming from a futile, desperate moment. I knew I would never follow through with them. I didn't have the strength to fight him.

The car lights shone on a dark house. It wasn't late, just 9:30. Vic must have decided to go to bed early. Good. I didn't have to face him. I could just go in, take off my tarnished finery, and slip into bed. No. Tonight I would sleep on the couch. Maybe.

Parking the car, I stepped carefully onto the icy driveway and made my way to the door. The knob refused to turn in my cold hand. Vic must have locked it. We had never locked our doors, despite the news of crime all around us. Oh, well. Taking the key ring, I held it up to the pale light of the winter moon, searching for the house key. It was gone. Had it ever been there? Had I ever had a house key? Confused, I looked again, feeling the shape of each metallic form. There were only three keys on the ring, two of which belonged to the car. The remaining key was foreign, its size smaller, its shape sharper than the one for which I searched.

The cold began to seep into my hands, through my thick cape and gauzy material of my fancy dress. Trying the odd key once more, I shoved and pushed and turned, all without success. Maybe it fell into my purse, I thought. Maybe it's on another ring.

Confused, not yet frightened, I returned to the car, turned it on to warm up, and emptied my purse onto the seat beside me. The dim light overhead displayed no escaped key. I turned the lining of my purse out, searched for hidden pockets that might hold a small piece of metal. Nothing.

Scooping everything back, I got out of the car once more, turned the doorknob once again. Nothing.

ASK ME NO QUESTIONS

"Vic!" I called, reluctantly resorting to the only action yet available. "Vic, let me in!" Pounding on the door, I watched as my breath created a cloud in front of me. Vic didn't come, didn't answer. After a futile few minutes, I returned to the car, wrapped myself in my cape, and eventually fell into an exhausted slumber.

"What are you doing out here? Get in the house! You'll make yourself sick!"

The sun was shining, its brightness glaring through the ice which had formed on the windows. Vic was outside. It was his voice that awoke me. Stiff, ice cold, I looked up at him with wary eyes. I had locked the car doors against—what? The only person of whom I was afraid stood on the other side of the door.

"Get out of there! What's the matter with you, are you crazy?" His face was just there, on the other side of the glass. "Stephani, don't be an idiot! Get out of the car." Turning on his heel, he marched back inside the house.

Slowly unwinding, I crept out. It was early, but not so early most of the neighbors wouldn't be up. Glancing at my rumpled cape and wrinkled dress, I thought, for a fleeting second, that I really must have been crazy, to spend the night in the car. But I was locked out! What was I supposed to have done?

Stepping gingerly over the concrete walk, I made it to the door without falling on the ice, and went on inside. "What were you doing?" Vic asked doggedly, innocently. "Have you gone completely off your rocker? You could freeze to death out there!"

"The door was locked," I said half-heartedly, my voice a whimper of bewilderment. "I couldn't get in."

"The door was locked? Since when! You never lock the door."

"It was locked," I insisted stubbornly, avoiding his accusing stare. "I tried it several times. I knocked, but you didn't answer. I couldn't get in."

Vic shook his head, his helplessness over my inadequacy fully apparent. "I don't know about you, Stephani. You get crazier every day. Pretty soon you'll be telling me I locked you out."

I couldn't voice the words. But you did, I thought. I know you did. Meeting his eyes in limp defiance, I stood in my wrinkled finery, the heat of the house hitting my frozen body with tendrils of warmth. I shivered.

"You'd better change," he said, his eyes on my pretty, now-wrinkled, blue dress. But his words held an entirely different meaning.

A week later, we were in Arizona, spending Christmas with my parents and younger brother.

Chapter 34

Our return to Reno after Christmas marked the beginning of the end of my marriage. The promised year was nearly over: I was exhausted, torn apart by the need to know the truth and the fear of what that truth might be. I could not handle the indecision, the deception, the uncertainty; and I could not face the possibility—no, the certainty—that my life had been a lie.

Vic was not one to give in easily: in 1980, he developed a new strategy, hitting me where I was the most vulnerable, the most fragile. In January he began going to church.

There was a new minister at the church I attended, a Bible-thumper of the old school. His sermons were fire-breathing epitaphs of the promise of hell should any Christian stray. He spoke of causing illness, even death, for people who crossed him, of the dangers of modern life and its lack of moral values. He emphasized the foundation of the home and the submission of the wife.

Vic ate it up, repeating phrases to me at home and in our bedroom. He told me about his many conversations with God, conversations reminiscent of Moses and the burning bush. Conversations which opposed any imagined dialogue I may have had with the Almighty.

"I talked to God today," he'd say upon his return from the woods, "and He said we were meant to be together forever. You are my wife. You must be submissive as a good Christian wife submits to her husband..." "God appeared to me today, in a tree. I was going to cut this tree down, it was huge, but God spoke to me and told me to wait. He advised me that you will always be mine, we're married in His eyes and nothing can tear us asunder."

These sermonettes would go on, sometimes for hours, interrupted only by the girls' comings and goings, dinner, and other household chores. Even then, I would find him following me, or standing behind me as I cooked, his voice intoning the commandments of his Lord.

They didn't stop with nightfall, either. I fell asleep each night with Vic's voice in my ear; I would awaken in the darkness and listen to the same phrases, the same sermons, over and over. Sometimes he talked while he made love to me, his sentences short and gasping, emphasizing God's admonitions with every thrust of his body. I would awaken to the sound and the feel and the weight of him and I would lie, trembling, while he asserted his power over me in the most intimate ways.

Vic had decided that he needed to become a "better" lover, and began fondling my body in ways that were foreign to me. It was as if he had realized that I needed more than the purely perfunctory act of intercourse—now, he tried to woo me with caresses and kisses.

But it was too late. I gagged at his kisses, repulsed by the taste of nicotine, smoke, and bad teeth. Vic had never taken care of his body, and nearly all of his teeth were literally rotting out of his mouth. I held my breath to keep the taste and smell at bay, twisting my head away from him as he licked and pinched in what he thought were techniques to bring me to arousal. I just grew colder. The fear and revulsion grew more intense, until I could not endure the sexual act without pain. My body rejected him.

Vic's campaign to win me back included a visit to our pastor, that fire-breathing minister who would not tolerate disobedience to God's will. Vic "confessed," although his confession was greatly abridged, and was baptized. I was trapped. "You have no Biblical reason to divorce him," Pastor Wilson told me, his voice stern and authoritative. "Vic has repented of any wrongdoing, he is clean before the Lord. You must forgive him or you will face damnation yourself."

January and February passed in this way, as I felt the strength to fight them dissipate. They were taking me apart, chunk by chunk, and I could not get the pieces of my self together. I had already lost the battle.

March approached, that same springtime that nearly always rejuvenated me, gave me hope. But this year there was no hope. I was beaten. I knew that it was only a matter of time before I became a Stepford wife, a robot like those women in a book I'd read, women who were replaced by robot lookalikes, whose only purpose was to serve their husbands. I knew if I gave him whatever he wanted, gave up the struggle to find myself, he would be happy and would probably give me some token of freedom. But I would never be allowed to step beyond the boundaries of the gilded cage he kept me in; the door would always be locked. I felt my spirit sink a little more each day, each day growing quieter, less autonomous, less able to make even the smallest decisions.

Yet, at work, I excelled. Now that I was working in a place that did not include Vic, I was able to discover talents and skills which set me apart from the robot that slept in my bed, cooked family dinners, and cared for four children. Work was the peace that saved my sanity.

And then one Saturday in early March, Vic came in with the mail. A letter, addressed to him, was the only envelope we received that day: Vic opened it, scanned it quickly, and exploded into a rage that had become all too familiar.

"They've blackballed me!" he screamed. "They're forcing me to retire! They can't do that to me! Not after all I've done! The bastards! The goddamned fucking bastards!" Crushing his hands together, he crumpled the letter and threw it into the fireplace, where a cheery blaze warmed the living room. Then he grabbed his coat and stomped out of the house.

Trembling, I had watched this display, waiting with trepidation for the verbal and physical assault that was sure to follow. When Vic left the house instead, my eyes were drawn to the flames across the room. The crumpled ball of paper rested in a corner, safe from the reach of the fire.

Swiftly, for I knew he could return any instant, I reached into that corner with the fire poker and carefully retrieved the missive from harm. I retreated to the bedroom, shut the door behind me, and began to unwrap the letter. I saw the letterhead: California State Forestry: District Headquarters. Puzzled, I unfolded the remaining paper and read:

Victor Charles Brian:

"You are hereby subpoenaed to appear before California State Court on the charge of arson..."

Blackballed? Retired? This letter was not from the Company. This letter was proof, proof that my husband of nearly fourteen years, my Victor Charles Brian, was nothing but a liar, a conman, a mental case. Which one? Or all three?

I stood, gazing at the paper, reading and rereading the words printed there. Over and over I relived the scene just past, heard his voice, the disbelief, the rage and hurt. He believed it! Whatever the paper said, he believed his words, saw what he saw, lived what he lived! What was he? What kind of a man was he?

I was stunned. Despite all my doubts, my suspicions, my prayers for release and my hope that he would just disappear from my life, I could not believe the proof in front of my eyes. Everything was a lie.

Slumping to the couch, I stared at that paper, thinking, hoping, I had misread it. He was merely wanted as a witness. Maybe it was a code, as all those previous letters were code. But the words didn't change, no matter how many times I read them. "You are charged with arson..."

ASK ME NO QUESTIONS

I recalled the Forestry officer who'd come to see Vic in October, investigating the fire that raged on Diamond Mountain. He'd taken paint samplings from Vic's truck. The tree markers Vic had given to the girls flashed into my mind. Could it be possible? Was this how it would end?

Yet, even with the "proof" held in my hands, I could not think of what to do. My brain would not go that far.

I was sitting on the couch before a burning fire, the television on but the volume low, the lights off. The children had been put to bed hours before, were sleeping soundly. I could hear a small, contented snore every now and then. My mind had not stopped racing. But my thoughts continued on the same track, over and over.... *He's not an agent for the CIA. He's not a victim of the Mafia. It's all a lie, a lie, a lie.*

The front door opened. I tensed, pretended to be interested in the TV program. "Hi, honey. Are you all right? I was wor-"

He grabbed my arm, his eyes opaque and his jaw set.

"Vic, what are you doing! Let me go!"

His reply was to grip me harder, drag me across the room, and, with the wild-eyed, glazed focus of a madman, gather me into his arms and throw me into the dark crevasse of our bedroom.

I hit the bed like a rag doll hitting concrete, slid across the quilted cotton bedcover I'd made with my own two hands, and smashed against the bookcased headboard of the bed I'd rescued from the Salvation Army thrift store three years previously; I'd moved it four times without nicking a splinter on its "authentic" walnut-stained finish.

The night was black, a solid absence of light that was impenetrable as I squinted hard toward the doorway. But I couldn't see him. The fire crackled cheerfully in the rock fireplace, the fire I'd tended so carefully only minutes before.

Where are you? I held my breath, I dared not breathe, I wanted to run but I was reeling from the blow against the headboard, my eyes saw fireworks in the darkness, and I couldn't make my body move.

I heard the door whisper shut, strained and heard his step on the orange carpet I hated almost as much as I hated living with the lies, then all I heard was the thud of my heart and the shudder of my breath as the fear rose quick and tangible and overpowering, and suddenly I had to vomit; I needed to throw up, but I couldn't move, couldn't flinch a finger as I heard first one shoe drop and then the other.

The bed creaked and I felt his hand brush my thigh. "No-o-o!" I screamed, and I smelled his smell, the smell of tobacco and sweat and rage, and I gritted my teeth as I fought him.

His hands on my shirt were gnarled and callused, hands I'd loved once, hands I'd snuggled safely inside as they enfolded me; hands that had held and slapped and bruised me over and over again. With one yank those hands tore the shirt from my back.

He laughed. The sound of it galvanized me into attempting, once more, to free myself, but my arms were pinned beside me, and he laughed, the sound of it filling the silence of the room as he ripped away all that I wore, not just the clothes, but whatever dignity, whatever pride I had left were gone, gone, in an instant, and I begged for my life.

"Please, please don't do this. Please don't do this…"

His laughter echoed in the room, and as the tears slipped down my cheeks I prayed, God please help me, please, God help me, but God watched and was silent. I looked at my husband, the man I'd loved for fourteen years, the man I'd given my life, and, as his hands reached toward me, I saw, against the flashing bursts of light, little pointed horns curve out on each side of his head. I saw the eyes of the devil.

"You won't leave me," he said, his voice quiet in the night, low and deliberate and more terrifying than anything I had ever heard. "You won't leave me alive." His eyes held me, those strange opaque eyes that impaled me with their intensity. His eyes glistened in the dark. I stared back at him, helpless, my own eyes bulging with terror, the fear so great I thought my head would explode with its force.

Pinning my arms with his knees on either side of me, he took my hair in his hand, caressed it, rubbed it gently between his fingers as if to savor the softness, and then, with a slow swoop of his head, he covered my mouth with his and kissed me. And as he kissed me, his grip tightened in my hair, pulled until the pain was more than I could resist and I opened my mouth to his.

He tasted like stale tobacco and rotted teeth.

Bile rushed into my throat. I fought it, swallowed and choked as his tongue licked the inside of my mouth, over my lips, moved to my face. He licked the tears as they slid from my eyes.

"Stop! Please, please stop."

The words were mere whispers in a black night. Somewhere in the back of my brain, lights exploded, fireworks in my skull. My head throbbed, my heart thudded, my stomach cramped again and again as I fought to remain conscious. I couldn't let go, couldn't give in to oblivion. I knew I would never wake up.

ASK ME NO QUESTIONS

Through a spotty red haze I saw him, all shadow in shadow, move down my body, his lips and teeth leaving a sticky wet trail as he licked and bit and kissed. I felt the cool night air against my skin and my entire body shivered when his mouth touched my belly. *Fight, Stephani. Fight. Don't give in to him. Don't let him win.* The thoughts came unbidden, a reflex from my soul. Logic flashed through the fear.

I bent one leg, brought a knee up between us, and gathered everything I had to shove, heaving, against his shoulders.

"Uumph!"

Thwack! The slap felt loud inside my head, the thud of bone against bone. The ringing in my ears increased. Logic fled.

"Don't try that again, damn you! You'll learn, if it's the last thing you do!" His breath was hot on my face. "You're my wife, and you'll always be my wife!" The words oozed from his lips, lips that moved just a skinbreadth from my cheek. "Even if you have to die in the process."

Reeling, I barely heard the words through the buzz inside my head, a buzz which became a roar as his hands closed about my throat.

"Yes!" I croaked. *Yes, I give in! You win. You always win.* The one word was lost in a moan beneath his hands. He couldn't see my capitulation, and if he had, couldn't have stopped himself. His eyes were the eyes of a madman, glazed and unfocused. I gasped, gulping for air, but there was no air.

His fingers tightened: I felt them, each digit meshing a grave-like indentation in my skin as they sought to crush the fragile bones, felt the bones begin to move beneath his hands. My lungs screamed for oxygen. I was defeated.

But more than all that, more than terror, more than pain, more than helplessness, I felt the insidious sense of fate, of acceptance. This was always meant to be.

My head whirled and I was sucked into a vortex of cold, black space, whirling dizzily, faster and faster until there was nothing but the roar in my ears and the pain in my chest as my heart pumped like the heart of a frightened bird, thump-THUMP, thump-THUMP, thump-THUMP, rapid erratic beats that filled my head with their frantic pulse. Then—nothing.

I opened my eyes. The pressure was gone. In its place was a vast, still emptiness. Slowly awareness returned, and I realized the scene I remembered wasn't a nightmare…He was still beside me, stroking me with feather-light sweeps of his callused hands, his lips and teeth leaving a damp trail on my skin. A trail of horror. Shivering, I forced my body to remain still, as if it were something outside my self. I endured, held my breath as the truth of his words registered in my brain: "You'll always be my wife…"

He would kill me. He wanted my mind, my will, to die. That was the only way he could possess me. And if I would not surrender that, he would murder me in order to keep me his forever. He had finally overstepped the bounds of reason. He was insane.

My skin burned where his lips had touched. The trail of his attack was written on my flesh. "I'm going to love you until you die, I love you, my wife…" His tongue professed an intimacy which belied the terror of his act. *Oh, God, help me. Please, God, help me die. I can't fight anymore…*

The scene rolled on before me, and I watched it from somewhere from outside myself. I saw Stephani on the bed, naked in the darkness, Victor covering her body with his own. I heard him say, "You know you love me, Steph. You know you can't live without me…"

And she replied, choking on the words. "Yes. Yes, Vic. You're right."

No, no! I screamed silently, my thoughts willing that woman to fight, and suddenly I was back inside her, and I felt the strength of that denial roll through my body like an evening tide. *NoNoNoNo!* It came from somewhere deep inside the recesses of my being, a silent scream which only my brain heard, only my heart responded to, a scream that seared my soul. *You will not win this war. Never!* And the tears trickled from my eyes.

The mattress heaved as he stood up. "I'll let you rest now, punkin. But don't worry, I won't leave you alone for very long."

I heard his footsteps retreating, heard the squeak of the door as he opened it and left the room. Then, clearly in the silent dawn, I heard the click as he turned the lock.

I was trapped. Worse, I was exhausted, traumatized, and helpless. Every cell in my body ached. I glanced at the windows enshrouded in darkness: even the heavy drapes seemed to hide secrets of their own. I could not reach out to those dark shadows to reveal the light beyond. I could not move to help myself. Instead I quivered and twitched and hid inside a shroud of blankets.

The door opened. My ears picked up the movement through the layers of bedding; every nerve in my body tensed, awaiting the next sound.

"Here, baby, I've brought you something to eat. It isn't often I get to fix something special for the woman I love." The smell of bacon wafted to me, beckoning. Bacon and eggs, probably hash browned potatoes. Vic's favorite breakfast. I gagged, pulling the covers tighter over my head.

ASK ME NO QUESTIONS

The drapes rustled open. I could almost feel the sunshine pour into the room. *Leave me alone! Go away and leave me alone!*

The bed sagged as he sat beside me. I forced my body to stillness when he touched my shoulder. *Be quiet,* I told myself. *Don't move.* The bedcover began to slip off my head.

"Come on, Steph. You have to eat. I've got great plans for us today."

Reluctantly I opened an eye. The sunlight brought instant tears. "Where are the girls?" I croaked.

"They're over at Jim's. Jim and Savannah said they'd keep them for the weekend. Give us a chance to be together. Come on, now. Up you go. Too bad we can't go fishing yet. But we'll find something to do, I'm sure." His fingers were busy as he spoke, busy with the blankets, the sheet, arranging the scene like a film director, folding the sheet just so on my waist, placing the plate and the fork on my thighs, punching the pillows up just right.

"Can I have my robe?"

"You don't need it. We're all alone."

"But I'm cold. Can't I just cover up while I eat?"

"I've got a great fire going in the fireplace. I'll just open the door a little."

Fear forced obedience. My mind raced, raced like a hamster caught in his wheel, going fast and getting nowhere. I choked the food down only because he insisted on putting the fork to my mouth, touching me and hovering over me with that promise in his eyes. The promise of more to come, more that I could not endure.

When I had swallowed as much of the greasy mess as I could, he took the plate, closing the door which let in the heat from the living room before he led me, tottering like a baby, to the bathroom. He turned on the shower, led me in, and retreated. "I'll be right here," he said. "I'll help you scrub your back."

In fourteen years, he had never "helped" me wash. In fact, he was something of a prude, never allowing the intimacies of marriage to interfere with his rigid sense of morality. The mysteries of a woman's toilette were beyond his realm of curiosity. This sudden change was more terrifying than his anger, which was at least routine in our lives. I shuddered as the warmth of the water splashed over me. *What is he doing?*

His hand reached in, he took hold of my shoulder to steady himself, and with the other, he began to stroke my back, building the lather with each completed circle.

My skin screamed.

"There, how's that?" Mercifully, he had no more sense now of fulfilling another's needs than he'd ever had. A few seconds, a gesture of simulated love, was all he could muster. He turned off the shower and handed in a towel.

"Come on, baby. Come to Papa. I'm going to take care of you. You won't have to lift a finger."

Enfolding me within the worn cotton, he began to wipe the sudsy water from my body, his arms imprisoning me. There was a time when I would have welcomed his attention, when I would have turned to him and unbuttoned his shirt in invitation. Not now, though. Now I knew too much. Water dripped down my back as he pushed me toward the door.

"I—I have to go to the bathroom," I stammered, halting.

"Oh, sure baby. Go ahead."

"I—I'd like to have some privacy."

His hand remained still; I held my breath as I felt it move on the small of my back. "All right," he said. "I'll be right outside. Don't be too long." That hand touched my cheek as he stepped around me to the door. "I'll be waiting," he said softly. His eyes flickered over me once, and then he shut the door behind him.

If only I could think! Even as I used the toilet, my eyes never left the doorknob. He was on the other side, he could open it so easily. A simple push. I flushed, washed my hands, and stood uncertainly before the door.

"All done?" He pulled the towel away from my body, tossed it on the floor, and pulled me toward the bedroom.

Once again I heard the door close, once again his hands pushed me down.

"I don't know what I was thinking, before," he said. "We can go fishing anytime." He climbed in beside me, his face inches from mine. I stared into his eyes, and I flew away, fled from this moment, let my mind escape while I forced my body to lie still beneath him.

The hours that followed were endless hours of torture. Vic was convinced he only had to "love" me into submission and I would forget about leaving him, forget the past, forget the lies. He prepared our meals, brought me wine and candles and flowers.

But he kept my clothes, unhooked the telephone, locked the doors. He accompanied me to the bathroom, aided me in the shower, washed my hair. He never mentioned the Company or the Mafia or anything outside our marriage. I remembered the long lunchtimes in the Nevada desert, the implication of the gun he kept by his side, the brooding silences and sudden violence in the past weeks. I watched the flat, cold, gaze of his eyes. I had never known such terror.

The first day, I wanted to die.

ASK ME NO QUESTIONS

The second day, I knew I would live.

I moved off the bed, slowly, quietly, willing my mind to numbness. *Don't think*, I thought. *Don't remember.* Moving to the door, I caught a glimpse of my image in the bureau mirror. *Oh, God. Is that me? That creature?* The reflection was vague in the dim light; the bedroom curtains were drawn against the weak winter sun. But I didn't want to see more. I didn't want to see the mottled bruises, the pink blotches, the ravaged eyes. My long pale hair frizzed out in a cloud about my face, tangled and limp. A harridan's face, a witch's hair. Slowly, forcing myself to move quietly, I opened a drawer, slid it just far enough to reach inside and grasp a piece of cotton flannel. I nearly had the nightgown out when I heard the doorknob turn. Caught.

"What are you doing?" he demanded. "You shouldn't be out of bed. You'll catch cold running around like that. Come on, let me help you..." Taking my arm, he led me back, one arm around my waist, guiding me. Tucking me in, he said, "We have all weekend. We're totally alone. I'm going to show you how much I love you, Steph, how much you love me."

He unbuttoned his shirt.

I tried. God help me, I tried to comply. I wanted to die. But something was growing within me, something that refused to give in. All the time that he "loved" me, I fought the impulse to strike him, fought the shudders of repulsion, fought the need to scream, and scream, and scream.

No one would come to my rescue. I knew that, just as I knew I could not fight him with my body. I had to beat him with my mind.

Against every instinct and impulse, I kept still, allowed him to "love" me while I concentrated on how I was going to escape.

Getaway.

My thoughts drifted. Pictures of our life together skated across the mirror in my mind. Behind those brief flashes, a child wavered, a toddler standing in a river, a fawn beside her, the forest behind her. Where is that child now? My resolve deepened. *You will not win this war*, I cried. *You will not!*

"See, Steph? I can make you happy. Just be patient, darling, just be patient. I'm the only man who can make you feel like this."

He moved over me, adjusted my arms and my legs, and was inside me. I felt a tear dampen my cheek.

I blinked the tears back. *I will not cry anymore!* Crying was weak. Crying didn't help. I clamped my teeth together. Every muscle tensed, every nerve screamed. Inside, I was dry, unresponsive. His flesh grated against mine. You will not win, I thought as his rhythm increased. You will not win this war.

"God meant for us to be together, Steph. Always. What God put together, no one can take apart. Remember? We made a promise to each other. No one can break that promise."

"Yes, Vic," I said. "You're right. You're always right." *No! No, no, no, no, no! God didn't put us together, He didn't create this mess.*

He rolled off me, spooned himself against me, wrapped his arms around me. "Let's just sleep awhile, baby. I'll hold you, I won't let go. We can just relax the entire afternoon."

Sure, sleep. I didn't think I'd ever sleep again.

But I did. I awoke to the sound of his voice, that odd, chanting mantra that was becoming as familiar as the fear in my heart.

"God spoke to me. He said we're meant to be together. Always. Forever. You'll never leave me, Stephani. Never leave me. We're meant to be together. Forever. God said so..." I heard the sounds, felt the words against my hair before I understood them. It was dark, the darkness of death, in which all light was closed out, curtained off, contained. Vic's arm snaked around my waist, clamped me to him in a vice-grip so tight I could scarcely breathe.

I moved the toe of my right foot, felt the prickles of numbness, stretched my left leg. It, too, was numb with the weight of immobility. Vic's arm tightened. "You'll always be my wife, always. What God has put together, no man will part. No man. You'll never leave me, Steph. Never."

I won't get away from him, I thought. I'll never get away. I could have laughed, if there was room to laugh within that embrace. I'd never wanted to leave, I'd only wanted him to love me. I'd fought heaven and all its angels to stay with him, to prove my love was enough. But love was never enough. Not with someone like Vic.

He left me, promising to return in a little while. My body ached with a weariness surpassing anything I had felt in the past. It was a deathly weight, a heaviness that chained me to the bed. What time is it? Has the night passed yet? It didn't matter. Nothing mattered. Was this what it had all been for? The years of sacrifice, of loving and understanding and giving in, giving up?

God, what a fool! How could I have been so blind! To think he really loved me! The tears began again as the pain inside my head exploded into a myriad of lights, so intense that the very act of opening my eyes was torture...It was too much. Cradling my head between my hands, I buried my face in the pillow. *Oh God*, I prayed, *Please help me. Please, please help me to die. I can't live like this anymore!* But I knew that praying was futile. I knew that God didn't listen anymore. I knew there would be no release. I escaped into sleep once more.

ASK ME NO QUESTIONS

My brain jumped into awakening, my dulled senses struggled to focus. What is it? Something was happening. I waited, straining my ears. My very skin seemed to listen, the nerves reaching beyond the confines of the flesh.

Someone was in the room with me.

I felt him then, felt the eyes upon me as he stared, willing my own to open. "Stephani," he murmured, his words just brushing my ear, "I know you're not asleep. You can't fool me, you know. I know everything. I know you love me. Show me you love me, Stephani. I know you're awake! Don't try to ignore me, Stephani! Your little games don't work!" I heard the anger swell from somewhere deep inside him, the frustration building. I knew there was no use in pretending anymore.

I turned over. He was lying just behind me, his head resting on one hand, his eyes unblinking as I turned to face him. Is that the face of the man I loved? Those burning eyes, that grim mouth. Where is Vic, the man to whom I gave my life?

He reached over me, grabbed my hair, and pulled my face to his. "Show me, Stephani. I know you still love me. Say you'll never leave...."

I groaned, gagged against his breath, his mouth on mine. His hand tightened in my hair, and then he was on top of me, inside me, and I could not fight, could not move, could not feel. "I'll never leave you," I said, my voice coming from somewhere far away.

And so the weekend wore on.

The third day I returned to work, dazed, confused, terrorized into submission. The subjugation, as far as Vic was concerned, was complete: I would not dare to defy him. Nor would I tell anyone what had transpired—after all, who would believe me? To the rest of the world, Victor Charles Brian was a model husband, a model father. So I believed. After all, hadn't he sent me flowers nearly every week for the past six months? Wasn't I the envy of all my co-workers? And hadn't he expressed his love and renewed faith in God publicly, in my own church?

Vic drove me to work. I wore no makeup: I had probably never looked as bad as I did that day. My hair was freshly washed; Vic had even helped me to curl it. I wore a pretty dress, a flowered affair with long, billowing sleeves and a high, buttoned neck. I hid my red-rimmed eyes behind the curtain of my hair, bent my head over the computer screen in front of me, the earphones securely keeping it in place. Last week's flower arrangement wilted on the divider beside me. Dying flowers. It seemed appropriate, so I left them there.

"Stephani," Jackie, my supervisor called out to me.

I glanced up, unwilling to meet her eyes. What now? I thought, annoyed.

"Mr. Craig wants to see you now."

Oh, God, not Eric Craig. He was the department head. He never called on one of us unless there was a problem Jackie had referred to him.

Reluctantly, I unhooked my earphones and slid out from behind my desk.

"Come on in," Mr. Craig invited, when I'd reached his office.

I crossed the room and seated myself at the chair facing his desk. Fleeting memories of another such occasion crossed my mind. Detroit Lakes Hospital. Donald Farrell. I blinked the image from my mind and looked shyly at Eric Craig.

"As you are aware," he said, taking note of my apparel, "there is an opening in Retail Sales. We'd like to promote from within the Classified Department, should any of you there be interested. I have heard, from Jackie, of your interest in advancement."

Oh, No! Not now, not when I'm at my worst...I blinked again, taking in Mr. Craig's words. He was considering me for a promotion! I could feel the adrenaline pumping my heart, accelerating my thoughts.

"Yes, I am very interested in advancement," I replied as calmly as I could. "I've done very well in Classifed, as I'm sure you know from my monthly statistics. I'm ready for a new challenge."

"Yes, we're aware of your outstanding work. What would you like to be doing in, oh, say five years from now?"

"I'd like your job," I blurted. My face flushed; the heat spread down over my neck.

Eric Craig smiled. "I'd better watch out, then." Again he seemed to take in my wan face. I wished I'd put on some mascara. My eyes still ached from crying. "Well, let's talk about the job opening we have right now."

We spent a few more minutes in casual dialogue. Mr. Craig's style of management was informal, friendly. I struggled to speak calmly, professionally. I needed to impress him with my knowledge.

"I think that'll do it for now," he said after fifteen minutes. "I have several other interested candidates. Thank you, Stephani, I'll announce the position by Friday. Keep up the good work."

He extended his hand, and I grasped it, giving it what I hoped was a firm shake.

Friday seemed eons away. I knew I looked terrible, but I told myself that Eric Craig knew what I looked like most days. Usually I dressed more conservatively, wore a little foundation and eye makeup. Usually I was not recovering from a weekend of rape.

ASK ME NO QUESTIONS

On Thursday I was once again called into the department head's office. I went there eagerly this time, sure that I would be told I was the new retail advertising salesperson. Despite the unchanged conditions at home, in which I was picked up daily from work and subjected to a nightmare of pretense with my children before retiring, trembling with apprehension and revulsion, to bed with Vic, I found I wanted to live. I just didn't want to live with my husband.

Stepping into Mr. Craig's office, I looked at him expectantly.

"Sit down, Stephani," he said. His voice sounded just the same as before—casual, friendly. I sat, and waited.

He took out his pipe, lit it, and met my eager gaze. "I've made my decision," he said. Did his eyes change a little? A shadow seemed to flit over them. "I've chosen to promote Annie Leu. I appreciate your interest, and I'm sure you will be among those who will advance as you gain experience."

Annie Leu! That sloe-eyed sleaze who used her body to sell advertising? Not her! The thoughts clanged in my head while I held a smile, blinking back tears.

"May I ask why you chose her over me?" I said, controlling the tremor in my voice. *I will not cry*, I told myself, barely listening to Mr. Craig as he leaned back, his face pensive.

"I'm not sure you're aggressive enough," he said slowly, as if thinking over the question. "And then there's the situation you're in right now..."

"Situation? What situation?" My heart hammered in my chest. *He can't know about Vic, about last weekend!*

"I understand you're having, uh, marital difficulties."

"I can still do my job!"

"I know, Stephani," he said, sitting straight again. "But we feel you will be more able to, uh, concentrate, once your domestic situation levels out." He frowned slightly, as if the subject was distasteful. "You're a valued employee. It won't be long and you'll be sitting in this chair," he smiled at the attempted joke.

I smiled too, my mouth sagging weakly as I kept my chin high. "You can bet on that," I said.

He reached his hand across the desk. "I'll be happy to help in any way I can. Keep up the good work."

I accepted his hand, shook it, remembering to grasp it firmly, and stood. "I'd better get back to work."

But I headed for the lady's room as I exited his office, where I closed a booth door behind me and let the tears flow. I'd needed that promotion. I needed the extra income. I had to leave Vic.

Another week disappeared into the mists; Vic's constant nearness, his continual babbling about God and submissiveness and foreverness were a growing weight on my spirit. The lessons in "sensuality" continued. "I think I know the answer to our problem," Vic said one night. "I'm a sensual person. You're not. I need a physical relationship. I can teach you to be sensual. I can teach you to enjoy my touch." He used the word "sensual" repeatedly, as if it were a new word in his vocabulary. I'd never thought of him in that context; I loved to touch, had longed for affection, for kisses, for caresses. Ironic that now, when I cringed at the mere thought of his hands and lips on me, he should come to this conclusion.

I had to get away from him.

Chapter 35

"We will be together for always. You know that...Always."

"Yes, Vic. I know that."

I parked the car in the driveway. Vic waited for me to get out before he did. We had gone to the grocery store; Vic had instructed me to drive, leaving him free to continue his rambling discourse on the future of our marriage. We'd left the children home, since Tiffany was, at fourteen, old enough to watch her sisters for an hour or so.

I opened the car door and began to slide out. Vic was faster—he was out, the door slammed, a bag of groceries in his arms. "Oh, my purse," I said, as though just realizing I'd left it on the seat. Swiftly I got back in, slid under the wheel, and jammed the key in the ignition. "Please," I whispered, "please start."

Vic had turned at my exclamation, but was hindered by the bag full of groceries. I was in the car and out of the driveway before he could stop me. I glanced in the rearview mirror. He stood in the driveway, his eyes blazing their message toward me: I'll get you for this.

I'm free! I'm free! My thoughts raced as I drove toward the freeway, toward freedom. It was the first time I'd been alone, without his constant hovering, in three weeks.

I turned onto the freeway and headed downtown, past the casinos, into the more exclusive residential area that was Elizabeth's. She would help me. She would tell me what to do.

I interrupted her dinner, but Elizabeth graciously, calmly directed me toward her attorney husband as if interruptions were an everyday occurrence. "I'll leave you two alone," she said, hugging me briefly. "You need to find out what your options are."

"Come on into my study," Rodger Bramford III said, gesturing as he spoke. He held the door open as I walked through, trembling in reaction to my precipitous flight. Reality was beginning to set in; I was taking my life in my own hands. I was taking action!

"Sit down, Stephani," Rodger instructed calmly. "Why don't you just start at the beginning and tell me the whole story."

"Well, I guess that means fourteen years ago," I said, as I tried to gather my thoughts. I'd never told anyone what I was about to tell Rodger. No one knew what our life was like. No one knew…anything.

"When I married Vic, I understood that he was an agent for the CIA. He'd told me, before our wedding, that our life would be different, that there would be things I didn't understand, and couldn't question. I believed him," I shrugged, embarrassed at my naivete. "I believed everything he told me, for a long time."

I recounted the years, the beginning of the doubts, the gestation of fear. "And then, a year ago, he told me he was actually working for the Mafia," I continued. "I wanted a divorce, and he begged me to reconsider. He said it would be over in a year, and we would be able to live a normal life."

Finishing my story, I sat, numb with fatigue, as I waited for Rodger Bramford's reaction. Would he believe me? Could he help me?

"How could you believe all this?" he said.

I glanced up, my face hot. *He thinks I'm stupid*, I thought. *Well, I was. But I'm not any more.* "I was sixteen years old," I said in self-defense. "I was very naive."

He sat in his comfortable chair, hands folded on his expansive desk, eyeing me dispassionately. I grew more uncomfortable under his lawyer's gaze. Seconds ticked aloud from the big, antique clock resting against the far wall.

"What do you want to do?"

"I don't know what to do," I replied, embarrassed still. "Do people like him ever change? Can we have any kind of life?"

"It's been my experience, from both research and from my courtroom experience, that people with this kind of personality disorder rarely change," he said, his eyes on the pencil in his hand. "It's a sickness, of sorts. I'm not a psychiatrist, but I've read that perhaps thirty percent of these people make the attempt, and the success rate is very small. They don't have a conscience. They don't really accept that they're doing anything wrong. The rest of the world is against them. They're just…surviving."

"Can I get an annulment? Based on misrepresentation? He lied to me. Our entire life has been a lie."

"An annulment would render your children illegitimate. I'm not sure that's what you want."

"No. I don't want that."

ASK ME NO QUESTIONS

I was silent again, as was he. He had no answers for me. He thought I was stupid! I waited, wishing I could just crawl through the floor. He waited. The silence grew.

"Well, when you decide what you want to do," he said after what seemed an hour, "call me. I don't handle divorces, but surely the legal aide could help you. I can probably get you an appointment with them."

His offer seemed terribly weak to me, as if he wasn't truly interested in helping me, but merely didn't want to offend his wife. I wanted him to solve my problem, rescue me from hell. But I couldn't tell him that. I couldn't tell him what life with Victor was like. He was a man, after all.

We exited the study, and I rejoined Elizabeth while Rodger excused himself and disappeared upstairs. "Well?" Elizabeth urged, leading me to the breakfast nook. A steaming cup of coffee awaited me there. I sat, facing her sunny, beautiful face, and I envied her security.

"Well," I echoed wanly. "I guess I need to plan a course of action. Right now I can't even get away from him, at least, not with the girls. We're prisoners."

"Okay," Elizabeth pursed her perfectly made-up lips, "Let's talk about that. Where would you go? And how would you get there?"

We talked and schemed for the next half-hour. I couldn't stay away from home for long. I didn't want Vic to take out his frustrations on the girls.

"This is what we've got," my friend finally said. "You're going to continue to do as he says until you can get all your ducks in a row. Pretend you're still under his control. Lull him into thinking he's got you where he wants you. In the meantime, convince him to allow you to visit your parents in Arizona. He'll probably let you go, as long as you leave the children here. Do you think he'll harm them?"

"No," I said uncertainly. "I don't think he'll do anything to them as long as he knows I'm coming back. He knows I won't leave them."

"He wouldn't let you take them with you, would he? Maybe you could convince him you're happy with him, and then you could just stay in Arizona."

"No. He doesn't trust me that far. The year is almost up, and I haven't given him my answer yet. Not totally. And I don't think I can convince him I love him." I shuddered, the memory of his hands around my throat shimmering in my mind.

"All right. Then you go to Arizona, and you tell your parents you're leaving him. You get their help. Then you come back, and you leave him as soon as the opportunity arises."

She seemed so sure of how it would work, so confident that I could do this. I nodded, grasping her hands in mine. "Thank you," I said, not meeting her eyes.

I rose and walked to the door, and, with a final wave, drove back to the dark house on Acacia Drive. However sure Elizabeth was, I had my doubts. But at least someone knew. Someone knew the truth. If anything happened to me, Elizabeth would know the truth.

As I drove toward home, the determination, and sense of empowerment slowly dissipated as the accustomed fear took hold. You can't beat him, the voice inside my head intoned. You can't beat him and live to tell about it. *Shut up!* my heart screamed. *Shut up and leave me alone! I will beat you! I will leave you!* The argument continued as the car headed steadily toward the house, my prison. I never doubted that he would kill me if he suspected any rebellion. But the madness in his eyes had convinced me I had no choice but to try.

When I stopped the car in the driveway, he was waiting.

"Where have you been?" he asked quietly. Too quietly.

"I just had to be alone for awhile, that's all. I just—drove around—then I parked over at the little city park and watched the ducks. That's all." My heart hammered in my chest. Look him in the eye, Steph. Don't look away.

He opened the car door, gestured me out. I stepped outside. As I stood, I found myself trapped by his arm on the door. I dropped my eyes and remained still. His hand came up around me behind my neck, where it circled lightly. But not too lightly. "I was worried. You shouldn't worry me, Stephani."

"I'm sorry. I just needed to get some air." My eyes remained on the button in the middle of his chest. My voice was hardly more than a whisper. I swallowed, the saliva stopping its progress down my throat to rest at the base of my tongue. I swallowed again.

"You'd better get supper started. The girls are pretty hungry." The reminder of my children, alone with him, brought a light film of sweat to my underarms, my back. Evidently the "honeymoon" was over.

"I'll get started right away," I said.

He dropped his arm from the car door, then, slammed the door and, with his other hand still on my neck, walked me into the house.

For the next three weeks, I plotted and planned and pretended that he had won his case. On March 19, 1980, we celebrated our fourteenth wedding anniversary. I dressed in the hot pink boa dress he'd gotten me for Christmas, clamped my eyes shut at the sight of it in the mirror, and followed him out the door. He was dressed for the occasion, too, slicked up and almost handsome in the dark blue navy suit he kept for special occasions.

ASK ME NO QUESTIONS

We drove to Lake Tahoe.

All the way up that winding road, I wondered if this was to be my last ride. So much could happen in the sixty miles between the two cities. The wooded mountainside would hide a body for years. He would get away with it, could get away with murder any day of the week. Who would question? No one knew the man that I knew. No one saw the anger, the cunning, the madness.

"Come on over," he said, patting the seat beside him. "I want to be able to hug my bride." I slid over, gritting my teeth as his arm found its way around my shoulders. "That's better, isn't it?" His lips touched my cheek. "Almost like old times."

I nodded. Almost, but not quite, I thought. In the old days, I loved you. I believed in you. Now, I'm just afraid of you.

The car rolled over the highway smoothly, the occasional lights from lakeside homes glistening through the trees. Soon the lights brightened and the casinos outshone even the stars in the sky.

Vic escorted me to a casino showroom, and before I could hazard a guess as to what he was up to, we were ushered to the show lounge; in moments, the lights were dimmed, and, as waiters scurried to serve sizzling filet mignon, an announcer's voice boomed over the room. "Ladies and Gentlemen, Caesar's Palace is proud to present—John Denver!"

John Denver, of "Rocky Mountain High" fame. My favorite singer. Vic had done this for me. He reached for my hand, the old smile on his face. If only I could wipe away the last few years. If only I could focus on this Vic, who loved me. Couldn't I do that? For our family? "You have no biblical reason to leave him," Pastor Wilson's voice whispered in my ear. "No biblical reason." Would God desert me if I left my husband? Would I lose the protection I'd always known was there?

"You fill up my senses like a light in the forest," John Denver's tenor rang out. Vic squeezed my hand, his fingers rubbing my ring finger. Tears stung my eyes. I would try. I owed him that much. I had to try to make the best of my marriage.

Vic had booked a room in a motel for the night; after the show, we drove the short distance to the room. As my husband slipped the sleazy dress off my shoulders, I straightened my shoulders as I used to, gritted my teeth, and determined I would return his love tonight. I would make the effort. Forgive and forget. Wasn't that what a Christian wife would do?

The room was dark; the lights from nearby casinos filtered through the tiny crack where the drawn drapes didn't quite meet. I slid my hand across the sheet on the other side of the bed. Empty. Vic was gone.

Where would he go? *This is our anniversary!* Indignation infused me. *Here I am, trying to forgive him, to forget all the reasons to leave him, and he walks out on our anniversary!* But deep down, beneath that trumped-up, self-righteous anger, was relief. Relief that he was gone. I could sleep, undisturbed. I closed my eyes and fell into a dreamless slumber.

When I awoke again, the crack between the drapes emitted a dim stream of sunlight. Vic was beside me, snoring lightly.

Moving slowly, I thought I'd grab a shower, get the cigarette smell from my hair—Caesar's Palace or not, the smoke was enough to kill a non-smoker such as myself. My nasal passages burned from two hours of inhaling second-hand smoke.

As I slid a leg off the bed, Vic's arm fell across my waist. *Caught.* His face inched closer. I couldn't escape. I slid my leg back under and gave in, my thoughts on Arizona, two weeks away. Arizona and freedom. Maybe the trip would clear my mind. Maybe a week away from him would give me a fresh perspective. Maybe I could rejuvenate my feelings for him if I could just forget the feeling of his hands around my throat.

And on it went. There were moments of clarity, when I knew without any doubts that I had to leave him if I wanted to live. Followed by hours of indecision. It had been years since I'd made a decision of any kind. Years since I'd felt any confidence in my own mind, or memory, or ability to think. Elizabeth was my strength. During our working hours, she would drop by my desk, give me a "thumbs up," or just ask how I was doing. Her presence empowered me to go through with our plan. Without her, I was lost.

At home, I walked in a daze. The constant presence of my husband served as a reminder of his strength, his ability to get his way, his uncanny talent for deception. No one would believe me; even Elizabeth, once Vic got to her, would think I was the crazy one. He was so convincing. Or so I thought.

Meekly submitting to him, I laughed and teased, and prayed that I could last until April, when he would send me to visit my parents. It would be the first time in fourteen years I'd ever gone anywhere alone, without husband or children. The children were his trump card: he knew I would never abandon them. My return was their safeguard—he wouldn't do anything to them, at least nothing physical, as long as I was coming back. Each of us knew this; both of us played the game as if we were unaware of the other's knowledge.

ASK ME NO QUESTIONS

If I could just hold on to my resolve. I had to be strong, stronger than I had ever been or ever thought possible. I had to believe I could succeed in leaving him with our children, once I returned from Arizona.

The day arrived. Vic drove to the airport with a cheerful smile on his face. The children accompanied us: Tiffany, her button nose hidden behind a curtain of silky fine hair as she gazed out the window behind me, solemn and still. Catlin, ten years old and trimmed to wiry toughness from five years in gymnastics, sat behind Vic, her steady grey eyes never leaving me. Deanna bounced between her sisters, a nine-year-old elf with chubby little cheeks and a ready smile. Except today. She stared at me from under blinking lids, her tears threatening to spill any moment. I smiled at her in encouragement. "I'll be back before you know it," I assured her. Her lips quivered and she blinked harder. I turned away, my throat tightening. *Will they be all right? Will they still be here when I get back?*

Jasmine squirmed against me, restless and impatient. At five, she was the least affected by the tensions around her, although her moods seemed to swing and dip in accord to mine. We had always been in tune with each other. I hugged her close, trailing my hand down her waist-length braid. How could I leave them? *I have to*, I told myself. *I have to tell Mom and Dad what's going on. I have to let somebody know—just in case I disappear. In case I don't make it when we leave him.*

Vic carried the suitcase as we all trooped through Reno International to my gate. I hugged each child separately and all together, and then I reached for my husband and hugged him, too. "I love you," I whispered. "Thank you for letting me go." The words had an ironic ring to them. I hoped he didn't notice it, too.

My flight was announced. I hugged everybody once more, and turned to leave.

"Don't worry, Mom, I'll take care of them." I turned back at the sound of Tiffany's voice. She was so tall, so slender, so forlorn. She grasped a sister by each hand, Deanna on one side and Cat on the other. Jas held onto Cat—Vic held on to Jas. I looked at them, my girls, and I gave Tiffany a smile, a silent message of hope, and I wished I could tell her it would all be over soon. Then Vic waved, his smile widening as I turned to corner in the tunnel.

I glanced once more, quickly, at Tiffany. "I'll be back before you know it!" I called.

Then I was hustled down the tube into the plane, and there was no turning back. I was squashed between the tourists fleeing Sin City, squabbling over seats and overhead racks.

I settled in, my heart thumping. *I'm actually going!* I thought. *I'm going away by myself!* And despite my concern for my children, despite the uncertainty of the future, despite the fear which clung to me as tight as oil on asphalt, I felt the first glimmer of hope, the first lift of fatigue, the first slight sense of certainty. We could do this. We would make it. And never, ever again would I live my life ruled by fear.

I glanced out the window. I could see him standing there, all four daughters standing close by. They waved. I returned the wave, knowing they couldn't see me but feeling better anyway. As the airplane taxied down the runway, I looked down at my hands, at the two identical rings encircling the third finger on my left hand, and I slipped them off. *For now*, I thought. *Just to get the feel of it. Just to get used to being free.*

The plane lifted, and I saw the expanse of azure blue sky beside me, ahead of me, and I released the breath I had been holding for fourteen years. *Thank you, God…Thank you.*

Chapter 36

So there you have it: the story of Stephani and Victor Charles Brian. The love story of the century. Of course, it doesn't really end there, with Stephani flying off into the sunset, her teary-eyed children hand-in-hand beside their father. No, that flight signified the beginning of another journey, a journey of recovery and regrowth for all five Brian women.

But as I flew over the Nevada desert that day, my thoughts were of relief and regret, sorrow and triumph. I resolved that, no matter what the future held, I would never live in fear again. The price was too high.

When I disembarked in Arizona, my unsuspecting parents greeted me warily, clearly unused to seeing me alone. We spoke little during the ride to their home, retreating into our own thoughts, leaving the questions until tomorrow. When I finally told them of my decision, Dad exhaled one word—"Good"—as if he had been holding his breath for a long, long time. Mom said, in her brief, economic way, "I wondered when you'd come to your senses." And Dad offered to drive back with me, to help me get out of the housed if need be.

I spent a relaxed a rejuvenating week with them and my younger brother, who was now a handsome, sought-after bachelor in Prescott: he squired me to some of the night spots in the evenings after work. I told him some of the story of the past fourteen years, but I couldn't bring myself to share much with my parents. I didn't really know how to talk about it, how to put voice to my experience as Victor's wife.

When I returned to Reno, I faced the devil at once: Vic noted the absence of my wedding ring immediately, and, without threats or rage or accusation, packed some bags and moved out. He was gentle, understanding that I "needed some space," and promised to "look after me." I knew that his behavior was not to be trusted, his words were veiled threats, but I took whatever gifts God would give me in exchange for momentary peace, and I steeled myself for whatever battles lay ahead.

As soon as they heard about my sudden separation, the people at the *Gazette-Journal* passed the hat and collected some two hundred dollars in a joint expression of "Good luck," and gave it to me without fanfare. I was overwhelmed by their generosity and kindness.

I changed churches, seeking out a less judgmental minister and a more forgiving doctrine, and I made friends with people who lived ordinary lives. This was only the beginning: I had yet to face what damage I had done to my children, to myself, and to my relationships within my family. I had yet to learn how to live without the watchdog eyes of the CIA and the fear of discovery. I felt like a modern-day Rumplestiltskin, looking out at a new and foreign world. Without Vic's control of my life, I had no structure, no boundaries. I was reborn, and the world into which I emerged was both exhilarating and frightening.

The children, too, had a huge transition to make. Their father was a giant in their lives in one way, and an ant in another—his personality loomed, always, over their lives, but in the day-to-day interactions, he had been largely absent. If I kept the children quiet and out of his way, he paid little attention to them. Now, they could be noisy, and they were. Now, they could defy me, and they did. In many ways, we were all lost, floating on a sea of ambiguity. It would take time—a long time—for us to find direction.

But we were together. The five of us were family. It was a start.